THE SECRETS OF FOLDER 42

A NOVEL BY
ABDELMAJID SEBBATA

Shortlisted for the 2021 International Prize for Arabic Fiction

THE SECRETS OF FOLDER 42

A NOVEL BY
ABDELMAJID SEBBATA

Translated from the Arabic by Raphael Cohen

The Secrets of Folder 42
First published in English translation
by Banipal Books, London, May 2024

Arabic copyright © Abdelmajid Sebbata
English translation copyright © Raphael Cohen, 2024
Al-Malaf 42 was first published in Arabic in 2020
Original title: الملف 42
Published by Al-Markaz al-Thaqafi al-Arabi, Casablanca, Morocco

The moral right of Abdelmajid Sebbata to be identified as the author of this
work and of Raphael Cohen as the translator of this work has been asserted
in accordance with the Copyright, Designs and Patents Act, 1988.

No part of this book may be reproduced in any form or by any means
without the prior written permission of the publisher

A CIP record for this book is available in the British Library
ISBN 978-1-913043-41-4
E-book: ISBN: 978-1-913043-42-1

Front cover artwork: Samuel Shimon

Published with support from Abu Dhabi Arabic Language Center,
through the Spotlight on Rights,
Abu Dhabi International Book Fair 2022

Banipal Books
1 Gough Square, LONDON EC4A 3DE, UK
www.banipal.co.uk/banipalbooks/

Banipal Books is an imprint of Banipal Publishing
Typeset in Cardo

Printed and bound in Great Britain by Clays Ltd, Elcograf S.p.A.

To Ruqaya Belmamoun, a fighter,
and Abed Sebbata, a wise man:
As usual . . .

Life just imitates novels . . .
    Rabee Jaber – *The Last House* (novel) – 1996

A Moroccan is unluckier than Sisyphus. He expends his life pushing the boulder of his oppression to the summit, then ends up crushed beneath it . . .
    Khalid Rafiqi – *A Moroccan Jigsaw Puzzle*
                                    (novel) – 1989

(0) If on a Winter's Night a Traveller

> *A writer never has a vacation. For a writer,
> life consists either of writing or of thinking
> about writing.*
>
> **Eugene Ionesco**

Wednesday, 6 November 2019
The railway station; Lamkinssia housing compound – Salé:

To me there's no difference between a writer and a chess player. Both are engaged in an intense mental struggle against their opponent on a deceptively small board that takes in the whole world.

Because, in both chess and writing, assessments of winning or losing are relative and not deterministic, I have had to raise the white flag rather than keep fighting a battle in which every circumstance has combined to defeat me. Even if I defended myself temporarily with "a tactical retreat" – which is a ridiculous expression and the refuge of every loser.

But I'm not a politician who lies to his audience to conceal the truth. I'm a writer who lies to his readers to reveal the truth.

I have no choice but to sign my confession, even if it is a statement of outright surrender.

I am unable to finish the novel I started writing on Monday, 1 April 2019, and that means – if I drop the guise of a writer and adopt that of the civil engineer, which I gave up years ago because it didn't suit me – the collapse of a structure whose foundations I did my utmost to strengthen, and whose schedule of works I always adhered to.

The structure collapsed leaving only one victim under the rubble: me!

Poor planning? Lack of funding? Or was the ground unfit for building in the first place?

All I can say is: I fell prey to an odious arrogance that made me believe I was master of my words and to a preposterous confidence in my ability to keep hold of the plot lines and follow the development of characters whose movement I controlled. But shockingly, they ganged up in secret to break their chains and start a revolution under a banner declaring: we have the right to decide our own destiny.

A unilateral ceasefire didn't hold and the peace talks to which I invited the other parties, who rejected all forms of peaceful dialogue, failed. A direct and decisive confrontation was inevitable.

Strength in numbers beats courage, and a helpless pen cannot withstand the siege of paper beings who have decided to continue their revolution to the end, while blaming the pen for manipulating their past, present and future.

Their intransigence drove me to threaten to issue a final, unappealable ruling condemning them to death. On this basis I would, with a single click, move the folder containing the draft of the unfinished novel, with its worlds, characters and events, to the Trash.

The response was loud and clear: If one day the people wish to live, then fate must respond[1]. And respond it did, but in its own special way . . .

---

[1] A line of poetry from the Tunisian Aboul-Qacem Echebbi's (1909–1934) poem "The Will to Live". The lines are included at the end of the Tunisian national anthem and were also frequently cited during the events of 2011 throughout the Arab world.

*

An almost empty railway station. A mobile phone displaying 21:24. A heavy rainstorm making it impossible to get home on foot, even though it's not far to the Lamkinssia housing compound.

I am so tired I have no need for a mirror to be shocked by my pallor, the black bags under my eyes and my protruding cheek bones. I've barely slept over the weeks I've spent filling my small notebook with plot outlines, arrows, remarks and incomprehensible sentences and words. Anyone who took a peek at it would think it was a child's scribbles. But despite all that I haven't been able to find the missing piece of the puzzle and add a single line to the unfinished draft on my laptop.

The publisher (whom I met in Casablanca) did not buy my excuses. He was keen on the idea when I first told him at the end of 2018, and approved of my choice of 2002 as the starting point for the action. He tried to go over some of the details with me, perhaps in the hope of helping, but in the end he apologised and gave me the freedom to do what I want.

Afraid that my laptop and my blue notebook would get wet, I hugged the leather bag close. I quickly exited the station and hailed a taxi – the only one waiting to leave. "Lamkinssia housing compound, please." Like all taxi drivers, who usually refused a fare from the station to the compound because it was so close, the guy's face showed displeasure. But the sorry state I was in from the rain – I had started to feel cold drips down my neck and chest – made him say, "Okay, let's go."

A middle-aged woman was in the front seat so I got into the back and quickly closed the door.

"I'll just drop the lady at the Diyar Estate, then we'll head to Lamkinssia." Busy wiping the rain off my glasses, I didn't reply. After a brief silence he continued, "I think being a taxi driver is the hardest job in the world. My wife's just gone into labour with our third child, but instead of going with her to the hospital to help, I have to go out in this rain to make money. Still, my mother's with her. It'll be a good opportunity for them to make up, or call a truce, after they fell out because of . . ."

The woman engaged with what he was saying, while I just muttered, and the driver realised that I wasn't interested in his personal life. The pair of them chatted away for a bit, but were interrupted by the screeching of the windscreen wipers and the intermittent distorted sound of a pop song coming from the radio.

The taxi stopped at the door of an apartment block. The woman paid her fare and said goodbye, wishing him, his wife and their third child well.

With a sharp turn of the steering wheel he caused a raggedy tramp to get soaked with dirty water and respond with a hail of filthy insults. The driver preferred to ignore them in favour of a new avenue of conversation with me: "Do you reckon Barcelona are ready for the post-Messi era? He couldn't carry the team for ever. He's thirty-two now, after all!"

God, I'm losing concentration. My head's about to explode. The only thing I have in mind is a warm bed and you're asking me about Messi!

His phone rang, sparing me the effort of passing that response on to my tongue.

"Hello, Mother. Any news? How are Naima and the baby doing? She has to have a caesarean! No way! I'm coming right now."

Clearly shaken, he ended the call. My impatience softened into real sympathy and I said, "Don't worry. She'll be fine."

"It's impossible! Naima's the strongest woman I ever met. She never complained of any pain, and her first two pregnancies were completely normal!"

We neared the entrance to the compound and I told him to stop and head to the hospital to help his ailing wife seeing as I could walk the rest of the way.

He thanked me warmly and asked me to pray for his wife and baby. Then he sped off, his tyres screeching against the asphalt.

I watched for a few seconds then gave an exhausted smile as I saw him pass the Umm Hani Estate and pull up next to someone else. Honestly, he had no hesitation in letting him get into the front seat before continuing like a rocket down the desolate streets of Salé.

Yes, he was distracted, worried about any harm coming to his wife and baby, but he was never going to lose out on any extra dirhams he might come across on his way to the hospital!

I turned on my heels and headed quickly towards the Khawarizmi neighbourhood. I went to put my hand in the left-hand pocket of my sodden trousers for my keys. But before my hand reached the pocket, my brain ordered it to stop with a sudden jolt, whose dreadful meaning I only understood too late. I had forgotten my laptop and my blue notebook on the backseat of the taxi!

* * *

World Culture magazine – May, 2002

Author of the Month: Christine McMillan (USA)

Note: To date none of the author's novels have been translated into Arabic.

Prisoner of Class 12 (novel) (1999)

> "Christine McMillan, with her impressive style and emotional honesty, has given us a concise depiction of the state of a society for which we do not know what the 21st century has in store." — Washington Post

High School teacher Gina does her utmost to stop her family falling apart and also fights to control her teenage students, who refuse to engage in dialogue with her or with her educational guidance.

The school is stunned by an armed assault carried out by a student named Eddie. He takes the members of class 12 hostage and threatens to kill his classmate Catherine after their relationship has failed. Gina finds herself in a standoff of uncertain outcome with her emotionally unstable student. A standoff replete with painful memories for both of them and a bloody gamble whose final outcome is hard to predict.

Will Gina be able to convince Eddie to back down or will she pay with her life trying to do so?

253 pages
Price: $16.00

Secrets of the Dark (novel) (2000)

"Christine McMillan: unrivalled pioneer of the new American realism." — *New York Times*

Laura loses her parents and her eyesight in a horrific road accident that she miraculously survives.

Unable to cope with her suffering, the twenty-something woman contemplates suicide but finds support from a mysterious young man who regularly visits her in hospital even though the two do not know each other.

Laura is able to confront her fears and she undergoes an operation to restore her sight. She then faces an unexpected and shocking dilemma: to follow her heart or submit to her strict upbringing and the teachings of her late father, once a leading member in the KKK.

What will she choose? And what is the truth behind the police finding strong evidence to suggest that the accident which killed her parents was deliberate?

223 pages
Price: $15.00

Silent Angel (novel) (2001)

"Christine McMillan continues to amaze us with new ideas and different styles, proving that she is head and shoulders above most novelists of her generation." — *The New Yorker*.

Everyone thinks that the Schwartzes are the happiest family in the world. Tom is a successful legal consultant, his wife Vera is beautiful and of Scandinavian descent, and they have a wonderful five-year-old son Johnny.

The life of this ideal family is turned upside-down after Johnny is afflicted with a strange itching. Is it a disease or a psychological condition?

Over the long course of treatment, many secrets are revealed and a crucial question is raised: were the Schwartzes really the happiest family in the world? Or was what was going on behind closed doors, a world away from what those on the outside imagined?

223 pages
Price: $15.00

(1) Things Fall Apart

> *America is a highly complicated country, although the ideas in circulation there are extremely simple.*
> Matei Vişniec

Thursday, 26 September 2002
Strand Bookstore – Manhattan:

"Nobody has the right to question your literary talent, Christine, but you don't understand anything about the ins and outs of publishing and the tricks of exclusive contracts. Please, don't make any promises that you know full well you won't be able to keep one day."

Those were the words that Brandon whispered in my ear three years ago. And I admit today that they were wise, honest and decisive.

The very same qualities that apply to an exceptional man with whom I've been in a fuzzy relationship (or was in, if I wish to be painfully accurate) for almost eighteen years. Yet I dealt with his words (and with him too, perhaps) stupidly, hastily and casually. The way I usually deal with all the major turning points in my life.

I greeted a youthful reader wearing a raincoat that was too big for him with a graceful smile. Then I asked him for his full name so I could write a dedication above my signature on the first page of his copy. At the same time, the bookstore assistant gave a subtle sign with her fingers, telling me there were still about twenty people left in line. That meant another half hour would be enough to finish the book signing. I might need a further twenty minutes to make my meeting with David Hersch at six, Manhattan traffic permitting.

My fingers had cramp from holding the pen, and I made a supreme effort to ignore the pain. I focused my gaze on a distant spot in the vast bookstore: the section for bestsellers. My novel, *Silent Angel*, had dropped near the bottom of the list for two reasons that reinforced each other. First, the book had been out for a year and most journalists and critics had lost interest as they sought new titles hot off the press. Second, *The Book of Illusions* by Paul Auster had been published three weeks ago and *Buick 8* by Stephen King had come out only two days ago. Either of those two stellar names on the cover of any book (even if all the inside pages were blank) was enough to generate record-breaking sales and unparalleled media and critical interest.

I might add a third thing. But my pride refuses to admit it.

The hands of my watch showed 5:30 as I signed the last copy – presented by an elderly Mexican lady, who asked me to dedicate it to her daughter living in LA. As I fulfilled her wish, I glimpsed the bookstore manager hurrying over. His apparent enthusiasm masked a degree of hesitation.

"On my part and on behalf of all the staff at Strand Bookstore," he began, "we would like to thank you for giving us the chance to hold a book signing for your beautiful novel, *Silent Angel*." Now overly pumping my hand, he continued, "We also congratulate you on the great success of the event, as confirmed by the record number of those in attendance, all fans of your distinguished works." His insincerity was unmistakeable.

I responded with a fake smile of my own and polite gratitude that prompted him to say, "We'll be in touch with your publisher and your agent to provide fresh batches of your three novels once the current stock runs out. Our media person will also send a piece to the major newspapers for publication in their literary supplements."

"You'll have to excuse me," I said in a firm diplomatic tone. "I'm very busy right now, but you can discuss all the details with my PA." Then I picked up my coat, signalling I'd had enough and was desperate to leave. Nonetheless, he stopped me with a nervous movement: "Ms McMillan, I do believe that our rivalry with Powell's Books in Portland over the title of best independent bookstore in the States is sufficiently well known that I can spare you the details. Today's book signing is a point in our favour, but we aspire to more."

I pretended not to understand, but his eyes gave away what he was hinting at. "We do hope that your next novel will contain a reference to our bookstore. There can be no doubt that the name of the Strand Bookstore appearing in a novel by a writer, all of whose previous titles have sold more than a million copies, would be a powerful boost to our publicity campaign."

I imagined exploding in his face: "And who are you to dictate what I include in my novels? Do you all want to make everything – including creative literary works – subject to the grubby laws of supply and demand?"

I remembered that I was up to my neck in a sea of those vile laws, but I controlled my nerves and said coolly, "Okay, I'll think about it."

Unable to suppress my fury, of their own volition my eyes glanced over at the bestseller section. I had to beat a retreat, deliberately ignoring the nonsense emanating from the obsequious manager, who did not hear me add in a whisper, "That's if I think about writing another novel in the first place."

* * *

Commendation

The administration of Firsts Private Elementary School is delighted to award a certificate of commendation to student Zouhair Belkacem in recognition of his outstanding performance throughout the school year 1993/4, culminating in him coming top of the school.

We wish him every success in future.

> The School Administration

"Morocco's Kasparov" wins Arab youth chess championship

(Al-Bayan newspaper – Sports Page – Monday, 16 June 1997)

Up-and-coming Moroccan champion Zouhair Belkacem (14), nicknamed Morocco's Kasparov, has won the Arab youth chess championship held in Rabat on 13-15 June.

The outstanding Moroccan youngster is also holder of the Moroccan youth title. Will our talented champion progress from the Moroccan chessboard to the international arena?

Attendance Required

The administration of Success High School urgently requests the attendance of the parents of first-year student Zouhair Belkacem to inquire into the reasons behind his repeated absences during the second term of school year 1998/9.

Would the student's parents please present themselves at the school upon receipt of this request.

The School Administration

Fight between teens at nightclub almost ends in massacre!

(*Al-Ghad* newspaper – Crime Page – Wednesday, 29 March 2000)

A violent altercation involving knives and glass bottles broke out among teenagers at one of the capital Rabat's top night spots, the Blue Night club, according to eyewitness reports.

An argument between two teenagers (including the son of a well-known woman lawyer) erupted over a young hostess. The girl rejected the advances of the lawyer's son, leading her friend to intervene. The argument turned into a violent fight, made worse by the intoxication of everyone involved. Several teenagers were injured and a number of young women fainted. The club also suffered substantial material losses. All of this in the baffling absence of any intervention on the part of the police.

Reprimand

The administration of Success High School, following the deliberation of its disciplinary board, has decided to issue a reprimand to third-year student Zouhair Belkacem and exclude him from the school for a period of 15 days, subject to renewal, as punishment for a fist-fight with maths teacher Abdurrahman el-Talibi, in transgression of all the rules of good conduct and respect towards teaching staff.

This decision affirms the school's requirement that all students behave properly, and its use of all necessary pedagogical methods to enable them to continue learning in the best environment.

The School Administration

Baccalaureat Examination 2000/1:

Full Name	National No.	Final Mark	Grade
Zouhair Belkacem	2xxxxxxxxx	42%	Fail

(1') The Adolescent

> *I believe that each body tells the story of its desire, its terror, and its disappointment.*
> **Milena Busquets**

Tuesday, 14 May 2002
Sidi Abed Plage – Harhoura:

Sunshine, golden sands, cool waters eyeing you seductively and begging you to take a dip before the beach becomes crowded in a month's time, perhaps less.

What in the devil's name made my mother come up with the idea of sending me to our beach house at Sidi Abed on the pretext that I would benefit from the perfect atmosphere to revise for my bac exams at the beginning of June?

She knows as well as I do that my father will reject the idea outright. He'll think that the atmosphere at home in our villa in the Hayy el Riad neighbourhood of Rabat is perfect for studying. The issue for him is not the place where I'm going to revise, but me, the messed-up, spoilt teenager who failed his exams last year.

But my mother also knows that the real reason he'll reject it has nothing to do with me. The beautiful beach house has become the arena where he chases after his lost youth with nymphomaniac patients from his clinic, and with good-looking female students of his who are seeking success by means other than diligence and hard work. She pretends not to know about his conquests, and hasn't come up with a way to curb his delayed adolescence, even if only for a couple of weeks, other than me.

Because my father realised that saying no to her means volunteering to walk into a minefield, whose detonations will send shrapnel flying on all sides, he gave in to her wishes, preferring surrender and the temporary concession of his clandestine playground.

That's life for the three of us: a sordid drama where we lie to each other, and each of us knows that the others know we're lying. We just pretend otherwise, obliged to play happy families for the benefit of others. It's like a game of tennis. It might go on a long time, but the first one to tire will pay in the end.

I stood in the doorway of the main bedroom of the beach house for a long time. My father hadn't bothered to tidy up after his last assignation, and my expert eye spotted an earring on the floor. I shoved it under the bed with my foot, worried that my mother would walk in. I had just heard her voice berating the new maid to hurry up with our bags.

"Leave the strident tone for court," I said. "Ghalia's only been with us for three weeks. She needs more time to get used to your shouting and your temper."

I gave a mocking laugh, which she backed up with a no less derisory smile: "Just look at her. She might be sixteen, anyway that's what the agent who supplied her said, but she looks as strong as an ox. No, I'm sure she's taking her share of the clover from her father's scrawny cow."

You've really gone too far this time, missus.

The maid deliberately dropped my bag in a clear expression of anger, and my mother retreated from her hurtful sarcasm, perhaps conscious of her mistake. Then she pretended the girl wasn't there and beckoned me with a finger to follow her into the hallway.

"It's six in the evening, and I don't think my meeting with the members of the association at Lalla Ghaitha's villa in Tamara will last too long. I'm hoping to make a grab for the presidency of the Blooming Rose Association for the Defence of Women's Rights. And I'm not going to miss the chance to spar with Nadia, a new little shit who dreams of beating me to it."

What rights are you talking about, mother dear? I overheard you talking to your friend about how you aimed to cement your mutually beneficial relationships with the wives of influential men, women who fill their spare time with stupid crap of no benefit to anyone.

I kept the thought to myself. Besides what do her Association, her friends, and her bullshit have to do with me?

"I'll leave Ghalia here to finish cleaning the rooms and the bathroom until I get back at eight to take her back home with me."

We were at the front door and I was shocked that she stroked my cheek, a gesture of affection that I hadn't seen for a very long time. Then in a strange tone, almost pleading, she said, "Zouhair, my love, you're facing a tough challenge. I barely managed to convince my friends that you failed your bac last year because of a sudden illness. Don't disappoint me again. It's your last chance. I beg you, forget about your quarrels with your classmates and late nights out with your friends. Concentrate on your studies and your exams, and I promise you that we'll do all we can. We'll use our networks so you can finish your studies at a French university. My relationship with your father isn't at its best, but I'm sure that your success will set the waters back on course."

She concluded her plea with a hot kiss to my cheek, so I made a show of seeing her off after she got into the car. Then I slammed the door behind me, causing the small house to rattle.

Go to hell the pair of you! You're the ones really responsible for fouling the waters. There's no point setting them back on course as long as they're not fit for human consumption!

I went back to the bedroom. Ghalia was dusting the windows with enviable application after having made huge efforts to clean the carpets of the villa in the morning. She had rolled her worn trousers up to her knees, revealing two strong calves whose veins stood out against the whiteness of her skin. The sleeves of her pink dress were also rolled up above two plump forearms. Her throat was adorned with a necklace of perspiration, droplets of which slipped unhurriedly down, preferring to nestle between her breasts.

Lost in her own world, she sang in a sad voice with a strange huskiness that only made it more beautiful and sexy:[2]

> "Okay, it's okay, it's okay
> Chaouia has enflamed me and made it worse
> So hard to leave my family and friends."

In an effort to stretch the cloth to the very top of the window overlooking the beach, she stood on the tiptoes of her bare feet. Her patterned scarf slipped down revealing surprisingly fine hair. Ignoring the strands falling over her forehead, she carried on singing, accentuating the words with pleasure:

> "Harbousha's no dancer and no whore
> Harbousha's a symbol of honour and dignity
> She heals wounds at hard times."

I kept quiet, wary of her noticing my presence and at the same time resisting a great urge to get closer and closer to her.

> "The oppressor will never give in
> The tribe will unite under one banner
> I swear by Fridays and Tuesdays I'll take my revenge, Uwaisa."

The last part annoyed me even though I did not understand

---

[2] A famous song from the Moroccan tradition. Harbousha was part of the rebellion of the Oulad Zaid against Caïd Aïssa, the provincial governor, in the nineteenth century. Harbousha is said to have sung it to him rejecting his advances, which led to her death.

what it meant, and I gave the door of the room a violent kick. "What are you doing here?" I shouted, making her jump and turn towards me. She gasped and her eyes widened in an indecipherable way.

A code that was effortlessly able to combine fright and flirtation.

"You've got the whole house to clean before my mother gets back," I whispered. My voice exposed my confusion, but she obeyed and left the room without saying a word.

Couldn't you find anyone but this time bomb to plant in our house, you stupid agent?

* * *

Articles from the original contract between American author Christine McMillan and publisher Charles & Clover – signed by both parties at the publisher's offices at 1230 6th Avenue, Manhattan, New York:

Article 8: The first party, represented by Charles & Clover, is committed to paying $250,000 in advance to the second party, represented by Ms Christine McMillan, who will thereupon receive her annual earnings from the sales of her works on a specific date and according to a specific percentage of profits to be agreed upon in Article 9.

Article 10: The second party, represented by Ms Christine McMillan, is committed to delivering a manuscript of one novel per year, and participating in the publicity tours organized by the first party, represented by Charles & Clover, inside and outside the United States for four years starting from the date of signing this contract.

Article 11: Any breach of this contract may expose the second party, represented by Ms Christine McMillan, to legal liability and payment of the penalty clause stipulated in Article 12.

* * *

(2) The Grapes of Wrath

> *There is nothing more useless than trying to prove something to idiots.*
>
> **Milan Kundera**

Thursday, 26 September 2002
Offices of Charles & Clover – Manhattan:

Who would have imagined that my star's rise in the firmament of literary creativity would be tied to a tragedy that shook every American to the core?

I put the question to myself as I drove through the intersection of 12th and Broadway (the location of the Strand Bookstore) heading towards Union Square.

I had been a plain high school literature teacher, doing her job in routine fashion at Columbine High School near Littleton in Colorado, and was now nearly forty years old. A woman who hitched up with Mike at a young age. He made her believe that he could make her the happiest woman on earth, and she believed that she was madly in love with him. Cindy and then Ronald were the rapid fruits of a hasty marriage. The result: a dull life with a husband who believed that happiness was sitting in front of the TV, belly hanging out, watching baseball games with a trashcan full of empty beer cans beside him. The two fruits lost their sweetness when they became teenagers, with all the difficulties and problems that this entailed. Then came the massacre of Tuesday, 20 April 1999, to turn over (or rip up) that boring page in my life forever.

I didn't have time to stop and stroll down Madison Avenue. The luminous digits of the car's clock showed 5:53. So I continued down 5th Avenue before taking a right towards 50th Street, leaving the Empire State Building and New York Public Library in my wake. I thanked my lucky stars that I managed to reach 6th Avenue on time and I rode the elevator in the offices of Charles & Clover up to the nineteenth floor. I was greeted by a secretary who ushered me into the office of David Hersch, director of publishing, at exactly six o'clock.

"Hello there, Christine McMillan, the creative as punctual as a Swiss chronometer." He had his back to me, but from the high pitch of his voice I could pick out sarcastic mockery. He turned on his heels and came over to me with firm, deliberate steps, then continued in a markedly serious tone, "The woman delighted with fame, fortune and literary glory who has forgotten a small article in her contract with the venerable Charles & Clover publishing house that required her to submit the manuscript of her new novel by the end of last month so we can prepare it for publication and enter it for literary prizes."

His hair was so glossy that I was half convinced he went to a women's hairdresser to have it styled. The prominent brow lacked wrinkles even though he was in his mid-fifties; his bulging eyes, I suspected, he had plucked from the sockets of a poor chameleon in the Nevada desert; his nose, it would be no exaggeration to say, was only an inch or two shorter than Pinocchio's; and his wide mouth revealed dazzlingly white teeth, even though his marriage to cigarettes was a Catholic one, divorce not an option. Sure, I'm also American, but I think of David Hersch with his irritating appearance as a classic example of the American hated by millions around the world, with or without reason.

I was primed for his incendiary opening and I sat calmly down on the large couch and pretended to contemplate a dreadful portrait occupying most of the wall opposite. I wondered how much the jerk had paid the artist to manipulate how the light fell and rework his features so he looked handsome and self-confident.

I squirrelled the stupid question into the furthest reaches of my mind, then gave him a rehearsed answer: "Charles & Clover is a major publisher. In the past it has handled titans on the scale of Hemingway, Fitzgerald, Wolff, Irving, Lessing and others, and I am honoured to work with it. You do know, though, that the primary source of my work's success is the quality of what I write and the ability of my words to touch the hearts and minds of readers..."

"The quality of what you write?" he interrupted, adding a drawn-out laugh that dealt a fatal blow to my composure. "In the US there are hundreds of thousands, if not millions, of talented people looking for a quarter of the chance you've had. We picked you out of the gutter from the small-time publisher who released the first few editions of your early work *Prisoner of Class 12*. Then we saved you from a dumb literary agent whose clock stopped ticking in the '80s and who rejected the limelight and preferred the role of anonymous talent spotter. Not so?"

His caustic words annoyed me, and I stood up and walked across the office to confront him directly: "I really was crazy when I dropped an agent who discovered my talent and encouraged me to take the risk of writing and publishing. As for what you call the life of fame and fortune, I've lost the taste for it. Your goddamn exclusive contract compels me to release a novel every year and take part in publicity tours that cover most of the US plus countries in Europe and Asia. I've been turned into a machine shorn of human feelings. I've had to give up my old life in Denver and stay here in New York to write novels. A kind of writing no different from flipping burgers, in my opinion. No, David, I won't play your suicidal game anymore..."

The director of publishing was stunned by my onslaught, but he composed himself with remarkable alacrity and waved a copy of the contract in my face, proof that he had prepared himself in advance to enter into a game of jeopardy in which we both knew who would win and who would lose.

"Listen carefully. Long experience has taught me that the biggest problem for novelists is that they handle life as if it were a novel they can control and whose events they can alter at will. You are bound by a contract that you signed with us when of sound mind. Just go over Articles 10 and 11."

I snatched the paper out of his hand with a violence that showed how worked up I was, and I forced myself to re-read and scrutinize what I well knew.

Yes, I signed the contract with my eyes shut. Stupidly, I agreed to its terms, heedless to advice and warnings, simply because at the time the contents of Article 8 made my mouth water.

"Calling your current agent, or even your attorney, won't help you in the slightest. The contract is watertight. I've persuaded the board to postpone publication of your scheduled novel until January. Come on, get your usual calm and enthusiasm back. Your lovely beach house in the Miami suburbs awaits. You have two months to submit a draft of your new book to the editorial department."

I thought he had finished, but he continued with contempt: "I also advise you to see a psychoanalyst. Perhaps they can help you cope with the early signs of menopause!"

A bitter lump stuck in my throat as I strode towards the door, which I flung open to the astonishment of the secretary. I got into the elevator, hoping its doors would close quickly, as if all the demons in the world were on my tail.

I sat behind the steering wheel of my car and picked up my mobile phone with trembling fingers.

No, I wasn't going to call my attorney or my current literary agent, or even Mike, but a number I hadn't forgotten in the three years since I had last heard the voice at the end of the line. After just two rings a calm, steady voice said, "Hello," and I burst into tears. "Brandon, save me! I need you!"

* * *

Practice question in physics – third year high school (baccalauréat) – curriculum of Moroccan Ministry of Education 2002:

The electrical circuit in the diagram below consists of:

G: Constant voltage generator of 10V = U_0
C: Condenser of capacitance 5μF
L_b: Inductor of impedance 0.8H with negligible resistance
K: Circuit breaker
1–1 The circuit breaker is set in position 1, charging the capacitor. Calculate the charge Q_0 of the capacitor.
1–2 The circuit breaker is set in position 2, at time t = 0.
1–2–1 Derive the differential equation describing the charge Q of the capacitor.
1–2–2 Find an expression for charge Q as a function of time.

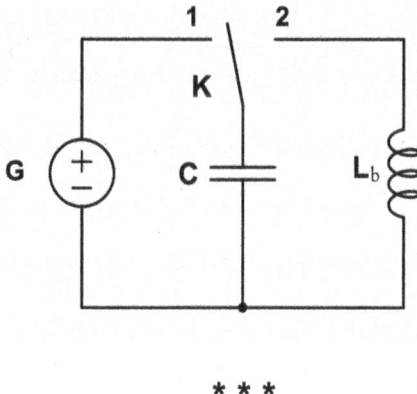

* * *

(2') The Assault

> *It's the same story always repeated: some guy who nobody listens to, nobody pays attention to, and he punishes the lot of them by forcing them to watch what he's capable of.*
>
> R. J. Ellory

Tuesday, 14 May 2002
Sidi Abed Plage – Harhoura:

Sprawled on my bed, fingers toying with my pen, exercise book next to me, I can't work out an easy physics question. No surprise really, when my desire to calculate the value of charge Q_0 clashes with my preoccupation to solve another more difficult problem: Why has my life gone so badly wrong?

To some I'm a prime example of a spoilt kid, whose life of affluence and luxury has stunted his mental capacity and snared him in boredom and laziness. But the truth is something quite different.

Zouhair Belkacem, son of distinguished doctor Younis Belkacem and steely lawyer Hanan el-Farisi was a good boy, polite and obedient, like Karim the model kid in our ridiculous school books. An outstanding student, who liked horse riding, excelled at chess, and basked in the admiration and esteem of his friends and most of his family.

But he was afflicted with two selfish parents blinded by greed, dreams of wealth and keeping up with so-and-so. They forgot the early years of their marriage as two happy young people living in a small house with simple furniture, and raced to climb the ladder leading to success. Even if getting to the top meant trampling over the backs of those they loved most.

Their only child was, in their view, too young to understand what was really going on around him. A father who took advantage of his profession for sexual ends, and a mother who made the law a servant of her own mysterious interests. The son, caught between them, suffered as he turned from a docile child into an unruly teenager bent on causing problems as a futile protest against the fact that he was totally lost.

I picked up the physics textbook in disgust and flung it away in hatred, as though it were to blame for my problems. Then I hurried over to my backpack in a desperate search for the beautiful cure . . .

A swig from a bottle of vodka I stole from my father's secret fridge, although it wasn't really suitable for a month of record-breaking high temperatures.

You Russians are fantastic. You invented a legendary drink that makes you fly to the seventh heaven.

No harm in a swig or two before my mother arrives to take Ghalia home, then the real evening begins and fuck the physics questions and the whole bac. It'll be an evening for me, in the company of sea and stars . . . and vodka!

The drink was burning my throat but urged me on. I stuck the end of the bottle in my mouth in defiance of the high alcohol content and the risk of losing control of myself before my mother came back. My body heated up after a few minutes and without my mind understanding the meaning, I blurted out, "Ghalia! The poorest, most beautiful girl I've ever seen, come over here!"

In a few seconds she appeared before me. I noticed the expression on her pretty face had changed from exhaustion to apprehension, whose main cause was the bottle, and I hid it behind my back. "What's the name of the godforsaken village that sprouts poor girls as incredibly good-looking as you?"

She raised her right eyebrow, either expressing her astonishment or her inherent flirtatiousness, no difference.

"When will Lalla Hanan be back? She's very late."

Her voice held an unmistakable note of fear, and I tried to reassure her with a more even response: "That's what my mother is like. For sure the temptation of chatting to her friends will make her forget the time she has to be back. No problem. What do you say we wait for her together?" With a sweep of my hand I invited her to sit next to me, but she didn't budge. "I can't do the physics question, but I'm sure you can help me, even though you're just an ignorant village girl who knows nothing about science. It's about a voltage generator, a capacitor, and an inductor . . ."

"Excuse me, sir. I have to go."

I ignored her interruption and continued, "Let's imagine that the voltage generator is me and the capacitor is the bottle that scared you . . ." I stood up fast to jump her. ". . . and the inductor with negligible resistance is you . . ."

The shock paralysed her, allowing me to put my arm around her waist and bring my lips up to her neck. But with astonishing agility she slipped away and squared up to me. "Who do you think you are, asshole? Keep away from me or I'll knock your teeth out!" she roared, then backed away and left the room at a run.

I gave a smile of pleasure, excited by her husky voice to try again. "Taming the bitch isn't going to be easy. Which only goes to show that woman epitomizes the mystery of life – it only gives you what you want if you deserve it."

Strange words, and I felt so hot it was making it hard to breathe. I pulled off my sweat-soaked shirt and went out into the hall after her.

"Don't play hard to get. I'm only thinking of what's good for you. What will you get out of hard labour for my mother if it isn't interspersed with some enjoyable times with me? Are you . . ."

I didn't finish what I was saying but turned it into a scornful laugh when my eyes met Ghalia's, wide in fury. With two trembling hands she gripped the handle of a kitchen knife, defending herself behind the dining table in the living room.

"I'm going to tell Lalla Hanan everything."

The cold liquor running in my veins gave me the courage to ignore her threat and move closer to her. I managed to grab her left wrist, confident that she was too much of a coward to attack me with the knife.

A bad idea, and I paid the price almost instantly . . .

The cut wasn't deep or serious, but my arm was swimming in bright red blood, and I lost it. "You insignificant insect, how . . ." Rage blinded me to everything but the heavy ceramic vase in front of me. I threw it at her and she just managed to avoid it, but the back of her head hit the window handle and she fell to the floor unconscious, her blood sullying her patterned headscarf.

My fit of rage and crazed lust gave me extra strength that caused me to forget the pain. I undid her belt and ripped open her tatty pink dress, the last obstacle to my assault on the gates of her impregnable fortress.

Hadn't I told her that to solve the physics question there needed to be an inductor of negligible resistance?

* * *

The Final Report – Episode on the Columbine Massacre – National Geographic Channel – 2007

Excerpt from minutes 18–20:

(Narrator in the background): April 20th, 1999 . . .

The rampage of Eric Harris and Dylan Klebold at Columbine High School is over.

Students are in shock.

(Student crying in distress): I was under a table and people were being shot all around me.

(Student, visibly in shock): They got automatic weapons, sawn-off shotguns and pipe bombs.

The dead include twelve students (four females and eight males), one teacher, and the two gunmen.

Throughout the school, police find pipe bombs and shell casings, evidence left behind in the worst school shooting in American history. The level of violence leaves police and school officials wondering:

Did the teachers at Columbine notice any warning signs?

That night, at Eric and Dylan's homes, police discover a wealth of evidence, including ammunition, metal pipes, fuses, violent essays and journals. They also seize a series of home videos made by Eric and Dylan in the months before the massacre.

In the days following the shooting, impromptu memorials appear around the school.

For the grief-stricken community, the most troubling question remains: Why did Eric and Dylan go on their murderous rampage?

* * *

(3) American Pastoral

> *Woman does not understand love. When she loves, she loves the wrong man.*
> Abdurrahman Munif

Thursday, 26 September 2002
Central Park – Manhattan:

Brandon did not disappoint me. He agreed to meet without the slightest hesitation, seeming to forget the problems that had wrecked our friendship for three years. I was relieved to see they hadn't changed him one bit – he maintained his resistance to having dinner with me at one of Manhattan's restaurants, always poking fun at their swankiness. He preferred to buy two bottles of sparkling water and a couple of hotdogs, which we would eat, as he put it, al fresco.

"Let's meet in thirty minutes in Central Park by the Lake." Thirty minutes was enough to go over some of our history.

I first met him in Denver in 1984 as part of a programme at college to help young soldiers coming back from conflict zones complete their education and reintegrate into civilian life. He was a handsome guy just turned twenty, tall, broad-shouldered and with good skin. His green eyes had an enduring sadness and he never seemed to smile, which gave him a singular attraction.

War had screwed up his present by killing his comrades and finished off his future by severing his right leg. Brandon had been injured in the 1983 bombing of a US military barracks in the Lebanese capital Beirut, a city I couldn't locate on the map, and I doubt he knew much about either when he was sent there at nineteen years of age. The wounded soldier came back from the hell of Lebanon traumatized and damaged. The medics had had to amputate his leg and replace it with a prosthetic, which he would have to live with for the rest of his life. I learnt this from reading the report attached to his file. Relying on him to talk about his past was a non-starter.

He seemed a nice guy, despite his melancholy. I got why he was introverted and loved solitude. I felt for him and did all I could to make things easier for him, motivated by a human impulse that went beyond what the university administration had asked of me. I showed him round the campus and gave him some advice about first-year classes. With a few friends I also helped organize a mini welcoming party. His new classmates gave him a round of applause, as a hero who had defied every difficulty to defend the flag with courage and valour. He reacted to this sentimentality with a rare ghost of a smile, which I later realised was one of cynical indifference.

My mission ended with the start of the new semester and I went back to my friends in junior year, also modern literature majors. That did not prevent me from meeting up with him from time to time, depending on my schedule and maybe on his inclination. Then, on my twenty-first birthday, he suddenly decided to open the first crack in his impregnable shell. He came to my party, bringing a small tasteful gift with him. It was a copy of *Mrs Dalloway* by Virginia Woolf, a recent edition in hardback, bearing a lovely dedication from him, which I did not need to be a graphologist to know he had written with an uncertain and trembling hand.

That really marked the beginning of our long friendship. Finally, I had come across someone who shared a passion that was of no interest to my circle of friends. Reading.

Brandon helped me discover new worlds. He taught me to dance with Zorba. He accompanied me on an exhausting tour of the streets of Dublin with Leopold Bloom, as Joyce had done in *Ulysses*. He wrapped me in an overcoat to bear the cold of Saint Petersburg in our pursuit of Raskolnikov, torn between *Crime and Punishment*. The allusions of Pessoa's *Book of Disquiet* he tried to unravel with me. Then he guided me through the labyrinth of *One Hundred Years of Solitude* to a brief encounter with *The Stranger* before we went back home like two people *On the Road* with Jack Kerouac in search of *The Great Gatsby*, avoiding everything that might draw us towards the maelstrom of *The Sound and the Fury* with *The Catcher in the Rye*.

At the time, I asked him why he was mad about books. The simplicity of his answer amazed me: "Literature isn't pure imagination like some people think. It's real life. And the most beautiful thing is the tightrope walk between reality and fiction. I don't reckon I would have been able to understand the absurdity of a life that has taken everything away from me unless I had held on to one end of that tightrope, which would lead me to unravel the riddle of life."

That's how our relationship developed. I did keep it within bounds; I wasn't going to give it a Hollywood ending.

My mom talked about signs from the universe and history repeating itself. She always told me the story of how she fell in love with my dad and married him in the early '60s after they were fated to meet on the steps of the college where they were both studying. Dad also encouraged me to get close to Brandon, expressing admiration for someone who reminded him of his youth as a soldier who also spent a few years serving abroad. Based somewhere more stable, he was luckier than Brandon and came home fit and well.

I got their message, but acted dumb. They understood that we would never be more than friends as long as I had given my heart to someone else.

Did I make the right choice?

I don't know . . .

It's too late to ask the question!

To begin with, all the girls like a teen rebel who's only good at dragging their dignity through the mud, and so keep the devoted good guy as a "friend". Only a klutz of a girl, who insists on ignoring the feelings of the good guy, keeps going with the rebel till the end, believing that he will change over time and turn into a mature boyfriend and then a perfect husband.

Mike was the rebel.

Brandon was the good guy.

And I was the klutz . . .

Anyway, the river of life flowed along and I graduated with honours from college and got a job as a teacher at Columbine High School. I married according to my heart, then had kids, and like any normal American mom suffocated in routine and boredom.

Brandon, though, was luckier (or braver) than me. He refused to submit to what he called the chains of savage capitalism. After graduation, he was happy to spend a few years gaining experience as an editor and proofreader at a big publishers in New York, then he set off to fulfil his dream of working as an independent literary agent, reading drafts, guiding and advising authors, then acting for them in defence of their rights and interests with publishers and the media.

He believed that happiness lay in turning his passion for reading and literature into a way of making a living, and he was pretty successful at it. That allowed him to do another job, one he loved as much as his first passion: being a guardian angel who vanished for long periods only to appear at just the right time to save me from the gales that fate was battering against the ship of my life.

The 1990s wasn't a merciful decade for me. In the early years, a sudden heart attack took my dad, and in the middle ones cancer stole my mother from me. Then at the end the Columbine massacre struck and the fragile cohesion of my family came unstuck.

Everyone was interested in what happened on that black day, and the innocent victims enjoyed sympathy and solidarity. Nobody understood the real motives why Eric and Dylan committed the horrific massacre.

And me?

Just another lucky lady who wasn't shot dead or injured, lightly or seriously. She wasn't the mother or relative of anyone killed or injured. Nobody cared about the imprint that the sight of dead bodies, the smell of blood, and the sound of gunfire left in her memory, or about her inability to rid herself of the deadly fear that gripped her the day she hid under a table with her students, waiting for two frenzied teenagers to reach the floor her classroom was on.

The effects of the massacre threw me into a deep depression and I had weeks of intensive therapy that sapped my strength and energy. I also suffered from the repulsive indifference of a low-down dirty husband who didn't take me seriously and couldn't be bothered to stand by me in my ordeal. He simply vented his outright annoyance at my being in a vicious circle swinging between insomnia and nightmares, followed by an addiction to powerful sedatives.

I reached a point where I could no longer bear the selfishness of a man who not for one second in all the years of our marriage I felt cared about me. I asked for a divorce and went to live alone in my parents' house, bereft at the fact that Cindy and Ronald chose to stay with their father.

Then Brandon turned up to save me from going crazy or killing myself.

He brought the solution with him, or the pen with which I wrote a new chapter in my life . . .

* * *

Blooming Rose Association for the Defence of Women's Rights holds outreach event to raise awareness about abuse of domestic staff

(*Al-Rai* Newspaper – Social Affairs Page – Monday, 1 April 2002)

The Blooming Rose Association for the Defence of Women's Rights held an outreach event with its members and other civil society activists on Friday 29 March at the association's base in Rabat's Agdal neighbourhood, to discuss the abuse of household staff, especially minors, and explore ways to protect them from all forms of discrimination and potential psychological and sexual exploitation at the hands of employers.

To this end, prominent lawyer and legal activist Hanan el-Farisi called for action to combat abuses in this unregulated sector and stressed the urgent need for legislation to provide a regulatory framework that ensures harsh penalties for anyone who violates the dignity of domestic workers. She also raised the issue of parents being subject to rapacious employment agents, particularly in overlooked rural areas where, owing to poverty, some families force their underage daughters to leave school early and send them out to work. According to the lawyer, this problem demands an immediate solution to limit its dangerous implications for the legal gains achieved by Moroccan women under the new dispensation.

(3') The Fall

Good and evil are our standard for judging people, but is that enough?
Donato Carrisi

Tuesday, 14 May 2002
Sidi Abed Plage – Harhoura:

Once she had come round, a few seconds was enough for Ghalia to take in the magnitude of what I had done to her. Then, for several minutes, she trembled in shock without making a sound while trying desperately to cover up her breasts, shoulders, and thighs with the clothing I had torn off when I attacked her in a burst of drink-fuelled lust that I had never imagined myself capable of.

I willingly admit to a long list of juvenile problems: staying out late clubbing and missing school in the morning; fighting with my friends for no good reason, leading to censure in and out of school; and, naturally, failing my exams last year was premeditated. But raping a defenceless cleaning girl in a scene of surreal horror that mixed sweat with blood, and groans of pain with moans of pleasure? The only explanation was that I was approaching the point of no return. If I hadn't passed it already, that is.

My fear equalled Ghalia's agony and I could not stop myself from shaking as I envisaged my mother's return and her furious reaction when she discovered what had happened in her absence.

I convinced myself that the girl would keep her mouth shut. She would never dare disgrace herself, unless driven by madness to risk the reputation that I knew was the most precious thing she possessed in the traditional community she belonged to. I approached her holding a white handkerchief soaked in alcohol in an attempt to clean the cut on her head and help her stand up.

A stupid move that lit the fuse of her fury and rapidly doused the spark of my absurd idea, that had only been a means to help me calm down.

Ghalia lashed out at me and intense shame paralysed me as I surrendered to her hysterical slaps and punches. I was stunned by her amazing ability to guess what I was thinking.

"I might be a poor village girl like you and your mother say, but you're going to pay the price for what you've done. I won't rest easy until I see you behind bars." She said this in a cruel tone that did not match her sorry state and the tears running down her cheeks. Words that had no relation to the humble domestic servant to whose name my mother had prefixed "the dumb cow" for the few weeks she had worked for us.

Had we been wrong to think she was illiterate and ignorant, understood nothing, and had never gone to school? The question evaporated in a flash when she suddenly stopped hitting me and rushed towards the front door and let herself out. I followed shouting, "Ghalia! Ghalia! Come back here. Don't do anything stupid. Please!"

The echo of my voice trailed off into the deserted emptiness while she ran like the wind, holding the hem of her torn dress up to her chest, oblivious to her hair flying loose. A blast of cold air stopped me chasing after her and reminded me I wasn't wearing a shirt. I went back inside to find one, wasting time that was more valuable than I imagined.

I went beyond the area of empty beach houses and reached the dirt track leading to the main road. The only light came from the moon and I fell over twice and only regained my balance with great difficulty. I kept calling Ghalia's name and surrendered to a despair that put paid to all my hopes of correcting my fatal mistake.

Would she look for the nearest police station or post to report me, or would the shock and her ignorance of the isolated beach area stop her thinking clearly and perhaps make her run off into the unknown?

My confusion soon ended when I was caught in the light of a torch while brushing the sand off my shirt. I retreated backwards and called in fear, "Who's there? Who are you?"

Half-shrouded in darkness, all that was visible of his face was a bushy moustache and two crafty-looking eyes, made more so by the put-on firmness with which he said, "I believe I'm the one authorized to ask that question. I'm the guard of the beach residencies and I'm going straight to the police if it turns out you're one of those chancers out for a quick fumble with their girlfriend on the beach. Things didn't quite work out as you planned, no doubt, since I spotted the shadowy figure of a girl get swallowed up in the dark before I could catch her."

Ghalia, no doubt.

The logic of his deduction was supported by the fact that many drunks and lovers sought refuge at this isolated beach that nobody bothered about outside the summer holidays. Still, he didn't let me disprove him as he continued with a sneer, "No worries. A bird in the hand is worth two in the bush!" He took out his mobile phone and I noticed that he was holding a thick stick. First, he waved it in my face, then poked its pointy end in my chest in a way that I secretly felt was hammy. When he also started dialling his phone, I got more nervous and had to play my hand: "Don't do it. Please. I'm Zouhair. Dr Belkacem's son. He owns number 6. The runaway girl is our cleaner. She ran off after I had an argument with her . . ."

I played my last card by asking him, "Also, I haven't seen you here before. Mouti is the usual guard. I know him well. So, who are you then?"

* * *

Email to Rachid Bennacer, PhD student in contemporary literature, from his thesis supervisor:

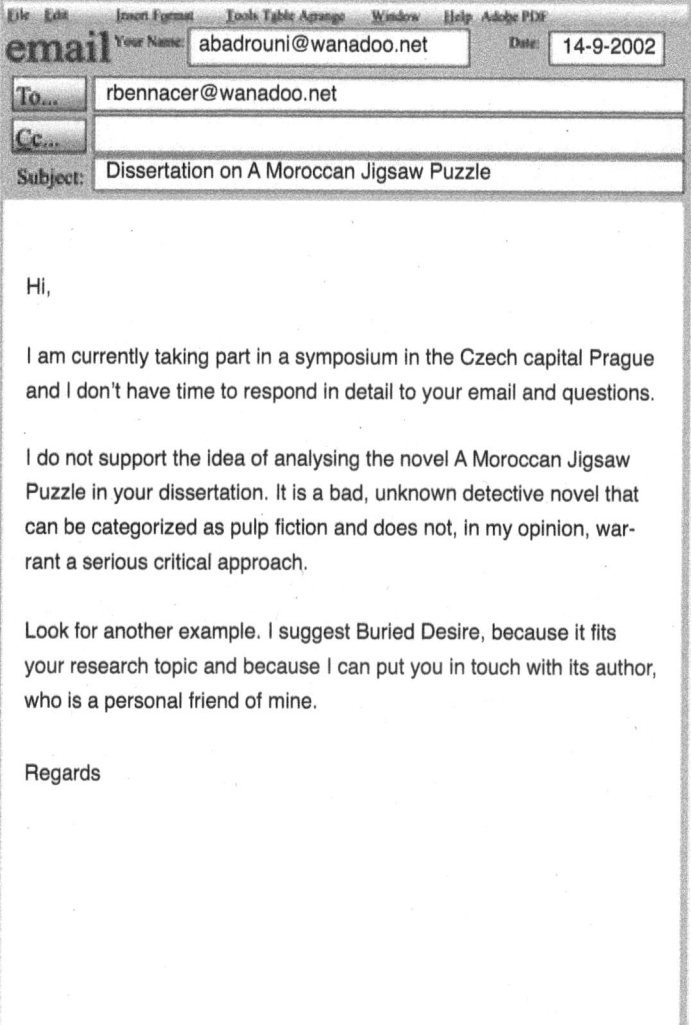

Hi,

I am currently taking part in a symposium in the Czech capital Prague and I don't have time to respond in detail to your email and questions.

I do not support the idea of analysing the novel A Moroccan Jigsaw Puzzle in your dissertation. It is a bad, unknown detective novel that can be categorized as pulp fiction and does not, in my opinion, warrant a serious critical approach.

Look for another example. I suggest Buried Desire, because it fits your research topic and because I can put you in touch with its author, who is a personal friend of mine.

Regards

Email to Rachid Bennacer, PhD student in contemporary literature, from Dr Fabien Bedos, French Arabist at the Sorbonne, Paris:

From: fbedos@wanadoo.net
Date: 20-9-2002
To: rbennacer@wanadoo.net
Cc:
Subject: Re A Moroccan Jigsaw Puzzle

Dear friend Rachid Bennacer,

Greetings.

Perhaps you wonder why I address you as friend even though I do not know you personally. But you are undoubtedly familiar with the precept that applies to all true lovers of literature: consider all those who have read a book you know as your close friends.

Turning to your dissertation, this is the first time that a Moroccan researcher interested in A Moroccan Jigsaw Puzzle has got in touch with me. It is an excellent novel, which I feel privileged to have read and translated into French, and I have presented it to my students as an example worthy of study and analysis.

The novel is appropriate for your thesis. It contains elements that fit very well with your critical approach to the subject of narrative techniques in new fiction. I find your supervisor's reason for dismissing it strange given that the author displays great talent and accurately observes societal changes in his country.

Great literature, however, is destined to remain eternal and always surprises us by reviving from nowhere, in defiance of ignorance and oblivion. Take the example of Franz Kafka, who instructed his friend Max Brod to burn the manuscripts of his work. The friend disobeyed his command and published them, leaving us the legacy of a literary artist who made a powerful mark on modern world literature, even though most of his stories and novels are unfinished.

Think of this then as an introductory email and rest assured that I will do all I can to help you make progress with your dissertation.

Warm regards,

Your friend Fabien

(4) Writing Degree Zero

> *Writing is like a magic trick; it isn't enough to pull rabbits from a hat, you have to do it with style and in an entertaining way.*
>
> Isabel Allende

Thursday, 26 September 2002
Central Park – Manhattan:

A shadowy figure appeared in the distance just as I reached that point in memory. I stood up to greet him and, with feigned delight manufactured to hide my great longing to see him, I said, "The long winter coat, the black hat, it seems you're . . ."

"The private eye Blue in *Ghosts*, part two of our friend Paul Auster's *New York Trilogy*."

Hugging him warmly, I commented on his response with an artless laugh. I invited him to sit down on a bench by the lake, snatching a few seconds to take in how the years had changed his features. To his face he had added a short beard, a little patchy in places, and wrinkles were creeping around his eyes. When he took off his hat I discovered some grey at the temples, which only made him more handsome.

Dear me, what a numbskull! Where had my brain been when I chose Mike over Brandon? Where?

"I confess that I would not object if the OED put my picture next to the entry for 'stupid'. It's the least I deserve." That was the best I could come out with, in expectation of a harsh response holding me to account for all I had done. But he confirmed what I had known about him for eighteen years by giving a gentle smile and pushing a hotdog and a can of sparkling water towards me.

My excitement affected my outward composure, and I took a cigarette out of a pack I kept in my pocket. I placed the filter between my lips, but he pulled it out of my mouth. "Don't believe the hype about smoking and creativity," he said dryly. "Cigarettes won't help you get over your crisis. They'll make it worse. Picture yourself on the back cover of your next book with blueish lips, scarecrow hair and dark rings around your eyes. The reader will think twice before buying a copy!"

I gaped in astonishment and he added in a serious tone, "Actually, I'm not at all surprised you called. Of course, you've fallen out with Charles & Clover because you agreed to an exploitative contract wrapped in financial inducement. It was obvious in *Secrets of the Dark* and *Silent Angel*."

"Did you really read them? What did you think?" I cried, revealing my excitement at knowing his impression of the two novels I had written after our connection ended. He winked with his right eye, took a bite of his hotgod and replied with his mouth full. "Which would you prefer, honesty or flattery?"

He read the answer in my eyes. "Both trash," he said in a resolute tone tinged with derision. "Don't be deceived by sales figures that belie the terrible decline in the literary quality of your works." He opened a can of sparkling water and gulped down half of it, pretending to ignore my shock. "The plot in *Secrets of the Dark* developed okay, but you spoiled it with a ridiculous ending only fit for a third-rate novel."

His snide remark grated on my nerves. "Readers need happy endings," I said defiantly. "Endings to restore hope in a better future . . ."

"Who said you have to write what they want?" he retorted firmly. "Hemingway, for example, could have ended *Farewell to Arms* with Frederic and his lover having reached the mountains and escaped the horrors of war with their love. But, against the wishes of the reader he chose to kill Catherine and her baby in childbirth. A powerful novel is able to reflect messy reality, the bad, the unfair, the bitter, even if the events are fiction."

"And what about *Silent Angel?*"

"It lacked sufficient preparation," he said baldly, "because you are obliged to write a novel a year. The plot is weak and flimsy. The characters are one dimensional and don't make the reader feel that they might exist in the real world. Also, you wrote it so fast, you made structural errors. Forgive me for being honest, but it only sold well because your name and photo were on the cover. That trick might not work next time."

The last thing he said made me lose control of the conflicting emotions inside me and I defended myself in the worst possible way. "You're casting aspersions on my talent because you don't accept my decision to dispense with your services after the success of my first novel, when Charles & Clover got involved and took me on with an irresistible deal." My temper made me spill a little sparkling water on my clothes and he moved closer to offer me a tissue to dab it off.

He replied with a cool indifference to the cruelty of what I had said: "But I'm confronting you with the fact that you've turned into a writer tailored to the bullshit of the postmodern age. A box-office star whose private life and sexy picture on the covers of fashion magazines are of more interest to readers than her writing. Sure, your phoney success will make you super rich so you can buy a luxury home in the suburbs of New York and a fabulous beach house in Miami, but it doesn't put you among the ranks of the great. To your publisher you're no more than a passing bubble. You won the admiration and sympathy of readers after your first novel, where you combined creative imagination with your bitter experience of the horrific massacre. They took advantage of your success and convinced you that you were too big to deal with an obscure agent like me. They also relied on your pretty face to adorn the covers of your books and boost their profits. But they will be the first to dump you when the interest wanes. That is unless you get back in control and make your next novel announce the rebirth of your writing talent, not write its obituary."

I felt a secret happiness at his expression "pretty face" and inwardly cursed my ridiculous petulance. I also moved closer to him, reducing the gap between my knee and his artificial leg to a matter of inches. "Auster and King have brought out new novels, while I'm uselessly roaming a barren wilderness in search of some fraction of an idea fit to turn into fiction. What's worse is I have to submit a goddam manuscript, of which I haven't written a single word, in two months' time. What am I going to do?"

His features softened under my imploring gaze and he placed his long fingers over mine, as if to protect me from a danger to come whose precise nature neither of us knew. "I've had faith in your talent, my dear, from the day I took the liberty of reading the texts, stories and thoughts you were writing as a young woman. You remember that, at the time, I encouraged you to play to your abilities while you preferred to hide behind your satisfaction with the role of reader and submit to luck, which had hitched you to a stupid husband, who was never going to accept your superiority. That required years of patience from me before I made positive use of the crisis you were going through and revived the dream of presenting you to the world as an outstanding writer, confident that the act of writing would succeed where drugs and destructive sessions with a shrink had failed."

His sympathy encouraged me to play on his masculinity with feminine weakness. "I need an idea outside the box," I said like a little girl looking for a lost doll.

He finished the rest of his hotdog, then rolled the paper napkin into a ball and said with the confidence of someone sure he has a solution to everything, "Outside the box, and maybe outside the

United States too..."

His gnomic statement spurred my curiosity: "What do you mean?" but he played casual, showing off his skill at throwing the paper tissue ball into a trashcan. He waited a long while before answering my question with one word that only set my mind ablaze with confusion: "Morocco!"

* * *

**Excerpts from the Moroccan Penal Code
(as in force in 2002):**

Article 475

Anyone who, without violence, threats or fraud, abducts or seduces, or attempts to abduct or seduce, a minor under the age of eighteen, shall be punished by imprisonment of one to five years and a fine of 500 dirhams. When a minor of marriageable age thus abducted or seduced has married her abductor, the latter can only be prosecuted on the complaint of persons having standing to request the annulment of the marriage and can only be convicted after this annulment of the marriage has been pronounced.

Article 486

Rape is committed when a man has sexual relations with a woman against her will. The offence is punishable by imprisonment for five to ten years.

If the rape victim is a minor under the age of eighteen, or disabled, or handicapped, or known to have weak mental faculties, or is a pregnant woman, the penalty is imprisonment for ten to twenty years

Article 487

If the perpetrator is a relative of the victim, if he has authority over her, is her guardian, in her paid employment, or in the paid employment of the persons designated above, if he is a religious official or minister of religion, or if the perpetrator, whoever he is, was helped in his attack by one or more people, the penalty shall be:
– imprisonment from ten to twenty years, in the case provided for in article 486, paragraph 1;
– imprisonment from twenty to thirty years, in the case provided for in article 486, paragraph 2.

* * *

(4') The Mother

> *Laws are spider webs through which the big flies pass and the little ones get caught.*
> **Honoré de Balzac**

Sunday, 28 July 2002
Hayy el Riad – Rabat:

I threw the plastic ball and Spike, the German Shepherd dog, shot off like an arrow to search for it among the bushes in the large garden. Medium size, fast, and very intelligent, Spike had been with me for five years and I had found no better candidate to be my only friend.

He came back with the ball in his mouth, wagging his tail in joy at having carried out his mission. I stroked his back and head. "What do you think, Spike? Where has Ghalia gone and disappeared?" I said to him, sharing the worry that for weeks had robbed me of sleep.

He looked at me with inquiring eyes and confirmed his puzzlement by giving a bark that showed his willingness to serve me in any way except listening to me speak. I threw the plastic ball as far away as I could and went inside through the back door before he could catch me.

My legs took me towards my mother's study and as if in a

hypnotic trance I went over to her bookshelves in search of a weighty legal tome. Finding what I wanted, I put it on the desk and started rapidly leafing through the pages until I reached the sections whose contents I could recite with my eyes closed.

Every article of the criminal code went against me. That girl, a minor, could have me thrown in prison and wreck my future if she proved to the police and the judiciary that I was guilty. Even if my mother were to intervene to save me from that inevitable dire fate, I wouldn't rule out her preferring death than seeing me marry a servant girl, which would be a scandal that would bring down the scorn and gloating of her friends, Lalla so-and-so and Madame blah-blah.

But none of that happened...

The case didn't reach the courts. Nobody knew the details. There was no sign of Ghalia after she ran away from the beach house, despite her threat to inform the police and avenge her violated honour.

I pushed the tome aside and, resting my elbows on the desktop, put my trembling hands on my head. I closed my eyes, waiting for the daily broadcast of the tape that recorded with total accuracy the details of that night and which my memory had produced with consummate professionalism.

*

My final words stilled the defiant workings of the guard's fingers eager to make the call. His intention to assail me with further questions was foiled by the sound of tyres crunching gravel. The car headlights shining in our eyes made us both turn around.

My mother was finally back. More than an hour late.

"What's wrong, Zouhair?" she said, rushing over with genuine concern having spotted the blood coagulating on my arm. She ignored the presence of the guard, who had taken a few steps back. Forgetting the difference in our heights, I took comfort in her embrace like a five-year-old. My words stuck in my throat and I failed to render any of them audible.

My tongue finally came unstuck under the crazed interrogation of my mother. I surprised her by breaking down and confessing to having, under the influence of alcohol, raped the cleaner. I was not oblivious to her shock at learning the girl had run off but, thanks to long experience, she pulled herself together and ordered me to get into the car. Then she told the guard, who had heard practically everything, to go inside with her. He obeyed without hesitation.

When they came back the clock showed exactly 10. They were carrying the bags we had brought with us a few hours before. My mother seemed calmer (or made a brilliant pretence) and simply gave a brief nod of acknowledgement to the guard, who waved goodbye to her. She did not speak until we had driven several kilometres down the main road to Rabat. "Tuhami is just a temporary guard standing in for his brother Mouti who's gone to their village to visit their sick mother . . ."

I was amazed she hadn't touched on the real issue, and had been expecting a boring disquisition accusing me of being mindless and not appreciating the seriousness of what I had done. Her neutral tone, which made it difficult to discover what she was driving at, confirmed to me that she wasn't actually talking to me, but rather following her favourite habit of thinking out loud.

I shrank into the seat to make room for her short, sharp sentences: "Ghalia hasn't kept quiet to conceal what happened. She's even threatened to tell the police. That confirms what the agent said. He warned me that she was a difficult character, although she's really strong and able to do the hardest housework without flagging or complaint . . .

"Ghalia forgot about her head wound and the sorry state of her clothes. Meaning she intends to carry out her threat . . . The few weeks she spent with us demonstrated that she has an excellent visual memory. I wouldn't rule out her having used it to memorize the way from Hayy el Riad in Rabat to Sidi Abed Plage . . .

"I asked her more than once how old she was. She said she was a minor under sixteen . . ."

We were only 100 metres or so from the house, when she stopped the car under a streetlight. She brought her thoughts to an end with one word: "Okay!" Then she turned to me. "Listen carefully, Zouhair." She said it so coldly, I got scared. "You've really gone too far this time. But I'm not going to punish you now, because I'm certain you will do exactly what I'm going to tell you. Understood?" Terror prevented me answering and she continued, "I'm going to take charge. Nobody is going to harm you and the cleaner won't carry out her threat, if you stick to my conditions: nobody must know the details of what happened; you just forget about Ghalia and don't get involved with the problem of her running away, which doesn't concern you; come back to your senses and concentrate on your studies so you pass the bac, as a preliminary to sending you abroad to university far away from here."

With her right hand on my seat she leant over so she could open the car door with her left and point with her index finger to the end of the street.

"There is one more condition. You get out, take the bags out of the boot, and go back to the house alone. I have a great deal of fine-tuning to do. Don't worry, your father's not here. He told me he was going out until late with friends. I'll tell him about the maid leaving later. Now get out of my sight!"

*

The ticking of the wall clock pulled me out of my reverie. I stood up heavily, returned the law book to its place, and left the room.

Long weeks passed and life went back to normal. My father resumed his series of adventures. My mother continued dividing her time between pleading in court and her campaign to become head of her silly association, while preventing herself uttering a single word about the night of the cleaner's disappearance, which seemed like a memory destined to be quickly forgotten.

I carried out my part of the bargain and passed the resit of the bac. I kept my mouth shut and didn't cause any new problems, manifesting what might be described as a radical change to my volatile and confrontational personality.

That wasn't enough to get rid of Ghalia's ghost . . .

My fears became obsessive. Every time the phone or doorbell rang, I imagined that the police were coming to take me away for questioning or that the village servant girl, not satisfied with having cut my arm, had come back with a bigger knife to kill me.

My mother refused to tell me what she had done after I had gone home that night. I searched her eyes for an answer to the riddle, but I was met with a provocative coldness that proved she had chosen the silent treatment as a novel way of punishing me for what I had done to Ghalia. It also made me understand that her calculations here had to do with the risks to my future and to her reputation, not with my having raped a maid, who to her could only have been of no account.

Her trained legal mind had command of all the details apart from one thing, which, at the time, I did not know sufficed to change the entry for the word 'future' in the dictionary of my life . . .

Because I failed the bac in the summer exams, my applications to French universities in Paris, Bordeaux and Lyons were rejected, and things were no better with Liege and Brussels in Belgium. That put her promise that I could study abroad in serious doubt.

Given my insistence on leaving, which I knew was the only way to end the terrible psychological torture I endured every day, my father could only find one solution to fulfil my wish (and perhaps also his wish to be rid of me).

I went up to my room in search of a few hours' sleep without nightmares. I ignored the barking coming from Spike, whom I had left on his own in the garden, and opened a drawer in my wardrobe. I ran my fingers over the patterned scarf Ghalia had left at the beach house when she fled and that I had taken with me during my desperate pursuit.

The long weeks that had passed had been unable to erase the faint traces of dark red blood spattering the scarf. A sign that time could not easily efface the events of the night of Tuesday, 14 May . . .

I put it carefully back in the drawer, unable to understand why I had kept it all this time. I flopped on to the bed. Next to me lay an orange folder. I went through the administrative and academic records it contained.

The folder bore a title that I had written in block capitals a few days before:

SECHENOV MOSCOW MEDICAL ACADEMY – RUSSIAN FEDERATION

APPLICATION PACK

---

* * *

**(*Al-Missa* newspaper – Investigations Page
– Thursday, 14 July 2011 – by Mohamed Ahdad)**

[. . .] At the height of World War II in 1942, after Germany under Adolph Hitler looked to have achieved victories on various fronts, the United States decided to intervene on the side of the Allies. Behind its intervention lay the American intention to tighten the screw on the Nazi advance by taking control of strategic zones. To this end it deployed significant forces to the Mediterranean front and, given its strategic geographic location, Morocco became a key airbase for staging American troops [. . .]

**(*Zamane* magazine –
Special Feature on US Military Bases in Morocco
– June 2015 – by Khalid al-Ghali)**

It took a whole year for the Americans to agree even to come to the negotiating table, a further year to accept the principle of evacuation, and a third to reach agreement on an evacuation date. This was the path that Morocco took between 1956 and 1959 in its negotiations with the United States over its military bases. Afterwards, Morocco persuaded the Americans to leave at the end of 1963.

Morocco led bitter negotiations before it succeeded in getting the Americans out. When Morocco gained formal independence in March 1956, it was still home to five US bases, among the largest in the world: Nouasseur, Sidi Slimane, Benslimane, Ben Guerir, and Kenitra. All of them were set up on the basis of a treaty that Morocco was not a party to: the agreement of 22 December 1950, during the protectorate, between French foreign minister Georges Bidault and US ambassador to France Jefferson Caffery. Right after independence, the Moroccan government declared that it did not recognise the legality of the US bases, even if their presence on Moroccan soil was a reality, and it called upon the US administration to enter into talks. The Americans ignored the Moroccan invitation for more than a year (March 1956 to May 1957) before finally agreeing to enter a negotiating process [. . .]

(5) Ask the Dust

Seeing a tree should not blind us to the forest.
Abdel Fattah Kilito

Friday, 27 September 2002
Denver – Colorado:

Things moved fast after Brandon mentioned Morocco and explained part of what he had in mind.

We telephoned to inquire about the next available flight from New York to Denver and left Central Park heading for JFK. Excitement stopped us from even going to my house or thinking about packing stuff we would not need anyway.

The plane took off at ten in the evening, and we took advantage of the journey to examine the idea of Morocco from every angle. And the idea was to investigate the time my dad spent there as a GI in the 1950s and write a novel inspired by a foreign place in a different age.

"What I'm going to say will seem to contradict what I said before about a writer not bending to their readers' wishes." Brandon was talking loudly, disregarding the silent admonishment of one of the cabin crew. "Yet it must also be admitted that Americans have gotten bored with all the usual subjects, which have been exhausted by cheap novels and done to death by Hollywood. The events of 9/11 proved to them that other people exist. People with different customs, traditions, and cultures, most of whom do not agree with everything Uncle Sam gets up to. Uncle Sam, whose half-baked modernity has made him believe he can impose his way of life on the whole world."

I squeezed his hand and, wary of annoying or waking the passengers close by, whispered, "Apart from the politics, which I don't understand why you insist on bringing into everything, I don't deny that it's an original idea. But turning the idea into a novel is going to be extremely difficult, and for reasons that I think you will accept." I took a deep breath. "Dad died years ago, and even if he were still alive, I don't think he would be of any use to us. I asked him once about his military service in Morocco and he was quite dismissive about the subject. He said that he didn't know whether he'd just struck lucky and served in a backwater, not in a war zone. He thought his real life began once he came back to the States and met Mom at college. We're dealing with a man who didn't have adventures or crucial turning points in his life that warrant putting down on paper. What do you say we write a novel about your time in Lebanon at the beginning of the '80s? Now that would be lively and exciting."

Once again I failed to spot the idiocy of what I had just said until it was too late. I tried to remedy the situation, but he got in first, ignoring my suggestion. "Life has taught me, Christine," he said, in a repetition of his performance by the lake in Central Park, "that we never know what other people can do, especially those we believe we know really well." His words roused the monstrous curiosity dormant inside me. "That makes it imperative we go to Denver."

His intention began to become clear, so I set another obstacle in his path: "For your information, my dear, we won't be as lucky as fictional characters who find a long-lost diary at the beginning of a novel to drive the plot. My father's only connection to reading was the bills and the sports page. He only ever picked up a pen to write a grocery list. Writing his memoirs? Out of the question." Brandon withdrew his hand in disappointment and looked away, occupied with the lights of Denver's suburbs which had started to appear in the small window. He concluded the discussion saying, "No one regrets what they've done. We regret what we haven't done. There's nothing to lose by looking for something useful at your dad's house."

After a four-hour flight we touched down at Denver International Airport shortly after midnight local time. Oblivious to the fatigue and jetlag of the sudden journey, we hailed a taxi that took advantage of the quiet streets to drive the twenty-five miles from the airport to the Uptown district close to the city centre in record time. The destination: my dad's house, which I left when I moved to New York.

The pressure of time did not permit me to indulge in nostalgic memories of a happy childhood. I ignored the desire to linger in every familiar corner of the beautiful house that my new (or phoney) life in the lights of New York had made me leave, and started frantically searching in the bedroom before moving on to the other rooms.

What a crazy idea, searching for something when you don't know what it is you're looking for!

Old clothes, films from Hollywood's good-old days that we watched together, records by bands I loved as a teenager in the wild '70s, baseball gear – Dad was a fan and loved following the leagues – fashion and cookery magazines that Mom subscribed to, my schoolbooks and university notebooks, and piles of books that I did not take with me to New York or to the beach house in Miami. Every item I touched exuded the beautiful fragrance of the past, and dust stuck to my fingers like a memory refusing to submit to oblivion.

I suddenly noticed that Brandon wasn't joining in the hunt, preferring to sit on the couch and watch me with a mysterious look that a relationship of eighteen years could not fathom.

"The attic is the favourite place to hide something in novels and films."

I didn't miss the irony of what he said and I replied with an all-too familiar irritation, "We're in real life here. We're not characters in a novel whose plot the writer is free to manipulate!"

He stood up with a lightness that did not fit his disability and came so close we were almost touching. "Maybe," he whispered in my ear, "but who said life is completely different from fiction?"

I almost surrendered to his breaths, which had paralyzed my capacity for rational thought and awakened feelings I believed I had buried forever. But the mountain of problems besetting me and threatening my future forced me to resist the overwhelming urge to embrace him and lay my head on his chest. Without speaking, I took a step back and headed upstairs to the attic that might conceal something I hoped deep down would be of use in our quest. It was a losing bet. All we found were more piles of discarded books, faded sheets, broken picture frames, and a broken lawnmower. Why I had been too busy or too lazy to throw it away, I did not know.

The dust was affecting my lungs and I coughed deeply. My eyes streamed with tears, from allergic reaction and covert sadness at three fruitless hours of effort. Brandon handed me his handkerchief to cover my nose. "Let's go," he said sympathetically and a little sadly. His sarcastic tone quickly returned. "All we're going to find here is enough layers of dust to give all the inhabitants of Colorado asthma. I'll just take a quick glance at the books. You know that anyone crazy about reading loves to check out the titles that other people own."

I didn't answer, preferring to leave without bothering to look back. We were wasting our time on nonsense. My father was a very homely guy, boring even. He came back from Morocco, finished college, married my mom, and got an ordinary job at a real estate company. His life was a world away from adventures and secrets and there wasn't a single incident for us to build upon and construct a decent novel with.

The problem solver had failed this time. He didn't provide the help I expected from him, despite the initial enthusiasm that had made us take a plane from New York to Denver without a second thought.

The only solution would be to turn on my computer, sit at my desk, search for some random idea and write a novel off the top of my head to settle my dispute with Charles & Clover before the next two goddam months were up. Brandon was only wrong about one point: he said that it would be easier if we were just characters in a novel whose author was serious about solving their problems and wouldn't allow himself to abandon them. Was Anna Karenina luckier than me when Tolstoy threw her under the wheels of a train as a radical solution to her suffering?

I exhaled cigarette smoke by the kitchen window in an effort to get my raggedy nerves back under control. My head, so crowded with jostling thoughts, was like a busy intersection in Manhattan.

"The million-dollar question for contestant Christine McMillan: who said, 'A man looking for a door in a hurry walks right past it?'"

I was tired of his flippancy and answered without turning around: "I'll call the airline and reserve two seats back to New York after sunup tomorrow, or today in fact. I'm going to sleep in my old room. You take care of yourself. The house is at your disposal."

He touched my shoulder and I flinched. At the end of my patience, I turned towards him. "Don't tou . . ." I began to say, but my annoyance turned to amazement when I saw he was holding a book.

"The right answer is Goethe," he said with great dramatic effect. "True, he lived between the late eighteenth and early nineteenth century, but I wouldn't want to exclude him having you in mind when he said it." He put the book on the kitchen table and continued in a neutral tone whose meaning was hard to discern, "You're right. Your dad didn't love reading like you, but that didn't stop him using books for purposes no one else had thought of!"

* * *

🔍 elkhabar.com – Home – Crime

Police investigate human remains at Sidi Abed Plage

Tuesday, 3 May 2016 – 09:43

Police have launched an investigation into the circumstances surrounding the discovery by construction workers of human remains on land bordering Sidi Abed Plage in Harhoura.

According to an informed source, the mystery began yesterday morning when construction started on a beach villa belonging to the wife of a prominent parliamentarian. While digging, workers were shocked to find human-looking bones and called the police. Some of the builders have refused to resume work at the site once investigations are complete in the belief that they might be cursed for life.

Immediately upon receiving the report, local authorities and the police attended the site to carry out all necessary procedures and gather evidence. The bones were taken to a laboratory for analysis and identification of the body as an initial step to solving a mystery that has traumatized local residents only a few weeks before the start of the summer season.

Comments (0) Opinions expressed in comments reflect the views of their authors and do not represent those of elkhabar.com

(5′) Life is Elsewhere

> *Ach . . . This world is not for us!*
> **Mikhail Lermontov**

Thursday, 3 October 2002
Sechenov Medical Academy – Moscow:

Would it be callous to admit that I wasn't sad to leave a Morocco for which I had not once felt what they call "patriotism" or a "sense of belonging"?

I don't know . . .

But I'm confident that the person who said "tar in my country is better than honey in another country" had a fertile imagination, and had never tasted either tar or honey to make the comparison.

I've been here for almost a month and I have a strong sense that I was created to live in this country. It would be no exaggeration to say that I wished I had been dealt a different hand. Then I might have had parents who were better than the two in Morocco who got rid of me (or I got rid of them, no difference). I was like a bad tooth to them. They chose to ignore it rather than seeing to it before it got worse, which ultimately left them with only one option . . .

Extraction and flinging it as far away as possible, namely Russia!

When I was accepted to study at the Sechenov Moscow

Medical Institute, I understood deep down that it marked a turning point, restoring Zouhair Belkacem to his old self: full of ambition and an honest desire to do the right thing, providing he was thousands of miles from the surgeon reliving his youth and the lawyer driven by a lust for power . . .

And Ghalia, of whom no trace had been discovered, as if . . .

As if the ground had opened and swallowed her up.

*

My temperament as a loner led me to avoid all contact with other Moroccan students, instead of mixing with them and benefiting from their experience in dealing with a different education system and in understanding alien customs and traditions.

I knew that decision was a bad one, but wasn't my number-one aim in leaving Morocco to get away from everyone and everything to do with it?

I preferred therefore to share student accommodation with a Russian called Sergei Kryachkov, who said he came from the Moscow suburbs but grew up in a city in Siberia I had never heard of called Tomsk. He showed me on a map and I learned it was over 2,000 miles from Moscow.

The guy was so skinny that if you saw him you'd think he had a disease requiring urgent medical intervention before he gave a thought to studying medicine. His fine blond hair was the colour of a wheat field and he wore black spectacles that gave his green eyes and smooth features a cute, childish look. In short, Sergei Kryachkov looked like the Russian Woody Allen!

He was in his first year, that is, he was a full year ahead of me (since the university required foreign students to become proficient in Russian before pursuing their degree subject the following year). I had no problems communicating with him though. On the contrary, mixing Russian and English was of benefit to both of us, especially as he had a passion for something that I believed I had left long behind. Reading.

Even though Sergei's timetable was full of lectures and classes that required laborious preparation and constant revision, I really admired his unbreakable habit of devoting an hour to reading before he went to sleep.

Whenever I looked at his bedside table, I would see a paperback novel, which changed every week, sometimes even twice a week.

Sergei's books made me curious and when I asked him about them he said they were from the university library and had mostly been on the shelves since the time of the now-collapsed USSR in the '70s and '80s.

Old copies, some of which had yellowing pages and were filled with the comments and doodles of previous readers. Yet they bore a strange pleasant smell that made you stick with the book to the last line, taking pleasure in the idea that, before you, it had been in the hands of a beautiful girl in Saint Petersburg or a lonely old man in a forgotten Moscow care home or even a prisoner exiled to the remoteness of Siberia!

I faced but one difficulty: dealing with the Russian language, which I had yet to master. So my roommate advised me to join the university library, telling me enthusiastically that special dual-language editions, Russian-English, of all the classics of Russian literature were available.

I thought it was a good idea, and as long as my first year was devoted to mastering the language of the locals, I could do no better than literature to improve my level with the help of great Russian authors to pave the way.

That's what I expected to begin with, but life with its customary absurdity chose to plant a landmine by the side of the road.

*

"I wouldn't claim to be an expert in world literature," said Sergei as we entered the university library, "but I'm quite sure that nobody writes like the Russians. You'll see for yourself."

Distracted from what he was saying, I wrapped my woollen

scarf round my neck and mumbled, "What I care about right now is preparing to face the savage Moscow winter. I already can't cope with 2°C in October, which you think is mere preparatory child's play. For God's sake, what kind of weather is this?"

Sergei laughed as he commented, "If the Russian cold can get into your bones, I have no doubt that its literature can warm your soul, but . . ." He suddenly cut himself short, in a way that did not match his calm, almost shy, personality. I followed his gaze with my eyes and discovered a young woman near the turnstile into the library.

I did not miss Sergei's signs of anxiety, and I was perturbed that his face had gone red, as if he'd drunk a whole bottle of vodka in one go.

"What's over there?" I asked. My roommate ignored me even though it would have been easy to give a truthful answer.

We moved closer to her and Sergei said hello while, like a scanner, I gave her body the once over from top to bottom. Two long, black-stockinged legs, above them a short red skirt revealing a narrow waist and a white woollen top that failed to conceal the fullness of her breasts. Her long neck she had chosen to cover with a red scarf that matched her skirt.

I took the opportunity provided by her talking to Sergei to observe the motion of her lips and study her features with the meticulousness they deserved.

Passing quickly over her ruddy cheeks, small nose, and fine chin, I lingered over the colour of her hair, which was blond like Sergei's and styled like Princess Diana's. As for her eyes, the only fitting description I could come up with, despite it being a cliché, was beautiful and the colour of the sea.

My final impression was that she was a gymnast or ballerina or even a tennis player, no difference. What mattered was that she did some sport that required rigorous physical exercise and had rewarded her with a fit body capable of driving anyone who saw her out of their mind before leaving her face to deliver the final blow.

She was holding a book like the pocket editions that my friend read. He even pointed at it and said something in Russian that I did not understand, although I noticed he stammered his words.

After giving him an answer, the girl quickly put the book in her bag and left, giving Sergei a polite smile and me a cold, expressionless glance.

I put my hand on the Russian's shoulder and whispered in his ear, "A month more or less and you've already fallen in love with her?"

"You don't understand a thing. She's Olga Kuznetsova, a classmate from high school. The way things turned out, we continued our studies in the same subject at the same faculty."

"And all the years you've known each other you haven't dared tell her your true feelings?"

Sergei kept quiet, trying to hide his embarrassment, so I changed the subject with another whispered question. "You pointed at her book and recited what I think is a passage from it. What was it?"

"'My soul has been spoiled by the world, my imagination is unquiet, my heart insatiate. To me everything is of little moment. I become as easily accustomed to grief as to joy, and my life grows emptier day by day.' It's Grigori Pechorin from Mikhail Lermontov's novel *A Hero of Our Time*."

The words hit home, describing as they did a suffering that had marked my tortured soul for years. I went up to the librarian, a woman in her fifties, showed her my foreign-student library card, and asked determinedly in English, "*A Hero of Our Time* by Mikhail Lermontov, the dual-language edition!"

Busy with a pile of paperwork, she replied calmly, "All the copies are on loan. The last one went to the young woman who just left the library."

"It looks like our time is worse than Grigori Pechorin's, the hero of the novel," Sergei commented, making fun of my disappointment. "We all feel despair and think we're heroes in a time not right for us!"

I didn't grasp what he meant by his obscure words and was only more determined to obtain a copy of the novel. I ran outside, unfazed by his astonished reaction.

The woman was standing in front a large notice board covered in university notices and she focused her attention on one which she read with great interest:

> Шахматный клуб организует университетские соревнования в воскресенье, **13 октября 2002** года в **Бетса Парке**. Желающие принять участие должны зарегистрироваться в регламенте офиса клуба на третьем этаже второго здания.
>
> ♘ ♔ ♙

"You almost ate me up with your eyes just now . . ."

Her chilly and uncensored words in impeccable English gave me a shock, but I ignored their implication and quickly redirected the conversation: "I understand from the notice that there will be a chess tournament at some place on 13 October. Excellent. It'll be a great chance to restore my glory on the chessboard after a long absence . . ."

"What do you want?" She trapped me with her question and her limpid blue eyes.

"Actually, I also want to read *A Hero of Our Time*, but it seems the last copy from the university library is currently in your bag."

"What's that got to do with me?"

"I'd like it . . ."

"Prove you're worthy then," she said, her grin failing to hide her defiant tone. "Beat me at the chess tournament, and I promise I'll give you the book there and then."

I gave her a sly smile back, having understood in a few minutes what my friend had for years failed to grasp.

Of course, I could very easily have obtained a copy of the book from the university bookstore or any other bookstore in Moscow. But the craving for a challenge was aroused and, aware of Sergei's approach, I said in a low voice, "If it's like that, I agree!"

* * *

An Attempt to Live – Mohammed Zafzaf – 8th edn (pp. 51–2)

The American soldiers continued singing. One of them reached for a bottle of beer, lifted it off the table, and poured it over the head of one of his friends. That man stood up laboriously and warily, but he was clearly the worse for drink . . . all of them were. The beer had soaked some of his clothes and he started shaking himself to get rid of it. The singing stopped. The munching on roasted corn kernels and snails also stopped and people turned to stare. The beer-dowsed American sat down again and their singing resumed. Some of the other patrons also went back to their own business. The dripping American, however, suddenly poured a bottle of beer over the first man. The two of them stood up and started grappling with each other.

"A fight's going to start," said Hamid.

"That's what we're hoping for," said his companion. "I've been longing for a fight between these cowboys."

"If it starts, it'll end in blood."

"What do we care? Let them all die."

* * *

(6) Portrait in Sepia

> *Reality sometimes forms an impediment to the novel.*
> Camilo Castelo Branco

Friday, 27 September 2002
Denver – Colorado:

The book had around 200 pages and, like many older editions, it wasn't especially well printed. But what really grabbed my attention was the square hollow cut out of the middle of the last hundred pages. Inside the space nestled four black-and-white photographs.

"How come your father ruined a valuable book to satisfy a narcissistic desire to hide personal photos?"

"The real question is why he chose this weird way of hiding them rather than simply putting them in the family album that I took with me to New York?"

"We can consider the answer to your question in two parts. The first concerns the method. Perhaps he was worried the photos might fall out or get lost if he just slipped them between the pages. The second concerns the reason. Here I have no doubt that the photos are highly personal and that your father preferred to keep them to himself and not have his wife and daughter see them because they're to do with his past, from before what he called his real life with the pair of you."

I nodded in support of his sensible theory and grabbed the photos to give them a thorough inspection.

Photo 1: A vast expanse of wheat fields and two sixteen-year-olds or thereabouts. Although I recognised my father's face without difficulty, it was still a bit of a shock since I'd never seen a picture of him so young. Then I turned my attention to the beautiful blonde girl with him. The fingers of her right hand clasped a book while she gazed at my father with an infatuation that was impossible for a woman like me to overlook. I also had a strong sense, based on his bored expression, that he did not reciprocate her feelings.

I turned the photo over to glance at the back. I found two lines of handwriting that I was able to read with the greatest difficulty:

A walk to remember

July 6th, 1947

Photo 2: In the background horrendously damaged shacks and small houses; a dark overcast sky; flat areas showing the aftermath of mudslides; groups of a few dozen people, mostly barefoot women crying and half-naked children. The camera lens was focused on my father, smiling as he carried a child aged five or six wrapped in a blanket and with his eyes half closed. I could almost feel the shivering of the small body in my father's powerful arms.

Written in faded ink on the back:

> **Morocco**
>
> **Taking part in removing rubble and pulling out victims of the Gharb's floods**
>
> **January 1958**

Photo 3: A bar or nightclub. My father with six bulky guys, four of whom are in uniform and two in civilian clothes, sitting playing cards around a table laden with beer bottles. Some of them look drunk. To the side stands a skinny waiter with a thin moustache. His brows are knitted, probably an expression of suppressed anger or annoyance at having been made to stand in the shot against his wishes.

Written on the back:

> **With my friends in Les Arcades bar**
>
> **Paul Howard, Bruce McBride, Eddie Stewart, Jeff Murray, Ernie Jones & Tony Wagner**
>
> **September 5th, 1959**

Photo 4: A tall young woman in her early or mid-twenties standing next to the door of a house, or more likely a villa. Good-looking and with her black hair in the bun-style fashionable in the 1950s and '60s. Hard to distinguish the colour of her sparkling eyes in the black-and-white photograph. She is wearing a modest dress that covers her shoulders and goes down below her knees, although it is quite tight. She is looking into the distance with a superior, aristocratic gaze and what might be considered the ghost of a smile adorning her small mouth, while deliberately ignoring the camera.

Nothing is written on the back of this photograph.

Brandon broke the silence. "Is your father from Texas?"

"Yes! How did you know?"

"Go back to the first photo. It's of a walk in the fresh air, but on the wooden table in the background there is a dish of chili con carne, the state dish of Texas. Beef, corn, and beans. Delicious."

"Do men only think about their stomachs and their . . ."

He interrupted me with a mischievous laugh that failed to hide his embarrassment, then continued, "We can deduce from the first photo that your father was in a relationship with a beautiful girl, and she was obviously infatuated with him. What's her name? Where is she now? How and why did her relationship with your father come to an end? Questions whose answers will be hard to find."

"I still can't believe my dad was involved with another girl, even though that would be totally normal for a kid that age!"

"Now compare the handwriting on the back of the photos. The writing on the first one is completely different to the rest, which leads me to believe that the girl wrote those words. The funny thing is that the phrase 'a walk to remember' corresponds exactly to the title of Nicholas Sparks' novel, which was recently made into a smash-hit movie."

I made no comment and he continued his review of the photos. "The information in the second photo is clear. A region of Morocco suffered flooding and landslides in 1958 and the US forces based there intervened to help. In your novel that will be the starting point for you to write about your father's heroism rescuing the victims. You know we love to burnish the image of the American superhero who . . ."

My fiery looks shut him up, and I took advantage to continue my own analysis. "The information in the third picture isn't as clear. My dad in an unknown bar with those he says are his friends, but actually I've never heard of any of them."

I lit another cigarette and, in defiance of his disapproving looks, made a show of enjoying exhaling the smoke. "Assuming the photo was taken in Morocco, based on the appearance of the waiter, who looks nothing like a typical American, we still don't know the address of the bar or even what city it's in."

He ended up ignoring my smoking and went back to reading what was written on the back of the photo. "Don't worry. I'll find the people whose names are mentioned in my own special way. Then we'll certainly find out more about their relationship with your father."

We reverted to silence for a few moments during which we looked steadily into each other's eyes before both exclaiming comically: "The fourth photo!" Our childish glee dispelled some of my confusion and anxiety, so I stubbed out the cigarette and propped my elbows on the table. I stretched my neck towards him, like a teenage student gazing dreamily at a teacher that she's secretly crazy about.

"It was lucky your mother died before the discovery of what her faithful husband kept hidden from her. Two beautiful, unknown young women. That would be too much for any woman to bear, even if it was in the past before she married him!"

"Another old love affair?"

"I don't know. But why did he keep the picture without any details of who it's of?"

I took his question as an opportunity to show off my skill as a woman able to pick up on the smallest detail. "You're right, but the woman is definitely Moroccan. If you concentrate on the door behind her, you'll see a small five-pointed star like the one on the flag in the background of the second photo. Underneath it there is a metal sign with Arabic writing, probably the name of the villa's owner. But it's not clear because of the poor quality of photography at the time."

Brandon looked impressed, but his response belied his expression. "Unfortunately, my brief stint in Lebanon didn't help me master Arabic. What's written might have led us to the girl's identity."

"Never mind. We'll solve the linguistic problem later. What matters is what am I going to do now? Time is really tight and every minute counts!"

"Answering your question," he said slyly, "requires you to formally reinstate me as your literary agent. And you should know, Ms McMillan that I do not offer my services for free!"

I smiled with delight, but he said with patent enthusiasm, "We have next to no time. You have to submit the text of your new novel in only two months. I'll get in touch with the veterans' association I belong to and search the database for the names of your father and his friends. If needed, I'll travel across the whole country to find the ones who are still alive."

"And me?"

He reached out a hand to play with my curls and, adopting the tone of a loving father giving an educational lecture to his daughter, he said, "You are a capable author. The photos are enough to create the seeds of a coherent plot. You'll open a new document on your laptop and for the next three weeks write a novel divided into two parts. The first is the story of a young guy who grew up in rural Texas following the Crash of 1929 and joined the army, which sent him to North Africa in the 1950s. He was forced to say goodbye to the girl he loved, who shed tears on his departure and swore to wait for him."

"What a sweeping imagination! Tell me, why don't you . . ."

He cut me short with a decisive gesture. "'It is as easy to dream a book as it is hard to write one,' said Balzac. I was created to be a reader, not an author."

The same answer as always.

"Fine. What about the second part?"

Like a man programmed to find an appropriate answer to every question, he replied, "That's the harder part. The scanty information we have at hand isn't enough. So you're going to follow the same path as your protagonist by going to Morocco for a further three weeks, during which you'll continue by presenting your hero's experience with an unknown society. We'll also imagine his meeting with a girl who puts his faithfulness to his girlfriend to the test, and in a way that suits your talents for probing the psychological depths of your characters."

He was silent for a while then took hold of my hand and continued lovingly, "I know that writing a novel in six weeks is an extremely hard task. We risk falling into the trap that spoiled your last novel – rushing it and using clichés. Yet I trust your abilities and have a strong sense that your curiosity as a woman will help you uncover the identity of the mysterious Moroccan girl and the nature of her relationship with your father. Was she an old girlfriend or is the story more complicated than we imagine?"

Words of encouragement, but what Brandon had overlooked was that Balzac's aphorism also applied to me. The existence of the idea did not mean turning it into a novel with a convincing plot would be easy. Besides, the information available to us so far was full of gaps and question marks. Was I going to knock at the door of every house in Morocco to ask about a beautiful girl who had been in her twenties in the 1950s? And did the fact that my dad had kept the photo indubitably prove the existence of a relationship between them? And what about the other, blonde, girl?

Brandon brought my hand to his lips and my resistance finally collapsed. My exhausted mind surrendered to my heart's fervent desire to defer the search for convincing answers to my sensible questions.

If only for a while...

*

Brandon slept like a baby. I watched the regular rise and fall of his chest and took a moment to enjoy contemplating his hair and beard. Then, so as not to wake him, I gently pulled the cover back, and a small portion of his artificial leg became visible. I lacked the courage to keep looking at it for long.

I slipped out of the bedroom and went into the kitchen full of energy. I sat down on a chair and took pleasure in the sting of a cold draft against my naked body as I put the book and the photographs under the microscope of my investigating eye once again.

I opened the book at the first page and found a dedication written in a tiny hand that the humidity of the passing years had not entirely erased:

> Every time has its own hero
> And you're the hero of this time . . .

Who and what was intended by these strange words?

An idea flashed in my mind and I brought the photo of my father and the blonde girl closer to examine the title on the cover of the book that the girl was holding. Many of the letters were obscured by her fingers.

> A H RO OF O R TI E
> MI H L L RM TO

I copied the letters onto a sheet of paper and, as if I were completing a crossword, it only took me a few minutes to fill in the blanks.

> A HERO OF OUR TIME
> MIKHAIL LERMONTOV

The translation of the work by the nineteenth-century Russian novelist in the photograph was the book I was holding in my hands, the one my dad had used to hide his pictures!

This sudden realisation threw me into confusion again and I went over to the kitchen window. I looked out towards the horizon. The first rays of dawn were visible, but I did not know whether in my present state I would be able to deal with whatever the new day might bring.

Hitler once said that starting a war is like opening the door into a pitch-black room. Nobody can predict what will happen. Didn't he know that his simile also applied to starting to write a novel?

* * *

Route taken by the two friends Sergei Kryachkov and Zouhair Belkacem from the state student accommodation to Bitsa Park, Sunday, 13 October 2002:

08:07

You're quite right to be proud that you're studying at a college that is part of a major state university founded in 1755 and that counts among its graduates a large number of scientists and intellectuals, Russian or otherwise, such as the mathematician Andrey Kolmogorov, the physicist Alexei Abrikosov, and the father of Russian aeronautics Nikolay Zhukovsky.

08:43

| The Kremlin |
| Кремль |

Of course you've heard this name before. We're now standing on Borovitsky Hill at the centuries-old heart of the capital. The czars' opulent palaces were built here, and most of them have now been turned into museums. Since 1917 the Kremlin as a whole has been the administrative centre for the Soviet authorities and then for the Russian ones post-1991, which makes it an international symbol for decision-making here.

09:01

| Red Square |
| Красная площадь |

This is our most famous square. It's where the big military parades take place and it was from here that our armed forces set off for the frontlines to fight the Nazis during the Great Patriotic War, and it's here that our fathers and grandfathers celebrated victory. If you look over to the right, you'll see the Great Tower and to the left the iconic Saint Basil's Cathedral with its bright colours and onion-shaped domes.

09:13

| Cathedral of Christ the Saviour |
| Храм Христа Спасителя |

This cathedral was built in 1860 but only lasted for 71 years after a minister in Stalin's government ordered that it be blown up with dynamite in 1931 because, as he put it, the Soviet people were demanding an end to the dominion of religion. It was a losing bet of course, since as soon as the Soviet Union collapsed it was rebuilt and reopened two years ago!

09:51

Kakhovskaya Line
Каховская линия
Kakhovskaya Station
Каховская

We are eight metres underground, and this is the last stop before Bitsa Park. I can see from your face how impressed you are. Every station on the metro is an amazing work of art that deserves to be looked at for a long time, but we're in a hurry, my dear!

09:58

Bitsevsky Forest Natural and Historical Park
Природно-исторический парк "Битцевский лес"

We've arrived at last!

* * *

(6') Dangerous Liaisons

> *I married Nadezhda Krupskaya because she was the only woman able to understand Marx and play chess.*
> **Vladimir Lenin**

Sunday, 13 October 2002
Bitsa Park – South Moscow:

When Sergei told me that the competition would take place in a park called Bitsa Park, I had no idea that this meant a green landscape covered with trees, and which the information board said spanned an area of 22 square kilometres.

It was also nearly 20 kilometres from the centre of the city.

"Whose bright idea was it to hold the tournament so far away? And at 10 o'clock on a Sunday morning?"

Sergei smiled in response. "All the green space is in front of you, but if you look carefully, you can answer your questions on your own."

We advanced a few dozen metres and I noticed a large number of hikers of various ages. There were children running and laughing; women busy chatting in pairs or groups; men exercising; old people sitting on benches, leaning on their sticks and staring silently into space.

"As I explained just now, as soon as the Soviet Union collapsed, the Russians rushed to restore churches and rebuild those that had been demolished. Was that a true desire to return to religion after decades of being forced to abandon it? I don't know. What matters is that lots of people are eager to go to Mass on Sunday, so it's only normal that the streets, metro stations, and parks are busy, even if on the morning of their day off."

I also noticed some tables made of wood, and others in stone with a chess board design on top. Now I understood what my friend meant, although I waited for his explanation.

"Bitsa Park and chess go together. Apart from in winter, when the lake freezes and the temperature drops to record lows, you'll never not find dozens of old-age pensioners and students who are passionate chess players competing in exciting games until it gets dark. And since you're an old hand, there's no need to remind you of Russia's international standing in the game."

"I know that," I said dryly. "Years ago, my nickname was Morocco's Kasparov."

Sergei's eyebrows shot up and he was about to say something, but held back when he noticed the woman standing a few metres away.

A few seconds was enough for me to recall the information I had picked up sporadically from my friend over the preceding few days, having made a deliberate show of indifference when asking the questions so as to avoid any possible misunderstanding between us.

Olga Kuznetsova was nineteen years old. She lived near Pushkin Square in the capital. My taking her to be a serious athlete had been exactly right, as she had done gymnastics for years, and it was no exaggeration to say that she had mastered chess not long after learning to walk.

Now that's what we might call a potent combination of the physical and the mental. Add to that good luck when it came to looks and a brilliant mind that had brought her top marks over the course of her education, and it goes without saying that she had achieved the heights of human perfection.

But I'm not a believer in goings-without-sayings, and, even though I'm still under twenty I stick to the most important of the series of rules that life has taught me: Life never gives you it all.

One night when we had stayed up very late, Sergei told me Olga had a temper and was moody. She would be friendly in a way that drew you closer and then rebuff you with sudden incomprehensible coldness. And that had led everyone to keep a certain distance.

All had tried their luck with her, and failed.

My roommate, under the sway of his heart, tried to justify her temperament, but he couldn't hide his resentment at, as he put it, her difficult character and conceitedness. He thought she was a faithful feminine reproduction of Grigori Pechorin, the hero of Lermontov's novel.

Or of Zouhair Belkacem, I thought to myself as I experienced a strong feeling that I would find myself in the pages of Lermontov's novel, which only made me more excited to read the book, the very copy that Olga had borrowed from the library.

There she stood in all her commanding feminine glory, her face radiant with a smile, as she listened to one of the tournament organizers. Sergei made to raise his hand to greet her, but I stopped him just in time: "Don't act so keen! It doesn't look as if all those novels you've read have done you any good!"

He gave an embarrassed smile as Olga turned towards us and came a few steps over. Forsaking hello, she directed her patronizing words at me: "Here you are. Ready to get thrashed?"

Picking up her tone of belittlement, I countered provocatively: "Who you do think you are? Judit Polgar? Don't compare yourself to her. She's miles better than you . . ."

"And miles more beautiful," I took pleasure adding.

Her face flushed in annoyance, but she kept calm saying: "The Hungarian Judit Polgar is the greatest ever woman chess player. It was her intelligence, not her looks, that defeated grandmasters, most recently Kasparov in an historic game in September."

I smiled triumphantly, relishing having achieved my aim of riling her.

I was all too familiar with her kind of woman, whose character is no different if they be in Morocco, Russia or the Amazon rainforest. Implicitly they are saying to you: "I'm beautiful and I know it. I know that 99 out of 100 men are friendly with me because I am beautiful, but I'm fed up with that silly game. Prove to me that you're different from the rest!"

That's what I did by making a show of indifference and playing with her nerves.

As for poor Sergei, he had spent years doing all he could to attract her attention. There was no question that she understood his hints, but she was content to treat him with cruel and hurtful disdain.

My decent friend did not understand that women despise those who display their submission to them. Even the fiercest feminist, who claims to be fighting male dominance, at heart hates a man who makes her feel stronger than him!

"The organizers want to end the tournament early," Olga said earnestly. "They're setting up for games of speed chess, no more than ten minutes a game."

"Why?" I asked with interest.

Sergei tried to answer but Olga got in first: "The man claimed that it was to manage the number of players given the available time. But we all know the real reason. No one would dream of staying here after dark for fear of falling into the clutches of the Bitsa Park killer."

The astonishment gripping me was only partly dispelled by Sergei's explanation: "Since last year the park has been the scene of a series of mysterious crimes. True, all the victims have been homeless people killed by a violent blow to the head, but the ever-growing number of attacks plus the police's inability to catch the culprit have made the inhabitants of Moscow very nervous."

As if there was nothing out of the ordinary about it, Olga changed the subject: "They've put up the list of games. Here, let's take a look."

The tables and chairs were neatly arranged, each table displaying the names of the two players in the first round, and since a number of foreign students were taking part, the names were written in English.

> Zouhair Belkacem vs Igor Fiodorov

"Who's the lucky boy then! Your first game is against Igor Fiodorov, the best player at Moscow State University and winner of a number of national championships!"

I clocked Olga's sarcasm and my anxiety grew as I made to shake hands with my opponent with his black hair, blue eyes and white waistcoat. He greeted me very warmly and respectfully.

Game on . . .

I was white and the Russian was black.

I tried to stay calm and focused, and played my favourite Spanish Torture opening. My opponent spotted it at once and played the familiar moves:

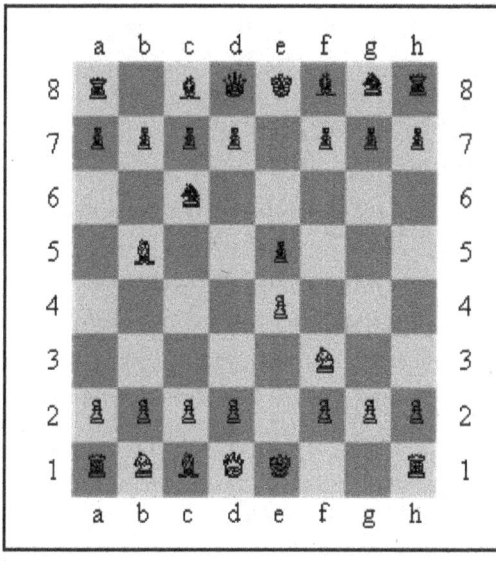

1. e4 e5
2. **Nf3 Nc6**
3. **Bb5**

*

I kicked open the door to my room in fury and flung myself on the bed with my face to the intensely yellow wall.

"Zouhair, there's no need to be so angry. You faced an unbeatable champion, and even though you were knocked out in the first round, the judges praised your high standard of play. Igor Fiodorov also gave you genuine words of encouragement."

I did not answer and Sergei continued: "Forgive me for reminding you that a few days ago you admitted that you hadn't played for ages. It's only natural that you'd lose. Chess, like any other sport, requires constant practice to maintain a level of mental fitness."

I preferred to turn into a mute statue while he finished what he had to say. "It looks like you want to be alone. Fine. I'll go and see some friends on the fourth floor."

I waited till he left the room before opening my backpack and taking out the copy of Lermontov's novel that Olga had given me at the end of the tournament.

"How pitiful you are, my big-mouth Moroccan. Here, take it. I hope today's lesson will teach you to keep your mouth shut next time."

Her gloating words had dripped with sarcasm and I refused to accept the book. But she insisted on opening my bag and dropping it in herself while Sergei looked on in amazed annoyance.

I recalled the ridiculous scene and threw the book away in irritation. It hit the wall and fell onto the floor. The corner of a folded sheet of paper was visible among the yellowing pages. My eyebrows curled questioningly and I went over to the book, pulled out the piece of paper and unfolded it. I imagined that I didn't understand the meaning of the few lines in her controlled, elegant handwriting, and I reread it several times:

> An unusual beginning must have an unusual end.
>
> Mikhail Lermontov – *A Hero of Our Time*
>
> Don't be sad. You faced a strong hero and managed to hold on to the end. I wasn't luckier than you and got eliminated in the third round!
>
> We will meet on Wednesday 23 October
>
> Olga

* * *

From the draft doctoral dissertation on contemporary literature with the provisional title "Narrative Techniques in the New Novel: An Analytical Study of *A Moroccan Jigsaw Puzzle* by Moroccan Author Khalid Rafiqi" by postgraduate student Rachid Bennacer:

[. . .] Similarly, a large number of contemporary novelists have been interested in the dichotomy between form and content, where the former is inseparable from the latter. Writers have created new narrative modes that are able to surprise and disorient readers, often by taking advantage of the novelistic genre's ability to absorb various other literary genres, thereby demolishing the boundaries between genres. The short story, verse, drama, epistle, newspaper article, and song are among those elements that novelists have incorporated into the body of their works.

Taking this as a starting point, in my research I have adopted an open approach corresponding to the dissertation topic, and undertake an analysis of the novel *A Moroccan Jigsaw Puzzle* by Moroccan author Khalid Rafiqi.

The text is subjected to a close critical reading that combines stylistics, structuralism, deconstruction and hermeneutics, while relying upon description, analysis, and interpretation in a move from the theoretical to the applied.

In my opinion, the novel, which was published in 1989, enjoys a very particular status, for apart from a notice of its publication that appeared in a Moroccan newspaper that closed down at the beginning of the 1990s, it received no media interest.

No critical reading of the work exists, be it an analytical article or a detailed academic study. Furthermore, even obtaining a copy of the only edition was no easy matter, since the problems of the book trade in Morocco led the small publishing house that produced it to close down a few years after its launch.

Despite all the obstacles mentioned, I decided to devote my dissertation to the novel *A Moroccan Jigsaw Puzzle* out of my conviction that it contains several elements that make it amenable to my approach regarding the development of narrative techniques in the modern novel, as I will elaborate in my research.

* * *

(7) I See What I Want

> *Love in the 20th century: a phone that does not ring*
> **Frédéric Beigbeder**

Monday, 21 October 2002
The Old City – Rabat:

As soon as David Hersch learnt of my plan to travel to Morocco to work on my new novel, he adopted an angelic attitude that did not suit him at all. He called to offer his assistance by utilizing his network at the State Department as well as the US Embassy and the big travel agents to provide the ideal circumstances for my stay in a country that I knew practically nothing about. He warned me of dangers that only existed in his head.

I understood that creep all too well and realised his true aim was to glean some initial information that he would sell to journalists eager to pounce on any news about me.

Because I worried about pictures of me appearing alongside ridiculous headlines such as "What is novelist Christine McMillan doing in Morocco?", "Christine McMillan goes back to the 1950s in her latest novel", or even "Christine McMillan turns to her father's past to confront her writer's block", I turned down his offer with fake politesse. I preferred to work on my novel and investigate my dad's past in peace, away from luxury and fuss. Under the influence of Brandon's lifestyle, I favoured simplicity. He called a small travel agency, which reserved me a room in a traditional-style hotel, whose décor as shown in the brochure I liked.

As soon as the taxi dropped me off at the hotel, a porter in his late twenties welcomed me in good English and guided me to the reception desk. I completed the formalities and went to my room. Without thinking about changing my clothes, I dropped onto the bed and fell instantly into a dreamless sleep.

*

I woke up feeling woozy, and my head only cleared after a bath that restored some energy to my exhausted body. I put my computer on the wooden table along with my papers and a notebook containing the outline of the novel. Then I set my watch to Moroccan time, as indicated by a clock on the wall: 4:30 pm.

I opened the file containing the draft of the new novel and read over what I had written in the previous weeks.

Early chapters of direct narration relying on the technique of an omniscient narrator. I don't deny that I had not the slightest difficulty in creating the context and events, although I was certain about the difficulty ahead in capturing the details of what happened to the novel's hero in Morocco.

I suddenly noticed that my mobile phone was vibrating, and I shuddered. But when I read the caller's name, a smile of happiness escaped my lips.

"Hi, Christine. If my calculations are correct, it's a quarter past five in the afternoon in Rabat, right?"

As if Brandon was standing there in front of me and not thousands of miles away, my fingers reflexively reached out to play with strands of my hair. "Right. And what do you think I'm doing now," I replied playfully.

He was silent for a few moments and I realised that he must be smiling as he sought the right words, before saying with mock seriousness, "I'm going to borrow a phrase that movie actors often use and ask you whether you want the good news or the bad news."

I excitedly moved my pen and notebook closer. "Well, my response is also the usual one: I want the bad news first!"

"Ernie Jones is in an old people's home in Cleveland with Alzheimer's. He doesn't even remember how to put on his pants. So there's no way we're getting anything about your father out of him."

I wrote Alzheimer's next to his name in my notebook and crossed him out too:

> ~~Paul Howard: Dead~~
> ~~Bruce McBride: Dead~~
> ~~Eddie Stewart: Dead~~
> ~~Jeff Murray: Dead~~
> ~~Ernie Jones: Alzheimer's~~
> Tony Wagner:

"That means our only hope is finding Tony Wagner," I added in a tone to encourage both of us.

"Those events happened a long time ago, and it's unlikely that any of those in the photo with your father are still alive. Paul Howard, Bruce McBride and Jeff Murray died of natural causes. Eddie Stewart died in a car accident at the end of the '80s. Ernie Jones has Alzheimer's. That only leaves us Tony Wagner."

"Great. So, what's the good news?"

Brandon replied excitedly, "I contacted an old friend in the Military Personnel Records Department. He understood that I didn't want to go through the bureaucratic process that might put us at risk of coming on the radar of press interest. So right off he gave me the names of the Moroccan cities where US forces were concentrated during and after World War II. That should make our task easier."

"Quick!" I cried eagerly. "Give me what you have!"

I had barely finished my words when the call abruptly ended. The phone's battery was dead, so I rushed over to my bag for the charger, which I plugged into the phone and then the socket.

Two seconds passed.

The charger fizzed ominously and I was afraid to touch it. My shock then turned to fury. Shit!

A short circuit or an incompatibility with the electricity system had blown the charger and damaged the phone at the same time.

I was so stressed out that it seemed every piece of furniture in the room was warning me not to touch it in case I got a fatal electric shock. I stormed out of the room and made for reception on the ground floor, venting my rage on all without exception.

Some tourists turned to look at me in amazement and the hotel receptionist's eyes nearly popped out of their sockets in shock and fright. He tried to calm me down in a staccato mixture of English and French: "Please ... *Madame* ... *Du calme* ... Don't panic!"

This coincided with the appearance from a side room of the young porter who had carried my bags. He was dressed to go out and had a backpack on, suggesting he was about to leave.

The receptionist exchanged some words in Arabic with him, and I guessed he was expressing his annoyance and displeasure. The porter stopped him with a gentle smile, which he kept up while he came confidently towards me.

Quite dark and with tightly coiled hair, his almond eyes sparkled with a mixture of gentleness and intelligence. His slender build also hinted at resilience and being used to strenuous tasks.

"What is the problem, madam?" he asked in beautiful English. "Is there anything I can do to help?"

"Your bad wiring has blown my mobile phone. Now what am I going to do?"

"First, let's check what happened. Then we'll sort it out!"

The guy did not wait for my answer and headed to my room on the first floor. I followed him, not oblivious to the envious looks he was getting from his colleague, the receptionist.

"There's nothing wrong with our wiring, madam. It's probably a fault with the charger." He said this one minute after switching off the electricity in the room and inspecting the charger and the phone. "Don't worry. Your phone probably isn't damaged. Fortunately for you, you're staying at a hotel near the Souq Legza in the old city. It has a host of geniuses able to fix any electronic device in the wink of an eye!"

*

I stifled words of thanks in my throat as I took back my phone along with a new charger. The guy was engaged in a brief conversation with a mobile phone technician of similar age, and then said to me, "Rest assured I'll be accompanying you back to the hotel. You'd no doubt find it hard to navigate back through the old quarters."

I just followed him, careful not to bump into anyone despite my annoyance at how crowded it was. He led me down a narrow side street, where I ended the silence that had continued for several long minutes. "I apologize about before. I just lost my temper. It doesn't mean anything. But I'm under a lot of stress which affects my mood."

He surprised me with an unexpected question: "You're a novelist, aren't you?"

I replied in amazement: "Yes. How did you know?"

He answered hesitantly, as if afraid I might be angry, "I saw your picture in a French literary magazine when the translation of one of your novels came out. I wasn't sure it was you when you arrived at the hotel, but a quick glance at the chaos on the desk in your room and the laptop open at a Word document, along with the notebook and scraps of paper full of notes confirmed my suspicion."

"Do all hotel porters here take such an interest in novelists and writers as you do?"

No sooner had that crass statement left my mouth than I regretted it. I bit my trembling lower lip with my front teeth while a flash of sadness flared in the young man's eyes. He tried to hide it by holding out his hand to introduce himself. "Rachid Bennacer, PhD student specializing in modern literature." Then with what seemed like a veiled reproach, he added: "And I work as a porter at a hotel to meet my expenses and help my family who live in a distant village."

* * *

A Hero of Our Time (novel) – Mikhail Lermontov (translated by J. H. Wisdom and Marr Murray) – Book V Chapter VIII

"Yes, such has been my lot from very childhood! All have read upon my countenance the marks of bad qualities, which were not existent; but they were assumed to exist – and they were born. I was modest – I was accused of slyness: I grew secretive. I profoundly felt both good and evil – no one caressed me, all insulted me: I grew vindictive. I was gloomy – other children merry and talkative; I felt myself higher than they – I was rated lower: I grew envious. I was prepared to love the whole world – no one understood me: I learned to hate. My colourless youth flowed by in conflict with myself and the world; fearing ridicule, I buried my best feelings in the depths of my heart, and there they died. I spoke the truth – I was not believed: I began to deceive. Having acquired a thorough knowledge of the world and the springs of society, I grew skilled in the science of life; and I saw how others without skill were happy, enjoying gratuitously the advantages which I so unweariedly sought. Then despair was born within my breast – not that despair which is cured at the muzzle of a pistol, but the cold, powerless despair concealed beneath the mask of amiability and a good-natured smile. I became a moral cripple. One half of my soul ceased to exist; it dried up, evaporated, died, and I cut it off and cast it from me. The other half moved and lived – at the service of all; but it remained unobserved, because no one knew that the half which had perished had ever existed."

* * *

(7') The Captain's Daughter

> *The world is a stage, but the play is badly cast.*
> Oscar **Wilde**

Wednesday, 23 October 2002
The metro; the Dubrovka Theatre – Moscow:

The carriage leaving Trubetskaya Station wasn't as crowded as I expected and we sat on facing seats. This enabled me to enjoy looking at the beautiful woman sitting opposite, although I pretended to do otherwise.

I did not know why she chose Wednesday, 23 October as the date for us to meet, although I reckoned she was giving me sufficient time to finish reading *A Hero of Our Time* before giving it back to her, which is what happened.

"No doubt Sergei has told you a lot about me. As everyone knows, Olga Kuznetsova is a stuck-up blonde who manipulates men, not one of whom has ever had his way with her. Right?"

My ears burned red hot with shame as I remembered my Russian friend and what might be deemed my betrayal of his feelings for the Russian girl, whom I had agreed to meet without his knowledge.

"I worked that out for myself and I wondered what had caused it. Perhaps you're orientated a little differently?"

She was silent for a second or two as she took in what I was hinting at, then gave a playful laugh and said, "You little shit! Of course not!"

She continued more seriously than at our previous encounters: "Imagine that you had grown up in a family headed by an officer in the Soviet navy who thought that his home was a barracks where he imposed a super strict regime on his wife and children. The boys went to military school and then on to Afghanistan to get injured or die there in the mid-1980s. I was the only girl, and I was forced to get my head around programs of study way beyond my level, as well as intensive practice at gymnastics, ballet, piano and chess strategy, and I was still only seven. What do you expect would happen if you are turned into a machine programmed to obey orders whose true intent you don't comprehend?"

"For your feelings to die at birth and for you to shun all human contact?"

She clapped her hands in agreement and looked at me with two dreamy eyes. "Exactly! That's what led me to what our friend Pechorin expressed so well: 'I was prepared to love the whole world – no one understood me: I learned to hate.'"

I remembered the quotation. Vague images ran through my mind that I tried to get rid of by silently contemplating Olga. I felt encouraged to share my own memories of human emotions with her. Should I tell her about a childhood ruined by my parents because of their selfishness?

I might have differed from her in terms of the real talents I possessed, but rather than nurturing those talents the surgeon and the lawyer preferred to ignore them so they could keep running after sex, power and money, and I turned out the way I did.

Should I tell her the details of what happened between me and Ghalia the night I raped her? She was just a poor village girl that I attacked. To escape her memory, I'd come to the most distant place on Earth.

Olga interrupted my long silence: "My father was an ardent

communist. He believed all the nonsense about Soviet superiority in the confrontation with capitalism and imperialism and all that bullshit which caused the demise of the country. Naturally, he was stunned by the collapse of 1991 and chose to immerse himself in far-flung missions with the Russian military. He would be away from home all year, but that ended two years ago."

"He retired?"

"No, he died in the infamous Kursk submarine accident," she said almost disdainfully.

Shocked, I cried out, "You mean the submarine that exploded in summer 2000 and some sailors remained alive? The Russian authorities dilly-dallied and they all died of suffocation. I remember the global media interest at the time."

She gave a sad smile. "Yes, but he was quite lucky and got killed in the initial explosion." She wiped away an imaginary tear and continued in a steady tone, "We've reached Barrikadnaya Station and we'll keep going to Proletarskaya on our way to our final destination at Dubrovka."

Her words were like an alarm bell awakening me from the slumber of sympathy with her sad story, and I reverted to my initial confusion. "Where are we going exactly?"

I assumed she would be bold enough to take me back to her house and, for a while, I imagined her lithe body in my arms. I quicky discounted the idea though, since with my basic knowledge of the city I knew she lived in the opposite direction to where we were going. Unless . . .

We were entering the next station when she took a small rectangular piece of paper out of her bag and handed it to me:

Норд-Ост

Билет

Дубровке

Среда, 23 октября 2002

"What's that?" I asked puzzled.

"Read it. The words are easy and clear enough for a beginner in Russian like you!"

I complied, slowly trying to link together the letters and words: "North... east... ticket... Dubrovka... Wednesday, 23 October 2002."

"It's a ticket to a performance of the show North-East at the Dubrovka Theatre."

"Lovely, but what does that have to do with me?"

"It's your prize for participating in the chess tournament, stupid. You were angry and left in a hurry with Sergei, so you didn't know that the organizers had allocated token prizes to all the players. I was given a copy of the novel *Chess Story* by Stephan Zweig translated into Russian, but I've read it a few times and preferred to swap it with another participant who was also eliminated in the first round. He wasn't interested in his ticket because he'd already seen the show. And I told one of the organizers that I knew you and could give you your ticket myself."

"All of that just to be alone with me?" I said in amazement.

"Do you have another explanation?" she replied through her smile.

*

The clock showed nearly eight as we took our seats in the vast, no, awe-inspiring, auditorium.

I estimated an audience of hundreds who had all come to see a show that began with a very professional crisscrossing of the spotlights, followed by a brief introduction and martial dances by lively actresses wearing heavy, brightly coloured overcoats.

I leaned over to whisper in Olga's ear. "What is this boring show?" I grumbled. "Is this the play that I got a free ticket to see?"

"It's a musical comedy adaption of Veniamin Kaverin's novel *Two Captains*. That is to say it includes songs and dance numbers that portray the events in the novel. It was written and produced by Aleksei Ivaschenko and Georgii Vasilyev. Are you going to shock me and say you understand nothing of the dramatic arts?"

I gave an embarrassed laugh and refrained from replying while I slipped the fingers of my right hand over the back of Olga's left hand. She made no sign of resistance or objection.

Then, in the second half of the show, came the turn of young men dressed in traditional military uniform to perform their dances. Next, masked men heavily armed with wooden weapons burst on the stage and asked the dancers to vamoose.

Really, I didn't understand any of it. It seemed that the only thing keeping me awake was the thought of what would happen between me and the gorgeous Russian once the show was over. Yawning, I said, "Is this the creative part of the show? A contemporary artistic trick? Masked men with rifles and hand grenades?"

Olga suddenly gasped in fear and ignored my question. The masked men were shouting in Russian and another language I didn't understand and started firing into the air, turning the whistles from some of the audience into dead silence, only broken here and there by women crying out in terror.

I didn't need to be proficient in Russian to understand what was going on, and be wide awake.

Real bullets that real gunmen were firing as they stood on a stage that had been showing make-believe. In other words, these gunmen were taking me and Olga hostage, along with hundreds of others in a theatre in the heart of Moscow.

* * *

A Moroccan Jigsaw Puzzle (novel) – Khalid Rafiqi – 1st edn (pp. 2-10):

Khalid Rafiqi

A MOROCCAN JIGSAW PUZZLE

– A novel –

Hope Press for Publishing and Distribution

To Veronica . . .

Any man who can write a page of living prose adds something to our life.

Raymond Chandler (1888-1959)

– 1 –

As they sunk in the mud Mustafa Mahmoudi's shoes turned into blocks of filth, and the splatters on his trousers ruined his appearance on the morning of Thursday, 23 July 1959. He ignored it, however, as a single question dominated his thoughts: how was he going to deal with a case the likes of which Kenitra had never witnessed before?

He wouldn't say he was comfortable with his job, accustomed as he was to solving cases of assault and battery, the pursuit of wretched prostitutes around the bars and streets of the town centre, and getting to the bottom of petty thefts, whose protagonists – usually ground down in poverty and unable to satisfy their hunger – resorted to copying Jean Valjean in Victor Hugo's *Les Misérables* . . .

But the discovery of a woman's corpse on the bank of the Sebou river and the early indications that she might be a homicide victim was something entirely unfamiliar.

His task was not going to be easy at all. Not because he lacked experience, but because he was certain that many people would refuse to cooperate with him to solve the crime.

He had been wrong when he assumed that his transfer to Kenitra would mark a complete break with his past. He forgot that he lived in a country where information had wings and flew. The townsfolk would know that he had worked previously for the colonial police and had joined the national security corps as a detective after its formation.

He might be shown respect, feared perhaps, but they weren't going to cooperate with him willingly. Behind his back, they nicknamed him "the colonialist", "the collaborator" and "the traitor" and it was going to be hard to win their confidence.

But was it his fault that he was a minor functionary in a country that found itself in dire need of retaining a large number of French doctors, teachers and civil servants to help run its affairs by "itself"?

Hadn't most of those currently holding the levers of civilian, military and police power previously cooperated with colonialism?

At least he wasn't as brazen as those who claimed to have belonged to the resistance and whose hands, stained with the blood of Moroccans, grabbed at the post-independence cake of privileges, and in the process created a picture of surrealistic distortion that had led to impotent governments, domestic and foreign political crises, struggles between yesterday's militant comrades, and uprisings in the countryside and various regions that had been supressed with iron and fire.

Nobody knew what other calamities awaited Morocco three years after "independence".

The police had done their job of clearing the area of curious onlookers and detained a skinny man dressed in rags, whose belly had clearly not been full for days.

The detective went up to him and exploited the fear so evident in his exhausted face to soften him up with the question, "Are you the person who first discovered the body?" The man seemed to have been struck dumb, and Mustafa shouted at him, "Speak!"

"Yes," practically sobbed the man. "And I also informed the police. I swear I don't know her and I've never seen her before. I was near the riverbank looking for snails to sell and buy something to eat. See, the bucket is my witness."

The detective glanced at a small blue bucket, split down the sides. It was indeed full of snails, some of which were trying to climb to the top with determination, if very slowly. The man calmed down a little and added, "She was lying on her front, barefoot and soaking wet. I don't think she drowned."

Mustafa gave him a hard stare, then said in a way that deep down he knew was the best to preserve his prestige, "Investigating the cause of death is no concern of yours, understood? We will continue this interview later, back at the station."

The man reverted to his original terror and was led aside by the policeman who had shown the detective the body.

The witness had not been lying. The woman lay on her front. She was wearing an off-the-shoulder grey dress that was soaking wet.

Mustafa put gloves on and drew nearer to look at the face. He found himself confronted by a young woman, in her mid-twenties he estimated. Despite the disfigurement to her features, the blueness of her lips, and the strands of hair plastered to her face, nobody could have overlooked – beforehand – her captivating beauty.

The accompanying policeman whispered in his ear, "The French forensic pathologist will arrive shortly."

Addressing himself, Mustafa said, "We're certainly going to need him. Perhaps his examination will take us somewhere, but I'm not so stupid as to overlook some preliminary observations. The body is not bloated and sufficiently far from the bank that we can rule out drowning. There's no sign of grass on her back, which suggests, at least on the surface, that she was thrown on her front and not moved. She also has a deep wound to her head, which may be the true cause of death. There is no sign of her shoes, although there are a great many footprints following the confusion around the discovery of the body."

"Who do you think she is?" asked his colleague. "One of the prostitutes recently arrived in Kenitra for summer? All the old faces are known to us!"

Mustafa stood up, took off his gloves, and replied, "I don't think so. Girls who sell pleasure have a particular way of putting on makeup and wear specific clothes to attract punters. Take a look at her dress. It's very expensive. No way some abject prostitute would own it. She's either from a rich family in the town or has come from outside."

A young policeman, one of those charged with clearing the crowd, interrupted with a salute and said, "Excuse me, inspector, sir. Regarding the identity of the victim, I know her well!"

* * *

(8) Jamila

The world is a book of which at every step we turn a page.

Alphonse de Lamartine

Monday, 21 October 2002
The Old City – Rabat:

I lowered my gaze in shame as I shook Rachid's hand and sought the right words with which to apologise. To mask my embarrassment, I asked him with interest, "What's your dissertation topic?"

We were almost back at the hotel, and he led me over to a stone bench. Then he took off his small backpack and slowly opened it.

He handed me a book with a white cover, devoid of any design or artistic picture, suggesting it was a limited local or university press edition. In a bold black font on the front was written:

Khalid Rafiqi

Un puzzle marocain

Traduit de l'arabe (Maroc) par Fabien Bedos

"For my dissertation I decided to work on narrative techniques in the new novel, including an applied example of the analysis. As part of my preliminary research I came across a novel entitled *A Moroccan Jigsaw Puzzle* by a Moroccan writer called Khalid Rafiqi. I read it and I liked it, and I realised that it fitted really well with what I was seeking for my research. Then I found myself facing an on-going set of problems."

The interest apparent on my face encouraged his desire to continue talking. "The novel was published at the end of the '80s and did not receive any media or critical attention. In a strange way it was just completely ignored, although that might be to do with this being a country where books don't sell very well to begin with, and where a chorus of half-writers make it their job to flatter each other in public and tear into each other in private. They form alliances to wage war against all those who refuse to join the chorus rather than concentrating on what matters, which is improving the quality of what they write."

The last acerbic part of what he said made me laugh, while he continued with an excitability quite the reverse of his previous unassuming shyness. "The final touch came with the withdrawal of my original dissertation supervisor. He was enthusiastic initially, but got a very well-paying position at a Gulf university and was replaced by someone else, who from the outset rejected the idea of working on *A Moroccan Jigsaw Puzzle*. He proposed that I study a novel written by one of his friends, but even a primary school student, let alone a postgraduate researcher in literary criticism, could judge how bad it was, lacking the most basic elements of fiction writing. The guy was seeking to make use of me in a complex web of favours and mutual interests that I refuse to be part of. The copy you're holding right now is the French translation of *A Moroccan Jigsaw Puzzle* by Fabien Bedos, a French academic at the Sorbonne specialising in Arabic literature. He read the book during a trip to Morocco for an academic conference and it impressed him. So he translated it into French and gave it to his students as an example worthy of study and analysis. The university published an edition, and I was able to get hold of a copy thanks to one of the second-hand booksellers here in the Old City after he got in touch with one of his Moroccan friends living in Paris."

He paused to catch his breath, then continued, "This translation is my last hope of persuading my supervisor to agree to me including *A Moroccan Jigsaw Puzzle* in my dissertation. That's for the simple reason that some people here consider anything coming from France sacred, not to be criticised or detracted from, even though we're talking about what is originally a Moroccan literary work written by a Moroccan like us!"

He ended his fascinating speech with a sigh that revealed the extent of his suffering. I tried to raise his spirits by patting him on the shoulder. "Your fierce defence of the novel has made me want to take a look at it. Is it all right if I hang on to the French translation to read this evening?"

He nodded his agreement and I thanked him. Then I stood up to head back to the hotel. "Actually, madam," he said, "my memory hasn't retained your name quite as well as it did your picture in the magazine!"

"My name is Christine. Christine McMillan."

It seemed that a startling question was about to escape his lips, but he simply said goodbye with a smile that restored his previous calm. "See you later. We meet tomorrow to discuss your opinion of the novel. I'm quite certain it will make you devour every page tonight!"

*

I ended a second call with Brandon, during which I explained why the first one had been cut short. He provided me with the names of the towns where US bases in Morocco had been concentrated. He had obtained them from a friend in the military archive office, and I wrote them down in my notebook:

> **Nouaceur**
> **Sidi Slimane**
> **Benslimane**
> **Ben Guerir**
> **Kenitra**

I set back to work, paying no attention to the need for rest until nearly midnight. I flopped onto the bed and picked up the copy of the Moroccan novel to flick through as an aid to quickly falling asleep.

I disregarded the French translator's introduction, afraid it might give away the plot, as some translators do for reasons my long literary experience could not fathom.

The certainty of the young porter had been spot on and the novel drew me into its world at once.

The events began on the morning of Thursday, 23 July 1959 with the discovery of a woman's body on the banks of the River Sebou in Kenitra. The police turn up under the command of a detective who understands that there's been a murder, based on the signs of a blow to the victim's head. This is confirmed as the cause of death by the forensic pathologist, who also doubts that the perpetrator transported the corpse to the riverbank.

A traditional opening then, familiar from many similar works of detective fiction.

The identity of the dead woman is confirmed, a certain Jamila el-Baroudi, the 26-year-old daughter of a prominent businessman in Kenitra. She is married to Saleh Belcadi, the son of her father's business partner, and is the mother of a five-year-old boy.

The detective begins his inquiries with the family. From the grieving father he learns that Saleh and Jamila live in their own house with their son, and that the husband is often away on business. As a result, the deceased woman and her son were used to moving between the marital home and her father's villa.

Saleh returns from a trip to Casablanca and is in a state of shock at what has befallen his wife. Through his tears, he offers to provide any assistance the police need to catch the killer, who has deprived him of the woman he loves and destroyed his family, as he put it.

The detective, named Mustafa Mahmoudi, continues his investigation by questioning the victim's neighbours. I admit I found this part strange!

In the plot of most American (or Western, in general) detective novels the neighbours are ignorant of everything to do with the family of the victim. The author thus usually resorts to creating the character of a crazy or nosy neighbour, who by chance is able to reveal the identity of the killer or kidnapper.

In *A Moroccan Jigsaw Puzzle*, however, every single neighbour knew the tiniest details of what was going on with the couple. It was really astonishing!

Had the author failed to fashion the details of his plot and so resorted to an easier solution? Or was he accurately describing the nature of a society that I was entirely ignorant of?

The neighbours agreed that the couple had a very bad relationship. It was clear to all that the marriage had been arranged to strengthen the business ties between two fathers who had demonstrated their ability to exploit every situation that Morocco had gone through - before and after independence - to promote their own interests and boost their profits.

Saleh was often away from home and he usually came back drunk. He beat and insulted Jamila in every way, confident in her silence, and what the neighbours took to be an inability to fight back following the birth of the child and the further consolidation of the relationship between the two families.

An old woman, whom it seemed was always stationed at the window of her house spying on all and sundry, confirmed that nobody had been present in the house on the night before the discovery of Jamila's dead body. This conflicted with Jamila's father's account that she had gone back to her house alone, having conceded to her sisters' request to leave her son to spend the night with them at the villa, as happened often in the family.

Had Jamila been killed after being snatched on her way back to her house?

For a few days the investigation made no progress. Then somebody dropped a stone into the still waters of the case. The detective received an anonymous, typewritten letter stating that Saleh had lied when he claimed that he had been in Casablanca the night his wife was killed, and that he should be questioned because he had concealed his presence in Kenitra from everyone for some unknown reason.

The letter threw Mustafa Mahmoudi into confusion. Its source was unknown and it had been found in his mailbox. It was impossible to gauge its credibility. Saleh was, after all, a businessman and the son and son-in-law of businessmen, and the field was rife with competitors and enemies. The letter also made Mahmoudi realise that he had made a mistake by not confirming that Saleh had been out of town on the night of Wednesday 22 July, but simply taken at face value what the victim's father had told him, which was that he had sent his son-in-law to finalise the details of a deal over foodstuffs in Casablanca.

The detective made up his mind. He kept shtum about the letter and called Saleh in again for questioning. Saleh seemed hesitant, his answers were contradictory, and he failed to provide any material proof that he had gone to Casablanca. The policeman pressed and confronted him with what the neighbours had said about the domestic violence. Saleh vehemently denied it, and the detective ordered that he be kept in police custody to make him confess.

Mustafa Mahmoudi was taken aback when Saleh's father and his lawyer burst into his office demanding the suspect's immediate release on the basis that there was no compelling evidence that Saleh had not gone to Casablanca. The detective knew this deep down, since a letter of unknown provenance was evidentially worthless.

He tried to buy time, but his immediate superior called and ordered him to release Saleh and seek the killer elsewhere. In other words, stop causing problems with a family whose wealth also included, as usual, a wide network of powerful relationships with post-independence authority figures.

Mustafa Mahmoudi felt furious, but he was obliged to carry out his orders, sending the case back to square one.

Who killed Jamila el-Baroudi?

Did Saleh travel to Casablanca on the night of Wednesday, 22 July 1959, or not?

If he didn't, then where had he been? And did that have anything to do with his wife's murder?

Who sent the mystery letter?

It really was a first-class Moroccan jigsaw puzzle!

The detective tried to bring the strands of the case together again, but failed. His interest waned as the weeks passed and other cases arose which, according to the author, were common in Kenitra at that time: theft from the port, and assault and battery at the town's numerous bars and cafés.

Then a case in the doldrums became a raging storm.

There was a road accident. A car crashed into a tree on the edge of town. The driver died instantly.

And the driver was none other than Saleh Belcadi.

Initial findings indicated an accident caused by driving under the influence.

While waiting for the final report, the detective went through the deceased's personal effects: identity papers, sunglasses, and an appointment book in his pocket.

Mustafa Mahmoudi went through the appointment book in detail till he finally found what he was looking for:

> **Rendez-vous avec Steve McMillan**
> **Mercredi 22 Juillet 1959 à 22h**
> **33137   42F**

I dropped the book in astonishment, unable to believe my eyes, which were wavering between wakefulness and sleep.

A meeting with Steve McMillan on Wednesday, 22 July 1959 at 10pm.

No way could the name be strange to me.

Steve McMillan was my own father's name!

* * *

TV programme Situation Critical – The Moscow Theatre Siege – National Geographic Channel – 2007

Excerpt from minutes 2–4:

(Narration in the background):

When the Soviet Union collapsed in 1991, fifteen states broke free from Moscow's grip.

The small, mostly Muslim state of Chechnya also demanded independence. But vital oil and gas pipelines from the Caspian Sea run through Chechnya.

The Russians refused to give up the valuable resources.

Over the next eleven years the small state fights two devastating wars with Russia. Two hundred thousand Chechens are killed and nearly half a million left homeless.

The territory lies in ruins. Only a heavy military presence keeps Chechnya under Russian control.

Chechen freedom fighters will do whatever is necessary to win their independence.

They'll even sacrifice their own lives to get the Russians out of their territory.

Their leader is twenty-five-year-old Movsar Barayev, a notorious rebel wanted by the Russians.

He was raised by a Chechen warlord and has been at war with the Russians all his adult life.

He is an Islamic fundamentalist who wants Chechnya to become an Islamic republic. In this rare home video he is seen training in the wooded hills of Chechnya, supported by Arab gunmen.

Now, Barayev and about fifty heavily armed freedom fighters are about to take the battle to the very heart of Russia:

Moscow.

* * *

(8') Celebrations of Death

> *In wartime humanity displays its worst, and also its best.*
>
> **Erri De Luca**

Thursday, 24 October 2002
Dubrovka Theatre – Moscow:

Total silence descended on the theatre that had been bustling with life only a few hours before. None of the hundreds present dared utter a word.

One figure alone assumed the right to talk freely ...

A guy in his mid-twenties, whom we understood was the leader of the armed group. Despite being the youngest, he seemed the toughest and most self-confident. He strutted the stage, his face visible, the muzzle of his gun pointing at the ceiling.

He was handsome: skin mimicking the colour of snow; eyes bright and alert; beard light and well-trimmed.

If the situation hadn't been so tense and dangerous, I would have said he would have made a good pop singer or a top Hollywood star, not an armed man part of a gang holding nine hundred people hostage inside a Moscow theatre.

I did not understand a word he said. The shock had caused me to forget my Russian. But evidently he had prepared himself for the presence of a significant number of foreigners at the theatre, and had one of his assistants simultaneously interpret his words into English:

"My name is Movsar Barayev. I am the leader of this group of heroic fighters. Russia has left us no alternative. For three years it has been slaughtering, burning and raping. It thinks it can frighten us and force us to relinquish our noble aim of freeing our land from occupation. But we will never surrender..."

A bitter struggle against the Russians, but what's it to do with me? Where's my guilt? Why should I pay with my life for a war that I have no part in?

Pressing questions assailed me, but an invisible inner voice forced me to bury them quickly under a counter question of its own: Isn't life's biggest problem that we only pay the price for our mistakes at just the wrong moment?

"We will keep fighting, until the last man, woman and child..."

The last sentence was like announcing the start of a new act of the play being performed before our eyes. If only it had been like that. Screams of panic and gasps of fear arose from the hostages once more when eighteen masked women entered the auditorium.

Lithe and cloaked in black, all that could be seen of their bodies and faces was their darting eyes.

Each one was carrying a pistol and a control unit wired to a suicide vest. None of that, I was astonished to see, affected the way they walked, which had lost none of its grace and feminine allure.

A terrifying spectacle that I defy any film director, no matter how experienced, to recreate. In fact, one of the fighters was capturing it with a portable video camera.

The one called Barayev took advantage of the general air of expectation and panic to resume his speech (with translation): "These are our comrade sisters in our holy struggle against the arrogant enemy. A brutal enemy that has deprived every one of them of a father or a brother or a husband. Our demands are clear:

either the Russian army withdraws from our land and declares a permanent ceasefire or we will blow up the theatre along with everyone in it. We have planted powerful bombs in the walls of the building that are enough to turn it into rubble in a flash. You may relay my message to the world via your mobile phones."

The silent panic of the hostages turned into sobs, especially among the children and women. I was reminded that Olga was sitting next to me when she said: "Get ready, our end has come. Not just because of their zealotry and insane desire to sacrifice themselves, but also because the authorities will not meet a single one of their demands. Blowing up the theatre and everyone in it is easier for the government to do than cowing to fighters who, let's not forget, humiliated the army and kicked it out of Grozny in 1996. The army certainly hasn't forgotten."

It was a dry comment, emotionless, and in English. I don't know how she managed quite so calmly to relay her thoughts to me.

I asked her in a hoarse whisper that failed to disguise my trembling: "And what are we going to do?"

"Sometimes," she replied with infuriating casualness, "the best thing you can do is nothing. Let's wait . . ."

The minutes passed heavily till the time reached 2am. None of us dared fall asleep. I felt a loud ringing in my ears, my heart was racing, and my forehead turned into a pump producing sweat non-stop.

The Chechen women, with their explosive corsets, took turns guarding us. Barayev was busy deliberating with his comrades. Then he said, "Your terrorist army treats our children over twelve as men able to take up arms and deliberately and viciously sheds their blood, burning the hearts of steadfast Chechen mothers. But we are not like that. We will demonstrate our good faith and honest wish to negotiate."

His words were accompanied by a prearranged signal to his men. They spread out among the seats and held out their hands to young children, who clung to their parents in a mixture of terror and confusion . . .

"We will release fifteen children under twelve years old." The leader of the armed men said this in an optimistic tone, and the children's confusion transmitted to the parents, torn between letting go of their children and ensuring their survival or keeping hold of them to face an unknown fate.

Sensibly, they accepted the first option.

The children formed a line, although most of them were unable to comprehend what was happening, in readiness to head for one of the theatre's entrances with the aid of an armed man.

At this point a woman in the audience stood up and addressed a plea to Barayev as she hugged a girl who was no doubt her daughter.

The commander came down off the stage holding his gun and he walked confidently over to the woman. All eyes were trained on him, which only boosted his self-confidence.

I did not need to be proficient in Russian to follow the dialogue . . .

The girl was over twelve, and her mother wanted her to be included among those leaving. Barayev categorically refused.

The woman was in tears, and our hearts ached for her, even though we were all in a pitiful state ourselves. One of the hostages tried to intervene to persuade the armed men to release the girl, who was thirteen years old.

The intransigent Chechen refused to back down, and in response to the woman's screams he could do nothing but threaten her, pointing his gun in her face. She went back to her seat sobbing and squeezing her daughter tight. The situation became electric again a few minutes later, given we now had a weak hope of the possibility of release and survival.

Gazing at Olga's pretty face was the last thing on my mind, but I shifted my bleary eyes between her lips and her breasts when she spoke: "The Chechen fighters reached the stage of despair after the army deployed in force in the villages and the Caucus Mountains, having learnt from its disastrous mistakes during the first war. Keeping hold of Grozny proved impossible for the Chechens, which obliged them to turn to kidnappings and hostage takings. This has all been well planned. They are releasing the children so as to gain international sympathy for their cause, which will put pressure on Putin and his circle and put what's happening outside this isolated and booby-trapped theatre under the spotlight. The police, the army, and the elite Spetsnaz have the building surrounded, for sure."

"Elite what?"

My question was interrupted by the entrance of the armed man who had evacuated the children. He sprinted over to his commander, who listened to him attentively, before rushing over to a radio. He tuned it in and turned the volume right up.

Slow minutes during which a cold, strong voice spoke, confident in all it said . . .

"It's an urgent address by President Putin," explained Olga. "He's saying that Russia will never bow to terrorists. Their demands are rejected. Withdrawal from Chechnya is not up for discussion."

The meaning was clear, but that did not prevent me stupidly asking, "Which means?"

After having shielded herself with the power of indifference, which quickly proved to have been an act, Olga's glacial tone was now tinged with fear: "In other words, he's saying: 'I will not sacrifice the gas pipelines and oil from the Caspian Sea in exchange for a few hundred hostages. Go ahead, blow up the theatre and everyone in it.'"

The anxiety transmitted to the armed militants. Movsar Barayev vented his anger by firing into the air, sparking renewed screaming and crying from the captives.

He issued his orders. Two women hostages had to carry a heavy, strange-looking object and put it down in the middle of the auditorium's rows of red seats.

A huge bomb. More than fifty kilograms. The Chechen contemplated it for a long while and then spoke. The translator relayed his words: "This is an invitation to all those with mobile phones, Russians and foreigners. As you can see, the Russian authorities are not trying to save you. Contact your loved ones and say goodbye to them. You might not see them again . . . . ."

Decisive words, which led all the helpless hostages to ask the logical question:

Is this the end?

* * *

A Moroccan Jigsaw Puzzle (novel)
– Khalid Rafiqi – 1st edn (pp. 171-6):

- 15 -

There were seven of them, swapping jokes and clinking bottles and cans of beer. The eighth was a girl under twenty. She recognised Mustafa as soon as she saw his face, and fled like the wind as if he were a monster come to eat her up.

The inspector ignored her and went over to the table. He placed a hand on the shoulder of one of the seven and asked quietly, "Are you Steve McMillan?"

Fair-haired, blue-eyed, and muscular, the man in his thirties had a grip that could crush the bottle he was holding. He looked up at the police inspector's hand with hooded eyes and in broken Arabic replied, "Who are you? What do you want?"

Mustafa was confident that the man could speak the local Arabic, if badly, as did most of the Americans working at the airbase, who patronised such places for a good time. "I'm an inspector with National Security. I'd like to ask you a few questions about your relationship with Saleh Belcadi, who died in a car accident a few days ago."

Steve said something in English, of which the Moroccan understood not a word. His friends laughed, infuriating Mustafa who was certain they were making fun of him. He miraculously steadied his nerves as he listened to the American's response: "As long as you're an inspector with National Security, hasn't one of your superiors told you that I'm a soldier in the US army and that only the American military police can formally question me?"

He was right in what he said, as the Moroccan well knew. Yet the constriction in his voice gave away his anxiety, just as the officer had wanted. "Who said it's a formal investigation, Steve? Normal questions that I hope you might be able to answer."

The soldier winked at his friends, in a sign that he had things under control. He stood up and loomed a foot taller than the inspector. They went off to a quiet table in semi-darkness, which made it more difficult to follow the soldier's eyes.

"Saleh is my friend. We always met here. Had a little fun, chatted about the rumours, you know, whether the US army in Morocco was staying or going. I was really sad about the tragedy to his family. The mystery of his wife's killing, then his own death in a car accident. Real scary!"

"Was your relationship with him limited to nights out here? Or did you meet elsewhere?"

Steve answered with a cagey question: "What are you getting at?"

"There are witnesses who confirm that you often met each other at his home. Was that a continuation of your drunken evenings, or did it have something to do with his business affairs?"

"Sure, I visited him at home. But just as a friend. I had nothing to do with his work and never asked about it." He said this with a confidence that suggested he was prepared in advance for every possible question, so Mustafa threw him a curveball. "What about his wife Jamila? Did you know her personally?"

The American kept quiet for a moment and reflexively rubbed the tip of his nose. "I might have seen her in passing once or twice," he said. "You know your conservative traditions better than I do. It wouldn't have been appropriate for her to sit together with us."

The detective had no choice but to play his ace: "Where were you on the night of Wednesday 22 July?"

"At the airbase as usual," he said with no trace of emotion. "And I have six witnesses. My American buddies sitting around that table, who can all easily confirm it."

The detective put his hand in his pocket and took out Saleh's appointment book. He flicked through in search of a particular page and waved it in Steve's face. "And I have a handwritten note by the deceased of a meeting between the pair of you on Wednesday 22 July at 10pm, even though he claimed that he had gone to Casablanca that day on business."

The soldier pushed the table away with force and it struck Mahmoudi in the stomach. "The meeting's over," he said coldly and provocatively.

He went back over to his friends' table, but Mustafa followed him doggedly. Forgetting the pain of the sudden blow, he shouted, "I haven't finished all my questions yet. What do the numbers that Saleh wrote under the note of the meeting mean?"

Steve turned towards him, fist raised. "My friends are waiting for me, and I don't have time to waste on you. Luckily for you, I'm in a good mood 'coz the right answer to your dumb questions is a punch on the nose."

The Moroccan curled his fist too, feeling angry at the disparity in strength and height between them. "Evading the questions isn't in your interest," he said, his voice unsteady. "Rest assured I'm not that powerless. I'll be on your tail until you are formally interviewed about your connection to the case."

The soldier resumed his tacit provocation, masked by an outward show of calm: "Listen good, Moroccan. Your country is lost, unable to stand on its own two feet after independence. You really need us. Whose advanced equipment was it that helped warn of the risk of floods in the western region? And who jumped in afterwards to rescue the victims? Who turns a blind eye to the smuggling of food, clothing, refrigerators and other stuff from the airbase? Why do your superiors stop you detaining the hookers and force you to let them go every time? Who spared you the headache of reviving the economy of a town, and perhaps a whole region, because we're here filling the cafés and bars and keeping the economy going with our cash and our goods? Who's giving you direct aid in the form of tons of flour and powdered milk? Who's training your pilots to fly the latest fighter jets? Rest assured, pal, your country won't put all of that at risk for your sake, but it'll hold you to account for having the gall to annoy me."

Mustafa swallowed the soldier's insults, but the sense he had had when he read the name in Saleh Belcadi's diary now turned into the absolute certainty that Steve McMillan was the key to the mystery of

Jamila and her husband's deaths.

    When, how and why? He could not answer any of those questions yet, but for certain he would. Whatever it cost.

* * *

(9) Story and Interpretation

Nothing was real except chance.
Paul Auster

Tuesday, 22 October 2002
The Old City – Rabat:

Strewn with sheets of paper, photographs and notebooks, the table had been transformed into something out of a wartime operations room. Rachid was silently reviewing the material.

I extended my tired gaze – it had been a long exhausting night and I had only gotten a taste of sleep around dawn – towards the horizon, where ancient houses and walls, modern buildings and chaotic traffic on both sides of the river formed a weird mosaic.

What is this insanity?

Steve McMillan, calm and taciturn to the point of being boring, a character in a book moving through the pages of a Moroccan novel!

Moving, speaking, laughing, having fun . . .

And committing a murder, and getting away with it!

"Actually, your name kept ringing a bell once I got home. Not just because you're a writer whose picture I saw in a literary review, but also because my memory connected it straight away with the character of the American soldier in *A Moroccan Jigsaw*

Puzzle."

"An unbelievable coincidence. One you'd only find in a novel, right?"

"When fate takes charge, you realise that those who find coincidence in fiction annoying haven't really experienced life, since life keeps astonishing us with more outlandish surprises. What's important is that I have got over my astonishment and considered what this new piece of information means for your novel and my dissertation."

He said all this without taking his eyes off the photographs. "How do you mean?" I asked.

Fist on chin in thought, eyebrows almost meeting beneath his forehead, whose furrows looked like the trace of an ECG, he seemed to have aged ten years.

Rachid was a fighter. I had only met him yesterday and knew little about him, but I was certain that life had not been kind to him and that he was struggling to stay afloat.

"I dealt with the text as a work of fiction, written by an author named Khalid Rafiqi, in which he combined the police investigation with an accurate portrayal of Moroccan society in the aftermath of independence. But the character of the soldier, whose name is the same as your father's, suggests two possibilities …"

I knew what he meant, but did not stop him from continuing. "The events and characters in the novel are fictional, unconnected to reality. Any resemblance to actual persons or events is pure coincidence – the usual disclaimer that authors of fiction use to defend against twists of fate. You know that ordinary people have sued writers for defamation because some character happens to have the same name as them!"

I interjected in irritation: "Yes, of course. My first novel *Prisoner of Class 12* was based on a real event, the Columbine High School massacre. I was one of the victims. But I played around with the course of events, changed the names of some characters and kept others real. In *A Moroccan Jigsaw Puzzle* there is no disclaimer and no detailed description of the character Steve McMillan."

He seemed hesitant, perhaps afraid, when he said, "Alternatively, the novel – ignored by everyone – is based on real events and its text expressly accuses an American soldier of involvement in the killing of a young Moroccan woman in Kenitra and of getting away with it in the end after the detective was removed from the case."

His hesitation turned into anticipation when he asked, "Don't these details remind you of something?"

I just gave a nonchalant shrug. Emotion and exhaustion prevented me from responding, so he answered his own question: "The novel *Who Killed Palomino Molero?* by the Peruvian Mario Vargas Llosa isn't a typical detective story, but it includes an investigation into the horrific murder of a young recruit. Lituma and Silva take on the case and their inquiries lead them into a maze of racism, conspiracy theories and what the author called 'the big fish devouring the little fish'. The story ends with their transfer faraway, even though they're close to solving the riddle. Some of the questions remain unanswered."

My patience over, I said, "Fine. What's your proof for the second possibility? I don't know anything about my father's past in Morocco and I came here in search of information. What, for example, proves that he was stationed at the airbase in Kenitra?"

Rachid picked up the photo of my father with the shivering child and pointed at the information on the back. "It says here that the picture was taken in 1958 and that US forces took part in the rescue operation after the floods in the Western Region. For your information, Kenitra is geographically and administratively part of that region, which is prone to flooding and landslides."

"That's not enough . . ."

He put the photo down, then examined the one of my father with his old friends. He turned it over to look at the writing on the back. "Okay, what's your comment on there being strong evidence that this photo was taken in Kenitra?"

The way he said it grabbed my attention, so I sat down on a chair opposite, propped my cheek on my hand and asked, "What evidence?"

"Les Arcades bar is mentioned in the novel *An Attempt to Live* by our Moroccan author Mohammed Zafzaf. It includes a scene of a fight there between a bunch of drunken American soldiers. Zafzaf used the hard facts of Moroccan reality in his work. Things he saw with his own eyes as a child and adolescent. The bar exists, or did exist during the '50s, in Kenitra, which is the main scene of the novel's action. Zafzaf lived there for a few years before he moved to Casablanca."

I grabbed the photo of the bar and examined it for a long while, until I imagined I could actually enter the scene, as happens in sci-fi series. "I don't think Brandon's going to come up with anything else, now he's confirmed that most of the guys in the photo are dead. I doubt it'll be different with Tony Wagner. So, what do you say we get in touch with the author of *An Attempt to Live*? His observations of the '50s and the assumption that my father worked at the Kenitra base will help us uncover more information on the subject. Perhaps he heard of a real crime that happened at the time, where the victim was a young woman whose body was discovered near the Sebou river."

"How are you going to get in touch with him when he's six feet under? Mohammed Zafzaf died of cancer in July last year, God rest his soul!"

He moved on to the photo of the anonymous Moroccan girl. Fear forced me to pose the booby-trapped question: "Are you thinking that . . ."

My shaking voice prevented me from continuing, so he carried on, ". . . that the girl in the photo your father kept for years is Jamila el-Baroudi? I don't know. The name of the villa, although it's written in Arabic so you and your literary agent were unable to read it, really is illegible. The photo dates back a long time and is of such poor quality it's impossible to make out all the details. Even if we could, I'm not sure it would help."

"That leads us to the clearest option. The riddle of *A Moroccan Jigsaw Puzzle* can only be solved by its author, Khalid Rafiqi. Only he can tell us whether its events are real or fictional."

Rachid stood up and put his hand in his pocket. He went over to the edge of the hotel roof terrace restaurant with a spectacular view over the city and dropped another bombshell: "It seems you didn't read the French translator's introduction or, naturally, the publisher's note on the back cover of the Arabic edition. The biggest riddle about *A Moroccan Jigsaw Puzzle* is its author himself. The publisher received the manuscript by post, and now years after the book came out, still nobody knows who Khaled Rafiqi is!"

* * *

> 🔍 elkhabar.com – Home – Crime

Medical Student at Souissi University Kills Unemployed Graduate and Hands Herself In

Friday, 27 May 2016 – 23:10

In a highly unusual incident, S. H. (23), a fourth-year student at Souissi Medical School, Rabat, handed herself in to city police, confessing that she had killed the man known when alive as R. B. (27), an unemployed graduate, by stabbing him a number of times in the heart and stomach causing his immediate death.

In her detailed initial confession, the student stated that blackmail and fear of scandal were the main motives for the horrific crime, since for months R. B. had been threatening to publish intimate images of her taken on a mobile phone. S. H. was adamant that she had no idea how the deceased had obtained the images.

Students at the medical school expressed sympathy and solidarity with their colleague, mentioning her good character and academic excellence. Meanwhile, her parents refused to give any statement to the website's correspondent.

Comments (0) Opinions expressed in comments reflect the views of their authors and do not represent those of elkhabar.com

(9') Confusion of Feelings

> *Death is not the opposite of life but an innate part of it.*
> **Haruki Murakami**

Saturday, 26 October 2002
Dubrovka Theatre – Moscow:

I made repeated, futile efforts to call my parents on my phone and inform them of my predicament, but the weak network prevented it.

Then the battery ran out and ended all my hopes of hearing their voices and perhaps saying goodbye to them for the last time . . .

We had been forcibly detained for more than fifty hours, and none of the hostages could take it anymore.

Tedious telephonic negotiations took place between Russian General Pronichev, whom the authorities appeared to have put in charge, and Movsar Barayev, leader of the armed group. The ebb and flow continued between them, which helped us keep our brittle selves together and cling to the faint hope of escaping the hell of Dubrovka alive.

Contradicting the prior declaration of Russian President Putin, the general promised to send negotiators to discuss the Chechens' demands. Barayev and his comrades were jubilant. His pressure had borne fruit and he told us that everything was going to work out all right.

There was a delay to the negotiators' arrival. The Chechens understood that the other side were procrastinating and looking to buy time before storming the building. So they resumed their menacing language and threatened to start executing us in stages. Or blow up the building and everyone inside, all in one go . . .

They were exhausted like us, and, as the hours continued to slowly mount up, they sensed the extent of their predicament. The pressure was driving them half-crazy and they terrorized us by firing into the air with or without reason.

They handed out sweets and drinks from a small kiosk attached to the auditorium. These were without flavour on a tongue that had lost its sense of taste, having been desiccated by fear, although reflexive chewing and swallowing did at least minimize the risk of passing out from hunger.

However, afraid of letting us out of their sight, they did not let us use the bathrooms. They made us empty our bladders and bowels in the orchestra pit, making the vast auditorium smell like a sewer whose stench almost caused hundreds of people to pass out.

On two occasions Barayev agreed to allow an ICRC medical team in. He was convinced of the need to release other children, as well as some sick people and hostages of Chechen extraction. That made the total number of those released more than sixty.

And without anything from the Russians in return . . .

Just a joke of an offer proposed by Putin and relayed by Pronichev: a guarantee that the armed hostage-takers would not be killed if we were released. The Chechen leader rejected it outright.

Intense hatred was directed at the Chechen fighters and the Russian authorities alike. Our fate was uncertain and we faced two scenarios, the best of which meant death. Either the armed hostage-takers would kill us because their demands had not been met, or government forces would storm the building and cause a massacre.

Honestly, there are a thousand ways to live, and only one way to die . . .

Some called their relatives under the gaze of the armed men, only to discover that they were assembled a few metres away pleading with the army not to launch an all-out attack that would result in their loved ones being killed.

An endless whirlpool and we were inside. We did not drown but no one came to the rescue either.

If I had been able at the time to give a fitting description of what I was going through, I would have said that the rapid flip-flopping of my emotions from optimism to despair caused my senses to dull and malfunction, like a switch broken by being pressed too often.

I cried like a child. I laughed like a loon. I prayed to a God whose existence I had forgotten. I cursed myself and my parents as well as the Chechens, the Russians and the whole world.

Then I resorted to silence.

Even Olga, the idiot who had caused me of my own free will to enter the pit of hell, I didn't blame her. As the hours passed, that idea seemed meaningless and futile.

She too was just a victim.

A victim of her fate, or perhaps of her bad luck, that had led her to think of getting involved with a fucker like me!

*

Relief finally came . . .

At 4am on Saturday, our torture ended with the broadcast of a news bulletin, which I understood from Olga to mean that the Kremlin, in a bid to save innocent lives, had agreed to negotiate directly with the armed hostage takers, after previous abortive attempts on the part of a famous singer and a former prime minister.

Barayev and his men were overjoyed. They shouted praises and thanks to Allah, lost some of their hardness, and regained some confidence. They moved between the stage and the lighting control room for deliberations and their positivity seeped into us, despite the exhaustion.

"Weird," said Olga doubtfully, after a few minutes' thought. My incomprehension led her to explain: "In 1995, when I was twelve, 200 Chechen fighters attacked a hospital in Budyonnovsk and, much like this, were holding around 2,000 hostages. The army stormed the place, causing the deaths of 130 people. But the incident was a mighty gain for Shamil Barayev. It forced that pisshead Yeltsin to negotiate a ceasefire and accept a de facto independent Chechen republic. That caused a major political crisis at the time. I'm talking about dark days back then, when authority had reached its nadir. But the situation is very different today. Could Putin agree to such a concession? Impossible!"

"Which means?"

New-found optimism prompted me to watch the fluttering of her long eyelashes as she replied, "Another trick. But this one is quite different to the earlier procrastination. They're planning something . . ."

I stretched out my stiff legs to get the circulation going, then said, "Leave the vacuous analysis to the loudmouth news channels. When the sun comes up, negotiators will arrive to solve their problems with the Chechens. They'll meet here or in the Kremlin, or in Grozny or in hell itself, and we'll leave safe and sound. I'll leave your jinxed country for good, disavowing any false sense of affection I acquired after coming here. I'm not going to remain in a country where theatres and hospitals are attacked with bullets and bombs. Wasting an academic year of my life is better than the loss of a whole lifetime."

I shifted my weary gaze between the hands of the clock showing five and the rows of red seats crammed with hostages. I noticed that most people, including some black-clad women fighters, were fast asleep. It was as though they wanted a few minutes' rest, confident of their imminent freedom.

These were crucial moments, during which the barrier between the armed militants and the hostages collapsed . . .

Between the aggressor and the victim . . .

Or between victim and victim perhaps . . .

We all resembled each other, paying the price for staying alive in an existence that might not have been in accordance with our desires.

Using my winter coat as a blanket, I did likewise and shut my eyes to the watchful, alert looks of Olga, darting left and right in search of what I did not know . . .

Within a few minutes, I had fallen into a strangely deep sleep that was punctuated by hallucinations, images and a cacophony of incomprehensible voices.

I dreamt that, in the midst of Olga's cries of alarm, one of the veiled women took off her mask to reveal a face all-too familiar to my memory. She pressed the button as the Russian special forces entered the auditorium, blowing up the place and everyone in it, as she doggedly sang in a voice with a sexy rasp: "I swear by Fridays and Tuesdays I'll take my revenge, Uwaisa."

My memory, wandering lost between consciousness and dreaming, did not manage to find a definitive answer to the source of the voice. It compensated for its inability by suddenly retrieving a forgotten image.

An image of me admitting my naivety when I thought that escaping to Russia would rid me of her ghost.

* * *

A Moroccan Jigsaw Puzzle (novel)
– Khalid Rafiqi – 1st edn (pp. 229-34):

– 20 –

Mustafa sat down in his leather chair. He ignored the files and reports stacked on his undersized desk and surrendered to the exhaustion caused by lack of sleep and by the critical question hounding him: did the pieces of the complex jigsaw puzzle fit together to form a picture?

No. He still lacked a few pieces. And they were all in the possession of the arrogant American.

He took a sheet of blank paper and jotted down some of his thoughts in pencil, summarizing the details of the investigation and enabling him to reconstruct the events of the night of Wednesday 22 July and afterwards. He relied on the confessions and details that Halima, Saleh's lover, and Safiya, Jamila's sister, had provided.

Saleh had pretended to travel to Casablanca on business, but in reality he had stayed in Kenitra with his lover. Their meeting had turned into a quarrel as a result of Halima's calling him out for delaying his promise to get rid of his stuck-up, spoiled wife and marry her. He had told her many times that he had only married to satisfy his father's wishes, then with the birth of their first child and the cementing of relations between the two families, his earlier promises became a fantasy.

Jamila, on her part, had taken advantage of her husband's supposedly being out of town and her father's belief that she had gone back to her house near his villa. She left her son with her sisters and secretly met with someone she knew very well: Steve McMillan.

Safiya said that her sister had gotten to know the American during his regular visits to the house. She fancied the idea of seducing him, thereby getting her own back on Saleh, who made her life a misery with his vicious beatings and insults. Jamila, a spoiled girl who had lived like a princess in her father's house (following the death of her mother when she was still a child), found it beyond bearing.

And sure enough, looks and smiles developed into clandestine rendezvous between the Moroccan woman and the American, out of sight of the nosy, of whom of course there were many.

An extremely risky game or adventure, Safiya warned her sister more than once of the consequences. But Jamila swore she had not crossed any red lines with the American, and was conscious of her son's and family's reputation.

It seemed, however, that her desire for revenge against a husband, whom she knew by feminine intuition was cheating on her, was stronger.

Jamila forced Safiya to keep her mouth shut for fear of a scandal that might destroy the family's future. Then disaster struck.

The woman's dead body had been found and the detective received the mysterious letter, which he later discovered had been put in his mailbox by a cleaner in her twenties who helped his wife every week with the housework. The girl had learnt (thanks to his wife's chatter) that he was investigating Jamila's murder. And it turned out that the maid was none other than Halima.

Illiterate, poor and miserable, she had got to know Saleh and had fallen in love with him years before his marriage. She had patiently put up with his lies until the argument that night, when she was finally convinced that she was simply a plaything for him to forget the reality of his being hitched to a wife he had no feelings for. He wasn't mad, though, to divorce Jamila and risk his family's wealth and contacts just to marry Halima. She pondered how to get her own back, and asked a professional letter writer to compose the letter for her. She put it in the detective's mailbox, thereby involving Saleh in the crime.

Initially, Mustafa started with what he had heard from the neighbours about the couple's deteriorating relationship. His questioning of Saleh would have revealed information that could have uncovered many secrets, but his family intervened to have him released. That ruined everything and resulted in his subsequent death in mysterious circumstances.

That was how Steve McMillan's name surfaced in the case. He was insistent that he would not cooperate, and the detective became sure that the investigation had been going down the wrong track from the outset.

Saleh had nothing to do with his wife's killing, however bad his relationship with her might have been. It seemed that the game of seduction between the American man and the Moroccan woman had descended into an attempted assault that ended in Jamila's death and Steve being forced to dispose of the body and meet Saleh afterwards as if nothing had happened.

What Halima did not know when she put the letter in Mustafa's mailbox was that Saleh's true reason for staying in Kenitra wasn't to meet her, but Steve, as Saleh had noted in his appointment book.

The car that Saleh had been driving when he died was a new and expensive 1957 Ford, but the technician confirmed that the brakes had been tampered with. Exactly as the detective expected.

These were logical deductions, but they flung the doors wide open to further questions:

Did Steve also get rid of Saleh?

Why?

Was it connected to Jamila's murder or something else?

And what did the numbers below the note of the meeting mean:

33137 42F

Most likely, 42F meant 42 francs, but what about the rest of the numbers?

Was it a deal to smuggle American goods out of the airbase?

The fathers of both the deceased denied that they dealt with the Americans. Had the son worked on his own account, at a remove from the interests of his father and father-in-law?

Would the strands of this complex case lead to something much bigger and more serious than the murders of a husband and wife?

Once again the image of Steve McMillan, subject and predicate of the case, appeared to Mustafa.

The telephone rang and he answered with a lethargy that evaporated as soon as he heard the voice of the caller. He hot-footed it out of his office, stopped at the police commander's door, and knocked.

He waited for the signal to come in, entered and saluted.

"Regarding the case of the deaths of Jamila el-Baroudi and . . ."

Forgetting their difference in rank, Mustafa interrupted. "All the evidence points to the involvement of the American soldier Steve McMillan in the killings of Jamila and Saleh. All that remains is to bring him in for questioning in cooperation with the American military police and . . ."

The major frowned and raised a hand to stop him. With a firmness tinged with sympathy, he said, "Write in your final report that Saleh killed his wife then committed suicide. Close the file and get yourself and your little family ready to leave in a fortnight's time. It's been decided to transfer you."

Mustafa jolted as if he'd been given an electric shock and mumbled in astonishment, "What? I don't understand."

The major stood up and stared out of the window as he responded, "You're one of the best men here, and nobody would deny that you've worked hard to erase the image of your past with the protectorate. I've always dealt with you like a son or a younger brother, so I'm going to be frank with you. It's rumoured that Eisenhower is going to visit Morocco soon. There will be talks on the withdrawal of US forces from Moroccan bases. Everyone wants those negotiations to go smoothly and without any problems."

"Major, sir, do you think that arresting a criminal who's killed two Moroccan citizens is a problem?"

"There are priorities," he replied absently.

Mustafa's face contorted as he shouted, "Or differences in worth, if that's the right expression. I imagine that if an American died, Kenitra would be turned upside down, perhaps all of Morocco too."

His chief turned and ended the discussion by saying, "Go back to your office. I expect your report in an hour."

The detective left the room almost in tears, so outraged he was at his treatment. He imagined Steve smiling gloatingly at him. He felt he was about to explode in fury and, picking up his jacket, he left his office without writing the report.

Lost in thought about an appropriate way to tell his wife that he was being transferred, he did not notice the large truck without license plates, whose engine started the instant he left the police station and which accelerated straight towards him . . .

THE END

(10) The Invention of Solitude

> *One does not find solitude, one creates it.*
> **Marguerite Duras**

Saturday, 26 October 2002
Habous neighbourhood – Casablanca:

We arrived at our intended destination and got out of a red taxi. Rachid ignored what I understood to be the driver importuning for a tip larger than the fare simply because I was a foreign tourist and, in his view, had to pay extra!

"Is this quiet neighbourhood really part of the same blaring city whose crowded streets we went through?"

"There's a good reason. Habous in Casablanca is renowned for its bookshops, which means it's tranquil all year apart from a rush when the schools go back." Rachid said this with a readily understandable sarcasm that did not conceal the distraction affecting him since we boarded the train in Rabat.

"What's up with you?" I found it necessary to ask. "Didn't we agree to look for more information about Khalid Rafiqi, starting with the address of the publishers, even though we know it's been closed for years? And we chose your day off for the task."

"The manager called me in and expressed his displeasure with what my colleagues are saying about my meetings with you.

Then he threatened to fire me, claiming he was being protective of the hotel's reputation, after incidents elsewhere in which dubious relationships developed between foreign tourists and Moroccans dreaming of crossing to the other shore."

He laughed nervously and continued, "Relationships that ended either with their dreams coming true or turning into nightmares after the tourists complain to the police that they've been tricked or conned. In some cases the Moroccans themselves are the dupes. That's when a cunning tourist leaves without paying a single dirham after having spent their holiday with a smart-ass Moroccan covering their expenses in full, out of greed for their goals, which evaporate as soon as the tourist's charter plane takes off for home."

To encourage him further, I joined in the laughter and took hold of his right hand in a friendly way in full view of some curious patrons at the Mauritania Café.

"With the greatest respect to the hotel staff and your need to help your family, an intellectual as smart and well-educated as you is too good to be working there."

"Better say he's too good to carry on living in a country where those in authority don't need bullets or drugs to finish off the cream of its youth as long as the game of slowly grinding them down is sufficient."

I felt he was making an effort beyond the powers of his unassuming character to express an inner emotional turmoil, but he was content to utter a couple of words to end the brief conversation: "We're here."

*

A young employee at the seventh bookshop we'd visited looked at us quizzically, then affirmed what we'd heard from others: "Yes, I remember Hope Press for Publication and Distribution with its small and elegant office very well. It was set up and run by a retired civil servant called Muhsin el-Fadili. He was a genuine example of a publisher who loved literature, but the project failed after a few years, and he was forced to bring down the shutters at the end of the '90s."

The guy in his twenties spoke to me in English while Rachid browsed the books on display. Running out of patience, I said, "We already know that. We're looking for him to find out some details about a novel his press published in 1989."

A man in his fifties, who looked somewhat similar to the younger guy, appeared. He asked him something while staring at me as if I were an alien just landed from Mars.

"We have no information about him. I'm very sorry but I cannot help you." The guy said this awkwardly, as he waited for the older man to return to a backroom. Then he wrote something on a small piece of paper on the desk and handed it to me in full view of Rachid, who was coming over carrying some books, most of which were weighty tomes.

In a low voice, the guy said, "I've written down Mr el-Fadili's address. It's nearby. He's over seventy and lives alone since his wife died and his children emigrated. He doesn't leave the house very often. He does the rounds of the bookshops, browses the shelves, and keeps up with what's new in terms of literature and ideas. He doesn't talk to any of his old friends. All of them, including my father, took against him, and some of them claimed he'd lost his marbles. But I don't agree. I met him more than once as a kid when I was helping my father at the shop. I only know him to be a kind and friendly man with an encyclopaedic knowledge of culture."

"It's only two streets away!" said Rachid once he'd seen the address written in a quick and unsteady hand. Then he took out his wallet and asked the guy how much the books were.

From the way his forehead creased and his brows shot up, it seemed he hadn't been expecting such an expensive price. I quickly intervened, handing a fistful of Moroccan banknotes to the bookseller.

"Not a word! Now's not the right time to play the self-sufficient, self-made man. And don't thank me like in a melodramatic film with ridiculous music. Take what you want. Think of it as a new kind of weird relationship between Moroccans and foreign women tourists!"

*

A quiet side street, like the tortuous narrow alleys in the Old City of Rabat. Whitewashed walls and dark wooden doors a stone step or two below street level.

A man selling fish, his face furrowed by the sun, pushing a rust-eaten bicycle and hawking his fish in what seemed a screech, pursued by a pack of cats on the lookout for a gesture of kindness or a moment's inadvertence to win one of the frozen fish.

A woman in her early forties wearing a white robe, its hem tucked into her yellow belt, stared at us suspiciously while cleaning the entrance to her house using an excessive amount of water and bending over so exaggeratedly that, to a crafted and nearly imperceptible rhythm, she revealed her ample bosom and the proportionality of her thighs and legs with her upper half. A show of strength that only a woman like her would appreciate.

We rang the doorbell more than once, then resorted to banging on the door. The rustle of a curtain in an upper window proved that someone behind it was spying on us. Then a little girl of about eight looked out of a window opposite and shouted, as Rachid explained, "'Don't waste your time. The bogeyman won't open his door to anyone . . .'"

He commented, laughing, "They've turned the solitary intellectual into a bogeyman to frighten their kids instead of encouraging them to get close to him and befriend him!"

Rachid cupped his hands around his mouth to amplify his voice as he called out in Arabic the name of the publisher, the name of the novel, and the name of its author, Khalid Rafiqi.

He gently tugged me away by the arm, muttering something I couldn't make out, but most likely expressing his annoyance at the forty-year-old woman's nosiness. As despairing as someone due to be executed in the morning, I followed him.

As expected, and with a nod to all those classic scenes in every film, drama, and novel, we had just reached the end of the street, when the door of the house opened, and a shabby-looking man with bleary eyes and sunken cheeks peeked out. His movements were slower than a Galapagos turtle's, but he called out to the Moroccan PhD student. They exchanged a few words in Arabic, and he paid me no attention. Then he allowed us in. The last thing I saw before the door shut was the woman picking up a broom to shoo away some evil-looking cats that had not managed to get their share of the fish, and were being punished for a crime whose nature the woman herself seemed ignorant of.

Stock scenes in films, dramas, and novels aren't always truthful, however.

Contrary to what I expected, I did not find myself confronted with a filthy, messy home, books strewn around, or a mad- and frightening-looking old man, who might surprise us with some sudden shock. Despite the building's age, the small rooms were neat and tidy. Every item of furniture was in its place, if a little dated. When we entered the living room, I was confronted by a huge bookcase and framed family portraits on the opposite wall as well as a television screen showing a news channel.

Without asking permission, Rachid made straight for the bookcase. He seemed amazed at the diversity of the contents, like a hungry man unsure where to begin with a table piled high with delicacies. The old man, as if we were old acquaintances, leaned amicably towards my ear, and said in faultless English, "They told you about a stuck-up, or loopy, publisher who lives on his own and never speaks to or befriends anyone since his venture failed and his wife died and his children emigrated. What they say actually suits me. It means I can live in peace. If your friend hadn't mentioned a novel I like a great deal, I wouldn't have opened the door!"

Weary and slow like anyone his age, there was nothing about

his appearance and dress – at least – that suggested any psychological problems, as we'd heard.

Rachid joined us. His eagerness had turned to puzzlement, prompting the publisher to comment, still in English to include me, "I quite understand the confusion that registers on the face of any true lover of literature as soon as they stop in front of a bookcase. Come with me now . . ."

While he was dictating titles to a revived Rachid, who wrote them down in his notebook, the television caught my eye. The broadcaster was anxiously commenting as scenes flashed past of tens, perhaps hundreds, of people crowded near a big building ringed by armoured vehicles and soldiers, along with the desperate efforts of nurses and doctors to provide first-aid to a large number of civilians.

Were they dead or unconscious?

I snapped out of it when Muhsin el-Fadili suddenly posed some questions unrelated to all that had gone before: "An armed group is holding hundreds of hostages at a theatre in Moscow. The Russian authorities are able to free them after fifty hours of captivity. The rumour is that they used a top-secret weapon to regain control. How did the hostages spend those horrific hours? Will their liberation mark the end of their suffering or just a new beginning for it? Don't you think all of that would make a suitably attractive opening for a fictional retelling, Ms McMillan?"

* * *

The Embassy of the Kingdom of Morocco
to the Russian Federation
Moscow, Thursday, 14 November 2002

NOTICE

In response to media speculation that has accompanied the disappearance of Moroccan student Zouhair Belkacem (born 1983) who is registered for the first, preparatory year (specializing in medicine) at the Sechenov Medical University in the Russian capital Moscow, and the proliferation of rumours that the missing person was present at the Dubrovka Theatre, scene of the hostage-taking by a Chechen armed group, the Moroccan Embassy declares that it has made inquiries in conjunction with the Russian authorities and can confirm that no Moroccan citizen is included among the victims or survivors following the freeing of the hostages from the abovementioned theatre. The Embassy has also been in communication with the Association of Moroccan Students in Russia, and learnt from them that the missing person declined to become a member, preferring to keep apart from his Moroccan colleagues and make friends with a Russian student, who has dismissed the theory that his friend was present for the theatrical performance.

The initial findings, therefore, do not indicate any connection between the student's disappearance on Wednesday, 23 October 2002, and the hostage-taking. Investigations are ongoing to discover his fate and reassure his family in Morocco.

In conclusion, the Embassy affirms that it is performing its duty thoroughly, with concern for the safety of all its citizens, contrary to the claims put about or fabricated by some newspapers of "deliberate negligence" and "shameful disregard" for the worth of a Moroccan citizen, in comparison with the embassies of other countries which, from the outset, kept tabs on their citizens held hostage at the theatre.

Signed
The Media Section, Embassy of the Kingdom of Morocco
to the Russian Federation

* * *

(10') Survivor

> *That you can see everything does not mean you know anything nor that you are able to do anything.*
>
> **Saud Alsanousi**

Saturday, 26 October 2002
Dubrovka Theatre; a hospital of unknown name – Moscow:

The cold stinging my limbs combined with my body's violent rejection of the alien object jiggling in my mouth and I regained consciousness in a sudden burst. I was lying on the ground, with a young doctor or nurse in white overalls above me. He had inserted his fingers into my mouth to stop me swallowing my tongue.

He spoke Russian, and I looked at him with the dumb expression of someone who didn't understand a word of what he was saying. My fear and physical collapse had combined to deaden the speed of my response and erase all I had learned of his language over the few weeks I had spent in his country.

The guy exchanged a few brief words with a colleague. Then the two of them simply carried me to a waiting coach with a large number of passengers in it. They sat me down on a seat by the window and, despite my blurred vision, I noticed a huge commotion near the main entrance to the theatre. Soldiers were mixed up with aghast doctors, nurses and civilians. Motionless bodies (or corpses?) were piled up on the pavement. A glance up to the sky showed the first rays of sunrise on a new day.

What had happened?

How had we been taken out of the besieged theatre?

Where were Movsar Barayev and his men?

Had they left by virtue of an agreement with the Russian authorities?

Had they surrendered?

Been killed?

Where had Olga disappeared?

My brain ignored the need to answer my pressing questions and commanded all my vital functions to bail on me. I fell back into unconsciousness, and everything around me went black.

*

I woke up to a pounding on my chest from massaging hands sheathed in yellowish-white gloves.

White walls, white bed, and an aged doctor with coat, hair and shoes of that colour too.

"Stop! You're hurting me, you stupid old man . . ."

My words startled the doctor and his face showed signs of surprise that made me realise I was speaking in Arabic. When I heard voices indicating activity outside the room, I uttered one word in English: "Water."

The doctor motioned to one of his assistants and the nurse filled a plastic cup from a bottle of mineral water labelled in Russian and handed it to me. The doctor for his part turned to English to communicate with me: "Are you okay? You're not Russian, then. What nationality are you?"

"I've got a bad headache and feel exhausted. And I can only move my limbs with great difficulty." He just nodded, in what seemed a sign prearranged with his assistants, and I continued,

"What happened? Why did I pass out? How did the operation to free the hostages end?" I was getting my focus back, and my voice raised to a shout: "Where am I? Where's my overcoat and my mobile? How will I call my family to reassure them?"

He chose to suck up my anger and answered my questions with words that meant nothing to me: "What matters is you survived. With you, like the others, I've used the drug Naloxone, but I don't know if it worked on you or you were only partially exposed to the mystery gas." He was silent momentarily, then asked, "Did you feel anything unusual at exactly five in the morning?"

"No, nothing. The hostages were in an optimistic mood after the news broadcast that the Russian authorities had agreed to negotiations with . . ."

"I mean physically," he interrupted with a force that perhaps masked his impatience. "Did you feel nauseous or have a headache before you lost consciousness?"

"Given the terror and foreboding that went along with captivity, I think I slept a little too well. It was only Olga who reacted negatively to the developments. She suspected that something was being planned behind the scenes."

He was about to continue his questions, when the door opened and two people entered the room. The blue cap of one of them showed he belonged to the police, while the heavy black boots and green jacket of the other indicated he was from the military. Both of them were holding sheets of paper that from up close I could make out consisted of lists of names in Russian.

They engaged in a short conversation with the doctor, and from the severe tone of the soldier, I understood that they wanted to be alone with me. The old man and his assistant left the room, and the blond policeman came over. He had a child-like face without moustache or beard, and I guessed he was in his mid-twenties.

His English was abominable, but permitted a minimal degree

of comprehension.

"Sir, we are very pleased that you have survived the nightmare of the Dubrovka Theatre. The operation ended with our special forces storming the building, releasing the hostages and killing all the terrorists. Relax, this isn't an investigation. We just want to confirm some basic information, understand?"

My vision, as distorted as an out-of-tune UHF television, shifted between him and the soldier, who looked like a block of ice. Then I said in resignation, "No problem. Go ahead!"

"Your name?"

"Zouhair Belkacem."

"Your age?"

"Nineteen."

"Your job or educational stage?"

"First, preparatory year student, specializing in human medicine, Sechenov Medical Academy, Moscow."

"Your nationality?"

"Moroccan."

Ordinary information, but I was taken aback by the dubious reaction of the policeman and his review of the list of names before having a brief word with the ice block and then returning to me to say in a tone that had lost much of its friendliness, "Sir, are you a dual national?"

"No," I said nervously.

"Do you have ID papers with you?"

"I lost my overcoat together with my mobile phone, passport, student ID card and wallet."

Confusion left its impression on his childlike face as he said in bewilderment, "Mr Zouhair, the list of foreigners at Dubrovka Theatre includes citizens from the United States of America, Ukraine, Austria, The Netherlands, Kazakhstan, Azerbaijan and Armenia. Their embassies all informed us of their presence among the hostages and monitored their fates blow by blow. Either the list I have has not been updated or . . ."

The second possibility was easy to predict, so I was not

stunned by what he said or by its coded derision: "Or the Moroccan Embassy has no knowledge at all that one of its subjects was at the Dubrovka Theatre."

The ice block said something in Russian, some of which I understood, but the policeman translated it in full: "As long as your ID papers are missing, as you claim, we are obliged to keep you here until we can confirm your true identity."

Then they left the room in step, not bothered about leaving me alone to tilt at windmills of confusion and doubt.

The drug Naloxone. A mysterious gas. Hostages at the theatre. A lost mobile phone and ID papers. Embassies concerned for the safety of their citizens, and others that knew nothing about them?

Had common sense decided to shed its overalls and tender its resignation?

They say that people are afraid of what they don't know. I had my doubts, given that I was now powerless to act, unable to feel fear, and lacking any mental capacity to construct a coherent picture of events from the moment I fell asleep in my seat at the theatre to the point of my answering the Russian policeman's questions.

Why should I bother exhausting my brain with the effort to understand?

Does anything about our lives merit that?

Apprehensions and strange disjointed ideas tied me up in knots. A vague voice intervened deep inside me, whose source, it seemed, was a man sitting on a comfortable chair behind a desk made of the finest wood, using low lighting to conceal his identity, and speaking freely . . . . . .

What's happened to you, Zouhair, has nothing to do with common sense. It's not possible that a person could experience such a succession of ridiculous calamities.

You aren't a person of flesh and blood. You are a character on paper, in a novel whose events are driven by an author who might be a sadist taking pleasure in drowning you in a sea of woes, or a fool who's pushed you into a maze that he himself does not know how to extricate you from!

* * *

**Events taking place elsewhere,
Saturday, 26 October 2002:**

Brandon sat down on the couch in the lobby and placed his hat over his knee, whose trembling was a sign of nervous excitement. He glanced between the clock on the wall and his wristwatch, as if comparing between them or urging them to speed up.

From his contacts in the Veterans Association, Brandon had found out that Tony Wagner was still alive and a resident of this old people's home in Detroit, Michigan. Clinging on to this last hope of finding even a single piece of information to assist Christine in her quest to uncover her father's past, there wasn't a minute to lose. Five of the Americans in the photograph had already succumbed to death, and after confirming that Ernie Jones had Alzheimer's, Wagner seemed like an oasis in a sprawling desert. And the greatest fear was that this oasis was no more than a mirage.

A bunch of explosive questions had kept Brandon awake the previous nights: What would come after the exhausting efforts criss-crossing the States? Would his "pro bono" assistance make up for the years he had waited for Christine to give him a single glance? He was a literary agent and best placed to understand the caprice and egotism of writers. Authors thought only about themselves and cared only for their own interests. Ambition often drove them to destroy those closest to them.

Why didn't Christine talk to him about her children, Ronald and Cindy, for example? They might as well not exist. Was it true she had lost custody of them to her ex-husband Mike? Or did she volunteer to give them up, in pursuit of her dreams that had come into being after her belated and dramatic entrance into the bright lights and fame of the literary world?

They had spent an unforgettable night together at her old family home in Denver. A night Brandon had waited eighteen years for . . .

With her golden hair, grey eyes, and freckles on her petite face, in his arms she had resembled a Barbie doll on the verge of forty. Some signs of aging were visible: fine wrinkles at the corners of the eyes and on her neck, a little excess flab around the waist, but the passage of the years had not managed to take away her physical vitality. Perhaps it had even increased his intense desire for her.

So much for her body, but what about her heart?

How did he know if her current feelings were real, or was she just exploiting what she had selfishly pretended to ignore for years in exchange for sorely needed help to produce her new novel, and so fix the problem with her publisher?

Hadn't he secretly noticed something akin to disgust on her face when she saw his bare artificial leg?

Didn't she always deliberately ignore talk about the future of their recent relationship, restricting their phone calls to discussion about her cooperation with a young Moroccan guy, going on about how impressed she was with his intelligence and diligence and how unhappy she was that his bad luck meant he had to live in a country that thought him worthless, but without really explaining?

Was she hiding something about her investigation? Or were those baseless suspicions that had taken root in the mind of someone who no longer trusted anyone or anything since that black day when his military base in Beirut had out of nowhere been rocked by explosions that caused the dead and injured to drop like flies?

All his worries evaporated, or he was at least able to sweep them under a rug in one of the chambers of his mind, when a doctor in his mid-thirties came into the lobby and shook him by the hand. "Mr Roland George, responsible for the health of our resident, Tony Wagner." The doctor gave a quick glance (one familiar to Brandon) at the prosthetic leg and asked him a question drenched in suspicion: "May I know the reason for your visit? And outside of visiting hours? We do not normally allow strangers to meet our residents!"

"I work for the office of Forster Legal Consultancy," Brandon replied with the innocence of someone prepared for possible obstacles. "And I have been sent to check on a few urgent details concerning our client Mr Wagner's assets." He backed his words by waving a small white card in his left hand and gripping the handle of a black leather briefcase with the fingers of his right hand, while adding confidently, "You can call the office to confirm my identity!"

The doctor turned towards the clock on the wall, which showed eight o'clock in the evening, and his doubt turned into an imperfect trust. "No, there's no need. It's just that this is the first time he's had a visitor since he was put in the care home. He's got three kids who've been swallowed up by the flurry of New York life. Not one of them can even be bothered to pick up the phone and ask after him."

"The whirlwind of America has caused many people to forget themselves, so forgetting their loved ones is hardly surprising," said Brandon in a friendly tone that removed any trace of doubt for the doctor, who responded with interest, "Very true. I should also point out that he is not suffering from any chronic disease, apart from the normal problems of old age. And if we exclude his difficult character, bad temper and lack of plain courtesy, then there's nothing seriously wrong with him mentally. He does, however, argue constantly with the other residents, and you can imagine the kind of fights between the very elderly."

Brandon laughed as he patted the man's shoulder and the doctor led him off to the room. He ended his words with a plea, "Please don't allow the meeting to last more than a few minutes out of consideration for Mr Wagner's comfort and so as not to disturb his usual bedtime."

The literary agent waited for the young doctor to leave. Then he smiled as he checked the card from the law office, which he had obtained easily from the receptionist there, and knocked on the door. A voice as grating as a horse-drawn wagon in Veracruz responded, "Go to hell, you sonofabitch."

Brandon had not expected quite such a crude reception, but his long experience dealing with a handful of the ill and mad who called themselves writers motivated him to use an alternative and time-proven method. A method that would help two people who had both spent years in the US military understand each other more easily.

He kicked the door open and burst into the room like a bandit. The terrified old man cried out, "Who is it? Who are you?"

Pink-skinned like a newborn and verging on the obese, the clippers of the years had condemned most of his hair to fall out and wrinkles had turned his face into a map of interstate highways.

His eyes widened when he heard the answer: "A sonofabitch you don't know, but who will kill you if you don't answer his questions about someone you know very well!"

It would have been possible for the resident of the old people's home to call for help from the medical team by pressing a button hanging by his bed, but the steady gaze of the person standing in front of him forced him to reconsider and pose the same question again: "Who are you?"

"Tony Wagner, you were a soldier in the ranks of the US forces which served at Kenitra Air Force Base in Morocco. My information is correct, is it not?"

He nodded and smiled. In the tone of someone whose interlocutor has lit the fuse of old memories that have a special place in his heart, he said, "Morocco! What unforgettable days those were . . ."

The features of the phony legal consultant relaxed as he sensed that the efforts of the previous weeks would finally be crowned with success. He opened his black briefcase, took out copies of the photographs he had found with Christine in Denver, and began showing them to Tony, who hunted on the bedside table for his glasses.

The literary agent put a finger over Steve McMillan's face in the picture at Les Arcades bar. "Sonofabitch," said the old man definitively. Brandon put his angry face back on, but Tony didn't retract and defended his cussing. "Yessir, I mean exactly what I said. Have you read the novel *A Hero of Our Time* by the Russian writer Mikhail Lermontov?"

The name of the novel struck like a hammer blow smashing into Brandon's skull, but he preferred to proceed cautiously when he said, "No, I don't know it. Novels are simply a waste of time in my opinion." The old man gave a mocking laugh and commented, "Because you're a stupid idiot of course! You will never know who Steve McMillan is unless you've read the story of Grigori Pechorin." With a speed belying his years and that stopped his interlocutor from even reacting to his harsh insult, he added, "Someone whose favourite hobby was destroying those he loved could only be a sonofabitch. If you look closely at the photos and try to make sense of them, you'll find yourself dealing with a novel called 'A Bastard of Our Time'. But that's too much for stupid idiots to understand."

Brandon made an extraordinary effort to steady his nerves and took back the pictures in an attempt to understand what he meant, but Tony ended his bafflement with a forcefulness mixed with a tinge of indifference. "Forget the bullshit now. I don't know you and I don't care about your relationship to him. But I'm so bored here, perhaps seeking refuge in the past will be an effective treatment for my loneliness. You want to know the truth about Steve McMillan as I knew him, a redneck country boy in Texas and a messed-up soldier in Morocco? Fine . . ."

He started to talk, recalling memories from more than fifty years before. Dreadful memories that made Brandon's jaw drop in horror and amazement and dealt a deathblow to everything that Christine knew – or thought she knew – about her father.

As he continued spilling the details, the literary agent took a decision that at the time seemed sensible: he would not tell Christine a single word that he heard from Tony. Ever.

* * *

(11) Masks of Reality and Masks of Fantasy

> *A classic is a book that has never finished saying what it has to say.*
>
> Italo Calvino

Saturday, 26 October 2002
Habous neighbourhood – Casablanca:

Astounded, I studied Muhsin el-Fadili's face and could find nothing more to say than, "Excuse me?"

The old man turned the TV off and changed the subject with the ease of someone essentially uninterested in my answer.

"Never mind. Returning to the subject of your visit, my memories about *A Moroccan Jigsaw Puzzle* vary between love and disappointment. I counted a lot on its success, but reality intervened. That was the first blow to a dream of mine which time proved to be ridiculous."

He sat down on the comfortable couch and motioned for us to sit, which we did.

"Every one of us has a dream he tries to fulfil in the autumn of his days. Some plan to own a house, in which they die a few years later; some go on the Hajj seeking purification of a soul, the extent of whose corruption one only admits after turning sixty;

another thinks about reliving his youth in rebellion against a domineering wife who for decades spewed bile over him by the barrelful."

Rachid suppressed a laugh and I just gave a smile that did not stop Muhsin el-Fadili from continuing. "I don't know whether a job at the Foreign Ministry was a blessing or a curse for a person with literature in his blood. I visited many countries and got to know different cultures and literatures. My view of the world and life changed. I came back to Morocco for good after I retired, hoping to pass on my experience to a country I love. My idea was to nurture the literary talent that I know exists aplenty and just needs someone to push forward. Nobody helped me. Only my wife had faith in my idea and she encouraged me to set up a bookshop and a publishing house after my children emigrated. I called it Hope Press for Publishing and Distribution, optimistic about achieving my aspirations . . ."

Rachid interrupted him with a tactlessness that annoyed me: "But sometimes, optimism is the worst crime that you can commit against yourself."

The publisher was silent for a long while, in what I imagined was the desire to rebuke Rachid, but he defied my expectation by saying, "No, the worst crime is that they have been able to sow the seeds of despair in the mind of a young man like you."

I manufactured a short cough as a sign of my desire to return the conversation to our main subject. Muhsin el-Fadili understood the meaning and stood up wearily and headed over to his library. He rummaged around for a minute and came back with a large envelope, which he handed to Rachid, and a newspaper clipping that he kept hold of.

"As soon as I received the manuscript of *A Moroccan Jigsaw Puzzle*, I read it carefully before showing it to the readers' committee. I knew I was dealing with something out of the ordinary. It wasn't the suspense of the detective plot that excited me as much as the despair between the lines. You feel as if the author is someone who's lost faith in everything: his past, his present and his future; and in other people. Writing is the only refuge he has to prevent the total collapse of his faith in himself. It really is a jigsaw puzzle, what with a crime, an investigation and a mystery, but with a purely Moroccan flavour that you won't find in other literary works."

"Seeing as he is a Moroccan writer, it's perfectly natural that he should write a novel full of despair. If it contained a single optimistic line, I would have classed it as science fiction right away." Another comment from Rachid that I ignored by casting a rapid glance at the envelope, my curiosity getting the better of my ignorance of Arabic:

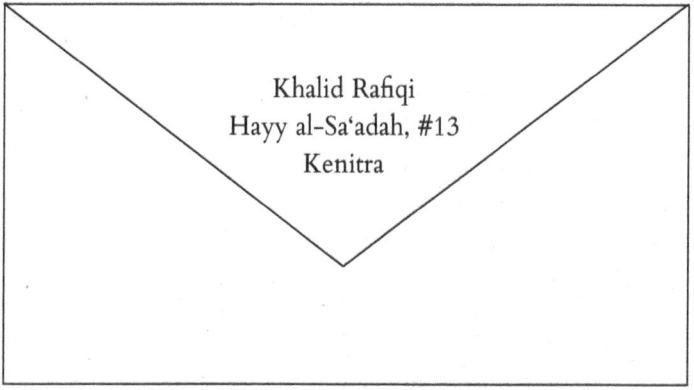

Khalid Rafiqi
Hayy al-Sa'adah, #13
Kenitra

"So you wrote to him after agreeing to publish the book?" I asked the former publisher.

"I drew up a contract and got in touch with the printers, the editor and the proofreader to start work, but I got a strange and puzzling shock."

"Which was?"

"The address of the sender doesn't exist," interjected Rachid, and the publisher clapped his hands like a child in response to his lightning insight.

"Exactly. The envelope was returned to me and I understood

from the post office that the address was made up. It didn't exist, or had done at some time in the past but no one remembered it anymore."

The young Moroccan researcher interrupted, saying with implicit sarcasm, "I would never have believed that a person who wrote a novel full of precise details plucked from the heart of Morocco's miserable reality lived in a neighbourhood whose name, Sa'adah, means happiness!"

I noticed the ghost of a wry smile on the corner of Muhsin el-Fadili's mouth. Then he leaned forward to address me slowly: "Your arrival thirteen years after the publication of the novel in search of answers to the question of the fictional and the real in its events, and your suspicion that your father might have committed murder, mean that *A Moroccan Jigsaw Puzzle* has not shown all its cards yet. It is asking you, in your capacity as readers, to cooperate to write further chapters of its story. Doesn't that remind you of anything?"

I answered him with silence, while Rachid gave it a shot: "*The Mystery of Edwin Drood* by Charles Dickens..."

Three seconds were sufficient time for my face to light up with understanding along with a flash of jealousy at Rachid's incredible insight. That pushed me to show off the breadth of my reading by explaining, "You're right. *The Mystery of Edwin Drood* is one of the world's most famous unfinished novels. Its mystery is still piquing the imagination of millions around the world. The action takes place in a fictional city, which Dickens called Cloisterham. Before Edwin's father dies, he betrothes him to Rosa Bud, another orphan, so they can both obtain a vast fortune when they come of age. Jasper, Edwin's uncle and choirmaster at Cloisterham Cathedral, brings the boy up. The two children grow up and we see them as two mature young people. Edwin suddenly disappears in mysterious circumstances, and Jasper starts searching for him. But we are shocked at the same time that the uncle, a decent religious man on the outside, is addicted to opium and is Rosa's secret lover. We also discover the fact of a meeting between

Edwin and Rosa the night before his disappearance, when they agree to end their engagement, which is a burden when they do not truly love each other. Then a character appears who presents himself as a detective called Datchery, whose features are somewhat familiar to the reader. It was the last novel Dickens wrote. He died in 1870 without finishing it. More than 130 years have passed and many people have worked on the puzzling mystery, turning it into an obsession that sparked what is now known as Droodian literature, devoted to resolving the complex mystery. Did Drood arrange his own disappearance, or did he die? And if so, who would the murderer have been? The uncle who wished to appropriate the fortune and marry Rosa, or somebody else? For your information, Rachid, there are currently literary competitions in a number of countries in which young writers are asked to come up with a suitable and logical ending to the mystery novel."

"Fantastic idea. And for your information also, I know a country where they organize beauty contests for donkeys!"

My failure to understand what Rachid meant, forced him to turn serious again: "Now we're confronted with a similar conundrum. We have a finished novel, but the author set to reveal its mystery is unknown."

While he made his comment, I went over to the library, turning to the arrangement of the books to gather my scattered thoughts. "If the sender's address was made up, then who is Khalid Rafiqi?"

"If we start," said Rachid confidently, "with the assumption that the crime was real, then the detailed description of the course of the investigation suggests that the detective Mustafa Mahmoudi, or whatever his real name, is the author. Perhaps he felt aggrieved after the closure of the case and his transfer to another city, even though he was close to bringing formal charges against Steve McMillan. So he wrote the novel to clear his conscience, using an assumed name to avoid any issues over his sensitive position. He fabricated an ending to make the reader think he had died and deflect any suspicion from him."

The publisher handed the newspaper article to Rachid while directing his words at me: "Back in 1988 I did not take into account the possibility that the novel dealt with a real crime. But then I came across an old newspaper cutting when I was throwing away a pile of newspapers left behind by one of the publishing house's employees. The short article led me to a completely different interpretation."

SEARCH FOR MISSING PERSON

The family of Rafiq Khalidi is appealing for help to find him 25 days after his disappearance in mysterious circumstances on Monday, 1 August 1988.

The missing person is a 35-year-old maths teacher at Salaam Middle School, Duwwar el-Hajj Kaddour, situated a few kilometres from Meknes, where he lives with his family. While he does not suffer from any psychological or mental disturbances, he has heart disease and difficulties with speaking and moving his limbs normally. He also has a large birthmark on his left cheek.

I took a close look over Rachid's shoulder, and once again the Arabic letters stood out. The young doctoral researcher did not give me the chance to ask and translated the clipping: "Rafiq Khalidi, a maths teacher living in Meknes according to the address given, whose family say they have lost contact with him since Monday, 1 August 1988."

The former publisher dropped onto the couch and added, "I received the manuscript of *A Moroccan Jigsaw Puzzle* by post at the end of November of the same year!"

I shifted my gaze between the two men in confusion. Then Rachid took a pen and a sheet of paper out of his bag. He wrote the letters in Arabic and English:

ر ف ي ق	خ ا ل د
خ ا ل د ي	ر ف ي ق ي
Ra F I Q	Kh A Li D
Kh A Li D I	Ra F I Q I

"I get it! Shifting one letter in the name Khalid Rafiqi was sufficient to change it completely into Rafiq Khalidi."

"But the similarity of the two names isn't enough to connect him to the novel and its author. Plus, the manuscript arrived months after he disappeared." Rachid said this with an insistence that angered me, and Muhsin el-Fadili forestalled him: "Do you really believe I didn't think about it? I went to Meknes myself and met with the family of the missing man Rafiq Khalidi to turn my suspicions into certainties!"

* * *

TV programme Situation Critical – The Moscow Theatre Siege – National Geographic Channel – 2007

Excerpt from minutes 35–38:

(*Narration in the background*):

Finally the moment the general has been hoping for. Now is the time to strike.

Within minutes special forces attach a container of the powerful anaesthetic to the theatre's ventilation system.

A fine mist descends on the auditorium. Hostages think it is teargas.

Two terrified hostages phone a local radio station: "They are gassing us! Please give us a chance! We beg not to be gassed!"

The rebels think they are under attack and start firing into the parking lot. Russian special forces don't shoot back.

The anaesthetic works fast. As soon as it is breathed into the lungs it enters the bloodstream. The blood carries the drug to the brain, where it affects the central nervous system. The victim slips into unconsciousness.

Outside special forces continue to wait . . .

* * *

(11') Morphine

This life is a hospital, where each patient is possessed by the desire to change beds.
Charles Baudelaire

Tuesday, 12 November 2002
European Medical Centre – Moscow:

The Russians took steps to rectify the initial confusion surrounding the presence of a Moroccan among the theatre hostages. Higher-ranking policemen with excellent English flocked to my room and made a great show of being friendly. They told me I was at the European Medical Centre, then asked me the same questions as the policeman with the childlike face, along with a few extra queries about places I knew or had visited in the Russian capital. They did not touch upon the hours of terror I had endured with Barayev's armed group.

I talked to them about a sightseeing tour of Moscow that my friend took me on and my participation in a chess tournament at Bitsa Park. They wrote the information down with perverse interest, although it all seemed secondary to my having been one of the victims of the siege.

What exactly were they thinking?

After a few days I was transferred to another room at the same hospital along with a new medical team, which monitored developments in my condition. They gave me what they said were stimulants to help my body regain its strength after a terrible ordeal that almost cost me my life in a way that Mikhail Lermontov – with his nonchalance and constant mockery regarding death – would not have been able to imagine.

My mental state did actually improve, but I was still in the grip of illness. Over the course of a few days I noticed the commotion in the hospital lessen as the chaos that had accompanied the transport of the freed hostages for treatment faded and relative calm returned.

I summoned up sufficient courage to ask some questions of my own and inquired about the value of keeping me and preventing me from calling my family in Morocco. A policeman, who looked like Anton Chekhov (whose picture I had seen on one of the paperbacks piled up by Sergei's bed) tried to reassure me. He affirmed that I was no longer in a critical condition and that I was being kept in for necessary medical observation while I waited for the completion of some administrative procedures allowing me to leave the hospital and return to the classroom at college.

If we had been in Morocco, I would have understood the reason, given that the expression "a delay in administrative procedures" had become quite normal and familiar in our comically dysfunctional reality. As proof, I offer my cynicism towards the Moroccan Embassy's ignorance of my presence among the hostages. I mean, I could have been angry.

However, things really had gone beyond the normal and reasonable.

My list of questions grew longer, as I sensed (as had Olga) a trap, in whose sticky threads a gang of spiders were cooperating to catch me. So I decided to satisfy my curiosity myself.

Answers were not long in coming, or at least some of them . .

*

A new day's sun rose, and along with it a morose cleaning lady came into the room. She gave the windows overlooking the backyard of the medical centre a cursory rub with some old newspaper.

I only knew the tiniest amount of Russian, deriving from my short presence in Moscow, but I have a mind that I think capable of acting intelligently . . .

I waited for the right moment, which came when the cleaner went out to answer a phone call, and looked inside her waste trolley. I extracted a page of an old newspaper and concealed it under my pillow as fast as my body would allow.

The cleaner finished her task and I gave her a fake, sweet smile, which vanished as soon as she shut the door behind her. I went back to the dirty, damp newspaper, whose contents were not therefore entirely legible, and spread it out on the bed.

It was the editorial page of a Russian newspaper dated Friday, 1 November 2002, that is six days after the end of the siege. It opened with a banner heading:

Скандал!

Российский спецназ использует секретный газ для прекращения захвата заложников на театре Дубровки, и жертвы превышают 100

The words outrage, gas, Dubrovka, and 100 victims indicated that some of the fog was lifting, and I was spurred to look carefully at some of the accompanying photographs. One of them showed someone speaking at a press conference; another the mangled corpses of Movsar Barayev and his group; a third a number of citizens at what looked like a demonstration holding up pictures of their loved ones from those among us at the theatre;

a fourth consisted of drawings of the structural formulas of chemical compounds, whose intricacies I was unable to fathom with what I had retained from chemistry lessons, and I ignored them. Then I made a real effort to decipher the letters and words at the beginning of the article and its conclusion on the other side of the page. I used logic and some guesses to fill in the gaps and understand what was meant. In that way I constructed a personal narrative of events, uncertain as to how closely it corresponded to reality.

Because the essence of truth is suffering, knowledge of the truth might be more harmful than ignorance, and naturally we are sometimes obliged to believe the unbelievable.

Olga's suspicion had not been out of place . . .

The Russian government had not been serious when it announced its agreement to negotiate with Barayev's group. It was just a ruse to gain valuable time. The Chechen fighters fell for it, and the Russians carried out their plan to storm the Dubrovka Theatre as they intended.

After they broadcast the news that the Kremlin had agreed to the Chechens' conditions, I fell asleep, not as normal but because the special forces (what Olga called the Spetsnaz) had pumped a secret gas into the building, probably via the air vents. This caused most of those present – me among them – to lose consciousness very slowly. Those who remained awake were unable to control their usual physical functions.

Troops stormed the building at around 5:30 a.m. on Saturday morning and killed all the armed militants. Then they started evacuating the hostages.

Most of the fifty Chechen fighters fell asleep. The remainder clashed with Russian special forces in a desperate battle, whose outcome was known in advance.

Why didn't they keep at least one gunman alive to interrogate? Nobody knew. Superficially, it was a clean, well-executed operation, during which not a single drop of innocent civilian blood had been shed. But blood loss wasn't the only route to the grave.

Scores of hostages were ferried to Moscow's hospitals on coaches provided by the city authorities. The doctors readied themselves to deal with gunshot wounds and blast injuries, but they were surprised by people losing consciousness and suffering from nausea and breathing difficulties. A number of them died after reaching hospital.

The doctors worked out that the victims had inhaled large amounts of an unknown gas. They conjectured that its composition was similar to a substance called fentanyl, and dealt with it using an antidote, Naloxone, which the elderly doctor mentioned a few days ago.

But the results weren't as effective as hoped . . .

The number of deaths continued to mount crazily and reached more than 100, including foreigners. Ordinary Russians and the representatives of foreign embassies were incensed. They demanded the truth and protested at the circumstances of the evacuation and the theft of the hostages' belongings.

My country's embassy had passed out of course!

The Russian health minister intervened and called a press conference on 31 October. He talked about a gas called Kolokol-1, which was completely different from fentanyl despite similar characteristics and 100 times more powerful than morphine. He stated that the Russian army had refused to disclose its composition or provide the ministry with an antidote, preferring to sacrifice dozens of lives rather than reveal its secret weapon.

This was horror in its worst manifestation: to be confident that you had survived a terrible nightmare only to discover subsequently that you had been tricked and dropped into an even bigger nightmare.

I had reached a crucial point in my efforts to piece together the jigsaw puzzle of the Dubrovka Theatre, and this coincided with the entrance of the police officer who looked like Chekhov along with the supervising doctor and a nurse assigned to the room. Just the right time then to recall the list of questions concerning my own specific fate, after I had found partial answers concerning the general course of events.

I was amazed that the officer paid no attention to why I was holding the page of a newspaper. He gently took it from me, scrunched it into a ball, and threw it away. "In consultation with the medical team," he said calmly, "we think you are out of danger, which means you can leave the hospital."

I failed to look happy. The nurse put an old coat and some tatty clothes next to me, while the doctor commented, "We cannot be sure that you are fully recovered. You are suffering from fatigue and some slight difficulty in moving your limbs as a result of inhaling a large quantity of the gas. But you are still only nineteen and have a strong constitution and obvious intelligence." As he said the word intelligence, he made a rapid gesture towards the discarded ball of newspaper.

Fuckers. I thought I was an intelligent person able to understand their trick with Movsar Barayev and his gang, but I've discovered that I'm a prisoner in a bigger trick! A trick whose real aim I am still unable to grasp.

"You'll get over any difficulty moving your limbs in time, and you'll come and visit us for physiotherapy sessions. So we'll be taking you back to the university accommodation in a wheelchair by ambulance."

Wow! All that for me, a valueless Moroccan whom no one cares about!

Fear crept into my voice as I shouted, "What exactly do you want from me? I'm just a college student whose bad luck put him in the wrong place at the wrong time!"

Chekhov's lookalike answered with an inscrutable smile followed by an expression that combined innocence with provocation: "Why so scared, my dear? Get dressed now, come on."

I had to obey him, convinced there was no other option. The nurse had to help me put on the rags because of my great fatigue.

I looked like one of the homeless down-and-outs from Moscow's poorer districts, not a medical student.

The doctor and nurse worked together to seat me in the wheelchair, then conveyed me to the ambulance outside the medical complex.

Because I enjoy, as they said, obvious intelligence, deep down I was certain that we were heading nowhere near the student accommodation.

* * *

What Rachid Bennacer wrote in his notebook summarizing what former publisher Muhsin el-Fadili said about his attempt to track down missing maths teacher Rafiq Khalidi:

- The publisher's thoughts after reading the article:

– <u>Khalid Rafiqi</u>, author of <u>*A Moroccan Jigsaw Puzzle*</u>, and Rafiq Khalidi, missing maths teacher, are the same person?? (tampering with the letter i – date of the disappearance and receipt of the novel manuscript close together)

– Coincidental resemblance between the names??

– Decision: go to <u>Meknes</u> and meet the family of the missing man Rafiq Khalidi.

- What happened on the morning of <u>Sunday, 11 December 1988</u> in Meknes:

– The publisher arrives in the city and looks for the address supplied in the article; first meeting with Samir Qassemi, close friend of Rafiq Khalidi and, as an Arabic teacher, a colleague at the same school in Duwwar el-Hajj Kaddour. The publisher understands that Samir also lives in Meknes and he wrote to the newspaper announcing the disappearance because most of the family are illiterate.

– Second meeting with the family of the teacher in the company of his friend. The conversation discloses that both the missing man's parents died before his disappearance and some time apart. An uncle moved with his family (from a desert area affected by the wave of drought in the '80s) to Meknes to live with Rafiq Khalidi.

– The family think it likely that spells and black magic caused the disappearance of the teacher in such a mysterious way!! (Rubbish . . . God spare us)

– Confirmation that the missing teacher suffered from a weak heart and difficulty speaking and moving his limbs. (Reasons why???)

– Categorical denial by the friend of the hypothesis that the missing teacher wrote novels, or had an interest in literature, along with a suggestion that he veered towards solitude and was obsessed with solving equations and maths problems that only he understood. (???)

- **What happened the evening of <u>Sunday, 11 December 1988</u> in Duwwar el-Hajj Kaddour:**

– A small village where everyone knows each other.

– They're interested in the issue of the well-liked teacher's disappearance and honestly want to learn his fate. (He's not mad as his family implied . . .)

– They spoke highly of Rafiq and Samir's friendship and their joint efforts to persuade families to send girls to school and their working together to encourage children to read and learn.

– Some students spoke of a cooling in relations between the two teachers, culminating in a violent quarrel and a complete severance towards the end of the last school year, only two months before the disappearance of the maths teacher. (Why did Samir Qassemi omit those details???).

– The publisher noticed (after returning to Casablanca) that many of those he met in the village suffered from problems walking and moving their limbs. (<u>Similar to the condition of Rafiq Khalidi???!!!</u>)

- **What happened on <u>Saturday 20 May 1989</u> in <u>Rabat</u>:**

– A few weeks after *A Moroccan Jigsaw Puzzle*'s publication and distribution to some bookstores.

– Muhsin el-Fadili accompanies his daughter Leila, living in Rabat, and her husband Ali to the maternity hospital in the capital when her contractions started. (~~Irrelevant chit-chat~~)

– While the publisher is busy talking to a refrigerator repairman whose wife has given birth to a boy they called Abdelmajid (~~and we care ???~~) he is surprised by Samir Qassemi rushing past him in the company of an exhausted looking young woman holding a newborn baby.

– He called out to him more than once, but the guy in his thirties pretended not to know him before hurriedly leaving the hospital. (What's Samir Qassemi's link with Rabat???)

– Muhsin el-Fadili checks the birth records at the hospital for that day and finds just one Samir. (The hospital records the mother's and father's names without the family name.) He is married to a woman called Lubna and they had a girl.

Lubna = Cherchez la femme!!!

* * *

(12) The Sleepwalkers

> *The only truth in life is feelings.*
> **Fernando Pessoa**

Sunday, 27 October 2002
The railway station – Rabat; Café Les Arcades – Kenitra:

We entered an empty first-class compartment, and as soon as the train started slowly pulling away from Rabat Ville station, Rachid piped up: "What do you think about what Muhsin el-Fadili said about the disappearance of Rafiq Khalidi?"

I drummed my fingers wearily on the table, then said, "An interesting story, but it's got nothing to do with our research. The publisher didn't find any evidence connecting the maths teacher to the novel."

He opened his scruffy backpack, rummaged intently inside it, and after a few moments shoved an old colour photograph in my face. "Take a look at the photo that one of the students at the village's middle school gave the publisher. It's Rafiq and Samir handing out sweets and books to the children. You can see how much they understood each other and cooperated to do their work as teachers. How did their fine friendship come to an end and why was that preceded by a violent quarrel of unknown cause?"

"That's their business," I replied indifferently, giving a discrete signal that I wished to concentrate on the matter in hand.

Without heed to my tone of voice, he continued, "The answer is obvious. '*Cherchez la femme*,' as Alexandre Dumas said in his novel *The Mohicans of Paris*. The relationship between two close friends would only be wrecked by their rivalry for the love of the same woman. I have a strong feeling that Samir Qassemi didn't tell the whole truth to Muhsin el-Fadili, and the woman called Lubna might have something to do with the quarrel and rift, and perhaps the disappearance too."

With a shout approaching a scream my hinting became a proclamation: "Let them all go to hell. Brandon called to tell me that Tony Wagner died years ago. That means our one feeble hope turns on finding an unidentified Moroccan waiter in a bar whose present situation we know nothing about!"

Then I burst into tears.

"I'll never get to the truth that has flipped my life over. Is it true my father was a murderer who escaped punishment? The time's nearly up and I haven't written a single word of my fourth novel. David Hersch will take it as a chance to wreck my future and cast me into oblivion, and maybe prison. Even if I sold my beach house in Miami and emptied my bank account, I wouldn't be able to pay a quarter of the penalty clause. And even if I acted on the Moroccan publisher's advice and wrote a novel about the Moscow theatre siege, everyone will accuse me of repetition and having run out of ideas, since I dealt with the theme of hostages in my first novel!"

My outburst shut him up, and after a couple of minutes he mumbled, "You're a creative artist, not a writer doing piecework. Literature is more sublime and beautiful than those worthless capitalist constraints."

My eyes clouded with tears as I replied dismissively, "Please, I don't need any lectures about the role of literature in our lives. Those I've already heard from Brandon are quite enough."

He inched a little closer and I felt the roughness of his trembling fingers as he took my hand. "Don't worry, everything will be all right. Perhaps you're right and we should focus on our research. After that you'll have to spend a few more days in Morocco as a tourist. Then perhaps you'd realise that your problem is more like a joke compared with what I and those like me have to endure here!"

*

We arrived after about thirty minutes and Rachid continued talking once we were on the platform. "For your information, the city today is nothing like Khalid Rafiqi's description of the 1950s in *A Moroccan Jigsaw Puzzle*. I read that Kenitra kept a special status after the evacuation of most of the American bases and some Americans stayed here until the beginning of the '70s."

The previous minutes had helped me calm down a little inside, and I responded to him: "My father came back to the States at the beginning of the '60s. Then he met my mom, and I was born in 1963."

"We'll see. Perhaps there's a specific explanation for his return."

"Will we find the bar?"

He brushed a lock of hair from his forehead and answered me with a strange awkwardness. "Actually, it's quite complicated. The month of Ramadan is approaching, a sacred religious occasion that will make the search difficult because Moroccans suddenly remember that drinking alcohol is forbidden. They'll get nervous and look at us warily as soon as we say the name of the place!"

"And the solution?"

He pointed to a young guy sitting on an almost broken bench and eyeing us with a mixture of apprehension and astonishment. "We'll ask Khalil to help. He's a friend from Kenitra who went to school with me years ago and knows the city very well."

A little overweight and more relaxed-looking, he differed from Rachid. They embraced and exchanged some friendly words in

Arabic before Khalil addressed me in halting French. "Please forgive me, Madam, but my English is poor and will never be as fluent as Rachid's. He was definitely the best student in our year. We nicknamed him The Mobile Library because his memory was so good and because of his amazing ability to connect everything with a book or novel he had read. He has a special gift, one not deserved by a country that doesn't seem it will appreciate those like him for at least the next hundred years."

He leaned towards me and pleaded theatrically, "I beg you, Madam, look for a way to smuggle him into the United States. Either he'll make it there and become an intellectual idol we can be proud of, or he'll come to nothing here between a bullshit job unsuited to his abilities and a dissertation that his supervisor may turn into torture. He'll end up unemployed and in bloody clashes with the police in front of parliament!"

I smiled as I took in the meaning of his words, while Rachid chastised him with an angry glance and some resentful Arabic words, which made Khalil turn serious: "Okay. You two are lucky. Les Arcades bar has become a café that still exists. It's very close to the busy Rue Mohamed V, and not far from here. We can walk there if you'd like."

*

I surveyed the patrons sitting on chairs arranged parallel to the sidewalk, whispering among themselves and staring with curiosity at my open white blouse, jeans and sneakers. Looking up, I read the large sign:

Café Les Arcades

Did my father spend many nights getting drunk and having fun with his friends here forty years ago?

If I excluded the dozens of goggling eyes, the café seemed very relaxed and nothing like what I had read in *A Moroccan Jigsaw Puzzle* or what Rachid had said Moroccan writer Mohammed Zafzaf described in *An Attempt to Live*.

He was right. The city had changed a great deal compared with what appeared in those two books. Nothing today indicated that a wild bar had once existed in this exact place!

"Wait here. There's no need for you to come in with us. We'll sort things out ourselves and ask the staff at the café about the waiter in the old picture."

I turned my face away to avoid the questioning looks of the café's patrons and, off to the right some 200 metres away, I caught sight of sunlight reflecting off still water.

Without a conscious decision, I made my way towards it with ponderous steps, like a sleepwalker. A couple of minutes later I found myself on the bank, surrendering to a solitude in which I was far away from Rachid, Khalil, Brandon, Khalid Rafiqi and the whole world.

It was without a doubt the Sebou River . . .

Had one of these two banks witnessed an American soldier called Steve McMillan steal along under cover of darkness, carrying the body of a young woman he had brutally murdered and intended to dump here?

Impossible . . .

I had no need for logic, research, investigation, evidence, or even Rachid's unspoken effort to condemn my father in order to satisfy an inner desire that I understood but pretended to ignore. A desire to blame the American for all the rest of the world's disasters just because he is more powerful.

My father isn't a killer. My feelings don't lie.

What insanity has driven me to doubt a humble man, whom my mother loved and of their love affair, she said, Hollywood itself wouldn't be able to recreate a single scene?

Why have I betrayed the memory of a father who played with me and gave me piggybacks as a child, who took me to the cinema and baseball games as a teenager, and then encouraged me to marry Brandon, the good guy, instead of chasing after that schmuck Mike?

And all because of the events of an obscure, forgotten-about novel that not even the fellow countrymen of its unknown author have read!

But I'm a novelist and know more than anyone that imagination only takes root and grows in the soil of reality, and that each of us has a secret garden on whose gate there's a sign bearing in large letters: No Entry.

Even if we assume that not a single sentence in *A Moroccan Jigsaw Puzzle* is true, why did Khalid Rafiqi choose the name Steve McMillan?

"What have you done, Christine? If it hadn't been for the nosy-parkers at the café who realised you had taken the path along the bank of the Sebou, we would have lost you!"

Rachid's sudden shout brought me back down to earth. He continued, red-faced and coughing and panting from the exertion: "It was much easier than we expected. All the staff at the café know Bashir, the oldest waiter there. They say that he's very old and can't work anymore. He's retired and stays at home with his elderly wife after most of his children grew up and went their separate ways in search of a livelihood. Didn't I tell you that everything would be all right?"

His friend Khalil added by way of clarification: "We'll need a taxi because the address is a little far. But I know the neighbourhood for sure. Let's go!"

* * *

From an earlier conversation between the two friends Zouhair Belkacem and Sergei Kryachkov:

"What are you reading this time?"

"A short story called 'The Bet' by Anton Chekhov, the best story writer in Russia and maybe the world. He poses an extremely important philosophical question in it. Which is the better punishment: the death sentence or life imprisonment?"

"A really interesting question. How did the author answer it?"

"The story here is a bet between a pompous banker and a young law student over that very question. The banker bets the student two million roubles that he can't stay imprisoned in solitary confinement for fifteen years."

"It seems to me that the Russians are a people obsessed with gambling. I've read a lot about Russian roulette, where a person gambles with their life against the barrel of a revolver. Horrific!"

"The young man agrees to the bet and enters a small room under guard. It was difficult to begin with since he suffered from loneliness and depression, but he trained himself to live with the situation. He studied languages, literature, science and the history of religions. His view of himself and of life changed completely."

"Then what happened?"

"The years passed and the bet was nearly over. The banker's wealth had diminished greatly and he realised that paying up would bankrupt him. He thought about getting out of the bet by killing the student, and he went to visit him in his room the day before the fifteen years was over. He found him sleeping, but stumbled across a letter, in which the gambler had written how he despised what he called empty material things and that the knowledge he had acquired over the previous fifteen years was more important to him than winning the bet. The banker was stunned by what he read and left. The next day the guards told him that the gambler had fled, perhaps sensing that his life was in danger!"

"Don't run to return the book to the library. You've made me want to read it!"

"Didn't I tell you that no one writes like the Russians? Okay, did you ever hear about Chekhov's gun?"

"He kept a gun and they found it under his bed when he died?"

"No, of course not. It's a basic principle of literary writing whose formulations differ but whose meaning is the same: if a gun appears at the beginning of a story, it has to be used at the end."

"I see. It means the writer is required to avoid prolixity and cuts out any sentence, or word even, that does not serve the story in some way."

"If you want my opinion, I would say that the genius concealed himself behind the story to say that the absurd has no place in the dictionary of life, even if we insist on inserting it among the pages to explain our ignorance!"

* * *

(12') Lord of Darkness

> *When the fates deal in human destiny, they heed neither pity nor justice.*
> Charlie Chaplin

Tuesday, 12 November 2002
A police station somewhere – Moscow:

As I predicted, the ambulance headed nowhere near the university accommodation. That was a gut feeling since there were no windows allowing me to follow the ambulance's journey across a vast city, only a few of whose landmarks Sergei had helped me get to know.

The vehicle stopped somewhere and the nurse and the policeman blindfolded me. Then they made me stand up, and my ears picked up the click of a key turning, followed by the skin on my wrists reacting to contact with cold steel. The only explanation was that I was being handcuffed like a bloodthirsty criminal or a dangerous terrorist, not a survivor of a terrible ordeal that nearly cost me my life!

Or had the final episode of this serial horror show yet to be written?

I felt two powerful hands grip me by the shoulders of the threadbare coat and push me roughly down a long corridor. I almost lost my balance as we went down a staircase which, from our twisting and turning, I understood was spiral and led to a level or cellar below ground.

The extreme pain gripping my limbs caused me to forget the chattering of my teeth from the bitter cold that the overcoat could not stop penetrating my bones. Then we halted and fear wiped away everything previous.

"Where am I?" I asked in English. Nobody replied, and when I repeated the question, the two hands pressed harder on my shoulders to sit me down on a chair that gave a low squeak. Suddenly and violently, they ripped off the blindfold.

I was in a small room whose dim lighting barely illuminated the spot I was sitting in. The wall behind me was yellowish-white. On both sides of me were small desks covered with piles of documents and papers. In front of me was a camera lens, wielded by a policeman and aimed at me like the muzzle of a cannon.

In an attempt to gather my shattered nerves, I said in a shaky voice, "What's happening here? You promised to take me back to the student hostel. What's changed? Why are you treating me like this? I haven't done anything!"

The policeman began taking pictures and I covered my eyes with my hand, unable to bear the rapid and repeated flash. Then I submitted in the realisation that all the shock in the world had come together to leave its mark on my face. I had no need for a mirror to confirm it.

Those present – the Chekhov double sitting behind his desk, another policeman and the photographer – remained impassive. It seemed that everyone apart from me understood what was really going on. In what almost became the plea of a slave to his master I shouted, "I'm innocent and have nothing to do with what happened at the blasted theatre except having been the unluckiest person in the world. Ask Olga Kuznetsova, if she's still alive. She'll tell you everything. Inform my embassy that I'm here, I beg you!"

It seemed the hospital policeman was the only one who spoke good English, since his mouth gave a cynical smile. Then he motioned to his colleague who came over and pushed me towards the desk.

The light of a small lamp just about illuminated the top of the desk and its immediate vicinity. The lookalike of the famous Russian story writer was seated behind it and the shadows gave him the appearance of a screen vampire from the 1950s. The other policeman stood up behind me with a key and unlocked the handcuffs.

The seated officer was busy filling in a form in Russian, heedless of my presence. My gaze shifted to the pictures stuck to a whiteboard behind him and I tried to focus on their details despite the poor lighting.

Horribly mutilated corpses of tramps lying on snow covered ground. Then pictures of green parkland covered with tall trees that I could not put a name to.

I knew that I had seen the place before, but where?

Why did I feel my memory was messed up and that my body was going to collapse at any moment?

What had the fuckers injected me with at the hospital?

The Russian turned the form over and I finally realised that it was a crime report, whose blanks he was filling in. Only the square for the photograph was empty – probably they were waiting to develop my photos and choose one.

The other policeman grabbed my right hand and made me dip my fingers in ink and press them on the paper. Then he did the same with my left hand. The man behind the desk finally spoke: "I may not agree with our great writer Dostoyevsky when he had one of his characters say that it would be better for useless people never to have come into the world. We were in a fix that might have ended the careers of all those working in the Moscow Security Directorate, but then your rotten luck sent us you. And what with your embassy's disowning of you, you were a gift from heaven!"

* * *

Details of what transpired at the meeting with Bashir el-Tahiri, former waiter at Les Arcades bar, as recounted by Rachid Bennacer:

The taxi took us to the neighbourhood. "Have to stop here," said the driver. "Can't go any further. That tent's blocking the way, as you can see."

Christine turned towards me inquiringly, but I waited to translate until after we had paid the fare and got out.

A large white tent, familiar to every Moroccan with its black design filled in with red, green and yellow. It would not be unusual for such a tent to be hired out for wedding guests to dance and sing in until dawn, before being moved the following day to another family, weeping and preparing for the funeral rites after a sudden death. A stark contradiction that I didn't think the American woman would understand.

A terrifying thought leapt into my mind: what if it was the mourning tent for the waiter? Didn't the worker at Les Arcades Café say that Bashir was very old and his health had declined after he retired? Christine would be devastated. She might even faint with the dashing of the last hope of obtaining information about her father and finding out whether he really had committed a murder forty years ago.

Her embassy would get involved. Events would go hurtling towards a diplomatic disaster. And the state wouldn't come up with any way to resolve it except sacrificing me as a scapegoat and . . .

Hold on . . .

Why has my unruly imagination taken me in this particular direction? Am I exaggerating? Or does having lived a quarter of a century in a country like Morocco mean expecting the worst at every moment?

I directed my gaze at the houses and spotted washing lines full of clothes dripping a mixture of water and washing powder. Also, the aroma of spicy broth, vegetables and chicken harmonized with the whistling of pots and the chattering of women unconcerned about their privacy, orchestrating a symphony that Beethoven was lucky never to have had any chance to hear.

Out of nowhere appeared a battalion of children, the youngest of whom could barely walk and the oldest some ten or eleven years old. They surrounded Christine, like the Bastille before its storming ignited the French Revolution.

Curiosity filled their eyes, while she was struck dumb in astonishment. She gave them a pale smile and her eyes sent out distress signals when she failed to understand what was happening around her. Khalil intervened to shoo the children away from her.

"What's happening here? Where's the house of Bashir el-Tahiri's family?" I asked one of them wearing a shirt, whose white colour had dirtied long ago. His big toe poked out of ripped sneakers and he stared at me uncertainly. When he said firmly: "Five dirhams!" I belatedly understood he was assessing the gains to be made from my having fallen into his clutches.

"Excuse me?"

"Five dirhams and I'll take you straight to the house!"

I told him off and he took to his heels. The others followed him like a flock of sheep whose shepherd has lost control of them, at the same time as a woman of similar age to the American and wearing a green kaftan came over and addressed us dismissively: "Aren't you two working for the caterers? Get a move on! Where are the boxes of apples and the crates of fizzy drinks?"

When she noticed the presence of Christine, her questioning took on a more derogatory tone: "And who's this blonde Christian girl?"

I huffed in irritation in the knowledge that she would not rest easy until she knew the tiniest details, but I relished leaving the snares of her desire dangling.

"We're looking for Bashir el-Tahiri's house. We want to meet him about some business of ours." As that was obviously all I was going to say, she was forced to head for the entrance to the tent, from where she waved her hand at someone. A few moments later a person, who looked almost exactly like the picture of Bashir taken forty years ago, emerged.

His son for sure . . .

The woman shouted out, using him as a defence, "These three are looking for our house. They're saying they want to see my father!"

His daughter then . . .

He checked us out with expert eyes, like any self-respecting Moroccan, then asked sharply, "Who are you? And what do you want with my father?"

I briefly explained that it was to do with an American woman who wanted to ask Bashir about her father, a former soldier at the airbase, because he knew him. Of course I made no reference to the subject of the novel.

He stroked his beard in thought as if searching for the solution to a complex mathematical equation, then said, "As you can see, it's not a good time at all. The tent is packed with guests and we're celebrating the departure in a few days' time of my father and mother for the Holy Land to perform the Ramadan pilgrimage."

His hesitation encouraged me to persist: "Rest assured, it will only take a few minutes. Then we'll be off without any inconvenience to speak of."

His face relaxed as he realised there was nothing to lose and, like a general giving a categorical order, he said sternly, "No! You will have dinner with us. Fawzia, accompany the American lady to the women's room. Treat her generously, she is our guest. You two, follow me!" After Fawzia had grabbed Christine's arm like a guard leading the prisoner to her cell, she said fearfully, "Rachid, what's over there?"

I suppressed my laughter as I answered, "Don't worry. They're just going to perform our Moroccan custom of honouring guests on you."

*

Most of the guests were busy chatting and drinking glasses of tea as they waited for dinner. The son led us to a large table. A man wearing a brilliant white jilbab was seated in the middle. His veined hand was holding a *sibha*, whose beads he passed through his fingers.

He was ancient, probably more than eighty years old. Forty-three years had passed since the photograph was taken, but he hadn't put on an ounce of weight and had only lost a few strands of hair, while the thin moustache had become a well-trimmed white beard.

The son whispered in his ear, and the man apologised to those sitting with him. Then he stood up, leaning on a stick and, as dictated by old age, walked slowly over to us and asked in a rasping voice, "I've heard that someone wants to meet me, and I don't expect it's to do with two youngsters at the beginning of life. Well then, what is it?"

I took the picture out of my pocket and showed it to him. He put on his glasses, which hung on a fine chain around his neck.

"Please, *ya hajj*, do you remember the people in the picture? We want to ask you about the American soldier Steve McMillan. His daughter has come to Morocco to gather some information about him, and we hope your good memory can be of use to us."

His silence continued for more than a minute, then he ended it with a sternness akin to his son's tone: "Khalid, get our guests some tea."

The son remained where he stood and the father banged the ground with his stick: "Move it!"

Khalid grudgingly obeyed, and Khalil hurried to take Bashir's hand in search of chairs a little removed from the ears of the guests.

"How did you get hold of it? I can't work out the date exactly, but I'm certain it's been more than forty years since it was taken!"

"It was in 1959 to be precise."

He shifted in his seat in a way that affirmed his willingness to knock on the gates of an abandoned fortress in his memory.

"God forgive me for what I have to say about those days, now as I am preparing to visit His sacred sanctuary. I wasn't too happy about working at that place, as proved by the obvious resentment on my face in the photo, but your generation knows nothing of life's harshness."

"The years come one after another and circumstances change, *ya hajj*, but life remains harsh for every Moroccan not born with a golden spoon in his mouth, or whose birth certificate doesn't bear a family name beginning with the sacred letter B."[3]

Khalil said this and I smiled, while Bashir preferred to ignore the remark and keep talking. "In the American era, Kenitra turned into a city that never slept. The Americans were mad for fun. They left the base and crawled into the city like a plague of locusts, filling the bars, cafes and cinemas."

I nodded my head in confirmation, given I remembered some of what Zafzaf and Rafiqi had described in their novels. "Were you directly in contact with Steve McMillan?"

"That's the first time I've ever heard his family name, but I remember him because he was the leader of his group of friends. A lively, enthusiastic youngster, he led his six friends in their capers and constant scrapes with other Americans and Moroccans. They would get drunk, gamble and chase the prostitutes in the bar and beyond, may the Lord forgive me . . ."

He ran the beads of his *sibha* more quickly through his fingers, and I rescued him from his embarrassment by praising him: "You have an

---

[3] Moroccan family names beginning Ben or Bel, indicating a connection with the court and the upper class.

excellent memory, *ya hajj*. So I hope you can provide some more answers. Was Steve an aggressive person?"

He gave an indifferent wave of the hand to conceal his pride, then told his son to move off once he had served the glasses of tea.

"Those days are hard to forget. I didn't like the excesses of that bunch. As you can see from the picture, they were hulking oxen confident in their strength and they ran riot as they pleased. They weren't afraid of anyone, except the Military Police patrols. But Steve wasn't bad or aggressive. He was really generous, at least with me. A few coins here, a pair of sunglasses or a wristwatch he no longer needed there. Once he even intervened to rescue me from a beating that his arrogant Moroccan friend was determined to give me because I had been slow bringing his order."

My disgust at the nauseating taste of the tea coincided with my hearing his last sentence and I exclaimed, "You said his Moroccan friend! How so?"

"Slimane Belarbi, God forgive him, was a perfect example of a spoiled rich kid. He was always in the bar, basking in his father's influence, and inseparable from the Americans, whom he thought would give him added value. Unfortunately, he came to a tragic end, and it seems his little family was cursed too."

My heart was pounding, and I found myself in turn caught by the usual Moroccan curiosity when I asked, "What happened?"

He smiled in a way that made me understand that the dam of his memories had broken and he wanted to spill more: "It started with a crime that shook the city. Everyone was talking about it. And that was a time when horrific crimes weren't an everyday occurrence. His wife Malika el-Farouki, also the daughter of a wealthy family, was discovered murdered in her house. Slimane was the only suspect, based on reports of how bad their relationship was and his doubts about her fidelity. When the police tried to arrest him, he escaped in his car. He died in the chase after his car hit a tree."

The mass of new information inside my skull made me feel dizzy and I said with interest, "Did you ever see Jam . . . Malika el-Farouki before? I have a picture and hope you can recognise her if possible."

I spoke while searching in my bag for the picture that Christine had found in Denver, but my suspicions were dashed when he said, "No, I only heard about her. I never met her and don't know what she looks like, sorry."

"Perhaps her picture appeared on the crime pages of the papers back then!"

Khalil pressed hard on my foot to curb my insensitivity, while Bashir hung his head and whispered in shame, "I didn't read the papers because I'm illiterate, son."

I gave up and closed my bag. My tone was calm again when I asked, "Okay, what about Saleh's, sorry I mean Slimane's, friendship with Steve McMillan?"

He fixed his gaze on his empty glass of tea and answered, "The smuggling business was booming. The base was huge and needed enormous amounts of supplies. The Americans sold everything: food, clothing, domestic appliances. The drinkers and gamblers among them might have to sell their valuable possessions for next to nothing to meet their losses. Moroccan businessmen weren't going to miss the chance to strike deals with them, and I have no doubt that Slimane was one of them. Perhaps he used Steve as a middleman. What I'm saying is based on what I saw at the bar and how often they met there. I don't know any other details."

With that the meeting ended. I got up to say goodbye and get ready to leave, ignoring the silent protest from Khalil, who was waiting for dinner. Then a nagging thought that had occurred to me the night before forced me to cautiously ask, "Sorry, *ya hajj*, you said that a curse pursued the family. Did they have children?"

Bashir relied on Khalil's hand again to help him stand up and he said, "Yes, one son aged five. I don't know his name, but the whole city knew his tragedy at the time. It's said he went with his old nanny to one of the villages to get him away from the sad atmosphere surrounding the death of his parents. But a tremendous fire burnt down the farm his grandfather owned there and the nanny was one of the victims. The fire went out and they didn't find the boy's body. His fate after that was unknown!"

"Do you know, or did you hear at the time, what that village was called?"

The answer was stunning, although an inner voice echoing inside me since last night had predicted it: "Yes, Duwwar el-Hajj Kaddour. And I believe it's somewhere near Meknes!"

* * *

(13) Remembrance of Things Past

> *Literature is the artistry to tell our own stories as if they were other people's stories, and to tell other people's stories as if they were our own.*
>
> Orhan Pamuk

Monday, 28 October 2002
Rue France – Rabat:

I toyed with the cigarette in my hands, but had no real desire to light it. My mind went over what the days, or even hours to come might reveal, based on the new information that Bashir el-Tahiri had provided and which was driving the story in another direction.

What I heard from Rachid should have relaxed me, since the retired waiter had passed on everything he knew about my father with the utmost clarity, talking about his rowdy nights out with his friends and their penchant for fun and games, while discounting the idea of him being aggressive. In fact, he confirmed he was a good and generous guy.

Most importantly for me, of course, was that there was no connection between him and the crime, some of whose details differed from what appeared in *A Moroccan Jigsaw Puzzle*.

Yet doubt still nagged ...

Why did the novel's author insist on linking Jamila's (or Malika's) murder with Steve McMillan the GI? Why did he change all the names and some of the events but keep Dad's name as he constructed his multi-stranded plot in a work of realist fiction whose reality is fictive?

Well, isn't he a novelist and isn't it his right to do what he wants with his plot?

Rachid appeared in the doorway of the restaurant and ended my train of thought with his smile. We greeted each other with a fist bump like two boisterous teens and he sat down in the opposite chair. "I looked for you at the hotel and one of your colleagues said you'd rushed out before five o'clock. Where were you?"

He didn't reply, so I continued, "A date?"

His smile became a laugh and, with a comic show of awe, he pretended to browse the menu, before saying evasively: "I was mentally preparing myself for this invitation to dinner, given it's an unfamiliar experience for a poor person like me. For years now my mind has consumed a hundred times more than my stomach. Even so, I can't decipher the symbols written on the menu of a high-class Moroccan restaurant. I'm extremely lucky to have gotten to know a renowned American writer. Thanks to her I'm able to enter posh places like this!"

I laughed along with him and tried to impersonate his style of answer: "And until now I haven't understood why that family was so generous with me. They don't know me and the impossibility of communicating was hilarious, but Bashir's wife brought me a bag full of nuts and fruit as well as a bottle of traditional perfume and a beautiful kaftan that fitted so well I was amazed!"

Animus slipped into his tone as he said, "Our women are experts at such things. One rapid glance from them is as accurate as the latest camera!"

I touched the edge of the table with my fingertips in search of the right words to apologise with and after a brief silence I whispered shyly, "I wanted to say sorry in a suitable way and came up with the idea of inviting you out for dinner. You alerted me to your suspicions about a possible connection between the novel and the maths teacher and I brushed you off. But Bashir's testimony proves your intelligence and insight."

With the straightforwardness of someone not expecting praise, he said, "All I did was go over the details in the novel and what the publisher said about his visit to Meknes and the village. I realised we had made a terrible mistake when we ignored the presence of a five-year-old child, Saleh and Jamila's son. He played no part in the action, but we did not wonder what happened to him after the death of his parents. Then in 1988, some thirty years after the events of the novel, the newspaper published the report of the disappearance of the maths teacher in his mid-thirties. My mind quickly put the two pieces together, and I asked Bashir. He remembered Duwwar el-Hajj Kaddour, which confirmed I had been on the right track since the beginning."

Not content with what he had said, he added a few seconds later, "But this discovery proves nothing so far . . ."

I waited for the waiter to leave after setting down the plates, and said, "Really? If the boy who went missing thirty years ago, Khalid Rafiqi, author of *A Moroccan Jigsaw Puzzle*, and Rafiq Khalidi the maths teacher are one and the same person, then the question marks are sprouting like mushrooms. What's the child's connection with Meknes? How come he returned to Duwwar el-Hajj Kaddour all those years after his disappearance? How did he know the tiniest details of what had happened to his parents? Why did he play around with the events? Why did the maths teacher's family keep quiet about his origins? And why did his friend exclude the possibility of him having written a novel?"

Rachid spread a paper napkin in front of him and scrabbled for a pen in his bag as he answered: "I've tried to find answers, but haven't been able to. One thing I can be sure about relates to your final question: Rafiq Khalidi's family and his friend Samir Qassemi lied to the publisher. Perhaps they played a part in his disappearance. And I wouldn't rule out that it was them who published the missing person's notice just to deflect suspicion. Another observation, which might be just the burp of a mind that loves to come up with possibilities, is that the difference between the birthdate of the child Lubna was carrying, 20 May 1989, and the date of Rafiq Khalidi's disappearance is around nine months. Till now I haven't shaken off the sense that Lubna holds the key to the mystery of the disappearance and possibly the solution to the whole case."

I leant forward towards him and saw he was drawing a rough table on the paper napkin:

Truth	Fiction
Malika el-Farouki	Jamila el-Baroudi
Slimane Belarbi	Saleh Belcadi
Murder of the mother at home	Her body found by the river
Husband accused immediately	Suspicion then accusation
The American not involved	The American killed the couple

"What's that?"

"I'm organising my thoughts, setting out the areas of similarity and difference between what appears in *A Moroccan Jigsaw Puzzle* and what I heard from Bashir. And I'm trying to connect that with the notes I wrote summarizing what Muhsin el-Fadili said about his attempt to track down the missing maths teacher."

I was relishing the taste of the salad, but unable to ignore a real feeling of admiration towards the young Moroccan absorbed in reviewing his papers and notes with such concentration that he quite forgot the various delicious dishes in front of him.

He made a mistake a little while ago, though. Women all over the world have an expert eye, as accurate as any advanced camera, not just Moroccan women . . .

His shoes are old, and judging by the nail marks in the soles, he's had to repair them more than once instead of buying a new pair.

His leather jacket is fake and its black has faded and he hasn't worn anything else since we met, but it is clean, which means he takes as much care of it as he can.

His striped shirt and blue pants are pressed, but they don't fit his slim build.

His backpack is tatty. The left shoulder strap might go at any moment. And it never leaves him.

He looks exhausted. He hasn't had a proper rest since meeting me. But his eyes shine with an excitement that helps him follow the developments in the case with me as if it were his own.

Initially I was irritated by his melancholia and despair, but then my grumbling turned to sympathy . . .

How serious is my problem compared to his suffering and those like him?

He came from the boondocks to go to college and was at the top of his class. He was on the path to success, then had to work as a porter at a hotel. To help his family out he puts up with the pressure and bears the abuse of his boss who threatens to fire him. Plus, he clashed with his supervisor, who probably hasn't even read the novel Rachid suggested and causes difficulties rather than helping and encouraging him . . .

Khalil was being bold when he half-seriously suggested to me that I look for a way to help his friend leave a country that doesn't seem to appreciate people like him.

It's so unfair for a country to force its people to hate it and look for the slightest chance to leave . . .

"When will we go to Meknes to meet the maths teacher's family and his friend?" I asked the question in an attempt to make him snap out of it and eat his food. Without lifting his eyes from the papers, he replied, "We don't need to do that. Their answers will be no different from what they said to the publisher fourteen years ago . . ."

I suppressed my annoyance at his nonchalance and added, "We don't have another option. I understand your wish, or what you call your sense, regarding Lubna, Samir Qassemi's wife, but you'll only get to her via him!"

He put his pen down on the table in what I suspected was submission to his failure to crack an intractable problem that his notes and tables could not comprehend. His tone carried no conviction when he responded: "I've obtained her address. She lives in Rabat . . ."

My mouth gaped in shock and I shouted in excitement, "Rachid, you're hiding something from me. Where did you go at five o'clock? Out with it!"

"To the faculty, to confirm certain information that suddenly came to light to explain everything and turn the course of our research upside down."

I slid my chair back and stood up while signalling to the waiter with my right hand to bring the check. "Let's go, then. And remind me to punish you later for your lame playing with my nerves. You . . ."

His reluctance to get up surprised me and I cut myself short to ask, "What are you waiting for?"

After a protracted pause he said, "I'm very sorry, but the new piece of information might lead us to discover the involvement of your father in a forgotten disaster that killed thousands of Moroccans and destroyed the future of tens of thousands more . . ."

I had barely taken in the horror of what he was saying when he struck another blow: "And the author of *A Moroccan Jigsaw Puzzle* was one of the victims . . ."

* * *

The distance between Moscow and the city of Krasnokamensk (Siberia) as given by Google Maps:

(13') The Spectre of Alexander Wolf

> *Struth lads, why do we stay here? What are we doing here? We live, but we are not people; we die, but are not dead men.*
> **Fyodor Dostoevsky**

Thursday, 1 June 2006
Outskirts of Krasnokamensk – Siberia:

The days, months and years pass, and human beings adjust to everything.

Everything...

A warder banged his stick against the iron door, announcing the end of lunchbreak. I swallowed the rest of my crust and scoffed bitterly at the bowl of cold soup. Then I stood up slowly and took my place in the lines of prisoners heading back to the capacious dormitory.

I paused in front of the broken mirror in the bathroom, and I was confronted by a face that could not possibly belong to someone only twenty-three years old: sunken eyes, prominent cheek bones, cracked lips, patches of fuzz that I might at a pinch condescend to call a beard.

In one hand I was carrying a bucket of water and in the other a mop. I draped a floorcloth over my shoulder and started work.

Four years, which seemed like four hundred, paying the price for crimes that had nothing to do with me, and living an existence that no sane person could call a life.

The charge?

That I am a human being of no value. The Russians wanted to get rid of the headache caused by a series of brutal crimes keeping them awake at night, and they could find no one better than me to make the angry residents of Moscow pipe down. They exploited what happened at the Dubrovka Theatre siege to concoct a plan of such fiendish cunning that only the mind of the Devil himself could have hatched it.

I quickly cleaned the bathroom ignoring the waves of nausea, which the past years had inured me to. I was able to continue without covering my nose with my hand to fend off the stench of the remains of what intestines fed only on bread and soup excreted.

When I took part in the chess tournament at Bitsa Park, Olga and Sergei talked about some unsolved murders of homeless people, whose bodies, all mutilated in the same way, had been discovered in various out-of-the-way spots in the park. The number of deaths was spiralling to an all-time high and the Russian police were powerless to do anything.

Then along I came to save their arses . . .

I went back to my bed exhausted and wrapped myself in the sheet, despite the relative easing in the temperature to a few degrees above zero. I took out a number of newspaper cuttings that I had patiently and painstakingly collected over the previous years from newspapers discarded by the warders after reading them.

Initially, the Russian authorities treated me as one of the victims from the theatre, but the loss of my identity papers and the Moroccan Embassy's ignorance of my presence there swept my fate in another direction . . .

I was forced to wear rags and be photographed. My facial features were slightly manipulated using advanced software at the police station. Then came the official announcement that the

Bitsa Park serial killer had been arrested. He was said to be a homeless Russian with no family or friends. They also made up a name for him.

And with the stroke of a pen, hey presto, Zouhair Belkacem turned into Alexander Gazdanov!

I remained locked up in the secret prison at Moscow police headquarters, where the atmosphere soon calmed down. Popular pressure ended and, as if nothing had happened, life returned to normal at Bitsa Park and in Moscow as a whole.

Of course people's fear was ultimately linked to their ability to walk around safely and visit a green space they loved. As to the murder victims, they had all been homeless and nobody cared about them in the first place!

Even so, the police prepared for every eventuality, fearful that the press might start nosing around. They stated that the case concerned a serial killer who would only appear before the cameras after the investigation and when the standard procedures had been completed, prior to him standing trial and the Russian courts giving their verdict. They published one picture of me taken in the police station, which I saw afterwards on the front page of a newspaper. I could have sworn it wasn't me, even though I remembered every detail of the circumstances in which it was taken.

That was a clever attempt to gain time and quell the people's anger. The police expected that they could either apprehend the real criminal at the first chance and close the case, or that he would be deterred and stop what he was doing.

Their belief in the second option only lasted two months, since someone came across another body . . . followed by a second . . . and a third.

The case exploded into life again and presented the police with two equally bad choices:

If they announced that I had died in prison, by suicide or poisoning, it would be understood by all that they had disposed of me to conceal their terrible mistake.

But if they actually released me, then my true identity would of course be revealed.

Evidently, the police were facing a narcissistic criminal who did not accept that they had announced the arrest of someone else. He wanted to prove his continued existence, and always in the same bloody way, like a signature distinguishing him from others: a fatal blow to the head with a hammer or a vodka bottle.

So, without preliminaries, they claimed I had been released, while really deciding to transfer me to another prison far from Moscow where nobody would know me or care about my case . . .

A high-security prison called G 14/10 on the outskirts of the city of Krasnokamensk in Eastern Siberia, more than seven thousand kilometres from Moscow and very close to the Chinese border. Or, to be more precise, the ends of the Earth . . .

"Don't you ever put down those clippings? You're wasting your time for nothing!"

I turned towards the bald man in response: "Vasili, keeping abreast of developments about the Bitsa Park serial killer has become a hobby for my entertainment. The case remains unsolved, although I know it won't do me any good. I am going to live, die and be buried here . . .

"Four years have passed," I added bitterly, "during which I believed I was a ghost, a phantom that does not exist, whose fate and future are of no interest to anyone. Perhaps my mother came to Russia to look for me after I disappeared, but logic says she will never find me . . ."

He did not comment, and I felt the urge to keep talking. "When the Moscow police invented the name Alexander Gazdanov, it did not occur to me that it was a compound name until I had been inside prison for a year and a half. I'm still puzzled now. Did they create the name by chance or did the cunning policeman who knew the details of my story make it up deliberately . . ."

"How do you mean?"

"Gaito Gazdanov is a Russian novelist who wrote a book entitled *The Spectre of Alexander Wolf* which is about . . ."

He interrupted, eager to show off his knowledge: "Ah yes, I read it when I was young and I saw a copy in the prison library. The novel tells the story of a man who kills a soldier and steals his horse during the Russian civil war. Years pass and the narrator moves to Paris where he learns of the existence of a book by an author called Alexander Wolf, which deals with the details of exactly that incident, but from the point of view of the victim. He searches for the author, and when he finds him he realises that he is his old adversary. At that point begins a perplexing psychological game between reality and fiction concerning their fates!"

"You have to imagine," I said, smiling, "that the same feeling has possessed me since Barayev's armed group stormed the stage, or perhaps since I submitted to my desire to chase after Olga and seduce her to obtain a copy of *A Hero for Our Times* by Mikhail Lermontov. Am I a real person, or a character in a novel like Grigori Pechorin or Alexander Wolf?"

With genuine regret he replied, "I'd love to give you some hope, even a faint hope, but trust me, I'm Russian and I know exactly how things work here. Your story is a complicated one, and you might stay here forever. If I hadn't suffered injustice like you, I wouldn't have believed a word of what you told me, starting with you assaulting the poor cleaning girl in Morocco to when you arrived at Krasnokamensk."

I said dismissively as I followed his blazing eyes, "You're getting out in a few weeks. They only sentenced you to five years. You'll soon forget everything."

"Do you think I'm happy about that? They've destroyed my professional future. I was a journalist who chose to tell the truth and express my opinions freely. So I was punished for writing an article critical of the way the authorities dealt with the Kursk submarine crisis, which caused more than 118 submariners to die because they were reluctant to accept British and Norwegian assistance to rescue them, simply because it was a nuclear submarine that the enemy should not have access to." I remembered Olga saying that her father had died with the crew on that submarine. "Is a single human life cheaper than those trivial secrets or . . ."

Vasili broke off as a clean-shaven man in his forties walked past. The man had salt and pepper hair and was wearing small spectacles and a tracksuit that fitted his bulky frame. He walked with the confidence of someone who didn't much care about being here with us. He nodded his head in our direction in a brief greeting, which I returned with a reflexive spasm.

Vasili leaned towards me and whispered, "Of course you know he's Mikhail Borisovich Khodorkovsky, oil king and Russia's richest man. Do you know why he's in here with us?"

"Wasn't he given an eight-year sentence last year for tax evasion?"

He pursed his lips scornfully, "Rubbish. He was brave enough to back one of Putin's opponents, so he was sent to Siberia as a punishment. But as you can see, he has sway over everybody, and his stay here is more like a holiday camp than prison."

What Vasili was saying wasn't far wrong. And I had absorbed it from my first day here.

Things at Krasnokamensk Prison ran according to a caste system. At the top of the hierarchy was a group called Kremliniki, and Khodorkovsky was probably the most prominent of that bunch of the rich and powerful who issued orders that were obeyed without discussion. The prison administration relied on them to keep the prison in order. Then came the Blatniyeh, basically gangsters with connections inside and outside prison. Directly beneath them came the Muzhiki, most of whom were guys whose physical strength allowed them to prey physically, or even sexually, on the weakest group the Opuschenniyeh, or the shamed. The parcels that the families of those downtrodden prisoners sent would be seized and divided up among the Muzhiki.

Of course, I belonged to the bottom caste. I had neither

influence nor physical strength. And were it not for the mumblings that I had committed a series of horrific crimes at my young age I would have been assaulted in another way.

You had to assert your status, according to the level of brutality of the crimes you had committed.

Perhaps that was the only benefit I gained from my undeserved criminal reputation . . .

"Come on, put the cuttings away and concentrate on chess. Let's play another game. I'm very keen to beat you after our last draw."

He didn't wait for my response but waved the wooden board in front of me to get me interested. I put the newspaper cuttings back under the pillow and helped him put the pawns on the board to begin another round in our long series of matches. It was an effective way of killing time, which had taken an oath to stop in this forgotten spot.

"How many people has the Bitsa Park killer murdered so far?"

I moved the first pawn as I answered: "Sixty, between 2001 and 2006 and at random rates. Months might go by without a single body, or a black month might see victims drop like flies. And always in the same big park, but at different locations. What's interesting now is that he's stopped targeting tramps and is hunting people from higher social classes."

"That's a whopping number. Does he want to get into *The Guinness Book of Records* or what?" he replied sarcastically. "He's almost totalled the number of squares on a chessboard – 64!"

His last words made me stop moving my hand, which was holding the second pawn. I raised my eyes towards him and exclaimed in astonishment, "My God! What if what you just said is really what's going on in the criminal's mind!"

* * *

Info Card for the substance Triorthocresyl Phosphate:

Chemical Formula:

$C_{21}H_{21}O_4P$

Description:

Colourless, odourless chemical compound containing organophosphorus

Uses:

- Plastics manufacture
- Component of engine lubricants
- Insecticides
- Mineral oils

Medical classification and direct effect on the human body (according to the severity of the case):

- Neurotoxin that damages nerve tissue
- Attacks nerve cells and impedes their normal operation
- Disrupts the muscle and joint control necessary for any movement
- Nausea, vomiting, and diarrhoea to begin with, then inability to move muscles of the extremities (partial and total paralysis) once the substance overcomes the nervous system
- Loss of vision and memory, involuntary shaking of the limbs, problems speaking
- Other complications such as diabetes, hypertension and heart conditions
- Death

Cases of mass poisoning caused by the substance:
- Thousands poisoned in the United States of America in the 1930s after consumption of Ginger Jake alcohol contaminated with the substance
- A number of Australian and Canadian pilots affected by various diseases after inhaling the substance in vapour form while flying in the 1950s
- Thousands killed and tens of thousands poisoned by contaminated table oil in Morocco, 1959

* * *

(14) Fear and Trembling

> *Each woman contains a secret: an accent, a gesture, a silence.*
> **Antoine de Saint-Exupéry**

Monday, 28 October 2002
Hassan – Rabat:

I could have strangled Rachid given his insistence on maintaining a provocative silence. It was only by a miracle that I controlled my fury and my confusion. I did not speak until we stopped in front of the door of an apartment on the second floor of a small building in a modern neighbourhood whose architecture somehow suggested that its residents belonged to the middle class.

"Are you sure this is the Lubna we're looking for?"

"If my inferences are correct, yes."

"Inferences? Are you being funny with me?"

I broke off when I heard the sound of slow, firm footsteps coming towards the door, followed by a few moments' silence, which I understood as someone standing behind the door using the magic eye to identify who was there at an inconvenient hour.

Of course no one would think of visiting a woman they did not know at ten o'clock in the evening, and without a prior appointment, unless they were an impulsive young man or a crazy writer.

Or both of those together!

A woman's apprehensive voice asked who was there (which I understood without need for a translation). The scene of our meeting with the ex-publisher repeated itself to the letter: Rachid said a few words in Arabic, and I picked out the name of the novel and its author.

Another thirty seconds' silence before the door was unlocked and the woman standing there became visible.

The hallway was dimly lit and that did not allow me to examine her features closely, but the look of astonishment on her face was unmissable.

At first glance one might think she was in her early forties, but with my advanced feminine radar (to amend Rachid's nomenclature) I realised she was no older than her mid-thirties, despite the overdone mask of gravitas she was hiding behind, and the loose-fitting dressing gown she was wearing that made it very hard to check out her figure.

Rachid continued his exhaustive explanation most persuasively, and his face beamed when she uttered a brief final word and ushered us inside after giving me a nod and a few polite words of welcome in French.

A small apartment comprising three rooms, whose doors were shut. In the middle of the well-lit living room there was a couch and a low table, on whose glass top I noticed a fountain pen, paperback book, and small open notebook. Opposite the couch was a television, which was turned off, and on the wall above it hung a picture of a woman hugging a girl aged twelve or thirteen.

There was no sign or trace of a man's presence in the house.

She waved her left hand for us to sit down on the couch, and selected a chair in the corner for herself.

She could hardly be called beautiful with her sensibly coiffed auburn hair, small mouth, whose red lips barely moved when she spoke, and honey eyes framed – or more accurately, besieged – by large spectacles that made her look like the hated headmistress of a girls' boarding school.

Yet she was really attractive. And weirdly, her attraction was connected to the patina of sadness on her face. She also moved and walked with a powerful feminine grace, despite her evident attempts to control, or perhaps bury it.

Here was a woman, it occurred to me, doing all she could to suppress everything that marked her out as a woman. She did not want to enjoy her youth and was annoyed by the effect of her beauty. In fact, she wished for a time machine that would transport her directly into her fifties.

Her welcome in French encouraged me to break the awkward stiffness between us and speak to her in the same language: "Madam, the situation is most bizarre and you have every right to express your displeasure. But I promise you I will get straight to the point without any lengthy introductions. I am Christine McMillan, an American novelist, and daughter of the soldier Steve McMillan, the 'fictional' character in the novel *A Moroccan Jigsaw Puzzle*. Our research into its unknown author has led us to suspect that he is the missing maths teacher Rafiq Khalidi."

She shifted her gaze between us, and the suspicion and upset in her eyes suggested we were really close to our goal. I kept up the pressure to force her surrender: "Are you Lubna, wife of Samir Qassemi, the friend of the maths teacher?"

She interlocked her fingers in a despairing effort to control their trembling, then mumbled in a low voice, "How did you connect the novel to Rafiq Khalidi?"

I conveyed to her what had happened, from when I read the translated edition of the novel to the moment we knocked at her door.

Then I turned to Rachid, expecting to hear the missing part of the story. He adjusted his position and began with an introduction that reminded me of Hercule Poirot about to reveal the killer in an Agatha Christie novel: "The publisher had the solution to the puzzle in his hands at the end of the 1980s, but he failed to spot some faint clues, perhaps because he had lived out of Morocco for a long time, and some key details passed him by."

He avoided looking at us and stared at the glass table while gesturing with his hand to speak more comfortably: "When Muhsin el-Fadili referred to a number of the village's inhabitants suffering from symptoms similar to those of Rafiq Khalidi, I remembered what my father had told me years ago about the poisoned oil disaster that struck Morocco at the end of the '50s and caused thousands to die and tens of thousands to come down with a range of illnesses like paralysis, difficulty moving the limbs, diseases of the heart and arteries, hypertension, speech difficulties, and sometimes blindness.

"I called him this morning, and he confirmed what he had told me before. He added that at the time the rumour was that Moroccan businessmen had bought jet-engine lubricating oil from the U.S. Air Force bases near some Moroccan cities. They mixed it with table oil, then flooded the market, and the tragedy happened.

"He said it was a forgotten episode, which our generation knows nothing about since it was mysteriously covered up at the time, despite the dire effect on the victims."

My heart sank to the floor as I heard the dreadful information. The trembling of Lubna's fingers spread to my whole body, while Rachid digressed in French, giving a distinct resonance to the letter r.

"Today I had an appointment with my supervisor in his office at the university. I was going to tell him the fascinating information we had uncovered about *A Moroccan Jigsaw Puzzle*, in the hope that he would agree to my using it as an example in my dissertation. But he failed to show up, and did not even bother to call and apologise.

"Then I had the idea to meet a history professor who had taught me one of the subsidiary classes during my second year. I asked him about the toxic oil disaster, and he gave me information that corroborated what my father had told me, along with some more precise dates, locations and events. He then advised me to read a dissertation on the subject written by a female doctoral candidate which had gained her praise and a distinction.

Like a student who gets the answer to a mental arithmetic problem first, I blurted out, "And that researcher is Lubna!"

"Yes," replied Lubna blankly, and to me that made her seem uninterested in Rachid continuing his explanation: "The professor told me he had supervised the dissertation in the mid-90s and more than once had considered recusing himself, given the gravity of the topic and how it touched upon certain details of a politically sensitive nature at the time. However, the passion and determination of the student to find the truth spread to him and he backed her and helped her confront some difficulties.

"She challenged the backdrop of social exclusion and the enforced silence about the nature and consequences of the disaster. She contacted families of victims and went through the archives. She read the interview records of those accused, summaries of their trials, and newspaper articles published back then. She corresponded with Moroccan researchers and American historians. She even went into the analysis of the toxic substance responsible for killing and disabling the victims, although that was part of medicine and chemistry and not really history.

"The man was being accurate when he said that he found himself dealing with a woman who wasn't doing normal academic research but was involved in a sacred battle, which would either end with her victory or her martyrdom . . ."

My expression was a mixture of astonishment and admiration when I looked at the woman seated opposite me as she asked absently, "And how did you get my address?"

"The professor talked about the woman with a great deal of esteem and saw her as a one off. Because I was also one of his best students, he took me to his office where he gave me a copy of her dissertation and showed me a souvenir photo of her thesis defence. He told me that her personal life was a complete mystery to him and he wished he knew the reason for her almost manic interest in the toxic oil disaster. Just once she had agreed to his offer of a lift in his car, because it was pouring with rain, and she asked to be dropped off at a private school close to Hassan Tower that takes students from kindergarten to secondary. Let's say I know the school and I stood watching the gates at exactly six o'clock this evening. And I in fact spotted Mrs Lubna el-Afaoui coming out in the company of the girl she is hugging in the photo on the wall. They then went into a building only a few hundred metres from the school."

Rachid's ears went bright red and I intervened to spare his embarrassment: "Madam, if it had not been for my colleague's determination to track you down, rather than travelling to Meknes to meet the missing man's family and his friend, I would not have disturbed you. I still do not understand the nature of your connection to the subject, but for me it's a crucial issue, and I therefore ask you, if Rafiq Khalidi really was Saleh and Jamila's son, or whatever their names are in the real world, and the author of *A Moroccan Jigsaw Puzzle* as well, why did he drop Steve McMillan's name into the action and bluntly accuse him of killing his parents, even though the testimony of another person who lived through that period refutes the accusation against my father?

"I am also a novelist and know that no one has the right to control a writer's imagination, but the presence of some real details in the novel sets us up against an infinite number of questions!"

A smile suddenly appeared on Lubna's lips, giving her face a beauty of a different cast. "Because you didn't take another possibility into account," she said. "Yes, Rafiq Khalidi, the missing maths teacher, whose family and friend Samir denied the theory that he might have written a novel, is the author of *A Moroccan Jigsaw Puzzle*. But the work was unfinished when he disappeared and another person took it upon themself to complete its final chapters and send it to a publisher under that assumed name."

"And who is that person?" we cried so exactly together it was laughable.

She cast a quick glance at the picture hanging above the television and answered innocently, as if indifferent to our reaction: "Me..."

* * *

🔍 elkhabar.com – Home – Crime:

Husband of activist lawyer vanishes in mysterious circumstances

Wednesday 6 March 2013 – 12:43

Police departments under the jurisdiction of Rabat Prefecture have opened an inquiry into the disappearance of Professor Younis Belkacem (59) a gynaecologist and obstetrician and professor at Mohammed V – Souissi University Medical School in Rabat. According to an informed source, the doctor was last seen on Saturday night when he left his villa in the Hayy el Riad neighbourhood without telling his wife, lawyer and legal activist Hanan el-Farisi (52) where he was going and without taking his blue Audi car. She informed the police after more than 24 hours had passed, during which his mobile phone was out of network coverage.

The disappearance was roundly lamented by faculty and students at the Medical School. A third-year student (who declined to give her name) stated that the professor was very well liked by his students and enjoyed a reputation for, in her words, being available and dispensing with excessive formalities.

It is noteworthy that the son of the doctor and lawyer has been missing in Russia since October 2002. At the time it was rumoured that he was one of the victims of the hostage taking at a Moscow theatre, a matter denied by the Moroccan Embassy in an official statement.

Comments (0) Opinions expressed in comments reflect the views of their authors and do not represent those of elkhabar.com

(14') In Cold Blood

> *Fear cannot be without hope nor hope without fear.*
>
> **Baruch Spinoza**

Tuesday, 20 June 2006
Outskirts of Krasnokamensk – Siberia:

After Vasili's joking remark, I spent a long stretch reviewing every detail of the Bitsa Park serial killer case, for which I had been framed. Using the information provided by the newspapers in my possession, I came to understand the truth of what had really been going on since 2001.

Of course it wasn't a question of any supernatural intelligence on my part, or of role-playing the detectives from crime-fiction novels available in the prison library.

I just took real advantage of the peace and quiet of the isolated prison and the normal desire to slay the boredom of an interminable present and a future that was missing from Krasnovamensk's lexicon. Fifteen minutes by a window overlooking the emptiness here would be enough to turn anyone into a philosopher with ideas to rival Nietzsche's lifetime works, and not merely into a detective training his mind always to think outside the box.

The serial killer worked according to a patient and well-designed plan, which nobody had understood over the previous five years...

He wanted to fill each of a chessboard's sixty-four squares, and settled upon Bitsa Park, well known for its chess games and tournaments, to perpetrate his run of crimes.

His choice of victims and locations within the park was not random...

The rule being that if a crime occurs, focus on the victim not the criminal!

Anyone who loves chess knows that the pawns are the least valuable pieces, and a player has no problem sacrificing them to deceive and lull their opponent before surprising them with an unforeseen trap capturing their most precious pieces before finishing them off with the killer move.

That's what the criminal did from the beginning when he embarked on the cold-blooded murder of a number of homeless vagrants, people whose disappearance or death would not cause any inconvenience or grief to anybody. He also took advantage of the laxity and indifference of the Moscow police, plus their thinking that by arresting anyone at all they could close the case.

After that, he moved on to the next step: the elimination of ordinary workers or employees with families, who would inquire after them once they disappeared and be horrified when a body was discovered, but whose voices were unable to exert sufficient pressure, unlike those of castles and knights.

The Moscow police only opened a serious investigation last February after the slaying of a teacher followed by a prominent engineer, both of whose rotten luck had taken them to the park of death. Their social status indicated that the criminal was targeting the educated class, that is the chessboard's bishops.

A brutal killer, deserving the harshest punishment of course, he might have been suffering from serious mental derangement. Tracking developments in the case, however, led me to really admire his philosophy. He was able to turn the tiny chessboard into a true analogy for the cruelty of life, which only acknowledges the strongest.

Even press coverage did got gain any real impetus until the teacher and the engineer were killed and everyone started wondering what was the point of the police, given the impossibility of guarding twenty-two square kilometres of green space, some of which was forest, especially at periods when the temperature dropped scarily.

I wasn't able to follow the finer details at the opportune time. The newspapers were few and far between, only reaching the remote prison several days late and there was a queue of prisoners who read them once the warders were finished with them. Mostly I would be the very last person to get hold of them. Nonetheless, I became aware of a young woman journalist, whose photo came at the bottom of a number of articles and investigations that dealt with the case with considerable interest from the beginning.

Yana Zharchinskaya . . .

Her name echoed in my head more than once as the strands of a plan began to take shape. I might have been a drowning man clutching at straws, but I wasn't going to miss the opportunity to clutch them.

*

Vasili closed his small backpack, put on his overcoat and, when he noticed me watching him, said encouragingly, "Keep looking at the glass half full. We've suffered enormously here, but things are much better than the real Siberian hell described by Dostoyevsky in *Memoirs from the House of the Dead*, and the horrors of what Solzhenitsyn described in *The Gulag Archipelago*. You speak Russian fluently now and have read most of the novels, plays and short stories in the prison library. You can also trounce me at chess. You remind me of . . ."

Smiling, I interrupted him: "'The Bet' by Chekhov. My friend and roommate Sergei told me about it at the university accommodation. I've had the chance to read it here, as well as his *Sakhalin Island*, in which he conveys the suffering of the prisoners in Siberia at the end of the nineteenth century."

I went on, with emotion, "I'm really happy you're being released at the end of your sentence. It can't have been easy for a journalist like you to be so far from your family simply for writing an article in which you expressed your opinion. Time here passes awfully slowly, but pass it does . . ."

He embraced me tightly showing genuine sympathy: "I don't think they'll leave me to my own business once I'm free. I'll work to leave the country with my wife and kids as soon as possible. I'll do everything I can to save you, even though I admit it's a difficult task. You've suffered an injustice and don't deserve what's happened to you."

I held back the tear of defeat that almost slipped my eye and said with ostensible resolve: "As I explained to you yesterday, in the latest newspaper to reach here they announced the disappearance of a thirty-six-year-old woman called Marina Moskalyova. She was last seen in the Kakhovskaya Metro station close to Bitsa Park. If my suspicion is right, Marina is the sixty-first victim, or the queen victim, the first woman the maniac has killed and he will follow her with another woman, in conformity with the rules of the chessboard."

He put his hand on my shoulder, as was his habit when he wanted to speak candidly about something: "I'm still not convinced by your strange deductions about the case, but I will carry out your wish and contact the journalist concerned."

"I could have asked you to go straight to the Moroccan Embassy, but the lack of any connection between the theatre siege and the crimes at the park, along with the loss of my real ID papers and the creation of a new name and identity for me, will make them inclined to believe the Russian version of events. And because I'm a Moroccan, I'm the first to exclude the chance of a Moroccan bureaucrat leaving his comfortable chair and cosy office in Moscow to travel seven thousand kilometres just to confirm my identity here in Krasnokamensk. Only the journalist has a chance of saving me."

"Okay. If we assume I manage to reach Yana Zharchinskaya and persuade her to rouse public outrage at your case, what will you do after you're released?"

I took a deep breath and told him what had haunted me all the years of my detention: "I'll go back to Morocco and look for Ghalia first of all. Then I'll get down on my knees and beg forgiveness for what I did to her before thinking about beginning a new life.

"The certainty that I am trapped in a vicious circle has taken root in me. A circle I opened with my own hands and only the fingers of the mistreated cleaning girl will ever close it . . .

* * *

What happened the night of the disappearance of maths teacher Rafiq Khalidi on Saturday, 30 July 1988, as related by Lubna el-Afaoui (in all the boring detail in which the world's women excel):

My mother added her final touches to my hairdo, then tenderly wrapped her arms around my neck without speaking. Seconds later her tears were falling on my cheek like drops of morning dew on a rainy day.

Now my heart rested easy and, sitting in front of the large mirror in my room, my senses confirmed that it is impossible for a mother not to shed tears of joy at her daughter's engagement.

Today I am the happiest person on the face of the Earth, and I do not believe anyone rivals me for the title except her.

"Hundreds of brides have been through my hands at the salon, and I thought myself lucky to work as a hairdresser and beautician as I waited impatiently for your engagement night. Thank God, my dream has finally come true, and I'm content with a few simple adjustments, given, my princess, that you are too beautiful to need the intervention of my fingers to make you look stunning."

A smile of joy escaped my lips, and she lovingly kissed my cheek. Then she asked a question that I knew she had been very reluctant to ask: "Are you sure you're making the right choice?"

My answer was ready: "Mummy, what other people say and think is nothing to do with me. He's partially disabled and speaks and moves his limbs with difficulty. I'm not going to blame a person I love for a fate that he had no part in. Rafiq has a wonderfully sensitive heart, a tongue that only says beautiful things, and the mind of a genius, the limits of whose abilities none of those foolish detractors know."

I winked at her and added, "And he's peerlessly handsome, according to your own testimony!"

I could not miss the anguish in her sigh, even if she tried to conceal it with a faint smile: "Just as I expected, you're exactly like me, darling. Your feelings are too strong for you to listen to anyone else."

"What happened between you and my father is not going to happen to me," I said firmly and confidently.

I quickly tried to tone it down, but she made a show of indifference that turned into serious maternal advice, which I had long missed after being deprived of her tenderness at an early age: "Life has taught me, my girl, not to trust crazy, raging feelings. What starts so strong and powerful does not always end like that. True love remains realistic and calm till the end. Your father made such a fuss, threatening my family that he would kidnap me if they didn't consent to the marriage. And at the time, of course, I was impressed by his audacity and mad passion, so I also applied pressure. He got what he wanted. Time passed and he found himself trapped in a pathological vortex of jealousy and doubt, which ended with him casting aspersions on my honour without any tangible evidence. He divorced me without qualms, but that wasn't enough. No, he took you and left Rabat for good to live in Meknes. For years I paid the price in terms of my self-respect and my reputation. And if it hadn't been for your insistence, I would even have been denied my right as a mother to attend your engagement."

After a few seconds' silence, she said in a voice unsteady with emotion, "I swear to you, my daughter, that I never cheated on your father. I don't know what kind of lies he's been planting in your head since you were a child, but I'm no different to your beloved Rafiq. I, too, had no say when fate made me exceedingly feminine. My every spontaneous laugh, pleasant word or dreamy look was an attempted betrayal in your father's disturbed mind."

I stood up from my chair in agitation and, stepping on the edge of my dress, I lost my balance and would have fallen over if she hadn't rushed to catch me in her arms. Very upset, she hugged me and our tears blended on each other's cheeks.

The pair of us sobbing gave me an extra sense of calm and freed me a little from my nerves regarding the long-promised night. The night marking the first step to being forever with the one I love . . .

"I'm going to leave you now. It's your night and you have the right to be alone for a while before the arrival of your handsome prince. Don't forget to say the Verse of the Throne and the two Suras of Protection. Many eyes will be lurking for you, and only the ever-wakeful eye of God will protect you."

She said this, then kissed me on the forehead and left the room, heading for the kitchen, tearing her face away from the eyes of my father, which were blazing with fury. I satisfied myself with a smile with only one meaning: please, Dad, I don't want problems between you two now. The guests are on their way!

I left the door ajar, opened a drawer next to my bed and took out a photo of Rafiq. I filled my eyes with his features as a final preparation for meeting him and his family.

I sighed with longing at the sight of my beloved's eyes in the photo and my memory replayed its tape from the beginning to the accompanying score of Aziza Jalal singing "Waiting for You".

*

I grew up in my father's care after he moved to Meknes and refused to get married again after divorcing my mother and making vague, unsubstantiated allegations that she was cheating on him. He lived convinced that all women were treacherous by nature, hard-wired to cheat given half a chance. He always treated me on that basis, and prevented me from mixing with boys at school. He rejected the idea of my making friends with the girls or even revising for exams with them. If it hadn't been for the court order allowing me to visit my mother in Rabat for short periods, my relationship with her would have been severed too.

I grew up alone, subject to his whims in choosing my clothes and his constant criticism of the way I walked and talked, which he would describe as flirtatious. I went through the changes of puberty on my own, and I gradually fell in line with his constant insinuations and judgements. So in turn I grew irritated at the signs of my femininity and considered them to be a permanent obstacle preventing me from gaining his trust, no matter what I did.

He did not resist my desire to get an education and allowed me to attend the Faculty of Arts after passing the bac, even though my efforts had not been directed at a specific goal but were just a means to escape my daily torment with him!

Torment that continued for years, during which another shameful contradiction in his thinking became apparent . . .

More than once I heard him say that he was waiting for the first guy to come knocking at his front door to get rid of me. But, at the same time, he surrounded me with walls of suspicion and doubt, even though I was subjected to another flood of mockery and disparagement at university because I was aloof and refused normal contact with others.

How could this guy come knocking, as my father had it, if he couldn't even notice me before thinking of asking for my hand in marriage?

Then along came Samir Qassemi . . .

I met him at a poetry evening at university. He wowed me with the force of his words and his amazing ability to get his ideas across in a winning way that no one listening would tire of.

A young man years older than me, it became obvious from my initial observations that he was extremely popular with the young female students brimming with hope and familiar rosy dreams, which he took advantage of by surrounding himself with a squad of them. They followed him around wherever he went like the children of Hamelin in the tale of the Pied Piper.

Astonishingly, he wasn't dirty rich or especially handsome, but he excelled with a weapon that a woman can rarely resist.

His way with words . . .

I asked some of my fellow students about him in a modest way and learned that he worked as an Arabic teacher at a high school while continuing his university studies with the ambition of achieving the highest academic qualifications.

Over the course of time, my feminine intuition (which the previous years had been unable to kill) gave me the sense he was trying to get close to me, and to begin with I led him on, armed with a mix of curiosity and a powerful desire to defy my delusional father.

Our meetings came thick and fast, then, at the university library and on campus. I found him to have a truly encyclopaedic knowledge of culture and capable of shifting easily between subjects. But he was excitable, with a tendency for frivolity, despite approaching thirty. He talked about future plans, from which nothing had come so far. His self-confidence almost reached the point of vanity, giving him a belief that he was the cleverest person in the world, whom circumstance had forced to descend from his ethereal heights to address us, the multitude of disciples and fools.

He was the first guy I got to know outside the circle of my classmates (which was tight enough), and although he used all his abilities and skills to seduce me – and he'd succeeded with others – the feelings buried deep inside any girl of my age did not move an inch.

Was it that I simply didn't like him, or did I have a problem? Was I unlike other girls because of my complicated personal and family circumstances and completely unable to relate to normal human feelings?

I didn't know the answer, because that moment did not come until Friday, 25 September 1987, at a quarter past five in the afternoon.

How can I forget the date and time when I first met Rafiq Khalidi?

It was a new academic year, which I began as usual with the trinity of unremitting lectures, constant forbearance towards my father's unpredictable temperament, and permanent evasion of Samir's persistent effort to add me to his fan club.

I left the auditorium after a boring, tiresome lecture, whose main points I was barely able to summarize, and as soon as I reached the gates of the university I found Samir waiting for me. I made a show of annoyance and frustration, in the hope that with his supposed intelligence he would understand I had no desire to see him.

Then I noticed that he wasn't alone . . .

He was around the same age as him or a few years older. Brown skin and very well-tended black hair, some strands of which lay on his forehead. His features were well proportioned with dark eyes nestling behind large framed glasses. Full, bowed lips, and a smooth face that I felt a secret urge to touch.

And a birthmark on his left cheek . . .

He was unbelievably handsome, his features combining a balanced masculinity and an almost feminine beauty. If I excluded the birthmark, the only similar image that I could find in the album in my mind was the young Mahmoud Darwish.

His clothes weren't terribly expensive or excessively stylish, but plain and practical while also not part of the incomprehensible fashion adopted by some that mixed unkempt hair, filthy clothes, and revolutionary values!

I went to shake his hand and got a shock that it was practically rigid and grasped my fingers with difficulty. His voice stuttered and slurred letters and words like a drunk: "Rafiq. Rafiq Khalidi. Hello . . ."

I felt a little apprehensive of him and I took a step back. I regretted my behaviour when I picked up the hurt at my spontaneous reaction in his look.

Samir patted him gently on the back as he gave me a quick wink indicating that he would explain everything later. "Rafiq Khalidi, my great friend and colleague at school where he teaches maths. Recently he has surprised me with his special interest in literature, since I long believed he was a prisoner of his numbers and impenetrable equations. We've come to attend the literary seminar on modern narrative techniques. What do you say about coming along?"

Rafiq's hurt looks touched my heart and I burned with a desire to accept the invitation, but my tongue articulated a different answer: "Sorry, but I have to go home early. I hope we'll all have the chance to see each other again. A pleasure to meet you, Mr Khalidi!"

I slipped away from them like a fugitive, casting curious glances behind me that only doubled my puzzlement when I saw that Rafiq moved unsteadily like someone under the influence.

Was he an alcoholic?

Samir was irritated when I asked him about his friend afterwards, then he told me everything he knew about him in full.

He said that Rafiq Khalidi came from a middle-class Meknes family. His birth had been difficult, which caused him a range of obscure problems with his health that affected his speech and the movement of his limbs. Fate, however, had compensated him with prodigious mental prowess and an obsession with numbers. His father had owned a timber yard, but was killed during the 1965 riots in Casablanca, simply for being in the wrong place at the wrong time, when he had gone to conclude a business deal there and been struck down by a stray bullet. His mother, a nurse, brought him up herself while confronting the ambitions of some members of her dead husband's family to appropriate the little wealth he had, in contravention of the laws of God and man. The boy grew up and excelled far above his peers. He was a stone's throw away from winning a university scholarship to Paris, but in the end that went to another candidate with inside connections and influence. Rafiq took it very badly. He lost faith in everything, especially after his mother's death, and he was left on his own to fight the ambitions of his uncle's family to get hold of the house where he lived alone. He was content to teach maths at a middle school in one of the villages near Meknes, where he met Samir, who tried to bring him out of his isolation and partly succeeded up to that point.

I didn't utter a word after hearing the story. Perhaps the emotion was visible on my face, because Samir added with a fake delight, whose unspoken message I did not fail to miss, that being handsome wasn't everything and that most of the women who had tried to get close to the maths teacher soon backed off.

But I was completely unlike the others.

Time also proved that Rafiq was no ordinary man either . . .

I showed renewed interest in the times they got together, and I did not miss a moment that enabled me to spend time in their company. I discovered that the two friends were different, opposites.

Contrary to what I knew about Samir, Rafiq was taciturn so as not to draw attention to his disability. He was modest, not bragging or showing off his amazing abilities to memorize things and the quickness of his wits. In fact, he didn't speak about them at all unless Samir pushed him to. Mysterious, like a book in a language no one understands.

Speaking of books, in his company we often seemed like two junior school pupils or even illiterates, and I say that without any embarrassment.

He was a fan of literary works we'd never heard of (because most of them had yet to be translated into Arabic) and interested in novels that experimented with new narrative forms. He said they tested the reader's intelligence and did not reveal all their secrets easily.

Then we realised that he was particularly interested in the works of the OuLiPo Literary Society, which was known for its revolt against the classical structure of the novel and poetry and its attempts to break down the wall dividing the foundations of mathematics and literature. He focused on the works of its leading members, the Frenchman Georges Perec and the Italian Italo Calvino.

Anyway, the succession of meetings led me to forget his difficulties moving his limbs, to get over my initial admiration at just how good looking he was, to overlook the significant age difference between us, and then penetrate his heart and mind.

Without my feeling his slow and silent infiltration into my own heart . . .

My instincts woke up from their hibernation, and I was amazed to discover that my mind possessed appropriate cunning to handle the situation, me, who had grown up in a weird atmosphere that almost caused me to forget I was a woman. I invented excuses, spontaneous incidents and chance happenings to meet Rafiq away from Samir's prying eyes. My heart was finally convinced that it wanted no one other than an exceptional man that none of the other girls understood . . .

And that no one other than me would understand and love . . .

I did not need much time until I was confident that my feelings were reciprocated, even if his feelings were tinged with a sense of guilt regarding his friend, and he was being honest when he put it bluntly: "I do not want to participate in creating a new love triangle, whose three sides are me, you and Samir . . ."

I reassured him more than once by speaking about Samir's multiple relationships with women and how his romantic feelings towards women weren't serious. He responded with strange and mysterious words, whose real meaning I did not grasp at the time: "Humans beings, my dear one, are enigmatic creatures. God has granted them a mind with millions of sealed dark rooms capable of concealing much. The hardest challenge is to hold on to the keys for every room, since no one knows what will happen if a single door is left open!"

Things between us developed quickly, until I was no longer able to live without him.

And that's a cliché I had often made fun of in Arabic films, but surrendered to with pleasure in the end.

To pledge your life, your present and your future to another's life, one whose soul has intertwined with yours to create a single being that believes those ties will only be severed by death.

At that point, Rafiq let me in on his little secret . . .

He had written a novel, and said he was going to give it the title *A Moroccan Jigsaw Puzzle*.

My happiness was indescribable and I felt proud to be associated with a fighter who defied the cruelty of his circumstances and wrote in a country that had entered the tunnel of the lean years of the 1980s, when the vast majority of people were struggling to make a living, let alone write novels or even read them!

I annoyed him several times with my desire to read the draft and understand the import of the strange title. But he refused, arguing that he was still at the beginning of the work and the idea was not fully mature yet. However, the pressure of my curiosity continued and every so often he gave me a few typewritten chapters. I read them and was blown away by the force of his literary style, and couldn't wait to know what would happen in the following chapters.

Of course it was no longer possible to conceal our relationship from Samir . . .

Rafiq took on the difficult task and took advantage of the end of the school year at the village middle school to inform his friend that he intended to get formally engaged to me at the end of July 1988.

Samir's incendiary reaction was unexpected, or not expected to be so extreme. He expressed absolute outrage and said that he had trusted us and did not want to believe an inner sense that something untoward existed between us. Then he accused his friend of betrayal and, behind my back, called me all kinds of names. Rafiq – and he was docile to the point of passivity – lost his cool and the discussion turned into a fight at the school. It ended with a complete break between them.

I felt pangs of regret at the ending of their beautiful friendship in such an unfortunate way, but that's life. It doesn't give you a thing without taking many others away!

*

"Are you unconscious or what?"

With a quick movement I hid the photograph when the crudeness of the tone hit me, and I replied, "No, I'm awake, Daddy. Is there something?"

My father shouted nervously at me: "The cripple and his family were due here at nine and they are more than forty-five minutes late even though they don't live very far away. Why are they so late? If they're messing with us, I'll teach them a harsh lesson, before punishing you for putting me in an embarrassing position in front of everyone!"

Then he grabbed my wrist and shook me hard. My mother, who was standing behind him, intervened and pulled his arm shouting, "Get away from her! She's none of your concern. Soon she'll be married and rid of you, you sick man. Perhaps being left on your own will help you think seriously about visiting a perspicacious miracle worker, or even a psychologist, to save you from insanity."

He raised his other hand to punch her as he cursed her honour and I shouted with all my might, "Stop! I beg you!"

The doorbell rang . . .

It was a fifteen-year-old boy who, out-of-breath and worked up, spoke to my father: "I'm Rafiq's cousin. My father is asking after him. Did he come before us? He said he was going to the flower seller to pick up the bouquet and he hasn't come back!"

* * *

(15) An Attempt to Live

> *Oh, love isn't there to make us happy. I believe it exists to show us how much we can endure.*
>
> **Hermann Hesse**

Monday, 28 October 2002
Hassan – Rabat:

Tears of sympathy rolled down my cheeks, while Rachid looked down in thought. After a minute or so, Lubna broke the funereal silence with a sad smile. "It looks like our evening isn't over..."

Even though she had not finished her story, I interpreted her words as a tacit invitation for us to leave, but she proved my hunch wrong by adding, "I'll make some tea and we can keep talking in the kitchen."

She cast a lengthy glance through the doorway of a darkened room and closed the door again. Then she beckoned us with her finger and we followed her across the hall.

She set a box of sugar cubes and some mint on a small table along with a teapot and clean glasses. Then, taking advantage of the time for the water to boil, she said, "I nearly lost my mind. The only explanation for Rafiq's disappearance was that something bad had happened to him. That night we searched the hospitals and police stations, but nothing."

"What about the flower seller?" I asked with concern.

She replied casually, "He remembered him well after he agreed to arrange the bouquet, but he did not see him that day, which means of course that Rafiq did not reach his destination after leaving the house."

Rachid finally spoke: "Didn't it occur to you that his uncle's family or Samir were behind his disappearance? Both of them had powerful motives to get him out of the way. The family because of their ambitions to appropriate the house and kick Rafiq out, and Samir because of a desire for revenge after their friendship fell apart."

She folded her arms across her chest and replied, "At first I couldn't think straight out of worry for Rafiq. Then my father weighed in to stop me taking part in the search. He poured curses on me, and my mother wasn't able to provide any help. But later on I was sure that something was not quite right."

"How so?"

"I felt the uncle's family weren't serious about looking for him, although they pretended otherwise. I remembered what Rafiq had said a few days before he went missing about how strange he found the sudden improvement in his usually turbulent relationship with the members of his family, who had agreed to come with him to the engagement. Then Samir suddenly turned up to express his shock at what had happened. He showed willing in helping to uncover his friend's fate and turn the page on the previous disagreements between us. He suggested putting a missing person's notice in one of the national papers."

Rachid pointed out that the water was boiling, and Lubna hurried to turn off the stove. I said in a deliberate tone, "That out-of-place compassion condemns both parties more than it exonerates them."

"You're right and I started to believe it myself. But an unexpected event shuffled the deck and forced me to take a step back." Our questioning looks besieged her, and she resumed reluctantly, "I was pregnant . . ."

I sensed she was making an enormous effort to summon up painful memories, and I gave her a smile of encouragement that helped her keep going despite her embarrassment: "My father found out. He kicked me out of the house and disowned me, ignoring all my pleas. I was forced to leave university and the city and return to Rabat, where my mother took me in and stood by me."

She turned her back, preferring to avoid looking at us: "She had hardly restored her good reputation and managed to show she'd led a decent life, when I rolled up like an ocean wave smashing a sandcastle. I only left the house occasionally and was often alone as my mother was busy at her salon. I was prey to toxic imaginings that something terrible had happened to my beloved, the father of my baby boy or baby girl, and he was dead. Only rereading the draft of his unfinished novel spared me from those obsessive thoughts, till I thought seriously about finishing and publishing it myself, in the belief that that symbolic act would be the one and only way for all of us to remain alive."

I shuddered like someone being electrocuted: "You finished writing *A Moroccan Jigsaw Puzzle* when you were pregnant?!"

"It took around ten weeks . . ." she replied proudly.

I expressed my indignation by saying, "Preposterous . . ."

Rachid turned towards me and corrected me: "No, it is possible. Kerouac wrote his famous novel *On the Road* in three weeks. Stendhal, author of *The Red and the Black*, was able to write another novel, *The Charterhouse of Parma*, nearly seven hundred pages long, in less than two months."

Then he asked Lubna, "Here we reach a crucial point: where did Rafiq's draft end? And where did your imagination take over to complete the novel?"

"The last thing Rafiq wrote in his draft was the detective Mustafa Mahmoudi reading the contents of Saleh's notebook after his death with its reference to a meeting with the American soldier and those strange serial numbers: 33137 42F."

I cried out in triumph, "So the detective, and along with him the novel, deducing that Steve McMillan committed the murders was a product of your imagination!"

She nodded her head in agreement, and Rachid winked as he whispered: "*The Mystery of Edwin Drood* . . ."

But she heard him and commented extremely calmly, "Exactly. It was similar to the problem of Dickens's novel with the narrative stopping at a very ambiguous point."

She handed us glasses of hot tea and put hers down as she digressed: "I don't deny that taking the decision to finish writing the novel was strange and not subject to any logic. I don't know if I was motivated by my emotions and my fear for my lost beloved or whether the psychological trauma of the pregnancy played a role. What matters is that after rereading the draft again I came up against several question marks. First, the puzzling dedication to Veronica.

"You felt jealous of course," I said wickedly.

Her smile remained faint, if less sad. "Absolutely. I was consumed by curiosity to discover the identity of this unknown Veronica that Rafiq chose to dedicate his novel to and had never mentioned to me before. Nonetheless, I respected the draft and left it unchanged. Then I moved on to another problem: the contents of the notebook. Here I went back to the novel *An Attempt at Life*, which came out in 1985, to get an idea about the atmosphere of the 1950s and the American presence in Kenitra. That wasn't enough for me and I waited for an opportunity to meet Mohammed Zafzaf on the fringes of a literary event in Rabat. I claimed I wanted to do academic research on his literary oeuvre, and he spoke to me in greater detail about Kenitra and the life of the GIs there. I wrote down literally everything I heard him say, and I can honestly confess that I was not happy at my failure to achieve a real understanding of those mysterious serial numbers despite all the effort I expended. Because of my lack of experience at the time, I chose to play the chords of a vague conspiracy and an open ending as an easy solution that would no doubt please a large number of readers. I finished it a few days before the end of November, and given my not insignificant knowledge of the publishing world thanks to my academic field, I opted for Hope Press for Publication and Distribution because of its good reputation. I put an assumed name on the manuscript and got a trusted friend to send it from Kenitra with that made-up address, since I was scared that publishing it under his real name would cause more problems."

"Practically no one read it after it came out," quipped Rachid, and I scolded him with severe looks, which he evaded by asking her, "What happened next?"

"The most difficult months of my pregnancy along with great fear for the future, and . . ."

Things were much clearer now and I pre-empted her, saying: "Samir came knocking at your door, presenting himself as a lover renewing the frank expression of his feelings towards you, and proposing to save you from an unknown future by marrying you and supporting your child."

She sighed in sorrow, "Exactly. I found myself forced to consent as a means to escape the looks and words of a society without compassion. That was a fatal mistake and I paid a very high price afterwards . . ."

*

We went back to the living room, and she picked up where she had left off: "Samir did not behave badly after the marriage was registered and he looked after me during my final trimester. My mother lightened up and she trusted him and praised him for sticking with me and for his patience travelling every week between Meknes and Rabat to see me. She forgot the existence of the person I loved, who had been missing since the night of our engagement. I'm not an ungrateful person, and I'm still thankful for everything Samir did for me at the time. But I could not overlook a strong feeling that he was working to an elaborate plan, whose details and purpose were unknown to me."

Rachid put his thumb and index finger to his chin in deep thought and said, "A plan that perhaps he felt was in danger after the ex-publisher visited Meknes and asked him about Rafiq and the possibility of his writing novels. Then came the meeting at the hospital on Saturday, 20 May 1989, when he made you leave in a hurry. Not so?"

She put her hand in the pocket of her loose-fitting dressing gown and replied slowly as she stared at a spot on the glass table: "I was carrying my daughter Jenan in my arms, and even though I was exhausted, I noticed the old man who called Samir's name more than once, but he pretended not to hear him. Afterwards he explained himself by saying that he had not wanted to waste time in vacuous small talk with people he did not know. But that contradicted what I knew about him being a man always seeking a multitude of casual social relations."

"Did you know the man was the novel's publisher?" I asked.

"No, and I forgot all about the incident until I made my way to Casablanca after I had weaned Jenan and regained my strength."

Finally, she decided to give her beautiful smile free rein, and added, "Criminologists say that most of those who commit murder return to the scene of the crime. And if we consider writing a crime, then I could not resist the delicious urge to go to the publishing house and cast an eye over copies of the novel in the place that had turned it from a manuscript into a printed book. That's where I saw the publisher, sitting behind his desk, Then I understood it all and joined the dots between the missing person's notice, the assumed name, the incident at the hospital and the publisher keen to discover the identity of the unknown author."

"What about Samir? What was your relationship like after Jenan was born? Did he really forget the seething love triangle of the past?"

"My final trimester and the need for my mother to take care of me were sufficient justification to stay with her, and he was forced to agree to my wish. But once I stopped breastfeeding, I was confronted with the bitter truth: logically I would return with him to Meknes and then be required to perform my marital duties like any normal woman."

Her eyes glistened as she said the last sentence, and I hoped she would explain more, although I understood what she meant. But her swift glances towards Rachid made me understand that she would only add more in purely female company.

"Didn't you consider that Samir's offer to marry you and adopt the little girl even though he knew everything that had happened was proof of true love?" said Rachid with interest.

Lubna instinctively stroked her auburn hair as she replied, "To begin with, yes. I appreciated what he did for me, in the knowledge that he risked setting up an asymmetric confrontation with a society that would look at him dubiously and show him no mercy. I might be the guilty party again for perhaps resorting to magic to rescue my reputation and force an unmarried man to marry me when I was pregnant with the child of another man who had disappeared the night we had been due to get engaged. Over time and living with him under one roof, however, confirmed that what came before Jenan's birth would never be the same as after, and that the motivation for his strange behaviour had nothing to do with love."

I smiled as I commented in the style of a writer able to grasp the profundity of human emotion: "Jealousy! He didn't love you as much as he refused to accept the idea of you preferring Rafiq over him."

Rachid leaned forward and spoke with a gravity that made me imagine him to be a psychoanalyst diagnosing one of his clients: "Maybe it wasn't really a close friendship between them but a concealed intense rivalry. Rafiq was taciturn and partially disabled, but the lively, self-confident Samir, who enjoyed enormous rhetorical skill and powers of persuasion, was unable to match the superior intellectual prowess of his friend. He found himself the loser in comparison, and that culminated in you choosing Rafiq rather than responding to his repeated efforts to seduce you."

"Exactly. Our marital relationship gradually turned into a sequence of psychological torture sessions and implicit comparisons between him and his old friend. He took photos of our outings or trips, despite their infrequency, with a perverse insistence. To my father and mother, he played being part of a happy family that lacked for nothing, but he didn't provide my daughter Jenan the care and attention any child of her age deserved. When I confronted him about it during a heated argument, he felt no restraint from thrusting a killer blow at my heart by saying that he felt nothing for her since she was the fruit of my relationship with his disabled rival."

Her voice quavering, she said in derision: "For your information, that intellectual, open-minded, enlightened teacher and university student, who achieved none of the items on his list of cultural and literary projects that he gave us headaches about in the past, refused even to contemplate me resuming my studies. He insisted that my connection with university was over, and that it was better for me to stay at home!"

Rachid gave a snort of laughter and said, "We're all hypocrites, we're all hypocrites..."

He fell silent for a long moment, then asked her, "Did Samir discover the existence of a connection between you and Rafiq Khalidi's *Moroccan Jigsaw Puzzle*?

"Basically not, since he acquired a copy of the novel later on and read it in secret, probably in search of something that in the end he didn't find, and he forgot all about it. He might have suspected something from what the publisher asked and the obvious similarity between the name of his rival and the pseudonym."

She continued with uncharacteristic venom, "You have to imagine my feelings when I'm sharing my life with a husband who is unaware that I am somehow a contributor to the writing of a novel that he's reading."

Then she turned to me as I asked, "Didn't all the contradictory behaviour make you feel any doubt? The only explanation for his making comparisons and belittling his former friend is that he knows Rafiq is still alive!"

Rachid backed me up: "We basically say, think well of your dead, and someone missing excuses himself. You're right Christine, our society treats the dead and missing with a certain subconscious respect."

"It was a dreadful struggle between intuition and logic. Intuition said that Samir was responsible for Rafiq's disappearance: logic said something like that was impossible, given the absence of any proof. Anyway, the situation worsened, what with our arguments growing more vehement, our quarrels becoming a daily ritual, and my constant demands for a divorce, until things came to a head one rainy night, three years after we married."

I watched her lips closely, like a child waiting for the end of her grandmother's story.

"He came back that night after a boozy evening out with his friends. I was asleep and had forgotten to close the drawer in my wardrobe. He discovered a packet of contraceptive pills."

Rachid lowered his gaze and the silence was ringing before she broke it with something like a justification: "Yes, in the beginning I was forced to accept his offer of marriage, but I never thought about having his child."

Her eyes misted over with tears and I moved closer to her and took her hand as I mumbled in sympathy, "In your heart you believed in the possibility that Rafiq would come back some day."

Her response was so emotional, I put my arm round her shoulder: "Yes. My heart and mind, my whole being, refused to believe the assumption that he was dead . . ."

After making an effort to display some strength in her tone of voice, she continued, "We quarrelled again. He started hitting me ferociously, and disgusted me with his hurtful insults and disgraceful slurs against everyone: me, Rafiq and Jenan. Then he went out and I heard nothing of him until the next morning, when someone called to tell me he'd been involved in a serious road accident."

My hand trembled on her shoulder, and Rachid failed to realise that his lower jaw dropped slackly, so intense was his concentration.

"I rushed to the emergency room where what I saw horrified me: a broken leg, crushed ribs and a face that had lost all its distinguishing features. The doctors told me it was hopeless. He had been hit by a speeding lorry as he walked drunk out of a bar. I was by his side for his final dying hours as he drifted painfully in and out of consciousness. As he lay dying, he kept repeating, and with immense difficulty, the name of the village where he worked as a teacher, 'Duwwar el-Hajj Kaddour, Duwwar el-Hajj Kaddour . . .'"

"But what's that village's got to do with it?" I cried dismissively. "And why did he insist on repeating its name before he died?"

"I didn't understand anything at the time and took it as the ravings of a man breathing his last. But Samir's death revived the mystery of Rafiq's disappearance when an unexpected surprise about his past came to light."

"What was it?"

"His connection to the case of the toxic oil . . ."

* * *

Video of the programme The World's Worst Killers – Special episode on the Chessboard Killer – French TF1 – Produced 2012

Excerpt from minutes 44 to 47:

Presenter: As a Russian journalist who covered the horrific case in detail for the Russian and British press, how did you feel when they announced the arrest of Alexander Pichushkin, the Bitsa Park serial killer, on Friday 16 June 2006?

Yana Zharchinskaya: Happy of course. I relaxed after months of constant work. Even the people of Moscow breathed a sigh of relief at last. They were able to return to their favourite park for walking and playing chess. It was funny that someone even got his sense of humour back. A nice bald old man followed me around for a few days after the case was over to tell me that he had been incarcerated in Krasnokamensk, and one of the other prisoners had been able to work out the puzzle by himself!

Presenter: Did you believe him?

Yana Zharchinskaya: Of course not! He just repeated what the police had concluded after their questioning of the killer and his confession. When he saw that his joke wasn't getting the expected reaction from me, he gave up and I never saw him again!

* * *

(15') The Tunnel

Life is a great surprise. I do not see why death should not be an even greater one.
Vladimir Nabokov

Sunday, 22 September 2019
Outskirts of Krasnokamensk – Siberia:

Aslan, the young Chechen prisoner, reached out with his small hand and touched my forehead for a few seconds. "You have a high temperature," he said anxiously. "You need urgent medical attention. I'm worried it's the same symptoms . . ."

The icy touch of his hand against my burning skin was enough to raise my heavy eyelids. In a daze I looked at his childish face and red beard and, after such a long silence that I might have been seen as congenitally mute, my tongue broke free of its stasis and I replied with difficulty, "Symptoms? Medical attention here? Since when has medicine been able to revive the dead? Will you perform the funeral rites?"

"You're delirious," he said. Whether there was anxiety in his voice or my exhausted mind was incapable of registering his tone, I could not tell. "I'm going to call a guard to come and take you to the prison infirmary."

I paid no heed to his going, and my eyes rolled in their sockets as they tried to focus on the ceiling. Then nausea overwhelmed me and I threw up the soup from lunch on the white tiles.

The act of vomiting forced my body to shudder violently, making me feel that my stomach would come pouring out of my open mouth. Then my strength failed me and my head dropped on the pillow like a boulder.

An illusory sense of relief flowed through my veins after my feeble body's tremendous exertion. My spongiform memory could do no better than replay the details of how thirteen years previously my attempt to leave this Siberian hellhole had failed...

After Vasili left prison, I waited for any news. And although I pretended to be in despair, my innermost being refused to surrender, clinging to the faint ray of hope that he could do something.

Once the storm has passed doesn't the ship make for the nearest port?

He was required to make contact with the woman journalist and exploit the popular outrage at the rising number of the butcher's victims to raise my case and force the police to release me.

The days on the alert went by and ended with a painful shock...

The newspapers reached the prison, out of date as usual, and I learned that the Moscow police has been able to arrest the serial killer on 16 June 2006, that is four days before Vasili's release.

Assuming he kept his promise to seek out Yana Zharchinskaya, and that the journey overland from Krasnokamensk to Moscow took around three days (as I had heard), he would have arrived a whole week after the arrest. In consequence, neither Yana nor anyone else would believe him if he talked about a prisoner 7,000 kilometres from Moscow, falsely accused of the crimes committed by a killer on the loose, and who was nonetheless able to solve the mystery on his own!

The press began giving the details of the police interviews with the murderer and the whole shocking picture emerged. Funnily enough, it corresponded exactly to my deductions.

Marina Moskalyova was the sixty-first victim. Her body had

been found on 14 June at a different location in the park. New this time was the metro ticket in her pocket, which provided the time and place of her last entry to a station.

They went through the CCTV footage at the station during the relevant time window and discovered that the woman met up with a man her own age, who accompanied her out of the station. She seemed very relaxed with him.

They learned her identity: a thirty-six-year-old woman living in a neighbourhood on the outskirts of Moscow with her young son. Witnesses stated that she had recently met a man in his early thirties, and that perhaps she had become involved in a relationship with him.

They had met several times and, before she went out for the last time, she left his mobile number with her son. The police had their man. They presented him with the evidence and the CCTV images, and first he confessed to killing Marina, then he boasted that he was the infamous Bitsa Park killer.

He was a thirty-two-year-old man called Alexander Pichushkin, who worked in one of the capital's supermarkets and lived with his mother in an apartment building that overlooked the park!

His home was searched and they found a chessboard, in whose squares Pichushkin had written numbers.

57	58	59	60	61			
49	50	51	52	53	54	55	56
41	42	43	44	45	46	47	48
33	34	35	36	37	38	39	40
25	26	27	28	29	30	31	32
17	18	19	20	21	22	23	24
9	10	11	12	13	14	15	16
1	2	3	4	5	6	7	8

Each number corresponded to a victim, and with astonishing accuracy he recalled the names and faces of those he had killed.

So the press nicknamed him the Chessboard Killer, but only after he had confessed to everything I had already deduced. He did, however, say that he would have carried on going beyond the squares on the board if the police had not caught him. When they tried to take him back to the origins of his criminal activity, he spoke about his passion for chess and his father leaving home and abandoning him. Then he summed it all up with a phrase that could only have come from a Russian, someone who grew up in the land of Dostoyevsky, Tolstoy, Lermontov, Chekhov and the rest: "Killing for the first time is like falling in love for the first time. Both are hard to forget."

In 2007, after his conviction on forty-nine counts of murder, a judge sentenced him to life imprisonment and he was incarcerated at Polyarnaya sova (Polar Owl) penal colony. Totally calm, he requested the addition of a further twelve victims, making a total of sixty-one, out of respect for the law of the chessboard that he adhered to!

Amusingly (if it's possible to include amusement here), the court ordered that the first fifteen years of his sentence be served in solitary confinement.

Just like the hero of "The Bet"!

Ultimately, his case was closed and everyone forgot him, while my case remained open and nobody knew a thing about it . . .

If it had been in my hands to do so, I would have requested a correction to the newspaper reports, adding another name to Pichushkin's list of victims: Zouhair Belkacem, a.k.a. Alexander Gazdanov, even though I was alive and "well".

It's often the case that we kill someone by keeping them alive . . .

Years went by, a thirteen-year-long tunnel that I entered with no light at the end and unable to go back.

Prisoners were released and others took their place. I heard about mobile phones with touchscreens and that took pictures, and the proliferation of instant messaging sites and social media where people expressed their views and shared images with their followers.

The world around me was changing and I was a prisoner of the void, without a present or a future. Governors, one after another, came to run the prison. They only knew what they read in the forged documents, which said I was accused of twelve murders...

The first four years of my detention were more lively, as I followed developments in the case of the serial killer. But then what?

What would I read in the papers now?

Change in power between Putin and Medvedev, another hostage siege at a school in Beslan, conflict with Georgia over Abkhazia and South Ossetia, crises with Ukraine and over Crimea, then intervention on the ground in the Syrian civil war that killed hundreds of thousands and made millions homeless.

All useless bullshit of no benefit whatsoever to a prisoner in the remotest spot in Siberia...

Of course I thought more than once about committing suicide, but two verses in the Sura of the Cow, which I read in a small Qur'an left behind by a released Chechen inmate, saved me from that compulsion:

> {Surely we will try you with something of fear and hunger, and loss of wealth and lives and crops; yet give glad tidings to the patient, (155) who say when they are struck by affliction, "Surely we belong to God, and to Him we will return." (156)} Verily the truth of God Almighty.

So I was more patient...

And because afflictions are sociable creatures by nature, a new, silent killer, unforeseen by me, infiltrated to crush what remained of the vigour of my youth.

*

Two guards joined forces to apathetically carry my emaciated body. One said to the other in annoyance, "When are they going to close this dismal place down. All of us, prisoners and guards, are going to die like rats!"

Traces of vomit on my beard, the disgust showed on the other's face as he looked into my glazed eyes. "He'll die like the others before him," he replied to his colleague. "What do you expect from a prison built on top of a region floating on a sea of uranium. The whole world has heard about the Chernobyl disaster, but what about what's happening here?"

"Funny you should mention Chernobyl, but I heard the American series is really good. It's received critical and popular acclaim, even though it's obviously biased against us in its discussion of the causes of the disaster . . ."

The other laughed as he replied, "In a few years' time they'll produce a second part called Krasnokamensk!"

Their banter turned to silence when we entered the infirmary. I shut my eyes to the unbearable brightness of the light and I heard the voice of the doctor saying with obvious indifference, "Put him over here and I'll see what I can do. You can both leave now . . ."

A whole minute passed, during which I managed to slowly open my eyes. Colours blurred in my distorted vision.

"Am I dreaming or what? Impossible! Zouhair, is that you?"

I looked at the blond doctor's face in disbelief. He was shaking me as he cried, "I'm Sergei. Sergei Kryachkov, your old friend in Moscow. Do you remember me?"

* * *

Letter from a Swiss nurse to her husband in Geneva dating from her time in Morocco. Lubna el-Afaoui translated it into Arabic and appended it to her dissertation on the toxic oil disaster of 1959, among the testimonies of foreign health workers concerning the effects of the disaster on the Moroccan victims. (The researcher preferred to translate and publish it unedited, despite it containing some personal and intimate details which may not be of any interest to the reader):

My beloved Loris,

I love you, and the only thing that distracts me from counting down the weeks, days and hours separating me from my return to Geneva and flinging myself into your warm embrace again is duty, which dictates I stay here until my humanitarian mission is done.

I know that things have gone contrary to both our expectations. I cut short our honeymoon in that beautiful hut in the Jura Mountains on the border between Switzerland and France and was forced to leave the passionate bed of our lovemaking after receiving that telegram from the Swiss Red Cross. The look of heartbreak so clear in your hazel eyes almost killed me, but such is my work, which you agreed to from the beginning ...

As I promised in our last all-too-short phone call, I am sending this letter to explain to you in tedious detail what happened from the moment we exchanged a final kiss at the airport until the second I picked up this pen to write.

On the plane I found it annoying the way some people talked disparagingly, almost contemptuously, of Morocco, simply because they come from a continent that they think grants them cultural superiority over others.

As long as they see this North African country from such a smug racist perspective, what motivated them to join the mission? Why do they knock the noble spirit of relief work that is blind to race, colour, ethnicity or religion?

Anyhow, as soon as we arrived we found a representative of the local Ministry of Health there to meet us. He welcomed us and arranged a slap-up luncheon in our honour, while affirming the Moroccan authorities' willingness to provide every assistance to facilitate our mission.

Actually, we found his behaviour a little odd …

We're on an urgent relief mission and the country is suffering the aftermath of a disaster, the likes of which I have never heard of before, and that makes the idea of organizing a party unimaginable, even if it was a nice expression of the generosity that we've heard Moroccans are renowned for.

The official rather limped over the subject of our delegation and complained of the paltry resources available and the inadequacy of the financial, technical and medical aid that has been trickling into Morocco's sea and air ports since the tragedy struck. There is also a lack of trained local staff able to deal with the complex situation, and he conveyed a message from the minister of health concerning the impossibility of his country meeting the needs of several thousand victims all at the same time …

Most of those present – nurses, doctors and experts of various nationalities, French, Swiss, Dutch, German, Canadian and Swedish – were shocked by what they heard, because it went against all the reassurances that we'd received in Switzerland concerning the cooperation of the World Health Organization and the International Red Cross to supply assistance – medicine, supplies, equipment, and kit for rehabilitating the injured – to those in need.

Some of us were bold enough to question the representative of the ministry, but he just repeated what he'd already said in different words and stressed how grateful the Moroccans were for our sacrifice and honest desire to help them in the crisis they were going through. Then he suspiciously withdrew!

We were told that the meeting in Geneva between delegates from the relevant Moroccan ministry and a group of Red Cross Societies had reached an agreement stipulating the creation of a specialist hospital to treat the victims as well as a number of feeder health facilities in the affected areas.

Anyway, I was sent to a centre near the city of Meknes and, after seeing the horror of what had happened, much worse than anything I'd heard, I no longer had a shadow of a doubt about how bad it was. Seeing is believing, not hearing …

I'm going to tell you everything, darling, as if you were watching a film at the cinema.

In rotten French the Moroccan driver explained that because the centre was located on the outskirts of one of the cities struck by the disaster, we had to drive along some unpaved roads. His battered vehicle jolted over and over, and the nausea I experienced made me be sick twice. I even had to take a strong sedative, which made me semi-anaesthetized and stopped me remembering the details of the route.

(I consider it my good fortune that you did not see me in the worst of states, something you have not seen before. Perhaps you would have had second thoughts about marrying me!)

The car stopped next to a building that seemed solid and well built, despite its obvious age. I thought we must be stopping for the driver to do something, but he gave me a shock by announcing that we had arrived at the designated health centre. He added that the building was originally a school built by the French during their presence in Morocco before it gained its independence and that it had been abandoned when they left. Some bright spark decided to turn it into an emergency medical centre for dealing with the aftermath of the disaster!

What about the agreement to build new facilities in carefully selected sites in a manner appropriate to the critical condition of victims of poisoning? No idea . . .

Devotion and the powerful desire to fulfil my mission (under whatever circumstances) stopped me engaging with the question, unaware that entering the place would confront me with an endless list of questions, the quest for answers to which would trap you in a set of Russian dolls, each question containing others!

I caught up with the brown-skinned driver who had walked halfway round the building towards the back entrance and I was shocked by the chaos, out of all proportion to the calm at the front.

Dozens of people of various ages, women wearing jilbabs or wrapped in a very large sheet, which I later learned is called a haik, and concealing their faces with a black veil so that only their eyes were visible, children barefoot or dressed in rags . . .

Men whose faces were all alike, old or young, because of pain . . .

Most of them walked with the help of crutch-like sticks, leaning on each other's shoulders. Signs of terrible, unbearable pain on their faces. Children, their heads shaved, crying and screaming either because of intense pain or their inability to cope with the heat, which I, accustomed as I am to a cool or moderate climate, had not anticipated.

I wondered why the sick and injured had been left like that, and suddenly two men appeared out of nowhere. One was wearing a white apron, suggesting he was probably a nurse, and the other wore a suit and brightly coloured tie and walked with a detestable swagger, an impression of arrogance only reinforced by the way he looked at me and whispered a few words in the ear of the man with the apron. That one started shouting and threatening the patients as he pushed them towards the wall as if they were a flock of sheep, not human beings, in the face of their desperate efforts to defend themselves and stave off their extreme pain.

A child fell over and gave a loud cry of terror and pain. His injured mother tried to help him, fighting her own difficulty in moving, but the man in the apron forestalled her with a shove that caused her to fall over too. All in the midst of the dazed remonstrances of the others, caught as they were between the abuse of the supposed nurse and coping with their serious health problems.

It was a horrific scene, Loris. Can a sane person treat another as if they were beneath them or as if they weren't even a human being?

I ignored the fatigue of the journey and the shock of what I had seen, and I lambasted the man in the white apron, expressing my blunt opposition towards him in clear and harsh terms. I know, Loris, that you get scared when I'm a little worked up, but the other arrogant man dealt with me belittlingly and used expressions in Arabic that nobody translated . . .

The Moroccan driver intervened and gently guided me inside the old building, where I found the French professor Gayle waiting to greet me along with Swedish expert Mellinson. They both said hello and advised me to have a good rest before starting work, which they hinted would be exhausting and under the most difficult conditions.

All of that, plus my inability to answer one very simple question: what is going on here?

My puzzlement did not last long, for I was also received by some of the women nurses working at the centre. Most of them, like me, had come from Europe as part of the humanitarian relief mission, but there were also some French nuns who had spent many years in Morocco and whose presence was not connected with the Red Cross or the disaster alone.

From what they were saying, I understood that the general sense of the mission members was that someone was obstructing their work in a manner that was deliberate and definitely premeditated ...

The agreement mandates the construction of new health facilities, but old, abandoned and unsuitable premises have been used ...

The WHO recommends providing the centre with advanced technical equipment and a specific number of beds and sheets. Then the equipment arrives and some of it is broken. The sheets are worn and ripped and the beds don't conform to the agreed specifications.

And that's saying nothing of the ongoing theft of supplies allocated to the victims ...

It's the same old one-two: not performing the required tasks in proper fashion, and having the appropriate justification ready ...

The nurses talked about a struggle going on behind the scenes, the heavy price of which is being paid by the disaster victims.

A political party wants to monopolize the issue of the toxic oil disaster for its own narrow political objectives. So, among ordinary Moroccans, those who did not have the good fortune to spend even a single day behind a school desk, ridiculous rumours are being promoted: we're conspiring to kill them; our medicines are poisonous or mixed with alcohol and pig fat, which are forbidden in their religion; and our real aim is to take them away from Islam and propagate Christianity among their children.

What is this nonsense, Loris?

There are so many victims and the situation cannot tolerate any procrastination or delay, yet they totally disregard our enormous efforts, just as they've disregarded the people themselves, while they scrabble over gains that I see as trivial!

I am a nurse experienced at dealing with wars and natural disasters. I've been working for years with the International Red Cross. I visited divided, exhausted Berlin at the end of the '40s, Korea during the war that ended with its partition at the beginning of the '50s, and Suez in Egypt only a few years ago ...

I promise you that the extraordinary nature of what I've been through here in Morocco is beyond my modest powers of description, even though it's a country that, unlike those I mentioned before, has not endured a conventional war of destruction!

The nurses informed me that the arrogant man who accompanied the man in the white apron is a party official. Having given himself bogus authority to supervise, his only task is to visit the centre from time to time. He incites the male and female Moroccan nurses, whom the delegation has been charged to train to take over in future, to disobey our instructions and guidance, and to deal with us with unjustified wariness . . .

You also know, my darling, that I am a sociable person, and I have had no difficulty engaging with people at work. I have become friends with Sister Josephine, a nurse who has spent many years in Morocco, during which this north African country has become dearer to her than her original country, France.

Josephine filled me in with what's going on. Then she took me to meet someone whom everyone here at the centre has fallen in love with, and I'm no exception to the rule . . .

Rest assured, my love, I'm speaking about a five-year-old boy, who enjoys our sympathy, just as his mysterious story invokes our bafflement.

He is also a victim of the disaster. One of those who survived . . .

The nurses, the nuns and Professor Gayle took it in turns to ask him his name, but he refused to answer. He just shook his head when he was asked about his parents' identity.

In the midst of their questioning, this mystery child shocked them with intellectual abilities way beyond his years. He understood our instructions with the greatest of ease, whether in Arabic or French. He has a powerful visual memory and learns astonishingly fast. And he has an amazing obsession with numbers . . .

Josephine took an early interest, and she got him some colourful toys, blocks with the Roman alphabet, and a set of picture books for children. The child studied the drawings and tried to read the contents, but with a striking habit: he arranged the books according to the colours of their covers, and he repeated the operation in a different way every morning. From this they understood that he had assigned a particular colour to each day of the week.

The medical staff and the patients too watched the child, with his slow clunky steps, make a walking tour of the beds to count them. He also counted the patients trickling into the centre. He would be highly upset if someone was missing from the medical team or an extra person had joined, as if it disturbed the numerical harmony he wanted.

He adjusted the balance of the world around him in his own unique way . . .

My arrival at the centre coincided with the second phase of his physiotherapy. It's true that I treat all my patients – be they temporary or permanent and required to stay at the centre because of their worsening condition – with equal attention, as demanded by the nature of my relief work. But I won't hide from you that I lavished special care on that child of unknown identity.

My God, he's so lovely, Loris!

His soft black hair tempts you to stroke it. His dark eyes bright with intelligence and innocence, the birthmark adorning his left cheek, his beautiful voice which, because it is so slow and such hard work for him, makes you sad.

We will have an angelic child like him, won't we?

I would stretch him out on the large mat and help him do exercises to strengthen his puny legs and other ones for his tiny hands by getting him to squeeze his fingers around coloured balls or pieces of pliable rubber. Then I would warm his atrophied muscles with large infrared lights.

He took care to arrange the rubber balls according to their colour and size. He counted them every time we began to train his muscles and asked to change the colour in accordance with the correspondence between the day of the week and a specific number he had in mind.

Strange requests, all of which demonstrated an almost pathological subjection to a rigid numerical system . . .

As expected, my extra concern for his condition naturally put me into fierce conflict with the party official . . .

During every one of what he considered his tours of inspection, he would upset us by harshly preventing the child from reading the books and looking at the pictures, claiming that they originated with the nuns, whose main concern was the propagation of poisonous ideas among Moroccan youth. I just laughed in his face and he was forced to leave the innocent child alone.

Don't worry, Loris, I'm as strong as you've always known me. I can stand up to him and stop him achieving his aims. But for how long? We won't be here for ever. From the administration of the Red Cross and the World Health Organization we hear rumours of six months, or a year maximum, but in the end we will leave, and what I fear most is the fate of that little boy and dozens of the injured after we've gone . . .

We are training the nurses and are preparing treatment schedules and cards for each patient. That should make the task of the Moroccan team easier after we've left. But the presence of that odious official and his ilk makes me very scared for the victims and their future treatment.

Nonetheless, I will be optimistic and put my trust in a merciful power that will not forget these poor people during their painful ordeal.

I will be back soon, my love. The bed in the hut in the Jura Mountains awaits. I still have so much to tell you . . .

Your true love, Veronica
17-11-1959

(16) The Absurdity of Fate

> A writer's first novel is typically akin to a testament.
>
> Éric Neuhoff

Tuesday, 29 October 2002
The Faculty of Literature and Humanities – Rabat:

I had always believed that the longest hours of my life were on Tuesday, 20 April 1999, when I and my students hunkered behind chairs and desks at Columbine High. We shook with terror as heavy gunfire continued and we expected Eric and Dylan to come and finish us off at any moment.

Then along came the slow hours that followed my first meeting with Lubna to rival those of Columbine . . .

When she looked at her watch with a graceful, studied movement, we suddenly realised that it had gotten very late, and staying any longer would be inappropriate. We said goodbye awkwardly. The scene seemed to correspond to when Scheherazade stopped talking in the tales of the *1001 Nights*. Lubna, however, promised to continue the story the next day and suggested we meet at the Faculty of Literature and Humanities at two in the afternoon.

After we left, Rachid made his objection plain. He had to work at the hotel until six, and it would be very difficult to get his boss to agree to let him leave early. I promised to relay to him every word I heard from her, like a good tape recorder, as he had done with the elderly waiter in Kenitra.

I spent the night and the following morning in my room at the hotel, counting down the minutes till it was time to meet. I went over the possible information and revelations Lubna might disclose about the complex case.

I also moved an idea that had seized me last night into the column headed: for immediate implementation . . .

My new novel would not be about my father's past in Morocco, but about my own journey to Morocco in search of his past!

*

Lubna seemed more relaxed when we met at two o'clock on the dot, although her external appearance was unchanged from the evening before: the same practical hairstyle, dreary, bland clothes and deliberate avoidance of any hint of adornment to remind those she encountered that she was still in her mid-thirties.

She greeted one of the guards with a warmth that indicated she knew him well, then invited me to sit down at a discreet spot in an empty lecture hall, which a class had just exited. On the table in front of us, she set down an Arabic copy of *A Moroccan Jigsaw Puzzle*, which I was able to recognize from its old-style printing and yellowing pages, another thick publication with an Arabic title, whose contents I could not discern, and a folder containing a large bundle of papers.

Her every action demonstrated that she was used to being alone. She filled the emptiness in her life with her daughter Jenan and immersed herself in a job, whose exact nature I did not know.

"I was a little anxious yesterday, afraid of my daughter waking up and hearing our conversation. She's thirteen now, so I try to balance the need to tell her the truth and the difficulty of dealing with a girl of her age."

"She's very pretty and looks like you, as I saw yesterday from her picture. I bet she's a lot like her father too, no?" I said this in a tone of encouragement, although I felt a pain inside given how long it had been since Ronald and Cindy had bothered to call or ask about me. She just gave a ghost of a smile to conceal the gleam in her eyes and deftly changed the subject: "I left Samir's house in the worst possible way. I was haunted by his family's bad-mouthing of me as a cursed devil woman who brought bad luck and destruction wherever she went. In their eyes I had caused the disappearance of one man and the death of another. So I chose to abandon everything, including my legal rights, and go back to my mother.

"A rerun to the letter of the scene of you going back to your mother's house in Rabat. How absurd!" I said with nervous humour.

She leant her elbows on the table and clasped her fingers in front of her as she shifted her gaze towards the large blackboard.

"What's really absurd is for other people to make me into something that fate never intended me to be. That was my mistake from the outset, when I agreed to marry Samir to escape the gossip of a society whose wheels of condemnation never stop turning whatever you do . . ."

She continued absently, "It wasn't easy for me to deal with my new situation as a widow under twenty-five, but I finally felt in control of my destiny. The first decision I took was to resume my studies at the Literature Faculty in Rabat and take on part-time, temporary jobs that would help me bring up my daughter and contribute to the household expenses. Then I could reopen the case of Rafiq's disappearance."

I felt I was on the path to understanding, so I said, "You went to Duwwar el-Hajj Kaddour . . ."

She gave a pleasant laugh, and I understood that my French pronunciation of the name had not been spot on. However, she quickly turned serious again, as if her laughter had been a flagrant sin that deserved punishment.

"I did not understand why the dying man was so insistent in saying the name of the village, so I went there and met the inhabitants. They welcomed me and treated me generously when they learned that I knew Samir and Rafiq. The mother of one of their former students insisted on inviting me for lunch."

"You Moroccans are very generous. I noticed that myself when I went with Rachid to Kenitra in search of the waiter."

She shrugged her shoulders in a gesture, whose meaning I did not get, and continued, "It was a small two-room house. I discovered that the former student's grandfather was bedbound, completely unable to move. Because Moroccans are experts in the art of talking about their problems, the mother told me all about her struggles caring for her disabled father, a victim of the poisonous American oil, and how his condition had deteriorated from extreme pain when walking and moving the limbs to total paralysis. She said that a large number of the village's elderly suffered from the same symptoms. I went back to Rabat in shock, and I asked my mother about the disaster. She said it had happened quite a few years before I was born and that Meknes and its district were one of the worst affected areas. She gave me more or less the same information as your companion Rachid gave last night. I wasn't satisfied, or to be precise, I had a sense that this subject directly concerned me, and without consciously deciding, I made a beeline for the unfinished draft of *A Moroccan Jigsaw Puzzle*."

She opened the folder, which contained old typewritten sheets of paper, and said, "I reread Rafiq's draft and it was easy for me to reach a more sensible conclusion . . ."

I interrupted her, "Rafiq Khalidi's real aim in writing the novel was not to produce a conventional work of crime fiction, as you did, but to revive the forgotten case of the toxic oil . . ."

As harmoniously as a professional choir, Lubna completed my sentence: ". . . of which he was a victim, a fact he kept from me. A loud alarm was ringing inside, linking what I had seen and what the student's mother said about the old man, and what I knew about Rafiq. The same symptoms without exception, difficulty in walking, problems speaking and a weak heart muscle. But the question was the nature of his relationship with Saleh and Jamila, Steve McMillan and the rest of the novel's characters, given that he came from a family who lived in Meknes, nowhere near Kenitra."

"Didn't you think about Saleh and Jamila's son, even though he was only mentioned in passing and plays no part in the action?"

"Of course I did, and as a result I decided to proceed in my own way and delve into Rafiq's past without reference to his uncle's family."

"How so?"

She took a deep breath that coincided with my realisation that our suddenly turning up on her doorstep had forced her to become a memory retrieval machine: "Before his disappearance, Rafiq used to go and visit an old lady who lived on her own, an old friend of his deceased mother. I had no problem locating her and I often went to visit her. She spoke with sadness about what had happened to the house after the uncle's family got hold of it. When I asked her about Rafiq, she said that his mother, her late friend, had been married to a self-made small businessman. She worked as a nurse and when she failed to become pregnant, which was having a bad effect on her relationship with her husband, she decided to adopt a five-year-old child. That's why they tried to kick him out after the mother's death, seeing as he wasn't a legitimate son in their eyes."

"So he hid his true origins from you, then. Didn't he tell you anything about Kenitra and his real family?"

"No. But the seesawing between reality and what was supposedly a novelist's imagination could not be concealed from me. That was confirmed later on, when I was working on my thesis. I obtained old issues of a well-known Moroccan newspaper that had covered the disaster right away in 1959. Back then there were conflicting reports over the cause of mysterious cases of paralysis, or what ordinary people called knock-knee. Then two experts from Oxford University discovered that cooking oil was responsible and that it contained the substance triorthocresyl phosphate. After investigation it turned out to be present in engine lubricant for fighter planes that were stationed at the US airbases in Morocco, especially the Nouasseur Base near Casablanca. The oil was kept in drums with an identification number. Do you know what the number was?"

I was at a loss, but like a detective revealing her hand and solving the riddle, she said, "33137. The same number as appears in Saleh's notebook in the unfinished draft of *A Moroccan Jigsaw Puzzle.*"

I swallowed with extreme difficulty as it dawned on me that all the signs pointed towards my father's guilt. After a brief silence, I asked her, "Okay, why did you decide to write a dissertation on the disaster?"

She picked up the thick printed volume, browsed the pages for a few seconds, then said, "During my basic research on Rafiq's connection with the issue, it became clear to me that there had been a cover-up or deliberate amnesia around what happened, despite the disaster destroying thousands of lives. So I swore to myself I would uncover the whole story for the present generation, so it might be . . . might be . . ."

Emotion overwhelmed her and I took her hand as a sign of genuine support and completed what she had been unable to say: ". . . the best dedication to those gone . . ."

She wiped away a tear that slipped from her eye, forcing herself to maintain her composure. "I did everything in my power, as your colleague indicated yesterday, and as the halls and corridors of this university can attest. After considerable effort I reached the conclusion that the real disaster was not the thousands of people being poisoned, but the way they were treated afterwards. Your country refrained from making an effective contribution to the rescue efforts mounted by the World Health Organization, for fear that it would be directly accused of involvement in the scandal. Patients were kicked out of the treatment centres once the foreign aid team left, and they were morally betrayed when the Moroccan businessmen involved were released in dubious and questionable circumstances, even though some of them had been handed death sentences which were never carried out. I'm a member of one of the victims' associations, and last year for example we made the public prosecutor at the Rabat Appeal Court look into the matter, with the aim of obtaining a copy of the judgement of the Special Court of Justice for the years 1959 and 1960. We discovered that the criminal file for the case has disappeared from the court archives and that in the prison records there is no trace of the names of those accused. It is as if the case has never existed!"

My face went bright red, and I imagined that the spacious lecture hall was a prison about to suffocate me, and I shouted in distress, "Let's go, please!"

*

I felt better when we sat down on a bench in the faculty's small garden and a gentle breeze ruffled my hair. "Perhaps now I understand what Rafiq meant when he wrote in his novel, 'A Moroccan is unluckier than Sisyphus. He expends his life pushing the boulder of his oppression to the summit, then ends up crushed beneath it!'"

Lubna was about to respond when I noticed that a middle-aged woman was standing in front of her. She shook my hand then embraced Lubna, and they exchanged some words in Arabic that seemed warm and friendly before she moved slowly off.

"The dissertation also helped me to find out a piece of information that mattered to me as a woman. I'm speaking about the identity of Veronica, the woman to whom Rafiq dedicated his novel. My supervisor helped me write a letter to the World Health Organization in an effort to obtain living testimonies from foreign medical staff who took part in the relief effort. Because a lot of them were already dead, the WHO forwarded me the details of quite a small number of people, Swedes, Germans, French, Dutch, and a Swiss woman called Veronica Decker, a retired nurse who had worked with the Red Cross in hotspots around the world. I wrote to her and she responded enthusiastically to the idea and showed a willingness to cooperate. Then, by express post, she sent me some photographs and photocopies of personal letters she had exchanged with her husband during her time in Morocco. She had no embarrassment in providing them to me, as long as they would be of use to my research."

She took some sheets of paper protected by plastic out of the folder. I scrutinized their contents and learned that they were letters written in French. I was absorbed in reading one of them for a few minutes, and then exclaimed, "The detailed information in this letter leaves no doubt that the child in question is Rafiq! The physical description, the dazzling mental powers, and the sympathy with his heart-wrenching condition!"

She nodded and I had a sneaking feeling that she had offered all the information in her possession and that, along with this meeting, the whole case was coming to an end. I found no other way to conclude it than to ask her, "Forgive me, Lubna, I know this is personal, but I haven't shaken off an urge to understand this. How do you maintain your powerful hope for Rafiq's return, even after all these years? I'm a woman, and I know all too well that women always tend to think the worst..."

While thinking she played with a lock of her hair, an action that seemed quite out of character for this shy, reserved woman. Then she said, "I'll give you an example before I answer. Farida, the woman who said hello to me just now, is a university professor working at this faculty. She's a close neighbour of mine in Hassan. All of us know the story of her daughter Jehan, which exploded at the beginning of the '90s with the death of her fiancé, an officer in the military, when his fighter plane crashed in the desert. In due time she got to know a French doctor of Moroccan origins and a romantic relationship developed. They were close to announcing their formal engagement when the pilot suddenly reappeared and it was clear to all that he hadn't died but had been held captive for a long period. The doctor withdrew from her life and chose to go to Bosnia-Herzegovina at the peak of the war there, as part of a United Nation's mission. Things did not go as they ought between the bewildered Jehan and her former fiancé and they split up. Reports conflicted as to whether the doctor had died or was still alive. The war ended in 1995, but there was no trace of him. Jehan finished her studies and did brilliantly at her job, but she closed the door on any idea of getting involved with someone. She hasn't given up her faith in the missing doctor's return one day, although logic insists that's impossible . . ."

She let out a heated sigh and then with the calmness and confidence of someone certain she said, "We are all looking for a certain value to our lives, even though the matter is essentially straightforward. Life acquires its value from our ability to love and be loved. Without that, it's just a waste of time. The answer to your question, Christine, is hard and easy at the same time. I maintain my hope in Rafiq's return because waiting is a gift, at times maybe even an art!"

* * *

🔍 elkhabar.com – Home – Crime:

Sex, Blackmail and Murder: the solution to mysterious disappearance of husband of prominent legal activist three years ago

Thursday, 2 November 2016 – 19:33

When our website published three separate news reports at different times (see in chronological order the articles: Husband of prominent legal activist vanishes in mysterious circumstances, Police investigate human remains at Sidi Abed Plage, and Student at Souissi Medical School kills unemployed graduate and hands herself in) nobody, including our crime reporters, expected the clues were all connected to one case!

A Video Clip Shuffles the Pack:

We begin bringing the pieces together with the third report, namely S. H. (23) a fourth-year student at Souissi University Medical School handing herself in to the police after stabbing R. B. (27), an unemployed geology graduate, to death with a knife. Her confessions prompted the police to delve deeper, and members of the investigation team visited the deceased's home and searched his room. An expert from the forensic science division analysed the hard drive of the victim's laptop computer and retrieved explicit images and video clips of the female student, confirming what she had told the police.

Another video clip, which had been placed inside a hidden directory, came as a shocking surprise and changed the direction of the case!

According to a trusted source, the video had been filmed on a mobile phone and contained shots of a young woman attempting to drag a body wrapped in a blanket out of a bedroom. Technical analysis confirmed that the young woman was the student S. H., but she vehemently denied any link to the clip, which she said was fake, and stuck to her original story that she had killed R. B. because she was being blackmailed.

A Surprise DNA Result and the Intelligence of a Young Officer:

Meanwhile, the result of DNA tests performed on human remains discovered on a plot of land bordering Sidi Abed Plage (the second story) stunned investigators. The remains belonged to Professor Younis Belkacem, who had disappeared three years before, as we reported at the time (the first story), but no trace of him came to light and the police investigation reached a dead-end.

At this point, the intuition and sharp wits of a young police officer came into play. He resolved to delve into the personal life of the doctor, setting aside the formalities of his profession. He also undertook a thorough and detailed review of the female student's academic record to confirm two crucial facts: the professor's multiple relationships with women (despite his care to keep them under wraps) and that he had taught S. H. in her first year at medical school.

Two pieces of information that put a noose around S. H.'s neck. She cracked and provided new detailed confessions that allowed the police to fit all the pieces of the puzzle together.

A Suspect Relationship outside College Walls:

According to the female student, the story began during her first year at medical school when she got to know the professor. She admired him first as a successful and capable teacher and then as a handsome and very attractive man. Despite the significant age difference between them, she felt that he was becoming close to her in a way that went beyond the normal relationship between a female student and her teacher. Her folly drove her to risk giving it a go, all the while ignoring mutterings among other female students over the professor's multiple relationships with women and the talk about the mystery of his only son's disappearance in Russia in 2002.

The relationship between S. H. and her teacher developed. They met repeatedly at a beach house owned by the professor at Sidi Abed Plage, which he visited constantly, though to avert suspicions he did not drive there in his own car. The relationship came to an ominous end, when on the night of Saturday, 2 March 2013, the student was shocked by the doctor having a sudden heart attack (caused by over-exertion) that left him dead in bed.

Turning to a Friend for Help:

S. H. was on the verge of collapse, afraid that it might be possible to link her with the discovery of her lover's body. Then an idea flashed in her mind: to call R. B., a young man she had met on social media who had more than once expressed his liking for her and his desire to get closer to her. She had only responded with aversion and rejection because of his lamentable social position.

After making his way to the beach house – at the female student's request – R. B. was stunned by what he saw. But he composed himself with amazing speed and ordered S. H. to wrap the body in a blanket to help carry it outside under cover of darkness and bury it in a nearby plot of land using the garden tools he found in the residence.

R. B. and S. H. completed the desired task, taking advantage of the dark night and the absence of the local security guard, and disposed of the body of a doctor whose sick lust had led to his demise. They then cleaned the house to remove any evidence that the deceased had been there.

The Price Tag:

S. H. believed she was rid of the nightmare for good, but only a week later she received a video via WhatsApp that R. B. had taken without her knowledge. The video showed her on her own trying to drag the blanket-wrapped corpse of the doctor, and was accompanied with the explicit threat of sending it to the police!

The price for R. B.'s silence was obvious: submission to his desires and his demands for money over a period of three years. During that time, he drained her body and distraught mind, making use of the video and other intimate photos that he took during their encounters, to threaten to expose her first as a criminal and then as a loose woman, nothing like the image she promoted of herself as a successful student well-liked among her fellows at medical school. Her academic performance suffered and she isolated herself by limiting most of her social contacts. The biggest bombshell came when she fell pregnant, despite all the precautions she had taken.

A Disastrous Fix:

S. H. confronted her accomplice R. B. with the fact of her pregnancy. He responded coldly and indifferently, which only doubled the devastated student's determination to take her revenge. So she pretended she wanted to see him and as soon as they were alone together in a dwelling owned by one of his friends, she suddenly stabbed him, killing him instantly. She then handed herself in to the police, having realised that her future was ruined for good.

S. H. was brought to justice in the midst of widespread shock: among her fellow medical students who had previously supported her; the doctors, teachers and patients at the professor's clinic who were his friends; and the family of R. B. who blamed everything that had happened on their son's unemployment, a university graduate who had knocked at every door with his degree certificate in search of a respectable job commensurate with his qualifications, but in vain, so forcing him to walk a minefield that ended with him dead and buried before turning thirty!

Comments (7) Opinions expressed in comments reflect the views of their authors and do not represent those of elkhabar.com

1 – Salima: I'm confused. I don't know who to feel sorry for in this dreadful tragedy!

---

2 – Abdelkadir: If you're in Morocco, don't be amazed.

---

3 – Abu Rabie: This is the result of sending our daughters to university.

---

4 – Hassan el-Maghribi: The girl student is the cause of it all and deserves to be punished. The proof is her ability to seduce a thirty-year-old guy and an old man in his sixties.

---

5 – Liga Lover: Who should get the golden ball, Messi or Ronaldo?

---

6 – Um Rayyan her husband's princess: My YouTube channel presents recipes from Turkish cuisine. Sign up to my official page on Facebook.

---

7 – Amin: The doctor's son is really lucky. I bet he went to Russia, got involved with a gorgeous blonde like Maria Sharapova and forgot all about Morocco!

(16') My Escape to Freedom

The free man is really one who owns nothing.
Jules Verne

Monday, 28 October 2019
Nur Sultan Nazarbayev international airport – Nur Sultan
(Astana formerly):

I could not stop my fingers trembling as I took back my passport, and one of the security staff came over and asked, "Are you all right, sir? Do you require any assistance?"

I made light of it and replied, "No, nothing. I guess I didn't sleep too well last night."

His mouth flashed a dazzling smile and he said warmly. "You'll get plenty of sleep on the plane. Have a good journey, and we hope you come back to Kazakhstan again!"

He then directed me down the walkway to the departure lounge. I looked for an empty seat and clutched my small bag closer. I happened to turn towards the monitor screen, which confirmed the need to wait forty-five minutes until the bus would come to take the passengers to the plane bound for Dubai.

I opened my passport and reread my fake details, whispering inaudibly, "Bastards, they really are master forgers!"

I stretched my legs in relaxation and closed my eyes, confident that my escape from the hell of Russia had become a reality, not fiction.

I would finally enjoy a good night's sleep, something I had been deprived of not for just one night, but for an entire seventeen years!

*

The succession of shocks I endured during my incarceration at Krasnokamensk was enough to stop me believing that my old friend was in front of me at the infirmary. Plus, the severity of my illness helped further complicate the situation, which forced him to handle me more circumspectly, and so I was busy for a time seeking a convincing explanation ...

The line dividing fiction from life is barely visible, and if what is happening to me is make-believe, then one must recognise that structurally, all novels contain a turning point!

In just one session of treatment, it would have been impossible for Sergei to share the finer details of the past years with me. So he concealed the fact that he knew me and impressed on the guards that they had to bring me for further treatment sessions.

Sergei Kryachkov, my intellectual friend and companion at the university hostel who was dazzled by the literary culture of his country. He fell in love with a girl but was not brave enough to confess to her what was bubbling in his heart. So I responded to her temptation and stole her from him like any other bastard, thereby rewarding his trust with undeserved betrayal.

He had put on weight over the years and acquired a gruffer voice. His blond beard had also grown longer, but he still wore thick glasses. My visual memory found absorbing his new image as a thirty-six-year-old difficult.

For his part, he found it difficult to recognise me to begin with, given that prison had turned me into a walking skeleton. It seems, however, that some distinguishing marks, which time had failed to erase, remained in spite of everything.

Olga Kuznetsova met her death at the Dubrovka Theatre siege as a result of complications from inhaling the gas. The drug Naloxone failed to save her, like dozens of others. The university held a memorial for her, and she was buried in Moscow's Vagankovo Cemetery along with other victims of the operation.

It did not occur to anyone that I had been there with her, especially when the authorities denied it and the Moroccan Embassy stated in its belated communiqué that Zouhair Belkacem was a Moroccan student who had gone missing for reasons unconnected to the hostage-taking.

There was also a new explanation, whose reasonableness convinced everyone: I had fallen victim to a criminal gang active in the capital that took advantage of my recent arrival in Moscow, killed me for whatever I had on me, and dumped my body somewhere.

My mother did not believe what was being said and travelled to Moscow several times to look for me. She met Sergei and subjected him to something akin to an interrogation about my movements and relationships before my disappearance. She met representatives from the Moroccan Embassy and the Association of Moroccan Students in Russia, who were unable to provide her with a single useful piece of information.

She did everything she could, Sergei always by her side, but to no avail. She returned each time to Morocco alone, her hopes of finding any trace of me, or even my dead body, dashed.

I asked Sergei if my father had accompanied her on her many trips to Moscow. He said no, something which I found odd and that troubled me.

My Russian friend finished his studies and began to practise at a government hospital in Moscow, and he was busy writing his first novel. Understandably, he forgot all about me. Then his relationship with one of his fellow doctors became serious and they got married and had a beautiful baby girl, whose birth seemed to herald a happy future.

Until his life was turned upside down . . .

I know that's an overused cliché, and experience proves that life is a series of upheavals that only end with you in a hole two metres long and one wide, but I haven't found any better way to express the change in my friend's situation.

The hospital management was involved in a medical business deal, whose details Sergei was following. He discovered the presence of medicines that were adulterated or out of date as well as large quantities of thallium, which he knew was only used to carry out poisonings.

He tried to object and refused to sign the documents approving the supplies, despite being promised a large commission. So they set out the options, one of which he had to accept: sign off the deal, exile to Siberia, or never see his wife and little girl again.

He chose exile, and when he arrived here a month ago to work as a prison doctor, he understood that the affair was much bigger that simply being punished by banishment from the capital.

They were planning to kill him slowly . . .

Sergei said that this Siberian city contained Russia's largest uranium mine. And leaving aside the figures and incomprehensible technical terms of interest only to experts, I understood that the increasing production (largely directed towards the Angarsk nuclear reactor close to Lake Baikal) had helped turn the city into a nuclear waste dump. Radiation levels in Krasnokamensk were ten times higher than normal, which explained the succession of prisoners' deaths recently.

My old friend thus explained to me everything that had happened over the previous years.

But what should I expect from just one person, when a whole state had forgotten me?

What was the point of what I was hearing, since the rule had been known for decades: nobody leaves Krasnokamensk Prison except as a corpse!

*

Sergei thought things over for a few days and came up with a single risky solution: to make everyone believe that I really had left the Siberian prison as a corpse ...

A solution with only two possible outcomes: the success of his attempt to liberate me from my icebound hell or, if the plan was discovered, the pair of us being sentenced to death.

My friend injected me with an anaesthetic that he had told me would cause me to lose consciousness and temporarily lower my heart beat, making it easier to smuggle me out of the prison. When he saw the signs of terror on my face, he reassured me that he knew what he was doing and that there were no side effects to worry about.

If the situation hadn't been so grave, I would have burst out laughing. Hadn't my body been turned into a site for experimentation that had gone on for seventeen years? An unknown gas one hundred times stronger than morphine, the drug Naloxone, mysterious drugs that weakened my muscles before I left the hospital in Moscow, radiation from nuclear waste in prison, and now an anaesthetic with an unpronounceable name!

There was nothing I could do. Doesn't the Moroccan proverb say, the dead can do nothing when their corpse is being washed?

Sergei put me in a black body bag, in which he concealed a few holes so I could breathe. Then he told the guards that after several visits to the infirmary for treatment my condition had worsened and I had died.

The Russian doctor exploited the fact that death was a commonplace occurrence for the administration, given the ongoing illness and deaths of prisoners and even guards, most of whom were old, and whose poor health could not take the heavy doses of radiation they were exposed to.

There were even unconfirmed reports that the authorities in Moscow had decided to close the prison and transfer the guards and inmates to other prisons. In his report, Sergei linked my death to the length of my stay at the prison and my weak body's succumbing to severe illness.

Sergei, as the person responsible for signing death certificates and supervising burials, stressed the need to dispose of my body fast, for fear that it should become what he termed a ticking dirty bomb and make the situation worse. When the ambulance carried me out of the prison to "bury" me in the city cemetery, I learned that there wasn't the slightest difficulty in bribing its driver and the two accompanying guards. All of them rued their rotten luck at having landed here and were united in their anger towards the authorities, who had yet to act seriously to transfer them.

They worked together lowering an empty coffin into the grave ready to receive my body. Having collected their fee from Sergei, the two guards returned to the prison as if nothing had happened . . .

*

"Why have you risked your life and future for me? What you've done could be discovered at any moment!"

"Do you think I'm foolish enough to trust two guards and an ambulance driver? They're willing to sell me out to anyone who pays more and might turn my time here into a nasty series of threats and blackmail. As I told you before, helping your escape from Krasnokamensk is a prelude to my own departure. I've got everything ready to escape with my wife and daughter. I didn't envisage staying in Siberia for ever, then you suddenly appeared, like a distant memory of a beautiful time, and I felt required to save you, even if that involved an uncertain gamble. But on your own testimony, we're a people who loves gambling, even if it means losing everything!"

"I don't deserve your sacrifice. I sold you cheap in exchange for my desire to get close to Olga . . ."

"Haven't I told you that you've been in prison so long you've lost the ability to understand life properly? Olga was a ridiculous adolescent love. She left my heart soon after her death. Time, my friend, can help us forget everything, especially when it's to do with love. That's reality, despite writers' insistence on believing the opposite."

"Sergei attacking literature and detracting from its value? Impossible!"

"Of course not. And the proof is that I've kept the draft of a novel that I will finish and publish later on. The most powerful lesson I've learned from literature is not to rely on it in our constant attempts to understand reality. Life is lived, not read in books."

"I remember how in your bones you believed in the greatness of your country and rejected any criticism of its methods. But you have been forced to give bribes and deal with people-trafficking networks to obtain forged passports and leave at the earliest opportunity..."

"The cunning of history is revealed in its ability to put any of us before two very complicated choices: to lose your life in exchange for sticking to your ideals or to lose your principles in exchange for staying alive. I will leave for Britain soon. Some here will accuse me of treason, but today I am married and have a daughter, neither of whom should be held guilty for my choices. What would be truly contemptible would be to sacrifice them to satisfy ideas that no one but me believes in."

"I'll never forget your kindness as long as I live..."

"Nietzsche says that someone who fights monsters must take care not to become one themselves. My only consolation is that what I have done for you proves that I have not lost my humanity. By the way, to assure you that I have not renounced literature, the novel *A Gentleman in Moscow* by Amor Towles came out three years ago. I recommend you read it as soon as you get back to Morocco, unless, that is, my country has turned into a terrifying nightmare for you and you never think about visiting it again, even if through the portal of reading!"

*

I sat down in my seat on the plane. Next to me there was a young blonde woman, whose European features indicated she was probably a tourist. Her eyes were glued to the screen of her mobile phone, but a look of reproach from a pretty member of the cabin crew forced her to put it in her handbag and turn towards me with a shy smile on her face.

I had lain low for days in an isolated house on the outskirts of the city of Irkutsk overlooking Lake Baikal. Sergei had rented it earlier to facilitate his subsequent departure and stocked it with everything I needed. My health improved a little and I regained a small part of my vitality, benefitting from the moderate climate and clean, invigorating air in a, to me, unknown part of Siberia, which I associated with frozen tundra, prison and death.

It would be too early to say I was well. My frail body was going to need more than a few days in the mountains to get its strength back. A long diagnostic journey awaited to determine its list of illnesses and complaints.

But I was free, and that was enough . . .

After that, I moved on to the suburbs of Tomsk, the city my friend came from. A relative of his welcomed me there and took very good care of me on Sergei's instruction. I shaved my head and trimmed my beard and stared into the mirror for a long time. I made really sure that Alexander Gazdanov had been buried forever in the empty coffin, allowing Zouhair Belkacem to be resurrected.

We waited for the signal from a middleman to take the overland route to the border with Kazakhstan, where another middleman gave me forged documents that Sergei had paid a fortune for. The guy spent days training me to use a touchscreen phone fitted with a technology called GPS, a new generation laptop, and Internet sites in their latest form, which differed from what I had been accustomed to at the beginning of the century. That was to forestall any unexpected event that might expose the truth of my ignorance of this strange technology. I crossed the Russian-Kazakh border without problems, then went to the capital and from there to the airport with a prior reservation.

The plane took its place on the runway in preparation for take-off, and the young woman said in English, "I wish they'd invent a technology that lets us use our phones during take-off. They made me interrupt a fun conversation with my friend in Munich!"

"Rest assured, they will invent it one day. The world is constantly developing, Miss, and everything is changing so fast. Astana itself is now called Nur Sultan!"

* * *

Some of what happened the night of Tuesday, 23 March 1965:

She styled her hair the way he liked it, flowing down unplaited over her shoulders as far as her lower back, and applied kohl to her eyes. Then she concealed last night's bruise under her eye with powder that she hid beneath the yellow blanket in the closet.

Fortunately for her, after a long unbroken sequence of days working at the clinic she had been granted a few days off. Otherwise the new bruise would have been the subject of jokes from those ugly female colleagues of hers who envied her. They took any opportunity (and there were many) to mask their gloating with manufactured pity and besiege her ears with advice. She had to demand a divorce, they all concurred, from a husband who had turned her face into a punchbag that he used to test his skills on an almost daily basis.

The doctor in charge (whose name begins with the sacred letter B) would take it as a perfect chance to renew his offer of a clandestine marriage once she had divorced her husband, or to at least embark on an affair away from prying eyes (a Moroccan area of expertise). All for the simple reason that his aristocratic mother rejected any possibility of her son marrying a wretched girl from society's lower class.

All of them could go to hell. She loves her husband and never considered the possibility of abandoning him.

She applied a deep red lipstick, the one that a few days ago in a sudden and rare moment of serenity between them, he had told her he really liked.

She remembered how he whispered in her ear as he said it. She bit her lower lip and sighed heatedly, in the near certainty that she was living with two husbands, or more accurately two men in the same body!

The first was a diurnal creature, one no different to the guy who had seen her for the first time – a few months before independence – leaving her family's house heading for work at the clinic, which was run by the Christians at the time. He swore he was going to marry her, even if that was the last decision he ever took.

The second was a creature of the night, like a troll in a granny's fairy tale, and she had been hitched to him for ten years. He would storm into the house every night after midnight to give her a sound beating and gratuitously insult her for all the defeats he'd suffered in life.

She put on a new dress cut off the shoulders and back that she had bought from a shop her friend had told her about. It stocked items smuggled in from the north at the border with Ceuta.

She felt the dress was a bit too revealing, even though she was at home. But she also remembered what her friend had said about today's men being dazzled by what they saw on cinema screens and how they lost their minds to a wink from Marilyn Munroe, a smile from Claudia Cardinale or a glance from Sofia Loren. This was, she said, a dangerous development that meant traditional forms of seduction were no longer sufficient to arouse men's instincts, and if she neglected to take care of her appearance, her husband would look elsewhere.

What her friend said made her angry because she was more confident in his fidelity than in the fact of her being alive.

True, he constantly insulted her, but she was sure that he wasn't sleeping with anyone else. And that was sufficient reason to endure his foibles. A woman cannot forgive another woman sharing her husband, but anything less than that she might forgive . . .

Anyway, her friend wasn't married yet and was expending the youth and femininity she had left to snare a victim to share the rest of her life with her. Still, she was very nice and a fiendish expert on sexual topics that women took the greatest pleasure in discussing at their closed gatherings.

Tonight would be a new beginning for their relationship. Spring had arrived and he was in a wonderful mood when he told her he would be leaving at dawn to deliver an order to Casablanca. He promised to head straight back for them to spend an unforgettable night together, and said that he had really been "missing" her.

She stood in front of the mirror bisected by a crack (the visible remains of a previous fight) to tie the belt of her white silk robe. She contemplated her body as if discovering it for the first time.

A thirty-two-year-old woman (if the calculations of the Moroccan civil registry office were correct), but she was exhausted. Bruises and scars were visible on her side, her left thigh and her upper back. Anyone who examined her features would see that the gleam had gone out of her eyes.

But despite it all, she clung on to hope . . .

Hope for what?

She didn't know!

During the first five years of their marriage, she told herself time and again that the cause of her husband's frenzied outbursts was her failure to give birth. She was afraid that he would give in to his mother and brother and divorce her, but was delighted that he stuck with her, although at the same time she was saddened by the fact that she wasn't infertile. A renowned French specialist, who had declined to leave after independence, had examined her. She had to keep quiet though, for fear of the effect on her husband's already precarious state of mind.

How would a traditional, practically illiterate man, who had made his little wealth himself after migrating at a young age from the countryside, accept that it was his fault?

She loved him or, more accurately, loving him was her oxygen, and so did the impossible to please him. A few years back, seeing as God did not wish to grant them a son of their own, she had been able to persuade him to adopt a child to ease their loneliness and give their lives a new spirit, even though she knew that his mother wouldn't like the idea.

Taking advantage of the closure of the health centre near the ten-kilometre point of the Duwwar el-Hajj Kaddour road that had been dedicated to the treatment of victims of the poisoned oil disaster and where she had been trained by foreign experts, she decided to keep a little boy whose origins were a mystery. He was five and had gained the sympathy of the relief team because of his marked intelligence and his suffering from a litany of health complaints that such an innocent and beautiful child did not deserve.

She chose the name Rafiq (kind one) for him, in the hope that fate would be kind to her and her husband.

The hands of the clock showed it was nearly midnight. She opened the door to her bedroom and headed with deliberate steps towards the child's room. She found him sleeping, although she was sure he was only pretending, as he always did.

He understood everything going on around him to a level far beyond his eleven years and had a penetrating, silent stare that had often been the reason her husband had stepped back from dealing with her severely.

She loved him from the moment she saw him and understood why patients, doctors and nurses at the centre (Moroccans and foreigners) were united in their love for him. Once she had been able to obtain custody of him after going back to Meknes and getting into a long struggle with complex administrative procedures to prove that he had been abandoned, she swore to herself that she would take care of him.

First, because he deserved it and, second, because she saw in him a prop to prevent her marriage falling apart.

His lofty, almost arrogant manner of speaking (despite his problems articulating) together with his command of many refined French words and expressions indicated that he came from a family that was rich, bourgeois or aristocratic, or whatever term meaning that he did not hail from the remote district around the temporary health centre. Perhaps he was there by accident or for some unknown reason he had not revealed or maybe didn't even know.

Bit by bit, the child relaxed with her and lost the fear that had accompanied him at the health centre. He began to reveal to her some of what he knew about his origins.

He said that his real name was Saleh and his father was called Slimane and his mother Malika. They had lived in a large house and were always quarrelling. A very tall and bulky blond man called Steve was always coming round to stay up late talking with his father and he sometimes played with him. He would always make sure to give him a delicious piece of chocolate.

He remembered the details of the last meeting between the giant man and his father very well. They had argued and Slimane had written some numbers on a piece of paper next to him, which the child had easily committed to memory.

33137

After the blond man had left, his father added some other words and letters to the paper, which Rafiq's or, as he was known before, Saleh's, memory snapped up:

33137 42F
STEVE MCMILLAN

Then he put the paper in his pocket.

A few days later, his mother left him at his grandfather's house and he was never to see her or his father again, particularly after he moved with an elderly nanny to a farm in a distant location. Playing with some children who entered a large warehouse and found a number of oil drums, the boy was amazed to see that the numbers written on them were the same as those his father had noted down on the piece of paper:

33137

Underneath the numbers were some words whose meaning he did not understand at the time, but his memory retained them and he copied them onto a piece of paper in front of his new mother:

US Army

A matter of days later, a terrible fire broke out at the farm and it was every man for himself. He got lost and nobody spared a thought for him until a man with a long beard and dressed in a jilbab found him. He looked after him for a while, then took him to the centre set up by the Christians since he was unable to keep him for good.

Rafiq spoke with passion to overcome the difficulties he had articulating his words but, despite the details he was providing, his adoptive mother did not grasp their meaning. So she chose to remain silent, afraid that he might reveal other information or even a longing to return to his real mother. She tried gradually to convince him that he needed to forget it all, now that he was living in a new home with a new mother who would never abandon him.

She was well aware that the closure of the centre, the expulsion of the patients, and the disappearance of the equipment for medical rehabilitation had put an end to any possibility of his being cured or even living with his chronic illness, even if in exchange he did enjoy awesome mental abilities. He had an exceptional memory which easily retained every line of a book his eyes fell upon, and his obsession with mental arithmetic and maths made him the envy of his peers.

On one occasion, Madame Dulagard, the Christian maths teacher at the government school, invited her to come and see her. The woman tried to explain many complicated technical words, of which the nurse with only an elementary school certificate understood nothing apart from talk of a photogenic or photographic memory, or something like that. She also said that the child's IQ was way above average and that he felt bored in class, understood all his lessons quickly, loved reading, and had a real desire for more.

This made it essential he be given the appropriate special attention and be immediately accelerated to the next level of education. She concluded by describing the child as a budding genius, comparing him to Touria

Chaoui, the first Moroccan woman to fly a plane, and when she was only seventeen.

The delight she felt at what she heard was mixed with fear arising both from her knowledge of Touria's tragic fate, treacherously assassinated before she reached twenty, and because of what an elderly neighbour where they lived before had said about the jinn taking possession of the boy's mind. The woman offered to accompany her to a sorcerer with the power to command evil spirits, as attested by all his disciples.

She had no hesitation in ignoring the neighbour's invitation, then thought long and hard before deciding to sell a small plot of land she had inherited from her father. She was determined to create the appropriate conditions that the French teacher had recommended, although living in a Morocco that had not achieved any of the many promises that accompanied independence was sufficient reason to crush any talent.

She bent down to kiss the child gently on the cheek, unconcerned as to whether he was really asleep or just pretending by shutting his eyes. A sudden violent knocking at the front door pulled her out of her reverie.

She found it very strange, given she knew that her husband, even if his stormy night time return usually turned into a scandal whose details the neighbours gossiped about, was able to open the door himself and not begin the session of shouting and beating until he had closed it behind him.

She rushed to see who was knocking, but realised she had to cover up her unseemly clothing. She went back and put on her jilbab, then slowly opened the door. One of her husband's men from the workshop was there. He addressed her awkwardly: "Good evening, Madam, forgive me, but is the boss at home?"

She shook her head. Her body started trembling as he said, "It's just that he promised the men at the workshop a bonus for their extra effort recently. But he hasn't come back from his trip yet . . ."

The last thing she heard before she fainted was, "Everyone is talking about the news that violent clashes have broken out in Casablanca. They're saying the army are roaming the streets in tanks to clear the angry protestors and that helicopters are firing randomly at everyone. I'm scared something bad has happened to the boss!"

* * *

(17) The Wretched of the Earth

> *There's not much pleasure in writing what you live. The challenge is to live what you write.*
> **Eduardo Galeano**

Friday, 1 November 2002
The Old City – Rabat:

My last night in Morocco . . .
I've packed my suitcases and confirmed my return ticket to New York at 11 o'clock tomorrow morning after calling Brandon. He offered to meet me at the airport. Also Rachid told me he'd be coming to the hotel early in the morning to say goodbye, even though Saturday is his day off.

I came to this country lost, worried and scared of the future, and I'm going to leave it taking a thousand and one stories with me . . .

Just ten days has been enough to learn a great deal. My perspective on the little details of life has changed after having paid scant attention to them when I was caught up in the rapid whirl of a New York life that robbed me of my humanity and my ability to empathize with the tragedies of others.

Sometimes a single day might fill the reservoir of memories with enough for an entire lifetime, something that Stefan Zweig understood perfectly and shaped into a wonderful novel, *Twenty-four Hours in the Life of a Woman*.

The idea of imagining my father growing up in Texas and working in Morocco no longer has any meaning. I've put aside all my earlier drafts and outlines and launched into a free-flowing narrative. I've decided to divide my new novel into twenty chapters. It begins with the book signing at the Strand Book Store and continues through my meeting with Brandon after a three-year break, my trip to Morocco in search of information about the U.S. military presence in the country during the 1950s and '60s, meeting Rachid and discovering the presence of my father's name in the action of *A Moroccan Jigsaw Puzzle*, then our trips between Rabat, Casablanca and Kenitra in search of the truth, our meeting with Lubna, and in the end reaching the heart-stopping shock of Steve McMillan's involvement in the contaminated oil disaster.

The decision has been so hard. It's not easy for any woman to condemn her father for committing a really serious crime, but I am motivated by a genuine desire to uncover the truth and an absolute belief that we sometimes have to cross red lines to do the right thing . . ..

This downtrodden people, thousands of its sons and daughters fell victim to a scandal that Steve McMillan was part of.

He wasn't directly responsible, just a middleman between Moroccan businessmen and senior officers at the American airbases. An ordinary soldier who did not grasp the Moroccan dealers' true reason for buying drums of airplane lubricating oil.

All of that is making excuses . . .

The disaster was horrendous, unbelievable, and caused the destruction of thousands of innocent lives, and as a writer I am required to convey all its details to my readers.

Whatever it costs . . .

The most dangerous thing about history is our inability to rewrite it, although we are able to read it more than once and in various ways.

I won't be able to bring the victims back to life, but I will do everything in my power to pull away the hands gagging their mouths, as long as I am convinced that writing is our most powerful means to say everything, including what we do not dare to say . . .

I don't want it to be a vacuous commercial novel, whose sales figures swell my bank balance and ensure that I can carry on playing the hateful American game of supply and demand.

I want it to be a word of truth for history, nothing else . . .

Even if only a single person reads it, that will be enough for me . . .

Even if it's the last novel I publish in my life, that would be fine . . .

What would publishing dozens of novels mean if I am unable to get my voice and the meaning of my existence across in even one novel?

John Kennedy Toole wrote a novel he called *A Confederacy of Dunces*. All the publishers rejected it and his dejection drove him to commit suicide in 1969. His mother did not give up and made publishing the novel her life's work. With the help of the writer Walker Percy, she succeeded in her quest and found a publisher. In 1981 the novel won the Pulitzer Prize and Kennedy Toole's voice was heard by the world, even after his death.

Will I be better than him, or than Lubna, the saint who confronted horrors and performed miracles and is still fighting till now?

Her only sin was that she loved. She was accused of being a whore, a witch, a jinx, without the slightest regard for the tragic disappearance of the man she loved, the trauma of her husband's death, and having to take responsibility for caring for her daughter on her own when she was still such a young woman.

But what do I know about love?

I used to think that I would only ever know and understand love if I looked for it in novels and in movie scenes, but Lubna proved my idea was stupid . . .

She endured and resisted, and overcame her tragedies, the

cruelty of her fate and the dictates of her society. She completed and published her missing lover's novel and deprived herself of the exhilaration of putting his name or her name on the cover. Then she wrote a brilliant dissertation about the toxic oil disaster to immortalize his memory and the memory of all its victims, but she did not gain the recognition she deserved. Nobody was interested.

She also shocked me when I learned that her PhD did not even enable her to get a job at her level, like a university professor for example. Right now, she's just an ordinary worker in the archives at a government ministry. Yet she hasn't given up despite that. Now that her own mother is dead, she's still raising her daughter, and she clings to the hope of the man she loves coming back, in the face of every logical proposition proving it to be an impossible hope.

She's sure about what she's doing, sure about what's in her heart, and willing to obey that heart's orders till the end . . .

A trivial problem between me and my publishers set me off crying and wailing and expecting the worst. Then I met Rachid, the smart, diligent guy who keeps fighting his morbid reality, his only weapons books and sarcastic humour about everything, even himself, even though he's drowning in a sea of nihilism and despair. I've gradually become convinced that he was right when he said that he and millions of other young people like him were suffering far worse and more bitterly because they had lost the most precious thing they possess: their faith in a future.

Rafiq Khalidi, the riddle that stumped everyone, lived through orphancy and homelessness as a child after the death of his biological parents. He fell victim to a disaster that destroyed his natural abilities to walk and talk. Then, once he thought he had struck lucky with a new family that adopted him, the father was killed during events that had nothing to do with him and he and his adoptive mother were burdened with the greed of the uncle's family who wanted to seize their house. He dreamt of completing his studies in France, which would allow him to realise his legitimate dreams, but the scholarship went to someone who didn't deserve it.

He sought compensation in friendship, but the battle to win Lubna's heart turned his best friend into his worst enemy...

Charles Bukowski was right when he wrote that writers' lives are more enjoyable than their writings. But now, neither they nor their writings are at all enjoyable.

I wish that my time in Morocco, and with it the events of my next novel, would end with the reappearance of Rafiq and his reunion with Lubna and Jenan, as a joyous reward showing that fate is not so unfair.

But that's life. It doesn't always reward us with what we want.

The novel will not therefore be action-packed in the American way and a long list of questions will go unanswered. I might find I have to amend the first outline and stop before chapter 20.

Where did Rafiq Khalidi disappear to? Did Samir and the uncle's family play a pivotal role in his disappearance?

Did they for example kill him, then bury him some place and agree to forget all about him?

Why did Samir insist on repeating the name of the village just before he died?

As long as the supposed aim of writing *A Moroccan Jigsaw Puzzle* was to uncover some clues about the contaminated oil case, how did Rafiq know the tiniest details of his father's relationship with Steve McMillan when he was only five years old?

The most important question I've preferred to keep to myself and not raise with Lubna: Did Rafiq really love her?

In my opinion, a love affair begins when we give the other person our most intimate secrets, otherwise it's just a question of mutual desires, at the end of which we may find ourselves feeling exposed, like the victim of a mugging.

Rafiq had the right to padlock the box of his past, but he was on the point of getting engaged to Lubna and even then did not tell her a single word about his true origins and having been poisoned by the oil!

Or was the unfinished draft of *A Moroccan Jigsaw Puzzle* his own way of confessing all his secrets?

I continued tapping away at the keyboard, oblivious to everything around me and focusing all my senses on the Word document until my mobile suddenly rang and brought me back to reality and to my chair at the small desk in the hotel room.

I was going to ignore it, but Rachid's name and number made me curious, so I pressed answer. His cry of excitement, practically a shout, hit me: "Before he died Samir revealed where Rafiq is, but no one understood what he meant for all these years. Christine, I think there's a chance, even if a slim one, that the author of *A Moroccan Jigsaw Puzzle* is still alive!"

* * *

The Bright Lights Guide
on Turning the Victim into a Slut

Time: Tuesday, 14 May 2002

Locations: The beach house in Sidi Abed and the police station.

Written and directed by: Lawyer Hanan el-Farisi

(1)

Arrival at the beach house to discover what occurred between Zouhair and Ghalia. Fear for the terrible fate possibly awaiting the teenage tearaway if the cleaning girl can prove she has been raped.

(2)

Calmly think about how to handle the predicament; any mistake could lead to disaster.

(3)

Exploit the position of Tuhami, the guard standing in for his brother Mouti. After all, he is unemployed without a permanent job. Bribe him and use him to execute the following steps.

(4)

Clean the house, dispose of the vodka bottle, and remove signs of the struggle between Zouhair and Ghalia.

(5)

Return Zouhair with his things to the villa in Hayy el Riad.

(6)

As long as the cleaning girl is determined to go through with her threat to inform the police, it is imperative to act quickly and report her as missing to the police station that is some thirty minutes away on foot, as well as to the gendarmerie post at the beach, even though Ghalia's knowledge of its existence can be discounted.

(7)

Arrival at the police station in the company of the guard Tuhami to discover Ghalia there, barefoot and her clothing in shreds. She tries to persuade the inspector to charge Zouhair Belkacem, son of Doctor Younis Belkacem and lawyer Hanan el-Farisi, with rape.

(8)

The law is clear: a minor cannot make an accusation in the absence of their parents or legal guardian.

(9)

Discredit the cleaning girl's account by saying she went to the house on her own to clean it, as confirmed by the guard, who says that Zouhair Belkacem was not present at Sidi Abed.

(10)

Testimony of adult man and woman against testimony of underage girl of sixteen: outcome a foregone conclusion.

(11)

Move from defence to offence: accuse Ghalia of attempting to sexually harass Zouhair and using him as a scapegoat for another relationship with a person unknown.

(12)

Ghalia spends the night at the police station until her father is summoned from the village.

(13)

Her father believes what he hears from those united in her condemnation. He goes even further and accuses her of immorality and tarnishing his reputation. Then he refuses to make a complaint against Zouhair, despite Ghalia's pleas.

(14)

Intervene in the role of saviour: mutually satisfactory closure of the case and payment of a sum of money to the father, with the advice to take Ghalia to a gynaecologist (Younis Belkacem naturally) to prove her lies and the absence of any sign of her deflowerment, in exchange for her giving up work at the villa and her father taking her back to the village, or to hell even, or whatever . . .

(15)

Persuade Zouhair to forget the matter without providing any more details, as a first step in getting him away from Morocco once he's passed his bac, in the fear that in a sudden moment of remorse he might do something foolish.

* * *

(17′) The Man Without Qualities

> *Fate shuffles the cards and we play.*
> Arthur Schopenhauer

Wednesday, 6 November 2019
En route to the Diyar tram stop – *Salé:*

I had a strange feeling of exhilaration when I left the agent's house, despite his insistence on keeping me there until the rain inundating the city stopped pouring. I touched the old striped scarf in my pocket, then discreetly thanked the man without offering any explanation for my desire to leave.

Neither he nor anybody else would understand that I missed everything here after an absence that had lasted for seventeen years, even if that meant walking alone through deserted streets beneath a sky whose clouds had taken an oath to spill their contents all day long...

How could I be scared of the night when I bear plenty of darkness inside me?

I am a zero, a nothing. My mother tricked fate by pretending that I had not been at the beach house the night I attacked the cleaning girl, but fate surprised her by scoring a goal in her net, when the Russian authorities claimed that I had not been at the Dubrovka Theatre.

I shapeshifted from the identity of Alexander Gazdanov in Siberia to that of Yemeni businessman Wajdi al-Mutawakkil according to my fake passport in Kazakhstan. The name Zouhair Belkacem does not currently exist in official Moroccan records, and it's going to take a great deal of time and effort to get it back.

But what's the value of names if the tortured soul remains the same?

As I expected, the agent knew nothing about Ghalia now, but he did know the village she came from and all the villages around it, since they were a rich seam that he and his ilk exploited to persuade simple people to send their daughters out to work as cleaners in homes in the cities.

One important step would finally lead me to end the cycle of torment which, as soon as I arrived at the villa in Hayy el Riad and embraced my mother a few days ago, I realised was still on-going...

The rain soaked my heavy Russian overcoat and I did not care that my feet were going through a pool of mud. My mind had floated far away, retrieving exactly what my mother had said the night of my return to Rabat.

*

We sat side by side holding hands the whole night, both of us trying to take in the horrors recounted by the other.

She screamed, lost consciousness, regained it, laughed, burst into tears, punched my chest, hugged me, kissed me, felt the bones sticking out of my cheeks, shut and opened her eyes several times, and repeated the strange names of Dubrovka, Naloxone, Pichushkin, Alexander Gazdanov and Krasnokamensk like a mad woman.

A natural response, and I had even prepared myself for it, but she wasn't the only one to get a shock.

She stunned me with the terrible news of my father's death and the horrible scandal accompanying it that had besmirched our family's reputation forever. I read a series of articles dealing with the issue on the small screen of her mobile phone, and followed the comments that ranged from regret and sarcasm to pernicious gloating from people I did not know and who had no connection to my family.

Astonishment stunted my ability to understand. Then I experienced an overwhelming sense of shame and along with it I grasped why the Russian middleman had insisted on drumming into me some details about advanced technology that I had missed the opportunity to learn. Technology had gradually infiltrated and taken control over the most intimate details and secrets of people's daily lives.

In this new world, everyone fed off each other's scandals and calamities. Perhaps the only benefit of my stay in Siberia was my ignorance of the whole shebang.

Time had not been kind to Hanan el-Farisi either. Tragedy and the cruelty of the years had formed an alliance to make her lose everything: attractiveness, vitality, a strong sense of being in charge, which she had imposed on everyone during the days of her lost glory in her assiduous effort to become head of the Blooming Rose Association, as a preliminary to standing for elected office . . .

Dry grey hair, a bent back, spindly legs, eyes on stalks, the opposite of the image of the forty-year-old woman I knew from before, a woman fixated to the point of obsession on looking elegant and glamorous.

Her dreams had evaporated after my disappearance and she was sucked into the whirlpool of constant trips to Russia in search of me and chasing up any clue that might lead her to discover my fate, with all that entailed in terms of time, effort and money. She neglected her work and abandoned her grand ambitions. Her star quickly faded, and her friends at the association, those who wanted to take her place and serve their own interests and strengthen their relationships with certain influential people in her stead, turned against her.

Then they gave her the cold shoulder and cast her into oblivion. And when she tried to live with her new reality, along came the disappearance of my father followed by the scandal of his tragic death to destroy her completely.

The villa itself had turned into something like an abandoned, haunted castle. Damp had settled in the walls and spiders in the corners. Every inch was covered in dust, including the large photograph in the main reception room showing us smiling to the camera, safe in the belief that fate would never dare think of harming us.

Gone were the days when the villa housed soirées and dinner parties, at which my mother hosted the wives of parliamentarians and big businessmen. Women who filled their waking hours with lavish parties and trips abroad, and whose chitchat did not go beyond flabby buttocks, nose jobs and their husbands' infidelities with cute secretaries.

Even Spike, the German Shepherd dog, could not bear being alone and shepherdless, and had died years ago.

O God, how did my mother live in a grave like this on her own?

It was a question followed by another that I preferred to keep inside unsaid until I had regained my equilibrium after a night whose impact on my heart was no less than what I had endured over the preceding years.

The first rays of dawn crept into where we were sitting, and to conclude a night that I almost believed would never end, I had to say, "It's the curse of Ghalia, Mum. What we did to her is unforgiveable."

She turned her exhausted face away, a face like a wasteland, without rosiness, without a trace of moisture. Then she stood up in a despairing attempt to escape. But I grabbed her arm and forced her to sit down. The cascade of her tears came bursting down again: "I had to act like that to protect you. But I regret it terribly now."

"Things only started going bad after we did it, not before. I'm not well and I don't know what horrible surprises a routine medical check-up will reveal, but I am determined to look for the wronged cleaning girl, even if it's the last thing I do.

*

A loud honk of a horn made me turn round, and to my left I saw a small taxi. "Where are you going?" asked the driver.

His cry made me jump and I mumbled without thought, "Hayy el Riad."

"Hayy el Riad? Are you drunk or an idiot? This is a taxi for the city of Salé only!" Then he opened the passenger-side door and, pointing a finger, said, "Get in. I'm going to the maternity hospital, but the pitiful state you're in has made me feel sorry for you. You're about to turn into some sort of amphibian. I'll drop you at the nearest tram stop and you can continue from there."

As if hypnotized I obeyed his command. I closed the door and he took off at speed.

"I promise you that being a taxi driver is the hardest job in the world. My wife's pregnant with our third child and she's suddenly having contractions. Rather than taking her to hospital and being with her, I'm forced to go out chasing after a living. My mother called me a few minutes ago and told me that Naima has to have a caesarean. There's nothing I can do, her life and the child's life are more important than anything of course."

I repeated his last words like a robot: "Yes, more important than anything of course."

"She wanted to know the baby's sex months ago, but I said no, I'm content with God's will. If it's a boy, she's insisting on calling him Yanis, a weird name whose meaning I don't know, but it's the name of the hero in a dubbed Turkish soap opera that she's a big fan of."

My lack of response to what he was saying seemed to annoy him and he shut up. After a few minutes the taxi pulled up at a tram stop and he turned on the interior light. "Seven dirhams . . ."

I felt in my right-hand coat pocket for some money, but not finding any I tilted sideways to check the other pocket, and exclaimed, "There's a leather satchel on the backseat. Perhaps a passenger forgot it!"

The driver also looked behind him at the backseat, then slapped his forehead and cried, "God, it's the guy I just took to Lamkinssia housing compound!"

He grabbed the satchel, then, with a sudden movement, handed it to me. "Listen carefully! Most likely, its owner has gone to the police station that you can see in front of you to report the loss of his bag. I think he's a student at university. The youth of today are very forgetful. But I have to go to the hospital. Don't worry, I'll explain everything to the duty officer afterwards. Here, write down my taxi number: 1099."

I was about to object, but his mobile started ringing.

"What, her condition is serious! Bleeding! I'm on my way. I'll be at the hospital in five minutes!"

His eyes pleaded with me, "Please, I'm begging you. The leather satchel, the police station, 1099. You seem a really good guy despite your sorry state. Naima. Goodbye."

He locked the door and shot off.

What is this madness?

Where is the police station and how can I go there to hand in the leather satchel when I don't have Moroccan ID papers? I might get sucked into an interrogation that I just don't need right now?

What a nightmare!

Why did I agree to ride with him in the first place? Wasn't I comfortable just walking on my own, even if all the rain in the world soaked me?

I sat fretfully down on the bench at the tram stop, unsure whether to look for the police station in question or just leave the satchel on the bench and forget all about it. But my compassion for the bag's owner made me drop the second option, and I put it inside my sodden overcoat.

An old black satchel, medium size and quite light.

An irresistible impulse to open it and take a peek at what was inside took hold of me. I discovered a laptop and a small blue notebook . . .

* * *

Excerpt from the evening news on Al Maghribia TV, Friday, 1 November 2002:

[...] The probe, launched by NASA as part of an ambitious project in 1996, is still expected to reach Mars early next year, although communication with the robot rover designed to collect samples from the planet has been lost due to battery failure. A media spokesperson for the space agency stated that the new project would enable scientists to look for tangible evidence of water as well as conduct comprehensive research into the surface terrain, the composition of the atmosphere and the levels of dangerous radiation, in preparation for a human mission in the future.

Returning to national news, in Duwwar el-Hajj Kaddour, located on the outskirts of Kenitra, a group of local women has set up a cooperative for growing and selling snails. The project has been endorsed by the village's residents and stresses real engagement with sustainable development in the context of a participatory approach that aims to encourage the establishment of small and medium sized enterprises in disadvantaged villages and rural areas. Our report on the issue is by [...]

* * *

(18) Beggars of Miracles

Love feeds on patience not desire.
Amin Maalouf

Saturday, 2 November 2002
Duwwar el-Hajj Kaddour – outskirts of Kenitra:

The incessant sweeping of the windscreen wipers made a monotonous noise. Lubna had the courage to break the monotony in French (out of a desire to include Christine in the conversation) even though she was simultaneously paying attention to the muddy landmarks along the road and concentrating on driving her small car: "I can hardly believe it. Another village with the same name! It's been fourteen years and that possibility never occurred to me!"

I answered from my seat in the back, "Me neither. But the report on the news was conclusive. The village really exists and perhaps Samir's last words were a misunderstood pointer."

Seated next to Lubna, Christine did up the top button of her coat and commented in real alarm, "What matters now is we arrive safely. We might get trapped by the rain at any moment and the car isn't equipped to handle these steep roads."

Lubna didn't utter a word, and like her I enjoyed a whole ten minutes of silence before I pointed into the near distance: "There it is! Just like the attendant at the petrol station said: the small tower of the mosque and simple houses clustered around it."

Lubna steered the car towards the entrance to the village and I added in explanation: "The main feature of these villages is that they are tiny and have very few inhabitants. The grocer will know them all for sure and might give us a detailed report on the past, present and even future of every person here."

That last bit was a bad joke, which neither of them were in the mood to get. I indicated to Lubna to park the car next to a low crumbling wall, seeing as taking the car down the narrow alleys would be impossible.

"Christine, would you prefer to wait in the car or come with us?"

"You bet I'm coming with you," she shouted vehemently. "Don't bother translating. We'll sort it out according to how things go!"

I preceded the two women in our quest for the grocer's shop, putting up with the rain in my face and on my old coat. A layer of filthy mud coated my shoes and it was gradually soaking into my socks.

We found a small, poorly stocked shop. Its owner, stuffed inside a woollen jilbab, was huddled in a corner sipping a mug of tea. Next to him was a boy who might have been six or seven.

"Hello. Excuse me, is this Duwwar el-Hajj Kaddour?"

He did not move an inch as he answered ponderously, "Yes. Can I help?"

"We're looking for someone here called Rafiq Khalidi."

He put his hands in his pockets and stood up slowly in a show of annoyance, as if my sentence had made him leave his bench in a nuclear research laboratory. "What did you say the name was?" he asked again.

"Rafiq. Rafiq Khalidi."

He shook his head. "No. There's nobody in the village goes by that strange name. The few families here are well enough known. Do you have any other details?"

"He's around fifty, moves his limbs with difficulty, and suffers from heart problems."

Lubna interrupted me and added eagerly, "And has a beautiful birthmark on his left cheek . . ."

I stifled a smile as the grocer replied in a dry tone, "There is only one cripple in the whole village. He never leaves his house and he lives with his dumb mute of a sister in a small house on the edge of the village."

I stepped back in disappointment, but Lubna surprised me with a rapid question: "Can you show us to the house?"

He shrugged his shoulders indifferently, then whispered in the little boy's ear causing him to run out of the shop.

After a couple of minutes, a tall, strong young woman wearing a faded pink coat appeared. Her features suggested she was a little under twenty.

"Ghalia, come here and take this guy and the two women to Daouia's house. They're looking for someone and they think it's her brother, that cripple even whose name we don't know . . ."

Lubna rapidly translated the gist for Christine, while the grocer posed a patently sarcastic question: "Aren't you going to take some sugar loaves[4] with you for the man and his sister?"

I was no less sharp-witted than him in my response: "No. We'll buy them once we're back in the city."

I tried to induce Ghalia to talk about the mute woman and her brother once we were sufficiently far away, and she said, "Daouia lived with her husband in their house for years, from before I was born even. After her husband died, her brother suddenly turned up, even though nobody had heard about him before. That caused the inhabitants to natter and gossip. Rumours quickly spread, but repeated visits by the village women proved that the man's legs were paralyzed and his speech impediment made it impossible to understand what he was saying. So they left him to his own devices, although the women all agreed that with his

---

[4] Traditional gift presented by Moroccans on any occasion.

handsome features, he didn't look anything like Daouia. Personally, I don't care what they say. The mute woman and the crippled man are just two miserable souls with nobody to provide for them. So I make sure to visit them from time to time to look after them and help Daouia with the housework."

After a minute's rapid walking and jumping over puddles of water and mud, she said, "We're here!"

She banged on the rusty blue door, which reverberated at the blows with an artillery-like boom.

A short woman opened the door. Over fifty, she was wearing a ragged grey sweater. Ghalia spoke to her using signs, and the woman glanced at us with two sunken, fearful eyes, unable to move or speak as she gave Christine's features, so unlike those she was used to in the village, a hard stare. She only let us in to comply with Ghalia's request.

I went down the narrow passage after the mute fifty-year-old, and was the first to enter a dank, dark room. I was struck by a bad sense of anxiety that was replaced by the shock of seeing the person sitting in an old wheelchair in front of me.

A thin, dark-skinned man, grey at the temples, a sad look on his face, and on his left cheek a birthmark that gave him an unmistakeable handsomeness.

His black eyes narrowed as he looked at the crowd standing in front of him, which suggested to me that he had very poor eyesight.

My mouth gaped open in astonishment when Lubna emitted a cry that combined joy and anguish in equal measure: "Rafiq!"

*

Darkness quickly descended after the sunset call to prayer. The onslaught of thunder and rain continued for hours, during which we gathered around Rafiq, listening to his detailed account of how Samir and his uncle had engineered his disappearance. The whole atmosphere instantly reminded me of the story *Blood Valley* by Abdelmajid Benjelloun.

It took the maths teacher such a long time and so much effort to deal with his speech difficulties and his frequent coughing fits that I thought he might be dying, although that was his "normal", familiar way of speaking. Lubna was practically eating him alive with her tear-filled eyes. She only interjected in order to help him complete a word or difficult phrase, and that was done with unparalleled alacrity.

Was she truly the same glum woman that we had met at her house in Rabat and in whose company Christine had heard the remaining episodes of the story at the Faculty of Literature?

I believe that love does not exist outside of what I read in novels, but what I was seeing in front of my eyes right then would force me to reconsider . . .

Suddenly bomb blasts rained down or, more accurately, violent bangs at the door of the house, about to unhinge it.

Ghalia dashed off to open it, and I heard the voice of a young girl crying out: "My brother Hassan and the rest of the children are trapped in the school in the neighbouring village!"

I left Rafiq in the room with the women and, oblivious to the rain and the two puddles forming in my worn-out shoes, I caught up with Ghalia and the girl who were both running and found myself before a gaggle of the village's inhabitants standing close to the covered space outside the mosque. Their jumbled voices turned into the din of a weekly market:

"The teacher has a mobile phone and he said that he and the children are all right for now. But for how long? The floods have completely surrounded the building!"

"Raise your hands in prayer . . ."

"Its weak foundations won't hold. The torrents will sweep it and everyone in it away!"

"Keep quiet, you jinx!"

"What shall we do?"

"We called the civil defence and they promised to come. But no one's come!"

"Let's go, we'll save the children ourselves!"

"Impossible! The inhabitants of the neighbouring village weren't able to intervene. They also called the civil defence but without any result."

"Our children's lives are in danger!"

The scene ended with the appearance of weeping women repeating the names of their children. The wailing expected in such circumstances then began.

I understood it all and ran back to Daouia's house in my practically split shoes and burst into the room shouting, "Christine, can you make a quick call to your embassy?"

* * *

Pages from the blue notebook that Zouhair Belkacem found along with the laptop in the leather satchel:

05–01–2019

Initial concept:

– Motive for writing: all the affronts to Moroccans' dignity (oppression – futility – youth's loss of hope for the future)

– Subject: <u>Contaminated oil scandal of 1959.</u> (Research information and gather sources)

– Narrative form: literary "detective" story. (A forgotten novel – search for the missing novelist)

– <u>Create an organizing thread that brings the motive, subject and narrative form together.</u>

14–02–2019

Plot outline 1:

– American woman writer suffering from writers' block (<u>classic opening but right for driving the action towards what I want</u>)

– Her publisher threatens to sue her if she doesn't submit a manuscript of a new novel as per her contract (~~with a comparison between the position of the writer there and here? No basis for comparison of course!!!~~)

– Her friend and former literary agent gets involved (romance subplot???) and suggests she writes a novel whose events revolve around the period her father served as a soldier in Morocco during the 1950s (<u>nod to the change in taste of readers in the United States after 9/11</u>)

– She comes to Morocco to pursue the idea and solve the riddle of some mysterious photos of her father that she found at the family home in Denver (avoid repeating the idea of the father having written his memoirs as is the case in *Towards Zero*)

– She meets a PhD student in literature whose supervisor has stopped him working on a particular novel in favour of another novel written by a professor colleague (flattery and mutual interests)

– The writer is interested in the subject and borrows a copy of the French translation to read.

– She is shocked by <u>the presence of her father's name for one of the characters in the novel</u> (turning point)

11–03–2019

Plot outline 2:

– Search for the author to question him: a missing person – the publisher received the manuscript of the novel in the post – made-up return address.

– The investigation begins and the writer cooperates with the young PhD student to solve the riddle of the disappearance.

– Clues to the disappearance of the maths teacher unfold (tricks with the names): family secrets – a love triangle – love's role in destroying friendship.

– Discovery of the relationship between the author of the novel and the American soldier, then coming across the <u>contaminated oil disaster of 1959.</u>

– The shameful affront to Moroccans' human dignity, then linking it to the present reality (nothing's changed of course!!!)

– Return of the missing writer in the end.

1 April 2019: Start Date

Basic structure of the novel:

Time:

– 1959 (U.S. presence in Morocco and the oil disaster)

– 1988 to 1989: the publisher receives manuscript of the novel and the disappearance of its author.

– 2002: arrival of the American writer in Morocco and beginning of investigation into the novel *A Moroccan Jigsaw Puzzle*.

– Check dates for accuracy (use the calendar on the computer)

Place:

<u>United States of America:</u>

– New York (Manhattan)

– Denver

<u>Morocco:</u>

– Rabat (traditional hotel – the old city)

– Casablanca (Habous) (meeting with the former publisher)

– Kenitra (main location for American presence in Morocco) (the novel *An Attempt to Live* by Mohammed Zafzaf)

– Meknes and outskirts (city whose inhabitants were worst affected by the contaminated oil disaster)

– Check everything to do with neighbourhoods, streets, cities and details of community life (food, clothing etc.)

Main characters:

– Christine: American writer (the narrator) (all the events are from her perspective <u>unless a chapter demands a different narrative technique</u>) (highly strung – impetuous – good-hearted – lost)

– Brandon: Christine's friend and literary agent (loves her in secret – very well read – tight-lipped)

– Rachid: young Moroccan PhD researcher specialising in literature (intelligent – quick-witted – shy – sarcastic – nihilistic)

– Other characters according to the course of events: (the ex-publisher – waiter at Les Arcades bar – author of the novel – his friend – the woman he loves)

Headings:

– Each chapter to be headed with the title of a novel or book by another author, plus a quotation appropriate to the chapter's contents.

– Leave looking for a suitable title until the writing and review of the novel is done.

Division of the chapters:

– 20 chapters.

– Insert stand-alone documents before the beginning of each chapter (summary of the writer's previous novels – story written by the writer – articles from her contract with the publishing house – excerpt from the PhD student's dissertation – chapters from the novel by the missing writer – articles and research on the contaminated oil case . . .)

– Average of 6 pages per chapter (5 or 7, according to what the action permits while avoiding anything too long)

– Font Times New Roman 12 point, Word, size A4

25-10-2019

~~1 2 3 4 5 6 7 8 9 10~~

~~11 12 13 14 15 16~~ 17 18 19 20

– What next? (Meeting with Lubna el-Afaoui and understanding the connection between *A Moroccan Jigsaw Puzzle* and Rafiq Khalidi, Steve McMillan and the contaminated oil case)

– Where did Rafiq Khalidi disappear? Samir Qassemi and the uncle's family are <u>responsible for his disappearance</u> of course.

– They killed him and concealed his body in <u>Duwwar el-Hajj Kaddour</u>, and that's why Samir said the name of the village before his death? (Possible, but I want him to come back. Poor Lubna doesn't deserve so much suffering!!!)

– Acceptance of fate and seeing him as lost forever for some reason? (Impossible: I won't repeat what happened to the unknown narrator in *Towards Zero*)

– He decided to disappear of his own free will? (No ~~logical~~ reason exists for that. He was getting ready to become engaged to the girl he loved and was writing a novel he aspired to publish and begin on his path as a writer . . .)

– He lost his memory? (~~No, a million times no . . . this isn't a Turkish or Mexican soap opera~~)

– He went to the United States and killed Steve McMillan by poisoning him, then killed himself? (Stupid idea)

– Conclusion: either I find a solution to the problem of <u>the return of the missing writer</u> or <u>everything I've constructed falls apart!!!!</u>

* * *

(18′) Journey to the End of the Night

Read until you stop distinguishing between the text and yourself.
Jón Kalman Stefánsson

Wednesday, 6 November 2019
Hayy el Riad – Rabat:

I went over to my mother's bedroom and quietly opened the door so as not to wake her up. There she was, kneeling on a prayer mat in the dim light and holding a large Qur'an in her hands. She read in a whisper:

"{And if God afflicts you with some hurt, there is none who can remove it save Him; and if He desires good for you, there is none who can repel His bounty. He strikes with it whomever He will of His servants. He is the Forgiving, the Merciful. (107) Say: 'O people, the Truth has come to you from your Lord. So whoever is guided, is guided only for the sake of his own soul, and whoever errs, errs only against it. And I am not a guardian over you. (108) And follow what is revealed to you, and endure patiently until God gives judgement, and He is the Best of Judges.' (109)} Verily the truth of God Almighty."

If the price of some hurt was to remind me of the existence of a Lord able to remove it whenever He will, then I'm ready to suffer more . . .

My heart quivered in my chest when I read the name of the Sura at the top of the page: Younis. Then I kissed her head and she brushed my damp face with her thin fingers. She cast inquisitive glances at the black leather satchel I was holding in my right hand, but I just kissed her hand and left the room in silence.

I put the satchel on the office table and took out the computer and the blue notebook with trembling fingers. My mind was busy thinking about a suitable way to deal with the two items.

Flicking through the notebook while I had been waiting for the tram was contrary to the most basic principles of respect and privacy, although I've realised in the last few days that those rules are no longer of much value. I convinced myself that I did what I did with the aim of finding some clue, some name or address that would lead me to the identity of the satchel's owner, so that I could quickly return it to him without the need to hand it in at the police station.

I was ready for anything: a notebook full of phone numbers or appointments (although those have become extinct), lottery numbers, a list of bills, results of football matches, rough homework, personal jottings or even magic spells.

But a notebook with the plan for writing a novel was something that never occurred to me . . .

The owner of the satchel is a novelist, then!

The tram arrived at the stop. I made up my mind as I got on: I would come back to the same spot tomorrow morning, seeing as on a rainy night looking for a police station, whose location was only known to a batty taxi driver, was an impossibility.

Turning the computer on was no problem, based on what I had learned over the previous days in dealing with my mother's phone and computer. The battery icon showed there was four hours' usage left.

A practically empty computer except for a folder numbered 42 containing twenty Word documents, also numbered sequentially: 1, 2, 3 etc.

What did the number 42 mean?

I noticed that the device did not contain any other files and provided no clue as to its owner's name. I realised it must be a small, secondary computer that the author used only for writing.

I began with file number 1 and the following lines came up:

---

(1) Things Fall Apart

> *America is a highly complicated country, although the ideas in circulation there are extremely simple.*
> **Matei Vișniec**

Thursday, 26 September 2002
Strand Bookstore – Manhattan:

"Nobody has the right to question your literary talent, Christine, but you don't understand anything about the ins and outs of publishing and the tricks of exclusive contracts. Please, don't make any promises that you know full well you won't be able to keep one day."

Those were the words that Brandon whispered in my ear three years ago. And I admit today that they were wise, honest and decisive.

Things Fall Apart is the title of a famous novel by the writer Chinua Achebe, though I've never heard of Matei Vişniec. But these details fit with what the author referred to in his notebook about using the title of a novel and a quotation to open every chapter in the planned novel.

I started reading and gradually got absorbed in the events of the novel with its clear style and short chapters. It seemed to be going according to how the writer had planned it in his notebook.

I don't deny that it's really gripping . . .

I engaged with the movement of the characters within the spaces delineated for them. Christine, with her impetuousness and disorganisation, set me on edge, despite the logic of her determination to clear her father's name. I admired Rachid's quick thinking, and completely understood his downright pessimism and inability to expect a better future for himself and those like him. Rafiq's tragic plight also evoked my sympathy, and I did not find Lubna's fighting spirit strange, nor that she clung on to the faint hope of his return.

Did Morocco actually go through that horrific experience: lubricating oil for American fighter planes being mixed with table oil and thousands of victims no one remembers today?

I say that with bitter cynicism. The horrors I lived through in the hell of Siberia long ago killed off any potential to be surprised by anything.

As the principle has it: kill once, kill a thousand times.

I would add that those who ignored the fate of one Moroccan, unjustly imprisoned in Krasnokamensk, would have been able to ignore the fates of thousands of others unjustly treated.

And all too often that deliberate ignorance has a greater impact on its victims than death . . .

I got to chapter 16 and the laptop gave me a low battery alert. That made me take a quick look at files 17, 18, 19 and 20, only to discover that they were all empty. The screen then went black, just as my watch showed three a.m.

Now I understood what was written on the last pages of the blue notebook.

There's nothing strange about writers having an answer to every question. They're liars by nature. In this case, however, the author really has failed to find a suitable way to reveal Rafiq Khalidi's fate and finish the remaining chapters.

He's right to insist on reuniting Rafiq and Lubna and end their suffering, which has gone on too long.

Fate isn't that cruel, and even if it were, then at least allow the imagination to treat us with compassion!

One point caught my interest, but I was unable to go back to it on the computer, so I swiftly returned to the notebook to make sure.

The writer stated that Duwwar el-Hajj Kaddour was near Meknes, but what I know personally is that it is located on the outskirts of Kenitra, based on what the employment agent told me when I met him just a few hours ago.

Ghalia comes from Duwwar el-Hajj Kaddour on the outskirts of Kenitra, not Meknes!

Any Moroccan knows that Kenitra is more than 120 km from Meknes, and I am very surprised that the writer could make such an egregious error . . .

But hold on!

What if there are two villages with the same name?

Doesn't that provide us with a new possibility for explaining what Samir tried to say on his deathbed?

I opened the desk drawer in search of pen and paper, as I surrendered to an idea no less crazy than what had happened over the last few hours, since I accepted the taxi driver's offer to drop me at the tram stop.

I read a lot of books in prison, but I never thought of writing a single sentence. Besides, my Arabic is so bad, I will probably make many terrible stylistic errors.

But I will solve the riddle of Rafiq's disappearance and set out my own conception of Rafiq's reappearance after such a long absence, as a prelude to my own encounter with Ghalia after seventeen years' absence of my own.

The village on the outskirts of Kenitra will be the beginning of the puzzle and its end, in this author's novel and in my own life . . .

* * *

Account of Rafiq Khalidi concerning the circumstances of his disappearance on Saturday, 30 July 1988 and subsequent events. (His words have been rewritten in the form of brief paragraphs, since his difficulty speaking makes him repeat letters and words and proceed very slowly):

– I left the house for the flower shop to collect the bouquet, as a final step before going with my uncle's family to Lubna's house.

– I was one street away from the shop when I bumped into Samir.

– My heart contracted in pain. Our last argument had been heated and our friendship had ended completely. I expected we would avoid looking at each other, as had happened on previous occasions, but he surprised me by coming over and embracing me. He congratulated me on the engagement and wished me a happy life with Lubna. Then he apologised for what had happened and said he wanted to turn over a new leaf. He invited me back to his house to drink coffee, which he made very well, as a sign of good faith.

– I was delighted by what I heard and agreed at once, seeing as there was still time before the nine o'clock start.

– As was our habit before the argument, he took me into the small study in his house. He presented me with a new copy of the novel *Life: A User's Manual* by Georges Perec. A small reconciliation gift, he said, in the knowledge that I was a fan of the author.

– He seemed in playful spirits and laughed when he said that *Life: A User's Manual* would be the most suitable choice for me if I happened to find myself on a desert island one day.

– We sat down to drink a cup of coffee and revive our glory days of literary discussion. Out of the blue, I had terrible cramps and extreme difficulty breathing. I was coughing violently and became certain that my end was at hand, without knowing or understanding the reason.

– My vision blurred as I was forced closer to the edge of collapse. Samir came over with a frightening smile on his face, the likes of which I had never seen from him before. I tried to scream, but my halting speech failed me, before I finally succumbed to unconsciousness.

– I came round in a poorly lit, dire-looking room somewhere totally unknown to me. I tried to stand, but the awful pain kept me prone. I was unable to move my legs, since for many hours I had not taken any of the painkillers that enabled me to walk.

– A rural woman in rags stood there staring at me dumbfounded. I addressed her as best I could with my speech impediment, and realised that she was a deaf mute and only capable of making a few vague signs.

– It was not long before the door opened and Samir appeared. He came over with calm, confident steps and sat on a wooden chair in front of me.

– He was a different person, totally unrelated to the close friend I knew. When he spoke, I discovered the extent of the plot against me which, unknown to me, had been hatched by my nearest and dearest . . .

– He said that I was fortunate because the first thought that had occurred to my uncle Kacem was to kill me and get rid of me for good, seeing as that was the only way for both of them to benefit: my uncle by taking possession of the house and destroying the proof that I was the owner following my mother's death; and Samir by getting Lubna all to himself. Samir managed to persuade my uncle that it would be better to send me far from the city and in such a way that I would never come back.

– He added that that wasn't due to any sudden pang of conscience, but that murder would bring into play the ancient Roman precept of *habeas corpus* (which my uncle of course did not understand). When the body came to light, that initial clue made anything possible. The body would be matched against the descriptions of those who had gone missing in the surrounding districts and its identity revealed. That would be followed by a hunt for the missing person's enemies, which would gradually tighten the circle of suspicion around them.

– He explained his idea to my uncle, saying that I took a pharmacy's worth of medicine, some of which helped me bear the severe pain of walking. Being deprived of them would render me completely paralysed. And seeing as my speech was halting already, getting rid of me without killing me would be easy. Then they could divert suspicions by posting a missing person's report in the newspapers.

– That I took medicine was a secret I had kept hidden from everybody except Samir (although my connection with the poisonous oil remained my biggest secret). In time my friend used that secret against me.

– He said that I was now in a godforsaken village and nobody would ever know I was there. I would not be all alone, because the mute Daouia, a distant relative of his, would take care of me and prevent me from dying of starvation, while herself benefitting from the presence of a man at home to protect her from carpetbaggers and gossips after her husband's death, even if I was disabled and paralysed and not to be feared at all.

– His final words dripped with malevolent gloating and before he left he added sarcastically that he wasn't really that evil so he was leaving me the copy of Perec's novel, which was only suitable for a reader forced into a long period of seclusion.

– Once he had gone, I was in a complete state of shock. I hoped it was all just a silly nightmare, from which I would wake up soaked in sweat on my bed. Not for a moment had I expected Samir to be so full of hate. His desire to take revenge and humiliate me was insane.

– I gradually got over my consternation and understood that it really had been a fiendish and watertight plan.

– House arrest in an isolated village I did not know. Plus, being deprived of the medicine that helped me endure the agony of my pain, which in the end would mean being unable to walk, and sharing the hardships of life with a miserable mute woman, like me confined to silence.

– My health deteriorated and I was no longer able to get out of bed. Pain in body and soul plus constant thoughts of Lubna, the only person left to me in the world, were crushing me.

– Samir visited regularly after that, until he stunned me with the news of his marriage to Lubna and then the birth of their beautiful daughter, whom he named Jenan. That wasn't enough for him, but more than once he eagerly showed me pictures of them together, confident in my inability to do anything, particularly as my difficulties speaking had grown worse, which stopped me even responding to his provocations.

– Three years of dreadful psychological torture went by, during which I saw my beloved with another man who made humiliating me into an art form. Then suddenly he was gone. I guessed he had chosen to completely ignore me as a final blow to end what little resistance I had left.

– Fourteen years have gone by with me like this, swallowing down agony and on the edge of oblivion, a prisoner of the walls and the body, captive to two gaolers à la al-Maʿaari, the blind poet. The only company I had was an old radio and a wheelchair that Daouia procured and which, with her gestures, she had me understand had belonged to an old woman who had died and whose children wanted rid of it. I became able to leave the room more freely and, after the poor woman managed to get me a pen and paper from one of the village children, I could sit at the table and try to write any old thing, even if it was only a child's scribbles, despite how hard it was for my stiffened fingers.

– Long years during which nothing changed, like a photograph of a room fixed in time in the fashion of Perec in his novel.

– That bastard was right, *Life: A User's Manual* is the ideal novel for a lengthy term of imprisonment. It's a novel without end that can be read more than once and in more than one way, which makes it an ever-renewing read.

– I read it many times. I took it apart and reconstructed it in my mind. I understood all the elliptical games and strict formal constraints of its author in his use of the Greco-Latin magic square and how he shifted from room to room in the building using the move of the knight in chess, and the secret behind his deliberate choice of 99 rather than 100 chapters.

– You might find it strange, my talking about a novel with such passion, but I'm no different to Dr B, the Nazi concentration camp inmate in *The Chess Player*. It was those small vivid details that brought me back to life. What that bastard did not realise when he sought to mock me by leaving the novel with me for fourteen years is that he handed me the weapon to defeat him. When I was able to solve Perec's complex riddles, I felt a strange sense of power and I was filled with the desire to take revenge against Samir and my uncle Kacem, even if that seemed impossible.

– Today, I am like Edmond Dantès in *The Count of Monte Cristo*. I never expected to be released from my prison after fourteen whole years – exactly the same number of years that Edmond spent incarcerated!

– Tell me Lubna, where is Samir? Are you still his wife? And more importantly than all of that, do you still have the unfinished draft of *A Moroccan Jigsaw Puzzle*? I have not forgotten it and am still determined to finish it!

* * *

(19) I Steal You Away

> *Human beings do not inherit dignity or abasement, but make them for themselves.*
> **Mario Vargas Llosa**

Saturday, 2 November 2002
Duwwar el-Hajj Kaddour – outskirts of Kenitra:

The rain continued to pour down and the men of the village thought it best to go inside the mosque and endlessly recite "*Ya Latif*"[5] once they had despaired of their ability to do any more than compel the wailing women to return to their scattered homes. I took refuge in the covered area outside the mosque and scanned the overcast sky for any sign of rescue that might or might not come.

About half an hour passed, then I heard a low noise gradually getting closer until it became a deafening roar. A few men rushed in fear to the doorway of the mosque, seeking the source of the noise. A large helicopter appeared, flying quite low and heading south. I addressed them confidently: "Rest assured, everything will be all right, God willing . . ."

---

[5] Literally, O The Most Gentle, one of the 99 names of God in the Islamic tradition.

After only a few more minutes a succession of ambulances and fire engines arrived, turning the entrance to the village into something akin to a military barracks. They were followed by a Land Rover equipped to deal with rugged terrain, from which emerged a man wearing a black baseball cap and a very expensive winter coat. He was obliged to skip through the mire to reach us, and his face turned grumpy when his trousers got splattered in mud. With the disdain of someone who only cares about himself he said, "The helicopter is customized to deal with weather disasters. Everything is under control. The children trapped in the school and their teacher will be rescued."

The villagers cheered and praised God, and, completely ignoring the mud and the risk of slipping over, some ran off towards the houses to tell the terrified mothers. None of that evoked the slightest sympathy from the man, who added, "Where's the American tourist?"

Those left in the mosque doorway exchanged puzzled looks, and I had no choice but to intervene and reply firmly: "The American tourist is safe and unharmed. What matters now is returning the children and teacher, who one assumes are Moroccans like me and you, safely to their families."

He focused his gaze on my shabby shoes for a few seconds before saying with manufactured coldness, "What kind of way is that to talk to me? Don't you know who I am? I am . . ."

"I'm a friend of the American woman," I quickly interrupted him. "And it was me who asked her to call her embassy, seeing as that's the only way to get your helicopters and rescue teams to operate in areas that any child in elementary school knows are geographically part of Morocco and not on Mars . . ."

His face swelled with blood till he looked like a tomato, and he lost his cool. He attacked me, grabbing my throat and shouting, "I'll teach you, you little beggar, so that you learn the ABCs of talking to your masters!"

His grip was vicelike, and perhaps I regretted my excessive forthrightness with him. I tried to wriggle away without success, but some of the village men intervened to get me away from him as they bellowed angrily, having finally understood what was going on before them.

He retreated, preferring to go back to where the ambulances were and give orders to the rescue teams. He pointed at me menacingly, "I'll be after you and you'll regret every word you uttered. Nobody will protect you from me. It's only a matter of time..."

Two men drew near to calm me down and I regained control of my nerves. "As usual for you lot," I whispered, "all you're good for is talk. One day we'll see which one of us regrets it."

Then an out-of-breath Christine appeared, her hair wet and all over the place, which provoked the amazement of those in front of the mosque doorway.

"Rachid, what's going on here?"

*

The second part of the evening session began once the rain had abated and all the children were safely back with their families. And first, to satisfy his superiors back in the city the official confirmed that Christine was with us.

I took turns with Christine and Lubna to tell Rafiq, who was itching to know what he had missed, everything that had happened. Ghalia and Daouia, meanwhile, collaborated in making tea, the official sponsor of all gossipy Moroccan evenings.

Lubna concluded her account by saying, "Your uncle Kacem died years ago and his wife is bedridden now, living with her divorced daughter and her five children. Her eldest son is in prison for robbery, while the youngest hasn't gone beyond the confines of the neighbourhood with his gang of mates since leaving school. In short, the glory days of that house are over." In a bashful and meaningful tone she added, "Along with all the beautiful moments it witnessed."

I leafed through the old copy of Perec's novel and noticed

Rafiq's comments and annotations written in the margins in a hard-to-decipher script like a nursery-school child's. "There are people," I said, "who don't see life the way we do. They don't give it any importance or value and are basically unable to stop themselves from committing acts of similar brutality. Please free yourself from the desire for revenge, sir. It won't be of any benefit, seeing as Edmond Dantès himself reached that conviction in the end."

Then I raised my head and smiled, "As Italo Calvino said, 'A classic is a book that has never finished saying what it has to say.' Fourteen years went by, then the novel *A Moroccan Jigsaw Puzzle* led us to you. As usual for all great works, they are not written but create themselves!"

Christine intervened, directing her words at Rafiq in French: "I know that no words of apology could ever suffice to express the magnitude of my sorrow. While I do not know the true extent of my father's involvement in your tragedy, I am willing to offer any assistance you require, and I propose to meet the costs of your treatment at the best hospitals in the United States of America."

Lubna squeezed Rafiq's hand as she gazed at his face with the adoration of a lover. Then she said, "I clung fast to the hope of his return, and he has come back at last. I won't lose hope of his being cured either. But the whole case needs a radical and final solution. Thousands of others are suffering in silence, forgotten by all."

The word 'forgotten' reminded me of a point that had slipped my exhausted mind, and I searched in my coat pocket for the photograph of the mystery Moroccan young woman. I handed it to Lubna, who helped Rafiq hold it between his shaking fingers. "One last point I'd like to ask about. This photo, is it of your real mother?"

He remained silent for long moments, then answered in his halting speech, "No. It's not her."

I pulled a disgruntled face and he added, struggling to connect the letters and words: "I was five years old when I saw her for the last time. I tried to find a trace of my family in Kenitra but without success. They all left the city at the beginning of the 1970s after what happened at the airbase and after the Americans left. Yes, years have passed, but I am quite sure that the person in the photograph is not Malika el-Farouki, my biological mother."

Christine looked at me quizzically, expecting my translation. I leaned back against the wall and let out a deep sigh expressing all my fatigue and confusion before saying to her in English, "It seems that the life story of your, as you put it, dull and boring father is still pregnant with mysteries!"

* * *

The most significant historical event of 1099 CE:

Fall of the city of Jerusalem to the Crusaders under Godfrey after a siege that lasted a little over one month from 7 June to 15 July. This occurred in the context of the First Crusade (1096–1099) and led to the formation of the Kingdom of Jerusalem.

The Muslims were unable to retake the city for 88 years, when it fell to Saladin after a two-week siege lasting from 20 September to 2 October 1187.

(19') Life: A User's Manual

Carry the book you're writing in your imagination, but keep your mouth closed.
Robert Masello

Thursday, 7 November 2019
Rue Mohamed V – Rabat:

I got off the tram close to Rabat Cité railway station and headed straight for the bookshop facing the parliament building, following my mother alerting me to the presence there of a large bookshop that opened years after my disappearance.

The sky was overcast, announcing its desire to shed its load again, without that having stopped a large crowd of young men bearing long banners and chanting slogans from massing in front of the building. The security forces had set up barriers to prevent them advancing any further.

The scene did not surprise me. It had already been familiar before I went to Russia. I had made fun of protesters whenever I passed by in my father's car, marvelling at their insistence on shouting with all their might to demand things the meaning of which I did not understand at the time.

Everything here has changed: the shop windows, the design of the old railway station, the new tramway; but the space in front of parliament remains the same, the only refuge for those whose glowing dreams for the future have turned into darkly realist nightmares in a country whose citizens are the cheapest things in it.

I say "things", and I'm sure I haven't made an error in classification.

I went inside the bookshop and the security guard asked me to put the folder and the black leather satchel into one of the compartments for visitors' possessions. I did so, then made a beeline towards a guy wearing a jacket bearing the store's logo.

"Please, is there a novel by a Moroccan author called *Towards Zero*?" I asked him.

"Yes," he replied, "it's by the writer Abdelmajid Sebbata. Would you like a copy?"

I nodded, and he led me to the fiction section and picked out a book. I estimated by eye that it was close to five hundred pages long, and said, "Yes please."

I checked out the cover with its clock hands and mixture of orange, black and grey colours. Then I read the blurb on the back.

The author is a young guy born in 1989, and the taxi driver also said that the owner of the satchel was a young guy.

I'm on the right track then!

The bookshop employee was occupied with another customer, so I went over and asked shyly, "Excuse me, I know my question is a little strange, but I need to meet the novel's author in person. Is there any way to find his address?"

He said nothing for a moment, a sign he was thinking, then replied, "Honestly, I don't know. But Sebbata comes into the store practically every day, although I've noticed his absence recently, as usual whenever he starts writing or translating a new novel and . . ." His eyes narrowed as if he was remembering something and added, "One minute please!"

He tapped on the screen of his mobile, then put it to his ear while saying, "I saved his number a while ago when he asked to reserve a copy of a novel we didn't have in stock. I'm calling him right now . . ."

After a few moments he said, "Hello, Mr Sebbata, how are you? It's . . . Ah, you knew it was me. You've saved my number then. Forgive me, but I have someone with me who would like to meet you at the bookstore. Is that possible?"

He passed me the phone and I heard a tremulous voice: "Hello? Who's this?"

I was no less nervous than him as I replied hesitantly, "Mr Abdelmajid . . . I am . . . the lost computer . . . the draft novel . . . the black leather satchel . . ."

*

Forty-five minutes passed, during which I walked up and down the aisles filling my eyes and memory with the titles of new books, fiction and non-fiction, until a young guy came through the shop doorway, quickly said hello to the employee, and turned to me. Every square inch of his face displayed signs of bafflement.

Thick black hair, which he did not seem concerned about brushing; two dark eyes, whose exhaustion was evident despite the large-framed spectacles he was wearing; a messy beard that reminded me of my days detained in Krasnokamensk and which he could have at least trimmed to look better.

He was wearing a blue jacket, black jeans and white trainers that were not suitable for the rainy weather outside.

He did not seem a hippy, for he looked quite smart, but he made you feel he lacked a touch of elegance and did not take sufficient care of his appearance, irrespective of whether his overlooking such details was a temporary phenomenon or a permanent choice.

The image I had in my head of the young writer was different to the person in front of me, and as I studied his features one name leapt to mind: Rachid Bennacer. He was very much like him, and a reader of the novel who then met its author would imagine that one of them had managed to have a certain effect on the other.

"Hello. Is it true that you've found my leather satchel with the computer and blue notebook?" He said this with fear and trepidation, but I smiled and shook his hand in an attempt to create an atmosphere of trust. "My name is Zouhair," I said. "Rest assured, it's safe and sound just as you left it yesterday in the taxi."

He emitted a sigh of relief that revealed the extent of his anticipation, then launched into a lengthy explanation: "It's my habit to remember taxi numbers by connecting them to famous dates in history. I didn't forget the number 1099. I looked for the driver at the taxi station, but his colleagues told me he was off work. I went to the police station believing that he would have handed the satchel in, but I came up with nothing. I don't care about losing the computer. It's an old model and of no use to anyone, but its contents are terribly important to me. I was tired out and distracted by some personal problems and, like a fool, I left it on the backseat of the car."

"The law of life is very simple: what we think we have we may lose in the blink of an eye, and forever . . ."

He raised and quickly lowered his eyebrows, perhaps sensing that it was a phrase similar to those that novelists put in the mouths of their characters. "But how did you get hold of me?" he asked. "Why didn't you just hand the satchel in to the police?"

"I'd say that my search for you was much easier than the effort Rachid and Christine had to make to discover the fate of the missing author of *A Moroccan Jigsaw Puzzle*. Your novel *Towards Zero* led me to you. You mentioned it several times in your blue notebook. I only knew the Agatha Christie novel of the same title, then I came to the bookshop to make sure. The rest you know!"

Astonishment gave his exhausted features a strange cast, and I said in a less excited tone, "Actually I should apologise. I allowed myself to take a peek at the contents of the laptop and the notebook, and I would like to give my humble opinion, if you would permit me of course."

*

We sat in a café near the bookshop that he had suggested, and until he had finished reading what I had spent all night writing, he did not utter a single word.

"This is really what I was looking for, an idea out of the box, as Brandon said to Christine in Central Park. I directed my attention to the village whose inhabitants (along with those of other villages and cities, of course) fell victim to the toxic contaminated oil, and I never expected there to be two villages with the same name, one towards Meknes, close to El Hajeb, and the other towards Kenitra. How did you know about that?"

"I know someone there who's dear to me, but our relationship ended because of me and I'm determined to visit them soon to make amends."

I quickly evaded any more questions by pretending to watch intently the protests of the crowd in front of parliament as the forces of law and order weighed in to disperse the demonstrators: "What matters now is your opinion. How did you find the ending?"

He removed his spectacles and rubbed his eyes, saying, "Your description of Rafiq's suffering in his prison for fourteen years is great. I also liked your use of the well-known idea of taking *Life: A User's Manual* to a desert island and reading it more than once in many different ways. It also makes me think that you've lived the two experiences yourself!"

I smiled as I recalled the copy of the novel that I read more than once in Krasnokamensk, but he changed his tone and went on to say, "But I didn't like your resort to Rachid as narrator instead of Christine. That violated the formal constraint I imposed at the beginning. Also, you stopped at chapter 19, although I understand the reasons. Nor do I understand why you introduced the character of the girl you called Ghalia. Overall, I think it's a pretty good ending, but it's missing something."

His needling annoyed me so I asked with a curtness I could not disguise, "What do you mean?"

Perhaps sensing his rush to judgment had been a mistake, he retracted in explanation, "It's a satisfactory ending for most of the novel's protagonists. Christine McMillan found an appropriate idea for her novel, despite the shock of her father having a certain responsibility for the toxic oil case. Rafiq returned to his beloved Lubna and their daughter Jenan, as well as Christine offering to take him to the United States for treatment as her symbolic contribution to atone for her father's sins. But what about Rachid?"

I replied spontaneously, "He'll persuade his supervisor that *A Moroccan Jigsaw Puzzle* was the right choice and he'll complete his dissertation on it as he wanted!"

He was silent for a long time and seemed lost in his own world, although his eyes were fixed on the protests in front of parliament. Then he said, "And then what? He'll come to this square demanding his right to live in dignity like those over there, and others whose worth is no more than 42 francs in a country like this."

My mind immediately linked what he said with the number of the folder in his computer, while he opened his blue notebook and took a pen out of his jacket pocket:

"Seeing as you're the first reader of the draft of the novel, and even helped write three of its chapters, I'm not embarrassed to share some of my recent ideas. A while ago I read Paul Auster's latest novel, *4 3 2 1*, and despite its size and multitude of events, it's based on a really great idea that appeals to all literary writers: what path would our life have taken if the decisions we made had been different? The author imagines four different life paths for the same character, Archibald Ferguson. Once he's a sporting hero, once an activist, once a writer, and once a journalist. What if we repeated the same thing with Rachid?"

"Great idea and possible to implement, but all paths here lead to one end." He gave a cynical laugh, and I added seriously, "Because Morocco is like a novel by Franz Kafka. The plot is simple, but going deeply into the action means entering a labyrinth of inescapable details. As soon as you get close to the denouement, you are stunned that the plot is unfinished in the first place."

"I'm sorry, Mr Zouhair, but the way you're talking suggests that your relationship with literature is much stronger than I imagined!"

I felt that his suspicion and his insistence would, sooner or later, succeed in stroking my desire to tell all. So I steeled myself and changed the direction of the conversation. "I noticed that you made a passing reference to the Dubrovka Theatre incident in chapters 10 and 11."

With the excitement of a five-year-old child he said, "Yes! I was thirteen when it happened. I followed the details with great interest at the time. The hostages, the negotiations, the mystery gas, whose identity the Russians have never revealed and that killed dozens. The plan to write a novel about it was deferred for several reasons, most importantly, the absence of any Moroccans among the hostages. So I contented myself with the publisher's remarks and his suggestion to Christine that she write a novel about it, seeing as the action of my novel coincided with the theatre siege in October 2002."

"You're mistaken, Mr Abdelmajid. There was a Moroccan citizen present at the Dubrovka Theatre on the night of Wednesday, 23 October 2002. He lived through every moment of the siege before his fate led him off to a Siberian prison that you have undoubtedly never heard of before."

He practically leapt out of his seat as he shouted, "A Moroccan in Siberia! Oh my God, who is he? Where is he now?!"

A flush of triumph suffused me at having managed to pique the curiosity of a novelist, and I said with a calmness dripping with provocation: "Sitting opposite you right now!"

* * *

What if?
(Two different endings for the character Rachid Bennacer)

Idea for the first ending: Zouhair Belkacem

Idea for the second ending: Abdelmajid Sebbata

Protestors seriously injured as sit-in by unemployed PhD holders broken up

(*Current Times* newspaper – Society page
– Edition of Friday, 2 April 2010)

Action to break up a sit-in by unemployed PhD holders on Rabat's Rue Mohamed V descended into violent clashes, causing injuries to protestors, including loss of consciousness. The injured were taken to hospital for treatment, and one person remains in intensive care after suffering a serious head injury.

The protestors had previously announced their intention to go on hunger strike as a symbolic gesture to draw attention to their on-going unemployment and marginalization and the deliberate wasting of their talents. This move met with no official response, and the PhD holders decided to escalate to a sit-in in front of parliament, necessitating the intervention of the security forces to clear the area by force.

(20) Introduction to the Psychology of the Oppressed Human Being

> *How sad to see great nations begging for a little extra future.*
> Emil Cioran

Thursday, 1 April 2010
Rue Mohamed V – Rabat:

All the protestors had dispersed. The placards bearing their slogans and demands had fallen on the ground and were being trampled by their and their pursuers' feet alike.

Rachid ran with all his strength. Tears fell from his eyes without his realising.

His PhD, with distinction, had been of no help to him. It was just a piece of stiff paper gathering dust that the flies had turned into a take-off and landing platform for their aerial jaunts.

The hotel manager had dispensed with his services after Rachid had refused to be turned gradually from a servant into a slave whom the manager (who relished torturing him simply because his own education went no further than elementary) wished he could employ for nothing.

They tried to convince him that his field of literature was worthless and that what he had achieved in his dissertation on *A*

Moroccan Jigsaw Puzzle and narrative techniques in the modern novel was just rubbish of no interest to anyone.

Perhaps they were right . . .

They said that holders of degrees in scientific and technical fields were more fortunate than literary types. But in time he realised that all were in the same unemployed basket. A seldom-found true equality.

He went to job interviews and they ruled him out, justifying their decision by saying he didn't match the requirements, and he gradually came to understand that the requirements might be a family name, a quiet phone call or big tits.

Someone suggested he join the youth wing of a political party as a means to get ahead and achieve his ambitions more easily. But he realised that having things easy meant arse-licking a bunch of the corrupt, who might exploit his abilities and set him up to burnish their image while covering him in their filth.

To be a bulletproof jacket for them to use when they needed then discard when they wanted.

Bootlicking was a talent which he did not possess, and he would never be any good at it even if he did think about acquiring the talent one day.

He clung to the hope of a better tomorrow, and got involved with a quiet girl, whom his mind fell for before his heart did.

The poor girl was very patient before submitting to her parents' pressure and the rapid falling of the leaves of her life. She consented to marry someone who had nothing to offer except residence abroad.

And he couldn't blame her for that . . .

Hadn't he believed all his life that love would remain just a beautiful lie created by literature?

He was thirty-six now and his future was still amorphous. There was no stability in his life and he was fearful for what the days to come might bring.

Suddenly he stopped, turned towards his pursuers, and shouted, giving voice to all the exhaustion and oppression inside:

"ENOUGH!"

He had barely finished his shout when a blow struck his head.

He dropped heavily to the ground and the other man, cognisant of the gravity of what he had done, retreated in fright to take shelter within the ranks of his colleagues.

Young men swarmed around Rachid's prone body and a young woman's voice broke as she shouted, "O God! Call an ambulance! He's bleeding badly!"

On the verge of passing out, his vision blurred and most of those crowded around him heard him blabbering incomprehensibly: "It won't arrive . . . It won't arrive . . . Unless Christine calls the embassy . . ."

* * *

Email to Rachid Bennacer, PhD student in contemporary literature, from Dr Fabien Bedos, French academic specializing in Arabic Literature at the Sorbonne, Paris

From: fbedos@wanadoo.net
Date: 15-11-2002
To: rbennacer@wanadoo.net
Cc:
Subject: Re

My dear friend Rachid Bennacer,

Greetings and Ramadan Karim to you and all your Muslim friends.

I have been a little delayed in replying to your series of emails about the surprises thrown up by your and American novelist Christine McMillan's research into the real identity of the author of *A Moroccan Jigsaw Puzzle*. Really, I'm still amazed at the unexpected turn of events, and it's simply impossible to go into the details by email or telephone.

I will arrange to visit Morocco at the earliest opportunity to meet Rafiq Khalidi and Lubna el-Afaoui in person. I will also be delighted at the same time to broach an important subject with you that I started thinking about from the moment I received your first emails some two months ago. It's a suggestion for a new supervisor for your dissertation, if that suits you.

Let's keep in touch then, until I let you know the date of my upcoming visit.

With my affection and esteem,
Your friend Fabien

(20') Le testament français

Even if they are born into rich families or win the Nobel Prize, writers are miserable people.
Roberto Bolaño

Thursday, 1 April 2010
The Sorbonne Paris III; a restaurant overlooking the Seine:

Rachid ended his lecture on unfinished novels, in which he had presented his in-depth readings of *The First Man* by Albert Camus, *The Castle* by Franz Kafka, *The Mystery of Edwin Drood* by Charles Dickens, and *Lucien Leuwen* by Stendhal, with a reference to the special case of *A Moroccan Jigsaw Puzzle*, the novel started by the writer Rafiq Khalidi before his disappearance, and finished by writer Lubna el-Afaoui, his lover and subsequently his wife.

He was about to leave when a lively student in her twenties detained him with some questions. He answered patiently and diligently, while avoiding her admiring looks. Then he recommended she review Georges Perec's *53 Days* as a modern example of an unfinished detective novel subject to the complex formal strictures of the OuLiPo literary group. Harry Mathews and Jacques Roubaud published the work in 1989 in an edition containing eleven finished chapters and the contents of a folder found in the dead writer's desk, that included references, drafts and organized notes for what was intended for the remaining twenty-eight chapters but precluded by his death in 1982.

Rachid gathered his papers and closed his bag when a voice speaking English made him start: "Does Dr Bennacer's time permit him to give some further explanations to an old student?"

His ears picked up the familiar twang despite the years that had passed since he last heard it in person.

He quickly raised his head and he beamed with delight when he saw the woman standing before him. "Christine!" he exclaimed with a happiness not devoid of shock.

*

She had not lost much of her attraction, even though she was nearly fifty. Wrinkles had crept around the corners of her eyes and her small mouth, but scrutinizing her tired features proved to him that she wasn't in the best of states.

Her silence prolonged and she pressed her face against the window of the restaurant overlooking the Seine as she contemplated the horizon.

"How are Ronald and Cindy, and Brandon?" he asked her warmly.

With an outward indifference she replied, "Ronald and Cindy are fine. We call and visit one another sometimes. As for Brandon, I kicked him out of the house and I don't think I'll be allowing him back."

He tried to act serious while making an enormous effort to ward off his cynical laugh. "The great American writer John Fante says that you can't be mean and still be a great writer. It's hard to find a man whose whole heart is faithful to you. If he was true in his love for you, forgive him . . ."

She turned to him and exclaimed contemptuously, "Who said I'm talking about emotional betrayal? It's something completely different!"

His fake seriousness turned into the utmost attention, and she continued, "Do you remember his interest in finding out what happened to my father's friends in the old photo?"

"Sure. He learned that they'd all died except for one soldier who had Alzheimer's."

She went on in annoyance, "He lied to me. Tony Wagner was alive. He went to see him at an old people's home in Detroit and he heard a lot about my father's past from him. He chose to keep quiet rather than be honest with me. But I found an audio tape where he'd recorded everything the ex-soldier said. When I confronted him about it, he claimed he did it for my sake."

He folded his arms across his chest and commented. "Perhaps he was right to do that. What matters here is what Tony said. Did he have new information about Steve?"

"Yes. He talked about his involvement in the deal for drums of poisonous oil and about the Moroccan girl he fell in love with, which we all know about. But he also referred to his past in Texas, before he went to Morocco, which is something we overlooked because we were so busy with the case of Rafiq Khalidi's disappearance."

"Do you mean that photo of him with the blonde girl holding a copy of Mikhail Lermontov's *A Hero of Our Time*?

The faint smile that passed her lips failed to conceal her agitation. "As usual, there's no question about your memory, even after all these years. The girl's name is Edith Bourgie and she's of French extraction. She escaped to the United States at the outbreak of World War II and settled with her family in Texas. She met my father, a teenage redneck, and fell in love with him. But he was pissed at what he saw as her intellectual and cultural superiority compared to his lowly level. He felt inferior and treated her really badly."

Then she gave a sigh replete with vulnerability and submission and added, "If only things had stopped there. He went off with the troops to North Africa, without telling her, on the very same day she had decided to tell him that she was pregnant. She wrote often to him in Morocco, and he received her telegrams and letters regularly. Then, in her last letter she told him she was going back to France with her family and her son."

Her partner in the conversation did not utter a word and she continued, "Tony said that Steve treated Edith's letters with indifference, thinking it was just feminine wiles. He only had to confront the truth when he came back to the States. He tried to locate her, even though he'd started a new relationship with my mom. But it was useless.

The picture became clear in Rachid's mind and he asked her cautiously, "Don't say you're . . ."

"Yes," she interrupted and pleadingly, almost begging, said, "I've come to France to look for her and my brother. And I won't find anyone better to help than you!"

* * *

Notes:

– The strange tale of Zouhair Belkacem is still playing on my mind. All sources affirm that no Moroccan was present among the hostages at the Dubrovka Theatre. Nonetheless, the compelling detail of his experiences in Moscow and Krasnokamensk and his fluency in Russian make me inclined to believe him.

– I do not understand why Professor Younis Belkacem was so indifferent. He did not accompany his wife to Russia to look for their missing son, but continued his numerous relationships until he died. It's as if his ties to his son had been cut, or weren't there in the first place. Has Zouhair concealed some background information about his father?

– I last met Zouhair after he came back from Duwwar al-Hajj Kaddour (outskirts of Kenitra). He did not find Ghalia. The residents told him that she had left years before. Accounts varied between those who said she was in Tangiers and those who swore she'd been seen in Agadir.

– There hasn't been a sign of him since then. He turned off his phone or changed his number, perhaps, and there isn't any other way to get in touch with him. I understood that he was going to spend all his time and effort following the tracks of the oppressed cleaning girl. I hope he comes back one day to tell me the outcome of his search.

– In my novel I refer to Lubna el-Afaoui's doctoral dissertation on the toxic oil case. Of course that is a product of the imagination, but I am obliged to point out the existence of a real master's thesis that was published (because of its excellence) in the contemporary history monograph series of the Faculty of Literature and Humanities, Rabat: The Poisonous Oil Disaster in Morocco (1959–60) by Madiha Sebaoui.

– That outstanding piece of research was of great benefit to me when I was gathering information and sources on the issue, and it allowed me to enrich the novel's plot with new ideas. I recommend that all those interested read it – it is available in the university bookstore for a token price. Especial thanks are due to novelist and friend Abdelkarim Jouaiti for his encouragement and for directing me towards this important source after the idea of my working on a fictional treatment of the toxic oil case enthused him. I also thank my friend, journalist Mohamed Ahdad, who was unstinting in providing me with information, as one of the few young journalists who took an interest and wrote detailed investigative pieces some years ago.

Abdelmajid Sebbata

05–12–2019

CONTENTS

(Or list of titles recommended by Muhsin el-Fadili that Rachid Bennacer wrote down in his notebook)

0.	**If on a Winter's Night a Traveller** by Italo Calvino	1
1.	**Things Fall Apart** by Chinua Achebe	9
1'.	**The Adolescent** by Fyodor Dostoevsky	15
2.	**The Grapes of Wrath** by John Steinbeck	21
2'.	**The Assault** by Harry Mulisch	26
3.	**American Pastoral** by Philip Roth	31
3'.	**The Fall** by Albert Camus	37
4.	**Writing Degree Zero** by Roland Barthes	43
4'.	**The Mother** by Maxim Gorky	49
5.	**Ask the Dust** by John Fante	57
5'.	**Life is Elsewhere** by Milan Kundera	63
6.	**Portrait in Sepia** by Isabel Allende	71
6'.	**Dangerous Liaisons** by Pierre Choderlos de Laclos	83
7.	**I See What I Want** by Mahmoud Darwish	92
7'.	**The Captain's Daughter** by Alexander Pushkin	99
8.	**Jamila** by Chinghiz Aitmatov	110
8'.	**Celebrations of Death** by Abdelkarim Jouaiti	119
9.	**Story and Interpretation** by Abdelfattah Kilito	129
9'.	**Confusion of Feelings** by Stefan Zweig	135
10.	**The Invention of Solitude** by Paul Auster	145
10'.	**Survivor** by Chuck Palahniuk	152

11.	**Masks of Reality and Masks of Fantasy** by Jabra Ibrahim Jabra	163
11'.	**Morphine** by Mikhail Bulgakov	171
12.	**The Sleepwalkers** by Saʻad Makkawi	181
12'.	**Lord of Darkness** by Rabee Jaber	189
13.	**Remembrance of Things Past** by Marcel Proust	198
13'.	**The Spectre of Alexander Wolf** by Gaito Gazdanov	205
14.	**Fear and Trembling** by Amélie Nothomb	214
14'.	**In Cold Blood** by Truman Capote	222
15.	**An Attempt to Live** by Mohammed Zafzaf	236
15'.	**The Tunnel** by Ernesto Sabato	247
16.	**The Absurdity of Fate** by Naguib Mahfouz	261
16'.	**My Escape to Freedom** by Alija Izetbegović	275
17.	**The Wretched of the Earth** by Frantz Fanon	290
17'.	**The Man Without Qualities** by Robert Musil	299
18.	**Beggars of Miracles** by Constantin Virgil Gheorghiu	307
18'.	**Journey to the End of the Night** by Louis-Ferdinand Céline	318
19.	**I Steal You Away** by Niccolò Ammaniti	329
19'.	**Life: A User's Manual** by Georges Perec	335
20.	**Introduction to the Psychology of the Oppressed Human Being** by Mustafa Hijazi	344
20'.	**Le testament français** by Andreï Makine	348

About the Author

Abdelmajid Sebbata is the author of three novels in Arabic: *Khalfa jidar al-'Ishq* (Behind the Wall of Passion, 2015), *Saa'at al-Sifr 00:00* (*Towards Zero* 00:00, 2017) which won the 2018 Moroccan Book Award, and this novel *The Secrets of Folder 42* (*Al-Malaf 42* [*File 42*], 2020), which was shortlisted for the 2021 International Prize for Arabic Fiction.

Born in Rabat, Morocco, in 1989, Sebbata has a Masters degree in Civil Engineering from Abdelmalek Essaadi University, Tangiers. He has written articles and translations on literary, cultural and historical subjects that have been published in print and online in Morocco and other Arab countries, and has translated into Arabic Walter Tevis's *The Queen's Gambit* and two novels by the French thriller writer Michel Bussi.

About the Translator

Raphael Cohen is a professional translator and lexicographer who studied Arabic and Hebrew at Oxford University and the University of Chicago. He has translated a growing number of novels by contemporary Arab authors including Amir Tag Elsir, George Yarak, Mohamed Salmawy, Ahlem Mosteghanemi, Eslam Mosbah, and Mona Prince.

In addition to translating *The Secrets of Folder 42* by Abdelmajid Sebbata for Banipal Books he has translated Abdallah Uld Mohamadi Bah's *Birds of Nabaa, A Mauritanian Tale* and Ghayla F T Al Said's *The Madness of Despair*, and translated and introduced Ahmed Morsi's *Poems of Alexandria and New York*. He is based in Cairo, and was a contributing editor of *Banipal Magazine of Modern Arab Literature*.

OTHER TITLES FROM BANIPAL BOOKS

At Rest in the Cherry Orchard by Azher Jirjees. ISBN: 978-1-913043-39-1 • Paperback & Ebook • 224pp • 2024. Translated from the Arabic by Jonathan Wright. After fleeing Iraq and settling in Norway, Said Mardan is haunted by painful and brutal nightmares about his murdered father. Will he find rest in the cherry orchard like his old neighbour Jakob?

Birds of Nabaa, A Mauritanian Tale by Abdallah Uld Mohamadi Bah. ISBN: 978-1-913043-43-8 • Paperback & Ebook • 192pp • 2023. Translated from the Arabic by Raphael Cohen. This first Mauritanian novel in English translation from Arabic is a tale of physical and spiritual journeys, introducing diverse characters, poetry, Sufi dancing and the world's first climate-change refugee.

Shadow of the Sun by Taleb Alrefai. ISBN: 978-1-913043-36-0 • Pbk & Ebook • 192pp • 2023. Translated from the Arabic by Nashwa Nasreldin. Impoverished Egyptian teacher Helmy is desperate to find a better life for himself, his wife and little boy, seeing no future in Cairo. He dreams of working in oil-rich Kuwait, and finally manages to get a work visa.

The Stone Serpent, Barates of Palmyra's Elegy for Regina his Beloved – An Eastern Serenade by Nouri al-Jarrah. Translated from the Arabic by Catherine Cobham. ISBN: 978-1-913043-29-2 • 2022 • 112pp • Pbk & Ebook. Syrian poet al-Jarrah restores to life an ancient story of migrant Syrian life, love and freedom, after a single line in Aramaic on a tombstone at Arabeia Roman Fort, Hadrian's Wall, sparks his imagination.

Things I Left Behind by Shada Mustafa. Translated from the Arabic by Nancy Roberts. ISBN: 978-1-913043-26-1 • 2022 • 128pp • Pbk & Ebook. This debut novel by a young Palestinian woman interrogates memories of growing up in order to liberate the narrator from the continual pain and tragic anguish of the "things" she left behind in her childhood in an occupied and divided land and family.

The Tent Generations, Palestinian Poems. Selected, introduced, and translated by Mohammed Sawaie. ISBN: 978-1-913043-18-6 • 2022 • 160pp • Pbk & Ebook. The 16 twentieth-century Palestinian poets are witness for today's readers of exile, displacement, disapora and occupation, through 1948, 1967 and 1973, war after war.

Sarajevo Firewood by Saïd Khatibi. Translated from the Arabic by Paul Starkey. ISBN 978-1-913043-23-0 • 2021 • 320pp • Pbk & Ebook. A searing novel exploring the legacy of the recent histories, connections and civil wars of Algeria and Bosnia-Herzegovina and the traumatic experience of exile for so many.

Fadhil Al-Azzawi's Beautiful Creatures by Iraqi author Fadhil al-Azzawi. ISBN 978-1-913043-10-0 • 2021 • 152pp • Hbk, Pbk, Ebook. An open poetic work, written in defiance of the "sanctity of genre", translated from the Arabic by the author, and edited by Hannah Somerville.

The Madness of Despair by Ghalya F T Al Said. Translated from the Arabic by Raphael Cohen. ISBN: 978-1-913043-12-4 • 2021 • 256pp • Hbk, Pbk, Ebook. The first of the author's six novels in English translation is a powerful saga of how psychological suffering and cultural displacement upsets very ordinary of aspirations for life and love.

Poems of Alexandria and New York by Ahmed Morsi. Translated from the Arabic by Raphael Cohen. ISBN 978-1-913043-16-2 • 2021 • 126pp • Pbk & Ebook. First volume in English translation for renowned painter, art critic, and poet.

Mansi: A Rare Man in His Own Way by Tayeb Salih. Translated and introduced by Adil Babikir. ISBN 978-0-9956369-8-9 • Paperback & Ebook • 184pp • 2020. This affectionate memoir of Salih's irrepressible friend Mansi shows a new side to the author, world renowned for his classic novel *Season of Migration to the North*.

Goat Mountain by Habib Selmi.Translated from the Arabic by Charis Olszok. ISBN: 978-1-913043-04-9 • 2020 • Pbk & Ebook • 92pp. The well-known Tunisian author's acclaimed debut novel, from 1988, now in English translation.

The Mariner by Taleb Alrefai. Translated from the Arabic by Russell Harris. ISBN: 978-1-913043-08-7 • Pbk & Ebook • 160pp • 2020. A fictional retelling of the final sea journey of famous Kuwaiti dhow shipmaster Captain Al-Najdi.

A Boat to Lesbos, and other poems by Nouri Al-Jarrah. Translated from the Arabic by Camilo Gómez-Rivas and Allison Blecker and illustrated with paintings by Reem Yassouf. ISBN: 978-0-9956369-4-1 • 2018 • Pbk • 120pp. The first book in English translation for this major Syrian poet bears passionate witness – through the eyes of history, Sappho and Odysseus – to Syrian families fleeing to Lesbos.

An Iraqi In Paris by Samuel Shimon. ISBN: 978-0-9574424-8-1 • Pbk • 282pp • 2016. Translated from the Arabic by Christina Philips and Piers

Amodia with the author. "A gem of autobiographical writing", "a manifesto of tolerance".

Heavenly Life: Selected Poems by Ramsey Nasr. ISBN: 978-0-9549666-9-0 • 2010 • Pbk • 180pp. First English-language collection for Ramsey Nasr, Poet Laureate of the Netherlands 2009 & 2010. Translated from the Dutch by David Colmer. Introduced by Victor Schiferli with Foreword by Ruth Padel.

Knife Sharpener: Selected Poems by Sargon Boulus. The first English-language collection for the renowned late Iraqi poet. ISBN: 978-0-9549666-7-6 • 2009 • Pbk • 154pp. Foreword by Adonis. Poems translated from the Arabic by the author. Plus tributes by fellow authors and Afterword by the publisher.

Shepherd of Solitude: Selected Poems by Amjad Nasser. Translated from the Arabic and introduced by Khaled Mattawa. ISBN: 978-0-9549666-8-3 • 2009 • Pbk • 186pp. First English-language collection for the late major Jordanian poet.

Mordechai's Moustache and his Wife's Cats, and other stories by Mahmoud Shukair. ISBN: 978-0-9549666-3-8 • 2007 • Pbk • 124pp. Translated from the Arabic by Issa J Boullata, Elizabeth Whitehouse, Elizabeth Winslow and Christina Phillips. First major English publication of Palestine's maestro storyteller.

A Retired Gentleman, & other stories by Issa J Boullata. ISBN: 978-0-9549666-6-9 • 2007 • Pbk • 120pp. Emigrant tales from the Jerusalem-born author and scholar.

The Myrtle Tree by Lebanese Jad El Hage. ISBN: 978-0-9549666-4-5 • 2007 • Pbk • 288pp. "This remarkable novel, set in a Lebanese mountain village, conveys with razor-sharp accuracy the sights, sounds, tastes and tragic dilemmas of Lebanon's fratricidal civil war. A must read" – Patrick Seale.

Sardines and Oranges: Short Stories from North Africa. Introduced by Peter Clark. ISBN: 978-0-9549666-1-4 • 2005 • Pbk • 222pp. The 26 stories from Algeria, Egypt, Morocco, Sudan and Tunisia are by 21 authors, all translated from the Arabic, bar one, Mohammed Dib's, from French.